# About the Authors

**Brenda Jackson** is a *New York Times* bestselling author of more than one hundred romance titles. Brenda lives in Jacksonville, Florida, and divides her time between family, writing and travelling. Email Brenda at authorbrendajackson@gmail.com or visit her on her website at brendajackson.net

**Lucy Ellis** has four loves in life: books, expensive lingerie, vintage films and big, gorgeous men who have to duck going through doorways. Weaving aspects of them into her fiction is the best part of being a romance writer. Lucy lives in a small cottage in the foothills outside Melbourne.

*USA Today* bestselling author **Katherine Garbera** is a two-time Maggie winner who has written 108 books. A Florida native who grew up to travel the globe, Katherine now makes her home in the Midlands of the UK with her husband, two children and a very spoiled miniature dachshund. Visit her on the web at http://www.katherinegarbera.com, connect with her on Facebook and follow her on Twitter @katheringarbera

# Billionaire Boss

# Billionaire Boss: Her Bachelor Billionaire

BRENDA JACKSON

LUCY ELLIS

KATHERINE GARBERA

MIX
Paper from
responsible sources

FSC

FSC C007454

This book is produced from independently certified FSC
to ensure responsible forest management.

For more information visit: www.harpercollins.co.uk/green

Printed and bound in Spain

**MILLS & BOON**

First Published in Great Britain 2020
By Mills & Boon, an imprint of HarperCollins*Publishers*
1 London Bridge Street, London, SE1 9GF

BILLIONAIRE BOSS: HER BACHELOR BILLIONAIRE
© 2020 Harlequin Books S.A.

*One Winter's Night* © 2012 Brenda Streater Jackson
*Caught in His Gilded World* © 2015 Lucy Ellis
*Billionaire's Baby Bind* © 2017 Harlequin Books S.A.

Special thanks and acknowledgment are given to Katherine Garbera for her contribution to the *Texas Cattleman's Club: Blackmail* series.

ISBN: 978-0-263-29852-9

# ONE WINTER'S NIGHT

**BRENDA JACKSON**

To the love of my life, Gerald Jackson, Sr.

Happy Holidays to all my family,
friends and dedicated readers.

A very special thank you to event planners
extraordinaire – Shikara Linsy, Sandra Sutton,
Tammy Griffih, and Tracy Hale. My interview
with you regarding the life of an event planner
and your patience in answering all of my
questions was most appreciated.

Pleasant words are a honeycomb, sweet to the
soul and healing to the bones. —Proverbs 16:24

# One

*A blistering cold day in early November*

It had snowed overnight and a thick white blanket seemed to cover the land as far as the eye could see. The Denver weather report said the temperature would drop to ten below by mid-day and would stay that way through most of the night. It was the kind of cold you could feel deep in your bones, the kind where your breath practically froze upon exhale.

He loved it.

Riley Westmoreland opened the door to his truck and, before getting inside, paused to take in the land he owned. *Riley's Station* was the name he'd given his one-hundred-acre spread seven years ago, on his twenty-fifth birthday. He had designed the ranch house himself and had helped in the building of it, proudly hammering the first nail into the lumber. He was mighty pleased with the massive two-story structure that sat smack in the center of his snow-covered land.

He was probably the only one in his family who welcomed

the snowstorms each year. He thought the snow was what made Denver the perfect place to be in the winter and why his home had fireplaces in all five of the bedrooms, as well as in the living room and family room. There was nothing like curling up before a roaring fire or looking out the window to see the snowflakes fall from the sky, something he'd been fascinated with even as a child. He could recall being out in the thick snow with his brothers and cousins building snowmen. These days he enjoyed moving around the mountains on his snowmobile or going skiing in Aspen.

Riley got into the truck and after settling his body on the leather seat he snapped the seat belt in place. There really was no need for him to go into the office since he could work from home. But he had wanted to get out, breathe in the cold, fresh air and feel the chill in his bones. Besides, he did have an important appointment at noon.

Since his oldest brother, Dillon, had slowed down now that his wife, Pam, was close to her delivery date, a lot of the projects on Dillon's plate at their family-owned business, Blue Ridge Land Management, fell on Riley's shoulders since he was the next man in charge of the Fortune 500 company. The next thing on the agenda was the planning of the employees' holiday party next month.

The event planner that had handled their social functions for the past ten years had retired and before Riley had taken over the project, Dillon had hired Imagine, a local event planning company that opened in town less than a year ago. The owner of Imagine, a woman by the name of Alpha Blake, had put together a charity event that Dillon's wife, Pam, had attended over the summer. Pam had been so impressed with all the detailed work Imagine had done that she passed the woman's name to Dillon. As far as Riley was concerned, you couldn't come any more highly recommended than that. Dillon trusted his wife's judgment in all things.

Riley was about to start the ignition when his cell phone buzzed. He pulled the phone off his side belt. "Yes?"

"Mr. Westmoreland?"

He lifted a brow, not recognizing the ultrarich, feminine voice but definitely liking how it sounded. He figured this had to be a business call since none of the women he dated would refer to him as "Mr. Westmoreland."

"Yes, this is Riley Westmoreland. How can I help you?"

"This is Alpha Blake. We have a noon appointment at your office, but I have a flat tire and had to pull off to the side of the road. Unfortunately, I'm going to be late."

He nodded. "Have you called for road service?"

"Yes, and they said they should be here in less than thirty minutes."

*Don't count on it,* he thought, knowing how slow road service could be this time of the year. "Where's your location, Ms. Blake?"

"I'm on Winterberry Road, about a mile from the Edgewater intersection. There's a market not far away, but it didn't appear to be open when I drove past earlier."

"And chances are it won't be open today. Fred Martin owns that market and never opens the day after a bad snowstorm," he said.

He knew her exact location now. "Look, you're not far from where I am. I'll call my personal road service company to change your tire. In the meantime, I'll pick you up and we can do a lunch meeting at McKay's instead of meeting at my office, since McKay's is closer. And afterward, I can take you back to your car. The tire will be changed by then."

"I—I don't want to put you to any trouble."

"You won't. I know you and Dillon have gone over some ideas for the party, but since I'll be handling things from here on out, I need to be briefed on what's going on. Usually my administrative assistant handles such matters, but she's out on maternity leave and this party is too important to hand off to anyone else."

And what he didn't bother to say because he was certain Dillon had done so already was that this would be the fortieth anniversary of the company his father and uncle had founded. This was not just a special event for the employees, but was important to everyone in the Westmoreland family.

"All right, if you're sure it won't be an inconvenience," she said, breaking into his thoughts.

"It won't be, and I'm on my way."

Alpha Blake tightened her coat around her, feeling totally frustrated. What did a person who had been born in sunny Florida know about the blistering cold of Denver, especially when it had snowed all night and the roads and everything else were covered with white?

But she was so determined to keep her noon appointment with Riley Westmoreland that she'd made a mess of things. Not only would she be late for their appointment, but because of her flat tire they would have to change the location of the meeting and Mr. Westmoreland would be the one driving her there. This was totally embarrassing when she had been trying to make a good impression. Granted, she'd already been hired by Dillon Westmoreland, but when his secretary called last week to say that she would be working with the next man in charge at Blue Ridge, namely Dillon's brother, Riley, she had felt the need to make a good impression on him, as well.

She turned up the heat in her car. Even with a steady stream of hot air coming in through the car vents, she still felt cold, too cold, and wondered if she would ever get used to the Denver weather. Of course it was too late to think about that now. It was her first winter here, and she didn't have any choice but to grin and bear it. When she'd moved, she'd felt that getting as far away from Daytona Beach as she could was essential to her peace of mind, although her friends thought she needed to have her head examined. Who in her right mind would prefer blistering cold Denver to sunny Daytona Beach? Only a person wanting to start a new life and put a painful past behind her.

Her attention was snagged when an SUV pulled off the road to park in front of her. The door swung open and long, denim-clad, boot-wearing legs appeared before a man stepped out of the truck and glanced her way. She met his gaze through the windshield and couldn't help the heart-piercing moment when she literally forgot to breathe. Walking toward her car was a man who was so dangerously masculine, so heart-stoppingly virile, that her brain went momentarily numb.

He was tall, and the Stetson on his head made him appear taller. But his height was secondary to the sharp handsomeness of the features beneath the brim of his hat. There was the coffee-and-cream color of his skin, his piercing dark brown eyes, a perfectly shaped nose, his full lips and a sculpted chin.

And she couldn't bypass his shoulders, massive and powerful-looking. It was hard to believe, with the temperature being what it was, that he seemed comfortable braving the harsh elements with a cowhide jacket instead of a heavy coat. It was in the low teens, and he was walking around like it was in the high sixties.

Her gaze slid all over him as he moved his long limbs toward her vehicle in a walk that was so agile and self-assured, she almost envied the confidence he exuded with every step. Her breasts suddenly peaked, and she could actually feel blood rushing through her veins. She didn't have to guess about what was happening to her, but still, she was surprised. This was the first time she'd reacted to a man since her breakup with Eddie.

The man made it to her car and tapped on the window. She all but held her breath as she pressed the button to roll it down. "Riley Westmoreland?" She really didn't have to ask since he favored his brother, Dillon.

"Yes. Alpha Blake?" he responded, offering her his hand through the open window while looking at her with what she thought was cool and assessing interest.

"Yes." She took his hand and even through her leather gloves, she thought it felt warm. "Glad to meet you, Mr. West-moreland."

"Riley," he corrected, smiling, and she felt her insides melt. He had a gorgeous pair of eyes. Dark and alluring. "The pleasure is all mine," he added. "I've only heard exceptional things about you and your work. Both Dillon and Pam speak highly of you, Alpha. I hope it's okay for me to call you Alpha."

"Thank you, and yes, that's fine."

"I've made all the arrangements with my road service. Keep your emergency lights on and leave your car keys under your seat," he said, taking a step back so she could get out of the vehicle.

She nervously gnawed her bottom lip. "Will it be safe to do that?"

He chuckled. "Yes, days like this keep thieves inside." He opened the car door for her. "Ready to get inside my truck?"

"Yes." She placed her key under the seat and then grabbed her purse and messenger bag. Tightening her coat around her, she walked quickly to the side of his truck. He was there to open the door and she appreciated finding the inside warm and cozy. It smelled like him, a scent that was masculine and sexy. She blushed, wondering why she was thinking such things, especially about a man she would be working for.

He closed the door just seconds before his cell phone rang, and she looked at the outside mirror as he spoke on the phone while moving around the front of the truck to get in the driver's side.

Opening the door, he climbed inside and proceeded to adjust the seat to accommodate his long legs before snapping his seat belt in place. The call had ended. He put his phone away and glanced over at her with a smile. She thought she would melt right then and there. "Warm?" he asked in a voice that was throatier than anything she'd ever heard.

*If only you knew,* she fought back saying. Instead her response was a simple "Yes. Thanks for asking."

"No problem." He then glanced into the rearview mirror before easing the truck onto the road.

The ensuing silence gave Riley the impression the woman was shy. And with her wrapped in a bulky coat and standing no more than five foot three, he figured she was probably short and stocky. He preferred tall, slender and curvy, but she had a pretty face that was eye-catching. She was definitely a looker. That had been the first thing he'd noticed. He was a sucker for a pretty face each and every time.

Deciding he didn't like the silence, he reached out and switched on the CD player. Immediately the soulful sound of Jill Scott filled the air. After a few moments, he concluded the music was not enough. To get a dialogue started, he asked conversationally, "I understand you're from Florida. What brought you to Denver?"

She tilted her head to look at him, and the first thing he noticed was her eyes. They were a chocolate brown and oval in shape. Then he was drawn to her hair, a beautiful shade of brown. The thick strands touched her shoulders and curled at the end. The coloring, whether natural or from a bottle, was perfect for her smooth, cocoa-colored complexion. And then there was that cute dimple in her chin, which was there even when she bore a serious expression.

"I've never been the adventurous type, but when my godmother passed away and left me enough funds that I could make a career change without going broke, I took advantage of it."

He nodded. "So what were you doing before you became an event planner?"

"I was a veterinarian."

"Wow. That was some career change."

She smiled. "Yes, it was."

He looked ahead, thinking that if she thought she would not have to explain why someone would stop being a veterinarian to become an event planner, she could think again. "How does a person go from being a vet to becoming a party planner?"

She pushed a lock of hair from her face and said, "Becoming a vet was my parents' idea, and I went along with it."

"Why?" He couldn't imagine going to college for anything other than what he wanted to do in life. He did, however, know how a person could get their dream career waylaid, as in the case of his cousin, Ramsey.

Ramsey had always wanted to be a sheep rancher, and he'd gone to school to study agricultural economics. The only reason Ramsey had taken a CEO position at Blue Ridge Management after school, instead of going into farming, was to work alongside Dillon to keep the company afloat when their parents had died in a plane crash. But once Ramsey and Dillon had made it into a million-dollar company, Ramsey had turned full management of Blue Ridge over to Dillon to become the sheep rancher he'd always wanted to be.

Riley's truck came to a stop at the traffic light, which gave him the opportunity to glance back over at Alpha just in time to see her gnawing her lips again and fidgeting with a sterling silver Tiffany bracelet on her wrist. *Umm, it seems "why" was another uncomfortable question,* he thought.

"I became a vet mainly to satisfy my parents. They own a veterinary clinic and figured I would join them and make it a family affair. I did so for a year, but discovered my heart just wasn't in it. They knew it, but still, they weren't happy when I decided to switch careers. However, they accepted that being an event planner was my calling when I put together their thirtieth wedding anniversary celebration."

"Did a good job of it, huh?" he asked.

She looked over at him and the smile that touched her lips extended from one corner of her mouth to the other and was simply breathtaking. "Yes, I did a bang-up job."

He laughed. "Good for you." He paused a second and asked, "Are you the only child?"

It seemed to take her longer than necessary to answer. "No. I have a sister."

He didn't say anything for a long moment and decided to change the subject. "So what do you have in mind for our employees' holiday bash next month?"

He listened as she went into the details. Some he was able to follow and some he could not. He was a visual person and couldn't use her words to produce mental images. He needed to see actual photographs to get the full effect.

She must have detected such from the expression on his face. "I had prepared a PowerPoint for today. But since we're meeting at the restaurant instead of your office, I—"

"Can still show the presentation. I called ahead and asked for a private meeting room."

"That's great. I have everything I need in here," she said, tapping lightly on the messenger case in her lap.

That caused him to glance down. She was wearing over-the-knee boots, a cute, dark brown leather pair. He glanced back up to her face and saw she was looking out the window, studying the scenery they were passing.

"I never come this way when going to McKay's."

He returned his gaze to the road. "It's a shortcut."

"Oh."

She got quiet again, and this time he decided to let the silence rule. He figured whenever she had anything to say, she would say it. In the meantime, he was perfectly satisfied to sit back and listen to Jill sing her heart out.

Alpha couldn't stop the fluttering in her stomach as she continued to look out the truck's window, trying hard to ignore the man behind the steering wheel. She would have to deal with Riley Westmoreland soon enough when they got to McKay's. She should have known he was drop-dead gorgeous, given Dillon wasn't bad on the eyes. And he seemed to be full of questions. At least he'd already asked two that she wished she could have avoided answering. The reason she had left Daytona was still too painful to think about and after the heated conversation she'd had with her parents last night, she preferred not to think of them right now, either.

Forcing thoughts of Daytona from her mind she saw that they were pulling into the parking lot of McKay's. It seemed the weather was not a deterrent for people wanting to dine at the popular restaurant. The parking lot was full, and Riley had to drive around back to find a spot.

She flexed her hands, liking how the gloves were keeping them warm, and tightened the coat around her as she prepared to get out of the vehicle and confront the cold again. She glanced over at Riley. He wasn't wearing gloves and it seemed the jacket was all he had. She couldn't help asking, "Aren't you cold?"

He smiled over at her. She wished he wouldn't do that because every time he did, he reminded her how long it had been since a man had smiled at her without her questioning his motives.

"Not really. Unlike most, I enjoy cold weather. For me, the colder the better."

She sat there and simply stared at him. He had to be kidding. "Why?"

He shrugged his massive shoulders. "Not sure. I guess I'm too hot-blooded to be bothered."

"Evidently," she said under her breath. If he heard her, he didn't let on. Instead, he opened the door to get out and she released her seat belt and opened her door to do the same. That's when she went sliding and would have fallen flat on her face if Riley hadn't acted quickly to catch her.

"I should have told you to be careful. The ice on the parking lot makes things slippery."

Yes, he should have told her. But if he had, there would have been no reason for his arms to be wrapped around her or for her to be holding on to him for support, feeling the heat of a hot-blooded man so close to her. And that same male scent that had nearly driven her crazy on the ride over wouldn't be doing a number on her.

"I think I can make it now," she said, releasing her tight grip on him.

He kept a firm hand on her arm. "I'll make sure of it." He then swept her off her feet and right into his arms.

# Two

Riley entered the restaurant carrying Alpha in his arms. The place was packed with a lunchtime crowd, and Alpha was certain she would die of embarrassment when a number of people watched them.

One man, who was on his way out the door, patted Riley on the back, chuckled and said, "You're still sweeping them off their feet, I see, son."

Riley grinned and replied, "Seems that way, Mr. Daniels." Riley then glanced down at her. "You should be okay from here," he said, putting her on her feet.

"Thanks." She refused to look up at him, but out of the corner of her eye she saw him take a step back. He was probably wishing he was someplace else since she hadn't cost him anything but trouble today.

"Welcome, Riley. The room you requested is ready," the hostess said, smiling, in a way that was a little too friendly, Alpha thought.

"Thanks, I appreciate it, and make sure we aren't disturbed, Paula."

Alpha shouldn't be surprised that the woman knew his name and that he knew hers.

"No problem," Paula said, gesturing for them to follow her. "We gave you the best room in the house." She looked over her shoulder, gave a dismissive glance to Alpha, then looked at Riley directly and said, "Because you deserve the best."

Alpha tried not to frown, wondering if that had been a deliberate dig. Didn't the woman know they were holding a business meeting? So why had she extended her claws?

Alpha felt a thrumming heat in the center of her back when Riley placed his hand there. Even through her coat and all the clothes she had put on to stay warm, she felt his touch and wondered if there would be a permanent handprint on her back.

She blinked when the door closed behind them, and it was then that she glanced around. The room was nice and spacious with a table for two in one corner. There was also a pull-down screen, a projector, speakers and everything else she would need to provide visuals of her plans for the party. And then there was the wall-to-wall window that provided a beautiful view of the mountains. How was anyone expected to work in here with such a gorgeous view?

"Do you want to do it first or eat?"

She swallowed deeply and drew in a deep breath, certain he hadn't meant "it" the way it had sounded. "Whichever you prefer—it's your call."

"In that case, I'll let Paula know we'll eat first. I'm starving."

She nodded, getting distracted watching him slide his jacket off his shoulders. Those massive shoulders were even more broad and powerful than she'd thought. At that moment, she saw firsthand how well his jeans fit his body, especially his tight, masculine thighs, and how they tapered down to his booted feet. He was definitely a hunk if ever there was one, a fine specimen of a man, hands down. He was a sample of pure masculinity, as raw as it could get.

Following his lead, she unbelted her heavy coat and shrugged it off. Then she peeled off her thick, wool sweater, unwrapped the scarf from around her neck and removed another bulky sweater. She had worn as much clothing as she could in order to stay warm.

Walking over to the coatrack to hang up everything she had taken off, she worked the kinks out of her neck and shoulders. Putting on so many garments had weighed her down and stiffened her muscles. She was flipping her hair back off her shoulders when she turned around to find Riley staring at her with an odd expression on his face.

She swallowed, feeling a bit uncomfortable at the way his penetrating dark eyes nearly swallowed her whole. She nervously licked her lips. "Is something wrong?"

Suddenly, a guarded look appeared in his gaze before he glanced out the window. When he switched his gaze back to her the look was gone. "No, nothing's wrong," he said in a brisk tone. "Excuse me for a minute while I let Paula know we'll eat first."

Alpha watched him leave while wondering what that had been all about.

Unnerved to the core, Riley closed the door behind him and leaned against it, releasing a deep breath. Every muscle in his body was thrumming with a need like he hadn't felt in a long time. He was glad the room he'd been given extended off a corridor for privacy…because at that moment he needed it.

Where in the hell had that curvy figure come from? He'd heard of a woman having an hourglass shape, but in all actuality, he'd never truly seen one. Until today.

He couldn't believe what Alpha Blake had been hiding underneath all those clothes. He'd almost dropped his chin to the floor when she started taking off that coat and those sweaters and then stood there in a pink, formfitting sweater dress belted at the waist, with over-the-knee boots. She looked so damn feminine that he'd been jolted with a degree of lust he'd never felt before.

Not only was she a looker, the woman had a body with luscious curves that could make a grown man weep. Lust, as sharp and keen as it could get, was taking over his senses, and the thoughts running through his mind were totally inappropriate, undeniably unacceptable and definitely X-rated.

Her waist was so small that if he blinked he might miss it. And her chest was a perfect size with nice perky breasts. The way the top portion of her dress pressed against those breasts had almost made his eyes pop out of their sockets. And then there was the way her hips flared from her small waist. They were smooth and shapely.

When she had walked over to the coatrack, he had taken it all in. He heard the heel of her boots clicking on the wooden floor and watched with deep male interest how her hips swayed with each step. He was convinced he'd never witnessed anything so sensual. And the shape of her backside filled his mind with all sorts of ideas.

Then she'd turned around and caught him staring. The look in her eyes had been unsettled, and he was sure the look in his had been cautious. That's usually the way it was with him when he'd been caught off guard and had to rebound. He was a man who, under no circumstances, mixed business with pleasure. But he'd wanted that rule to go rolling out the window the moment she'd taken off the coat and those sweaters. Okay, he would admit that it was a physical thing for him, but he couldn't help it. Westmoreland males enjoyed the physical.

"Need help with anything, Riley?"

Paula's question immediately snatched his thoughts back to the present. His gaze roamed up and down the short black hostess outfit she was wearing. Paula Wilmot had a nice body, but even hers couldn't hold a light to Alpha Blake's.

He and Paula had dated a couple of years ago. When it was time for him to move on, she somehow thought some injustice was being done. He had explained up front—as he did with all women he became involved with—that he didn't do long-term flings. Sex with no commitment. One month, six weeks at the most, was all the time he would put into an affair. Not enough time to get sentimental and clingy. That's the way he operated. He called it Riley's rule. Women knew up front what to expect—or not to expect—from him, and he liked it that way.

And the one thing he wouldn't tolerate was someone who agreed to his terms and then decided somewhere along the way to make getting a ring on her finger her number-one goal. All it had taken was a month with Paula to see what her intentions were. For some reason, she'd assumed she would be the woman capable of changing him. It wasn't happening. He'd wasted no time ending things and placing her on his Never Date Again list.

"Yes, please tell our server that my lunch guest and I have decided to eat before getting down to business."

Paula tipped her head to the side as a frown creased her brow. "And I can just imagine what kind of business you intend to get down to, Riley," she said curtly.

His gaze held hers intently. "Can you?"

"Yes. Do I need to remind you that I've been there with you and know just how you operate? So tell me. What does Ms. Frumpy have going for her? Good grief, Riley, I'm sure you can do better."

*Frumpy!* A vision of the ultrafine body of the woman he'd left in the room floated through his mind. He doubted he could do better. "First of all, this is a business meeting, Paula. Blue Ridge has hired Alpha to handle our holiday party. Secondly, none of my affairs, business or otherwise, are any of your concern." The only reason he'd told her the former was because he knew better than anyone about that vindictive tongue of hers. He refused to have her tarnish Alpha's reputation in any way.

Paula placed her hands on her hips. "One day a woman is going to come along and break your heart. I hope I'm around to see it."

Riley rubbed his hand down his face. Where was all this drama coming from? And why today? Hadn't he woken up in a good mood? "Fine, you've put a curse on me. I guess that means I won't sleep most nights worrying about it," he said, reaching out to open the door.

She quickly reached out and grabbed his hand. "Sorry, Riley, I shouldn't have said that, but you never returned my calls," she said in a frustrated tone.

He stared at her. "No, I haven't, and it's been almost two years, right?"

"Yes."

He nodded slowly, lifting a brow before turning to open the door, hoping she got it that time.

Alpha looked up from her laptop when she heard Riley returning. He glanced around and saw that she had set up the room for the presentation. "I thought we were going to eat first," he said.

"We are. I thought it would save time if I had everything ready so I can move right into my presentation."

He nodded as he sat down at the table. She was about to ask if he could see the huge screen from where he sat when the door opened and a waiter entered, carrying a pitcher of water and menus. Deciding she had wasted Riley's time enough for one day, she moved toward the table when the waiter began filling their glasses with water.

She took the seat across from him and was glad when the waiter handed her a menu. She needed something else, anything else, other than Riley to occupy her attention. She might be wrong, but he seemed upset about something. Was he upset with her?

She placed her menu down. "I'm sorry, Riley."

He glanced up from his own menu and arched a brow. "For what?"

"For getting off to such a bad start with you—having a flat tire, taking you out of your way to come get me, and then having our meeting place changed to accommodate me."

He gave his head a little shake. "No apology necessary. You haven't gotten off to a bad start with me, Alpha. I'm fully aware there are days that don't go quite as well as you'd like. You didn't ask for that flat tire, did you?"

"Goodness, no."

"Then don't worry about it. I'm just glad I was able to help. And as far as having to change our meeting place, McKay's is a favorite of mine, and I'll think of any excuse to get some of their chicken noodle soup. Have you had any?"

She shook her head. "No, I've only eaten their burgers and fries."

He smiled. "Then you don't know what you're missing. You need to try it, if for nothing more than a cup as an appetizer."

He had her curious. "Okay, thanks. I think I will."

She picked up her glass of water to take a sip and then she said, "So you come here often?"

"Yes. Tony McKay and I were good friends all through high school. We went to different colleges and he ended up taking a job in Phoenix. When his father died, he returned to Denver to help his mother close down the restaurant, but decided to stay and run it instead. He wasn't crazy about the job he'd landed after college and his management degree gave him plenty of ideas on how to take this place to a whole new level."

He paused to take another sip of his water. "Old man McKay would not have approved of the changes Tony made, especially with the expansion and keeping the place open until midnight. He didn't believe in change and fought it tooth and nail. Tony and I tried to convince him for years that the only constant was change, and so he might as well get used to it. We told him to embrace it like everyone else so he could stay competitive."

He chuckled. "Tony not only embraces change, but he's implemented a few precedents. Such as convincing our school board to add a culinary class to their high school curriculum and then giving students jobs to gain firsthand experiences while getting class credits."

"Smart move."

Riley smiled. "We thought so."

She glanced back at her menu. "So what else would you suggest other than my usual burger and fries?"

"Umm, you can't go wrong with their chicken. It's covered with the best gravy you can eat and comes with mouthwatering scalloped potatoes and hot buttered yeast rolls."

She couldn't help frowning. "That sounds like a lot of food."

"It is, but if the forecasters are right, you might be snowed in for the next day or two and leftovers would come in handy."

Was that excitement she heard in his voice? "You really do like it, don't you?"

"Like what?"

He glanced over at her, and the moment he did so she felt a zing in the pit of her stomach. Why was her body reacting so much to him? She was twenty-seven and knew all about chemistry between a man and a woman, but she'd never in her life experienced anything so potent. "The cold weather. I thought you were teasing about liking it, but apparently you weren't. Here I was, all bundled up like I was living at the North Pole, and you were wearing a lightweight jacket as if you could barely feel the cold."

He shrugged, and she couldn't help but admire the undulating movement of his shoulders beneath his shirt. "I guess I'm immune. I've been here all my life and was told I was born during one of Denver's worst snowstorms. I've always enjoyed playing in the snow."

He chuckled and the sound floated around the room with such a rich octave it made Alpha draw in a charged breath. "February is my favorite month because that's usually when Denver is the coldest."

Riley leaned back in his chair and her gaze was drawn to his hands. For a quick second, she recalled how those hands had felt when he'd picked her up and carried her into the restaurant. She had felt the warmth of them through the thickness of her clothes.

"Today is nothing compared to how things will get later on," he said, breaking into her thoughts. "Surely you understood what you were doing when you traded sunny Florida for Denver?"

Alpha drew in a deep breath. No, she hadn't fully understood. The only thing she'd known was that she needed to put as much distance between her, Eddie and her parents as she could. "I didn't expect it to be this cold so soon. I figured I would prepare myself for January and February, but it's still November."

"Yes, and Thanksgiving is right around the corner. Are you going back south for turkey and dressing?"

Not on her life. "No. I plan on spending Thanksgiving here since I have a couple of projects during that time." And they were projects she could have gotten out of doing had she wanted to, but she hadn't.

The waiter returned to take their orders, and she was glad for the interruption. She was getting too comfortable with Riley and had to admit that he made such a thing easy. He came across as a nice guy. Down-to-earth. A real gentleman, respectful. It was nice to know that for some men, sex wasn't the only thing on their minds.

# Three

Riley shifted in his seat, thinking that if Alpha knew all the things that were going through his mind, she would think he was as low as low could go. He had met her less than two hours ago and all he could think about was jumping her bones. No, jumping her bones was too quick and raunchy. He would love easing between those legs and then…

When he heard the sound of her lightly clearing her throat, he realized the waiter standing beside him had poured cups of coffee and was waiting to take his order. He glanced up at the waiter. George. The seventy-something man had worked at McKay's for ages and had waited on him plenty of times before with many of his other dates. Was that a smirk on George's face because the old man had finally caught him being taken with a woman?

"And what can I get for you, Mr. Westmoreland?"

"The usual, George."

"All right," George said, taking the menu from Riley.

Riley glanced over at Alpha and saw she was absorbed in

the beauty of the mountains that could be seen through the windows. "It's beautiful, isn't it?" he asked, studying her more so than the mountains he'd seen all his life.

"Yes."

Sitting this close to her, he could see just how beautiful, how stunning, she was. That wasn't a good thing. How was he supposed to concentrate on whatever presentation she was giving when he wanted to concentrate on her?

She broke eye contact while reaching for her coffee to take a sip and he did likewise. "So, other than the cold weather, how do you enjoy living in Denver so far?" he asked her.

"I like it. I'm grateful that the people here have been so kind. I didn't expect my business to take off like it has."

"I understand your work speaks for itself. My sister-in-law was definitely impressed."

She smiled. "Pam is super nice."

Their conversation was interrupted when George returned with their appetizers, still wearing that smirk on his face.

Alpha drew in a deep breath. She had done presentations quite a few times and knew there wasn't a shy bone in her body, but standing in front of Riley had butterflies floating around in her stomach.

She looked over at him to find him looking back at her. She forced a smile. "I promise to have you out in fifteen minutes."

"Take your time."

*He would say that,* she thought. Their waiter had cleared the table and filled their cups.

"The first thing we need to decide on is a theme for that night. These are the ones I came up with while trying to stay away from holiday themes. Because of diversity in the work-place, the last thing you want to do is offend anyone."

"So what do you suggest?" he asked her.

"A winter theme always works. These are a few that I've come up with," she said, clicking the remote in her hand to bring the screen alive. "As you can see, I have Winter Wonderland, Winter Delight, One Winter's Night and Winter Around the World."

She watched him study each suggestion. He shifted his eyes back to her, and she felt her stomach stir from the intensity of his gaze. "What's your favorite?"

"It's really your decision."

He nodded. "I know, but which one do you like the best?"

She glanced up at the screen. "Based on the fact that this year there will be a nighttime party in the ballroom of the Pavilion Hotel, instead of the daytime party you usually hold at the office, I like One Winter's Night. There's a sort of magical ring. I like it."

A smile curved his lips. "So do I. Let's go with it."

Alpha nodded, excited that he'd liked the same theme that she did. "All right. And as far as the ballroom at the Pavilion Hotel, I took a tour a few days ago. It will hold up to two thousand people," she said, showing an aerial view of the huge hotel, which was located midway between downtown and the airport.

"And it's a definite we have it for that night?"

"Yes," she said, smiling. "They were happy to accommodate us. The Westmoreland name carries a lot of weight."

Deciding to move on to the next point, she said, "I thought it would be nice to set the mood by having it be a dressy affair."

He lifted a brow. "How dressy?"

"Black tie." At the grimace on his face, she smiled and quickly said, "Not as bad as all that, Riley. I think your employees will appreciate it. It will make them feel special. Other than your family's annual charity ball, your employees probably never have anyplace to go where they can dress up and feel as if they're stepping out on the town."

He nodded slowly, and she knew he was thinking about the idea. She just wished she didn't feel that sexual chemistry between them even while discussing business. "Let's table that for at least a week," he suggested.

"All right," she said. "But I'll need a decision on the attire in order to determine what sort of decorations will be appropriate."

"I'll keep that in mind."

"Last but not least," she said, switching off the screen, "is the discussion of the budget. That handout I've given you breaks everything down. I inflated the expenses to allow for decorations. I'd rather operate on the high end versus a low one."

She paused a moment and then said, "Those are all of my ideas and suggestions. Is there anything you want to add or change?"

He shook his head. "No, I think you did a thorough job explaining things."

"Thank you," she said, crossing the room to place the remote near the television screen. That's when she dropped her ink pen and leaned down to pick it up.

For the second time that day Riley was slapped with a case of lust so thick he wondered how in the hell he was going to stand without giving away his body's reaction. She had leaned down to pick up her pen, and the way the material of her dress stretched snug across that gorgeous backside, he'd almost swallowed his tongue. Drawing in a deep breath, he used his hand to wipe away the perspiration forming on his forehead.

"Need help with anything?"

"No, thanks," she said, flicking a quick glance in his direction before returning to what she was doing. He continued to sit there, almost willing her to glance back at him, hold his gaze, feel his heat and not deny the potent chemistry flowing between them.

At that moment, he made a decision. "We'll need to meet

again next week, after I've reached a decision about the attire for the event."

He knew she was probably wondering why they needed to meet to discuss that when it was something they could cover over the phone. Instead of questioning him about anything, though, she simply said, "That's fine. Do you know when and where?"

"I'll call you."

She met his gaze and held it. He knew at that moment that if she hadn't felt the strong undercurrents flowing between them before, she did now. "All right."

Now that was where he disagreed with her. It wasn't all right, but he didn't know a way to change the path he seemed determined to take where she was concerned.

He watched as she re-dressed in her two heavy sweaters, scarf, huge overcoat and gloves. Was all that necessary? Evidently to her they were. If she wanted to stay warm the best thing she needed was body heat. Namely, his.

"I'm ready to go."

Glad he had gotten his body under control and that there was no sign of the lust that had overtaken it earlier, he stood. "Do I need to carry you out?" he teased.

Her eyes rounded and it amused him that she'd assumed he was serious. "No, and I'm sorry you felt the need to do so before. I'm usually not clumsy," she said apologetically.

"You weren't clumsy, Alpha. You aren't used to walking on icy, slippery surfaces and that's understandable. Will you do me a favor?"

She tilted up her head to look at him. "What?"

"Stop apologizing. You haven't done anything wrong."

"Thanks."

"Doing that must drive your boyfriend crazy," he said, deliberately fishing for information.

"I don't have a boyfriend."

"Oh." He placed his hand in the center of her back as he led her out of the room. So she didn't have a boyfriend. Hmm.

An hour or so later Alpha entered her home and immediately shrugged off her heavy coat and began peeling off her sweaters and gloves. It was then that she missed her scarf and figured she must have left it in Riley's truck.

During their ride back to her car she'd noticed he no longer seemed to be on guard with her, the way he had been at the restaurant earlier, and she took advantage by keeping the conversation going about the holiday party—One Winter's Night. The more she talked about it the more excited she got.

Once they reached her car, she saw her tire was fixed and her car keys were back where she'd left them. He wouldn't accept any money for having her tire taken care of, so she thanked him for lunch. After assuring him she would follow up with him in a week to discuss the attire for the party, she hurried off to her car. He had sat in his truck, watching her drive off.

Now she was home, inside the house she'd fallen in love with the first time she'd seen it. The last house in the cul-de-sac of a street where all the backyards faced the mountains, it was smaller than her place in Daytona but she'd always thought her condo on the beach had been too large for her anyway. Now she didn't have any wasted space, and the windows facing her backyard provided a gorgeous view of the mountains. However, there were days she missed the beach, until she remembered she had given up the beach for a reason.

Sitting down on the sofa, she began removing her boots. The first thing she'd done after buying the house was carpet the majority of the tile floors. The thought of getting out of bed and letting her feet touch cold tile had sent chills up her body. Other than that she hadn't changed a thing. Definitely not the extensive woodwork trim or the custom cabinets.

Moments later, taking her shoes in her hand, she walked

in bare feet to her bedroom while thinking about what had driven her here to Denver.

Eddie Swisher.

At one time, she had thought he was everything she had wanted in a man. In the end, she'd discovered he was nothing more than a puppet with his parents pulling the strings. She would never forget the day, a mere week before her wedding, when he had shown up at her place and dropped the bomb. A family meeting had been called and his family had voted. It had been decided that he couldn't marry her unless she vowed to disown Omega, her twin sister—the former porn star. After all, he had pointed out, her own parents had turned their backs on Omega. He couldn't understand why she wouldn't do the same. It had meant nothing to him that Omega was no longer in the business or that she had met a man who'd adored her regardless of her past. It was a past her parents and Eddie just couldn't get beyond.

At least he hadn't stooped to the same level as LeBron Roberts, the guy she'd dated before Eddie. When LeBron had learned of her twin's occupation, he'd assumed Alpha would miraculously transform into Omega in the bedroom. When she had dashed those hopes, he hadn't wasted any time in dropping her.

Her thoughts shifted back to Riley. He was a fine specimen of a man, definitely a threat to the peace she was trying to find. It didn't take much for her to remember those beautiful dark eyes, long lashes and the way his jaw curved whenever he smiled. She'd never been drawn to any male with such intensity. He took the word *sexy* to all new heights. She had been attracted to LeBron and Eddie but not to the same degree. It was something about his voice, the way he looked at her, his entire presence that made her think of long winter nights—with him.

She tossed the hair from her face, thinking she had truly gotten her drool-on today, whether he knew it or not. And it was best that he didn't know since it couldn't lead anywhere. She had definitely learned her lesson. When her relationship with Eddie ended she had vowed not to get seriously involved with another man. It wasn't worth the pain and hassle.

She dropped her boots in the closet and, leaving her bedroom, moved on to her family room. It was small and cozy. At the moment, she wanted cozy. She would curl up on her sofa and find something interesting on television. Or better yet, she could just relive her time with Riley. For just a little while, she would wallow in fantasies and then, later, she would get up and try getting some work done.

Riley sat on the sofa in his living room in front of his fireplace, drinking a cold beer while replaying in his mind his encounter with Alpha. Now that he had satisfied his curiosity about her, knew she was competent and could handle what Dillon had hired her to do, he could easily delegate any one of his supervisors to work with her. But he didn't want to do that, and for the life of him he couldn't understand why, especially when it was obvious the woman posed a lot of problems for him.

He knew that she had the ability to drive any man to distraction, which was the last thing he needed. No other woman had been capable of doing such a thing to him, but after meeting her today, he believed that she could, physically and mentally. The thought that he was even considering mixing business with pleasure was the first sign that he had messed up somewhere. He'd allowed her to get under his skin. But with single-minded determination, he intended to get her out.

He had learned his lesson by watching how obsessed his youngest brother, Bane, had been with Crystal Newsome and the heartbreak Bane had suffered when the teenage lovers had been forced apart.

Riley released a deep sigh. Bane had been the last child born to his parents, and everyone had assumed Bane would be a girl, the daughter their parents didn't have. Things didn't turn out that way. They'd gotten Bane. Personally, Riley had been happy about it. Who wanted a sister anyway? He had his girl cousins, Megan and Gemma, and as far as he was concerned, they were enough. So he'd become Bane's protector while growing up, or at least he'd tried. But he hadn't been able to foresee the pain Bane would suffer when, at eighteen, he fell in love with sixteen-year-old Crystal. Her parents had been against the match from the start and had separated the teens by sending Crystal away to parts unknown.

Riley would never forget that day for as long as he lived. A heartbroken Bane had ridden his horse out alone. When he hadn't returned at a reasonable hour, Dillon had gotten worried and sent Riley looking for him.

He had found Bane in an old abandoned shack that had been on the Westmoreland property for years. The moment Riley had entered the place he'd known it had been Crystal and Bane's love nest. But what had really gripped Riley's insides was the sound of Bane howling like a tormented and wounded animal.

Riley had actually felt his brother's pain and heartbreak that day. The sound had pierced something deep within him, and he'd wondered what there was about love that could torture and torment even a badass dude like Bane. On that day he'd vowed never to find out.

Without letting Bane know he was there, Riley had backed out of the shack and left, allowing his brother to grieve privately for the love he'd lost. That had been several years ago, but Riley's vow to never fall for a woman hadn't changed. That's when he had implemented Riley's Rule.

Reaching out, he picked up the wool scarf Alpha had left in his truck and brought it to his nose. It smelled like her. Sweet. Womanly. Enticing…so damn enticing. And the scent reminded him of all the heated desire that had warped his senses during the time he'd been with her. It was heated desire that was still slowly driving him insane.

He placed the scarf aside and picked up his cell phone to redial the number that had come through that morning. He felt his stomach tighten when he heard her soft voice.

"Hello?"

"Alpha? This is Riley. You left your scarf in my truck, and I want to get it back to you. Will you be home tomorrow?"

There was a slight hesitation and then she said, "Yes, but you don't have to come out of your way to return it, Riley. I have several of them."

"No problem. I want to make sure you get this one back. You live in the Arlington Heights area, right?"

"Yes."

"I'll be out that way tomorrow around two. Is it okay for me to drop by?"

Another slight hesitation. "Yes, I'll be home."

"Fine, I'll see you then."

Riley clicked off the phone. He was doing the decent thing by returning the scarf and nothing more. The thought that he was itching to see her again had nothing to do with it.

He brought the scarf to his nose once more. Yes, he definitely wanted to see her again.

# Four

"I should have been more forceful about him not returning that darn scarf," Alpha muttered as she glanced at herself again in the full-length mirror in her bedroom. "I guess, considering the layers of clothes I was wearing to keep warm yesterday, he figured I must need every piece."

Drawing in a deep breath, she licked her lips, wondering if she should put on lipstick. If she did, he might assume she'd gotten pretty just for him. She frowned, knowing that, in essence, she had. Wednesday was the day she usually did housework and seldom put anything on other than her sweats. But not today.

She had awakened and quickly straightened up, eaten lunch, baked her favorite cinnamon rolls, showered and dressed in a canary-yellow buttoned shirt that tied at the waist and a denim skirt that hit above the knee. A pair of striped, black-and-white ballet flats that she had purchased before leaving Daytona were on her feet.

"I look cute, if I have to say so myself," she said softly and then threw her head back and laughed. When was the last time she had gone to a lot of trouble to look good for a man? Why was she doing so now?

Okay, she thought, deciding to put on lipstick after all, she would answer the first question. The last time had been for her parents' anniversary party a year or so ago and the man had been Eddie. In all honesty, she had stopped thinking of her and Eddie as a couple long before he'd given her that ultimatum about Omega. They had begun drifting apart. Once she had gotten serious about becoming an event planner they had found excuse after excuse to not spend time together. It hadn't bothered her, and she had a feeling it hadn't bothered him, either. Yet neither of them had made a move to call off their wedding for those reasons.

Her thoughts drifted back to the second half of the question she'd asked herself. Why was she going out of her way to look good for Riley? It could be that a part of her wanted to feel like a woman—a woman any man could be interested in, a woman a man could and would notice.

He *had* noticed the other day, which surprised her when she'd caught him staring. She hadn't expected him to display as strong a reaction to her as she had to him. And she was certain she hadn't imagined it. It had been there in his eyes when she'd turned around. Although it had been quickly replaced with a guarded look, it had been there.

"Okay, for the first time in a long time I feel like a desirable woman, and I like it," she said, after applying her lipstick and pursing her lips to see the effect.

Even before they'd broken up, Eddie had stopped going out of his way to make her feel like she could rock his world. But with Riley the sparks had been there, and they were sparks that sizzled. They had both tried to downplay it, but hadn't been successful. And that was one of the things that concerned her. Would the sparks be there when she saw him again today?

She was about to take the comb and work with her hair some more when she heard the doorbell. Riley was early. A good five minutes early. Looking at herself in the mirror one last time, she tied her hair back from her face before quickly leaving her bedroom. She headed for the door, not sure if those five minutes were a good thing or a bad thing.

Riley glanced around. Nice house. The stucco structure with an A-line roof and carved columns on the porch suited her. The Arlington Heights area was one of the oldest in Denver, but he could tell her home had been added within the past ten years or so. She had a pretty nice neighborhood. Quiet. Serene. Mountains as a backdrop and snow-covered yard. It had snowed again overnight and was slow in melting.

On the drive over, he kept asking himself what he was doing. He could easily mail the scarf to her, return it when they met again next week or keep it for a souvenir. But here he was, standing on her doorstep like a lust-craved addict eager for one glimpse of her.

Okay, who was he kidding? He wanted more than a glimpse. He wanted *her*. In his bed. There was no reason for him to deny it because it was true. He had tried talking himself out of wanting her all through the night but had failed miserably. In the end, he'd figured that as long as he applied Riley's Rule he would be safe. And as for mixing business with pleasure, technically, she was on contract and not a real employee of Blue Ridge. Now, if he could get her to go along with his proposition, then an affair would be a surefire way of taking care of this desire before she had a chance to get deeper into his system.

He heard her at the door and knew she had looked out the peephole at him. He had felt her checking him out, which was fine since he planned on checking her out, as well. Chances were she wasn't covered in all those coats and sweaters today. Hell, he hoped not.

The door opened, and she stood there. He had to clamp his jaws together to stop them from dropping. If he'd thought she looked good yesterday then he was totally unprepared for how stunning she looked today. His gaze roamed over her, and he quickly decided that he loved her outfit. It emphasized her figure.

"Riley."

"Alpha."

She licked her lips, and his stomach tightened. Not for the first time, he thought she had a nice-looking tongue. He couldn't wait to taste it.

"You brought the scarf?" she asked, intruding into his thoughts.

"Yes." Did she expect him to hand it over to her right here and now and then leave? Did she not expect him to hang around for a few minutes? He hadn't thought of that possibility.

He pulled the scarf out of his jacket pocket. "Here's the scarf."

She took it. "Thanks." And then she asked the question he'd been waiting for, the one he had begun to fear she wouldn't ask. "Would you like to come in? I just made a fresh pot of coffee and was about to have a cup with some cinnamon rolls I made earlier."

He forced his feet to stay put and not rush past her. "Sounds good. Yes, I'd like a cup of coffee and rolls."

She moved aside and he walked in, inhaling her scent as he brushed by her. It was the same scent on the scarf. He glanced around her home, admiring the furnishings, crown moldings, spindle staircase and beautiful light fixtures in the ceiling. She had a great room with a huge fireplace, and he loved that a blaze was going inside of it, throwing warmth into the room.

"Would you like to give me your jacket?"

He glanced over at her. "Sure," he said, shrugging off his

jacket and handing it to her. She walked over to the coatrack, and he watched her every move. He had to clamp down on his lips to not let out a whistle. The woman had the most gorgeous legs he'd ever seen. When she turned around, there was no need to act innocent. He'd been caught red-handed checking out her legs.

He cleared his throat. "Nice shoes."

"Thanks."

"Different." Although he hadn't been concentrating on her shoes, they *were* different. Striped.

She glanced down at them. "Different but comfortable. Do you want your coffee out here or in the kitchen?"

He shoved his hands inside the pockets of his jeans. "Where do you usually take yours?"

"In the kitchen."

"Then lead the way."

And she did. He deliberately stayed a few paces behind her to check out her legs, waist and backside. And no, he had no shame. She had more sensuality in her walk than some women had in their entire bodies, and the male in him felt the need to take the time to appreciate it.

She was wearing flats, but with her shapely calves he could just imagine those legs in a pair of stilettos. Her skirt was a decent length, but if it had been just a tad shorter he would probably have already had a heart attack. At that moment, he felt blood rushing straight to his groin.

He walked into her kitchen and stopped, equally impressed by the custom maple cabinets, granite countertops and stainless-steel appliances. The high-top café table was facing a huge window overlooking her backyard, which included a view of the mountains.

"How do you take your coffee?"

He glanced over at her. "Black and as strong as you can get it."

She smiled. "My dad drinks his the same way."

"Does he?" he asked, sliding onto a bar stool.

"Yes. My mom prefers hot chocolate and so did I."

She brought the coffee to him with a tray of sweet-smelling rolls. They looked fresh, hot and delicious. Just like her. He took a sip of coffee. It was good, just like he figured she would be. He bit into a roll and closed his eyes. It was delicious.

He opened his eyes and found her smiling at him. "Hit a sweet tooth, huh?" she asked.

*If only she knew.* "Homemade?"

"Yes, one of my mom's old recipes. She likes to bake."

"It's delicious," he said, taking another bite and then gobbling up the rest of it while thinking he would love gobbling her up in the same way.

"You can have another. I ate a couple earlier."

"Thanks." He didn't waste time taking her up on her offer, grabbing another one off the plate and biting into it.

"Thanks for bringing my scarf back, but like I told you, you didn't have to do it. It could have waited."

Riley glanced over at her, thinking that, no, it could not have waited. He was one of those men who, once he made up his mind about something, there was no turning back, no hesitation and no stopping him. He hadn't been in an affair for about four months now, mainly because he'd had a lot on his plate at the office while taking over for Dillon. Now that he had things at a level where he could work without too much stress, he had time for some of the finer, more enjoyable things in life. All work and no play wasn't good for anyone.

"The reason I brought the scarf back, Alpha, is because I wanted to see you again. And I would have found any excuse to do so."

He watched her expression. She probably hadn't counted on him being so in-your-face honest. But he always was at the beginning of his affairs…and at the end.

She licked her lips. He was beginning to recognize that as a sign that she was nervous. She held his gaze for a moment and asked after taking a sip of coffee, "Would you have... found any excuse?"

"Yes. We're adults, and I don't like playing games. I believe in being up-front with any woman I'm interested in."

"And you're interested in me?"

He heard the surprise in her voice. "Yes, but you should have known that after yesterday. There is chemistry between us. A lot of it. I could barely watch you while you gave that presentation without getting turned on."

Maybe he'd given her too much information, but he wanted her to know just what he was dealing with. What they were both dealing with, because although she hadn't admitted anything yet, he had a gut feeling she was as attracted to him as he was to her.

She looked down and nervously began toying with her paper napkin, but he preferred that she look at him. He needed to know what she was thinking. "Alpha?"

She glanced up, and the look he saw in her eyes made his stomach quiver all the way to his groin. That same potent chemistry, that electrical sizzle, they had shared yesterday was present today whether she wanted it to be or not. It was just as strong and powerful...but he could tell she was fighting it tooth and nail. Why?

"We just met yesterday," she said softly.

He nodded. She had to do better than that. As far as he was concerned meeting just yesterday didn't mean a thing. People were into one-night stands. He'd done a number of those himself. "And?"

"And I'm working for you."

Okay, now she was trying to play the "it's not ethical" card, but it wouldn't work. "No, you're not working for me, at least you're not my employee. You're on assignment for Blue Ridge Land Management for a project that ends next month. As far as I'm concerned that has nothing to do with what's going on between us."

"There's nothing going on between us," she said, taking another sip of coffee.

Now she wanted to be in denial and he wasn't going along with that, either. He leaned back in his chair and stared at her. For a long moment he didn't say anything and then he said, "I want to know why you're sitting there denying what is so blatantly obvious."

Her lips began quivering, in anger or desire he wasn't sure, but neither curtailed the electricity sizzling between them. "And just what do you think is so blatantly obvious?" she asked in a quiet tone.

He reached out and placed his hand over hers. The moment he did so, he felt what she wanted to deny. A heated spiral of desire flowed between them, and she gasped softly. He wanted her to feel it. He needed her to feel it. And he knew by the look in her eyes that she had.

"What is so blatantly obvious, Alpha, is that I want you and you want me."

Alpha couldn't stop the chaotic fluttering in her stomach. Nor could she slow down the beating of her heart. What was Riley doing to her? What was he making her feel? All these incredible sensations that she'd never felt before were swamping her all at once.

She tried to force herself to think logically. She needed to make him understand something about her. "I've never been a woman to engage in casual relationships, Riley."

"There's a first time for everything, isn't there?" he asked, still holding her gaze as if he was looking deep into her very soul.

Yes, there was a first time for everything, but she wasn't sure she was ready for what she knew would be nothing more than a fling. But another part of her was demanding to know *why* she wasn't ready. She had moved from Florida to Colorado to start a new life. It wasn't that she hadn't gotten over

Eddie, because she had. So what was the holdup? Riley was ultrahandsome, much too sexy, and he was attracted to her. Why was she afraid to go with the flow?

He leaned in close to her. "In that case, I propose we take some time to get to know each other, but…"

She'd known there was going to be a *but* in there somewhere.

"But that we enjoy each other while doing so."

Her pulse quickened. She didn't have to ask how they would enjoy each other. The man was pushing all her buttons, in ways she hadn't known existed. He was making her consider doing things she'd never thought of doing before.

"With all of my affairs there are rules so we have a good understanding from day one," he added.

She lifted an arched brow. "What rules?"

He smiled. "First, there needs to be a time limit on how long the affair will last. Definitely no longer than six weeks."

She nodded. "What else?"

"There has to be exclusivity. I'm not into sharing. Neither am I into clinginess. This affair doesn't give us the right to crowd each other. We need to respect each other's space."

Evidently he'd had issues in the past. Well, he wouldn't have to worry about those issues with her. "Okay."

"And if, for whatever reason, the rules are broken by either of us, the affair ends," he said.

His rules were reasonable, but still… "I need to think about it," she said. At least he was being honest by letting her know up front what he wanted out of a relationship. She could appreciate that.

"That's fine. Since we need to meet next week to discuss some things regarding the party, you can give me your answer then. What about Monday? Hopefully the weather will be better and we can meet at my office. Let's say around ten. Is that time okay for you?"

"Yes, ten o'clock will work."

"Good." He stood. "I'm sure you have a lot to do today, so I'll be going. Thanks for the coffee and rolls."

She stood as well, thinking how his height seemed to dominate the room. She never thought her kitchen was small until now. "You're welcome."

He took her hand and held it gently in his while they walked through her great room back toward the door. Hand-holding was something she'd always craved but something Eddie had never delivered. He wasn't a touchy-feely type.

When they reached the door she turned to Riley, to again thank him for returning her scarf, but the words died on her lips. He had the most irresistible smile, one that showed his dimples. To distract herself, she looked over his shoulder at the picture hanging on her wall, but Riley lifted his hand to cup her chin and return her gaze to him. Then he softly trailed his fingertips along the lines of her jaw.

In that heated moment, when their eyes connected, she felt a sensual connection to him all the way to her toes. She wanted to take a step back but couldn't. Like he'd said, she couldn't deny what was taking place between them.

"I want to leave you with something to think about."

She didn't have to ask what that something was because she knew. The rippling of coiled anticipation in her stomach spelled it out for her. He was about to stamp his presence all over her, and she would do more than think about it, she would fantasize about it for years to come.

Her heart skipped a few beats when he released her chin to ease his arms around her waist and settle his hands right above her backside. Then he took a step closer while their gazes remained connected. There was a heated resolve in the dark depths of the eyes staring into hers. And when she saw him lowering his head, her feet—of their own accord—arched on tiptoes so she could meet his lips. All those amazing and incredible feelings she'd encountered since meeting him totally obliterated her senses.

The man had all but admitted the only thing he wanted from her was sex, but she hadn't decided whether or not he would be getting what he wanted. All she cared about for the time being was locking her lips with his, taking in more of his scent and acquiring his taste. She was tired of dealing with all these crazy emotions and sensations. She wanted relief, and she knew one place where she could find it.

*Right here,* she thought, the moment Riley's mouth aimed straight for hers.

His tongue entered her on impact, and she responded on instinct. Reaching up, she wrapped her arms around his neck and pressed her body closer to his. No kiss had ever made her feel like this. Riley was a master at using his tongue, and he was doing so with a skill that nearly brought her to her knees. He explored first one side of her mouth then the other. And he was doing it with such intimacy that she felt it deep in her bones.

He was taking her mouth greedily, as if this was his one-and-only chance. He was giving a whole new definition to French-kissing, and she moaned with every lick, every suck and every blatant stroke.

Alpha was certain she would lose her mind if Riley didn't let go of her mouth, and he seemed in no hurry to release it. Instead, he continued to take it in an even deeper kiss, stroking his tongue in a way that sent high degrees of desire spreading all through her. The hard bluntness of his arousal pressed like steel into her belly, and she moved her body to cradle it in the juncture of her thighs.

She knew he was intentionally driving her mad, branding her and leaving his mark. The heat flaring in her midsection was sending her hormones—which were getting his name stamped all over them—raging out of control.

And then he slowly pulled his mouth away. Heavy-lidded dark eyes remained steady on her. She tried to stop the way her stomach was quivering and found she wasn't able to do so. Nothing was capable of bringing a halt to the sensations stampeding through her.

"Now, a promise to you, Alpha. If you agree to what I suggested," he said in a low, throaty voice, "I'll make sure that we enjoy each other in a way no two humans have ever done."

He then leaned down and lightly brushed the tip of his tongue across her lips before opening the door and walking out of it.

# Five

Riley thought this had been the longest week of his life. Now the day had finally arrived when he would be seeing Alpha again. More than once he'd been tempted to come up with any excuse to pick up the phone and call her to see how she was coming along in her thought processes regarding the affair he'd proposed.

He would find out in a couple of hours at their scheduled meeting. He'd even arrived to work early, had advised the receptionist covering the lobby to send Alpha in as soon as she arrived. There was no need for her to wait. He was tired of waiting.

There was a knock on his door, and he knew from the three repetitive knuckle raps that it was his brother, Canyon. Dropping by Riley's office at the start of the workday was the norm for both Canyon and his other brother, Stern. Riley was eleven months older than Canyon and almost two years older than Stern. The three of them had been close while growing up, and although they didn't always agree on everything, they had deep respect for one another. Working for the family firm after college had always been their goal in life, and they enjoyed working alongside Dillon to preserve the legacy their father and uncle had begun. All his brothers worked in some capacity at Blue Ridge except for Micah, who was an epidemiologist with the federal government; Jason, who, along with cousins Zane and Derringer, was in the horse training and breeding business; and Riley's youngest brother, Bane, who was in the navy.

"Come in."

Canyon, who was one of the firm's attorneys, quickly walked in with his briefcase in hand. "I need to run something by you, Ry. It's that dispute we're trying to settle out of court with Shade Tree Developers. We're holding our initial meeting tomorrow."

Riley looked at his watch. "Okay, I have less than a half hour to spare, so make it quick."

Canyon lifted a brow. "And just what fire are you going to?"

Riley tossed aside some papers on his desk. "No fire, just an important meeting at ten."

"With who?"

If Riley didn't know of his brother's penchant for being inquisitive, he would have been annoyed with Canyon's questions. "I'm meeting with our event planner, Alpha Blake, about the holiday party next month."

"Oh," Canyon said with a smirk on his face. He took the chair in front of Riley's desk. Riley knew why the smirk was there. Dillon had tossed the responsibility to both of them and neither had wanted it. In the end, they'd drawn straws. Riley hadn't been happy that he'd been the one to lose, but now he was more than glad that he had.

"Okay, Canyon, what's going on with Shade Tree Developers?" he asked, deciding to steer his brother away from the subject of Alpha.

"I talked with one of their new attorneys today. She was brought on board a couple of weeks ago and you won't believe who she is."

"Who?"

"Keisha Ashford."

Riley scrunched up his face, remembering. "Is that the same Keisha you had that affair with a few years ago?"

Canyon shifted in his seat. "One and the same."

"Ouch." Riley remembered the affair hadn't ended well.

"Yes, that's what I said. However, she sounded pleasant enough."

Riley chuckled and leaned back in his chair with his arms raised and resting against the back of his neck. "They always do, even when they're about to cut off your balls. I told you to always be up-front with a woman. You set the parameters and the rules. Then there'll be less drama on the back end. That's why I have Riley's Rules. That's the only way I operate."

While Canyon rambled on with nonsense about not all women agreeing to rules, Riley's thoughts shifted back to Alpha. He had already spelled out his terms and she could take them or leave them.

He was hoping like hell that she took them.

Alpha stepped off the elevator onto the fortieth floor of the Blue Ridge Management building where the executive offices were located. She recalled the first time she'd come here, last month, to meet with Dillon and how impressed she'd been with the plush surroundings the moment she'd walked inside the building.

First, there had been the huge, beautifully decorated atrium with a waterfall amidst a replica of mountains, complete with blooming flowers and other foliage. Seeing all those flowers had reminded her of a spring day in Daytona when flowers sprouted everywhere. They were the first sign that the city should prepare for spring break, when all the college students would hit the beaches.

She liked the feel of the thick, luxurious carpet beneath her shoes. The first thing that caught her eye today, just like the last time, were the huge portraits of two couples that hung on the main wall in the lobby. They were Riley's parents and his aunt and uncle, who'd all perished in an airplane accident. Four beautiful people who had died young and left behind offspring who loved them. And speaking of love, the photographer who'd taken the photographs had captured the essence of love in both portraits. The way the two women were leaning in toward their husbands, the smiles they wore and the way the couples held hands showed that they'd truly loved each other. She would like to think that seeing these photographs gave the Westmorelands the strength to go on when others would have given up. She couldn't help but admire the way they had bonded together in a crisis, a response which had been so unlike her own family's.

She glanced at her watch and saw she was ten minutes early. The weather was a lot better than last week now that the snowstorm had passed. However, she knew that it was just the beginning and forecasters had already predicted a lot of cold weather ahead.

Alpha tried ignoring the stirring in the pit of her stomach when she approached a bank of offices. She drew in a deep breath when she reached the one with Riley's name elegantly carved in bold gold script. She had no reason to be nervous since he had given her enough time to make a decision and she had. It was one she would live with and not regret making.

She would have an affair with him because, whether she understood why or not, she wanted him. It was as if he had cast some spell on her and even when she'd tried talking herself out of wanting him, she couldn't. So against her better judgment, she would follow the cravings of her body. For once in her life, she would give in to her wants. Besides, after

Eddie had told her he wouldn't marry her, she had pretty much known she wouldn't set herself up for that kind of heartbreak again. A serious relationship with any man was totally out of the question. And she was curious about all that pleasure Riley had talked about.

Another thing she had taken into consideration was that she knew, at some point, she would date again. Although she was certain there were a lot of single men in Denver, she wasn't sure just how decent they were. She considered Riley both decent and honest. He'd demonstrated that by being up-front with her. He hadn't tried sugarcoating an affair or making it out to be more than what it would be. He wanted her. In his bed. Just like she wanted him in hers. No excuses. Just bald facts.

She let out another deep breath. Thinking that way was one thing but actually doing it was another. Growing up, Omega would tease her about talking a good talk, but when the time came to back it up, that was another story. Alpha hoped to do things differently this time around.

She opened the door to another elegant-looking lobby. A young woman sat at the receptionist desk and smiled when she walked in. "Ms. Blake?"

Alpha was surprised the woman knew who she was. "Yes?"

"Mr. Westmoreland has been waiting for you."

Alpha lifted a brow before glancing down at her watch. "But I'm not late."

The young woman chuckled. "Yes, I know, but he's checked three times to see if you've arrived, although I assured him that I would send you in the moment you got here. I guess this meeting is pretty important." The woman then picked up the phone and announced her arrival to Riley.

No sooner had the last word left the woman's lips than Riley's office door was snatched open and he stood there. This was the first time she had seen him in business attire. The transformation left her speechless. He was dressed in a gray suit and a white shirt. The printed tie brought both together and all three complemented the brown coloring of his skin. The cut of his suit did everything to emphasize his masculine build. He looked so handsome standing there, dominating the doorway in such a way that she had to force her breathing to slow. But she could do nothing about the way her blood was rushing through her veins.

The corners of his mouth curved in a heart-stopping smile. "Ms. Blake."

She released the breath she hadn't known she was holding. "Mr. Westmoreland. I have all the information we discussed last week," she said with professional decorum, for the benefit of their audience of one.

He nodded. "Good, I'm anxious for us to get started since we have a lot to cover." He averted his gaze from her to the woman sitting at the desk, who was watching them with interest. "Make sure we're not disturbed until our meeting is over."

"Yes, sir."

He then shifted his glance back to Alpha and stepped aside. "Ms. Blake, please come in."

The thoughts running through Riley's mind when Alpha passed him by were too dangerous to think about at the moment. Why did she always have to smell so darn good? Fresh, sweet and all woman.

She moved to stand in front of his desk and turned around. He remained standing with his back against the closed door with his hands shoved into his pockets. He studied her, thinking every single thing about her spelled *SENSUOUS* in capital letters.

"I've researched more information on the party and have a proposed budget for—"

"You look nice, Alpha," he interrupted her spiel to say. When she began nibbling on her bottom lip, he knew that he was making her nervous but he couldn't help it. He was obsessed, and at that moment he offered no excuses for being so. There was just something about seeing a woman in a business suit with pumps on her feet. Had she assumed her attire would make him want to get down to real business, without thoughts of making love to her? If so, the intent failed miserably.

"Thank you. Now can we get down to—"

"Business?" He gave a negative shake of his head said. "No, not yet."

He slid his hands from his pockets. She was right; they should get down to business. He could go even further and say there was really no reason they should be meeting today at all. The information she was here to give him regarding the party could have been done over the phone. He knew that and figured she knew that, as well.

"What have you decided?" he asked, tempted to walk over to her but knowing if he did he wouldn't be able to keep his hands to himself.

She averted her gaze momentarily and when she looked back, she said, "Maybe we ought to discuss this at another—"

"Alpha."

The menacing tone of his voice probably pretty much told her she could forget that suggestion. "All right, then," she said, placing her messenger bag on his desk. She then glanced over at him. "You were right about there being this strong attraction between us. I've thought about it and considered all aspects of what you've suggested, although, like I told you, I've never engaged in a casual affair—sex with no commitments—before."

"But you've reached a decision?" he asked, noting her expression wasn't giving anything away.

"Yes."

Both hope and despair flooded his stomach at the same time since he had no idea what her decision was. He said nothing, just waited for her to go on. When she didn't, he asked simply, "And?"

She nervously licked her lips again before lifting her chin. "I agree to it, but I have a few rules of my own."

That surprised him. No other woman ever had. He moved from the door to stand beside his desk. "Do you?"

"Yes. First of all, I don't want us to rush into anything."

"You mean not rush into sharing a bed?" he asked for clarity.

"Yes. Like I told you, I'm not used to engaging in casual affairs so it's not anything I can just jump into. I'm going to need time to get used to this."

He wondered how much time she would need. The affair was only supposed to last six weeks at the max. But then the last thing he wanted was a reluctant woman in his bed. Besides, there were ways of breaking down her defenses. "I can agree with that."

She nodded. "And another thing."

"Yes?"

She paused, as if she needed the courage to say her next words. "It's about that promise you made last week, right before leaving my house."

He knew what promise she was referring to and remembered it well. "What about it?"

"I'm holding you to it."

Riley said nothing. He only stared at her. But he wasn't *just* staring at her, Alpha thought. He was doing so in a way that was tantalizing her senses and sending electrified sensations all through her pores. Omega would never believe Alpha was letting any man affect her this way. Or that she was drawn to a man who was leading her down a road Omega knew well and had traveled down plenty of times. One that was naughty as sin.

"Now, can we get down to business and discuss the details of the party for next month, Riley?"

He shook his head. "No."

She lifted a brow. "No?"

He shook his head as he unbuttoned his coat to remove it and loosened his tie, tossing both on the chair across from his desk. "Not yet." Then, closing the distance between them, he pulled her into his arms.

She went to him willingly, opening her mouth the moment his lips touched hers. And when he slid his tongue inside, the memories of the last time they'd kissed magnified tenfold. She was convinced that no other man kissed the way he did. No other man could fill a woman with as much longing and desire as he could. Heat sizzled along her nerve endings, and her stomach tightened with each meticulous stroke of his tongue.

It was almost too late when she realized he had been walking her backward. Barely breaking the kiss, he eased her up by the hips to place her on top of his desk. He didn't let up, continuing to take her mouth with a hunger she felt in every part of her body. In response, she tightened her arms around his neck and moved in closer, needing the contact of his chest against hers, liking how her nipples were hardening in need.

"Mr. Westmoreland, I'm leaving for lunch now."

The sound of the receptionist's voice over the intercom seemed to boom across the room. Riley pulled his mouth away but kept it within inches of hers. "I hope you liked that," he whispered against her lips, tipping her chin up for better access.

A smile curved the corners of her mouth. "The kiss or the fact that your receptionist is taking lunch?"

He chuckled. "The kiss."

There was no reason to lie, so she said, "I did.'"

He traced her lips with his tongue before saying, "Good. Just thought I'd get a little head start on all that pleasure I plan on giving you."

She thought he'd gotten more than a head start. "Do you mind getting me down off your desk now?"

"Not at all."

And just as easily as he'd placed her up there, he had her

back on her feet. They were standing close. She could feel the heat of him all over her. "I've got a suggestion, Alpha," he said in a deep, husky tone.

She lifted a brow. "What?"

"I suggest we move our meeting someplace else, and I know just the place. Go home and change into something comfortable—like jeans and boots—and I'll pick you up in an hour."

"And just where are we supposed to be going?"

"Riley's Station."

"Where?"

"Just do it, okay?"

"And this is a business meeting, right?"

A smile touched the corners of his mouth. "Both business and pleasure."

When she opened her mouth to remind him of her rules, he quickly spoke up and said, "I know, you want to take things slow and not be rushed. I got it."

She was glad he got it. Now if she could only get her traitorous body on the same page.

# Six

Alpha tried keeping the butterflies from her stomach as she quickly dressed, knowing Riley would be there to pick her up in less than thirty minutes. "This is crazy," she muttered, pulling a burgundy V-neck sweater over her head. "All he had to say was 'let's go' and I'm going."

She stood sideways to look in the mirror at her perky breasts pressed against her sweater. It had been Omega's idea for her to wear a push-up bra with all her sweaters, and she would admit it made her girls look bigger than they really were.

She was about to put on lipstick when her cell phone rang. She grinned as she answered it. "Speak of the devil."

"Hey, and you were talking about me to who?" her sister said with laughter in her voice.

"No one, just thinking about what you told me, about ways a woman can make herself look sexy."

"Umm, you're trying to look sexy? Sounds like you've made some decisions about a few things."

Alpha leaned against the bathroom counter. When Omega had called last week she had spent over an hour on the phone telling her twin the latest about her meeting with Riley, how fine he was and his suggestion that they indulge in an affair. Of course Omega had been all for it, saying Alpha needed to rev up her love life. "Yes, I agreed to do it, and he's agreed not to rush me into anything."

"But no climax control, right?"

Alpha lifted a brow. "Climax control?"

"Yes, you plan to let the orgasms rip."

Alpha threw her hand to her mouth to keep from screaming with laughter. Her sister could be so outlandish at times. Um, in fact most of the time. "Behave, girl. And how is that book coming along?" Omega had decided to write a book about her experience as a porn star.

"Great. It's wonderful therapy for me."

Alpha didn't say anything for a minute and then asked, "Do you miss the business, Omega?" She'd always wondered but never asked. Nothing her parents said or did had made Omega give up her line of work until Omega had been ready to do so herself.

"I know it's hard for most people to understand, Al, but for me it was nothing more than a job—a job I needed while going through that rebellious period in my life. I don't want to think about where I'd be or what I'd still be doing if Marlon hadn't come along. He reminded me of who I was before I made those decisions, and he was willing to love me, no matter what."

Alpha loved her brother-in-law because she knew he loved Omega, no matter what her past had been. He didn't give a damn what others thought. He treated her sister like his queen.

Omega had been out of the business less than a year when she met Marlon. Alpha knew Omega was happy and could hear it in her voice every time they talked. The only dark cloud in her sister's life was their parents and their holier-than-thou attitude.

"The only thing I regret," Omega was saying softly, "is hurting you and the folks. Maybe one day they will forgive me. You never turned your back on me, even when the folks tried getting you to do so…and even when I cost you the man you loved because you wouldn't choose him over me."

Alpha nearly dropped the phone. "Who told you that? How did you know?" she asked, going back into the bedroom to sit on the edge of the bed. "I told you—"

"I know what you told me, and you lied. You and Eddie didn't just decide to call off the wedding because the two of you felt like you were drifting apart. I ran into Eleanor Sloan, in New York of all places, when Marlon took me there on a shopping spree. She approached me, thinking I was you, and you know Eleanor," Omega said of their high school friend. "She told me how sad she was for you now that Eddie had made you call off your wedding because of me."

Alpha tilted her head back and looked up at the ceiling. "When was this?"

"Last Christmas."

Alpha brought her head back down to gaze out the window and frowned. "And you've known all this time and never mentioned it," she accused. "Why *didn't* you mention it?"

Omega paused a minute before responding. "I couldn't say anything because I was feeling your pain. After the way I had lived those three years, here I was, about to marry the best man any woman could have, and there you were, you who'd always been the good girl and did everything the folks told you to do…even going to college for a career you didn't want to please them. I was the one who ended up with the fairy-tale marriage and getting a real prince and you ended up with a toad. It didn't seem fair. Life sucks."

A smile touched Alpha's lips. Life did suck at times, but a part of Alpha wouldn't change a thing. Because thanks to

Marlon, things were the way Alpha had always dreamed they could be for her twin.

Determined to get her sister back in a good mood, mainly because she didn't want Omega feeling sorry for her, Alpha said, "Yeah, must have been rough being a porn star."

"Oh, Alpha, you didn't have to go there."

She knew she'd succeeded in changing the mood when she heard the giggle in her twin's voice. Alpha laughed. "Yes, I did. Besides, had I been married to Eddie I wouldn't be having this fling and doing the no-climax-control thing."

Omega chuckled. "Okay, sis, you got me there. Is this Riley Westmoreland as hot as you make him out to be?"

Alpha remembered how he'd looked when she'd been to his office earlier that day. Yummy. "Trust me, he is. And I'll find out just how hot he is soon enough."

Omega went silent for a moment and then asked, "Will you tell him about me?"

She could hear the seriousness in her sister's tone. She had tried doing that with LeBron and Eddie and both men had ended up showing their true colors.

"Why would I tell him anything? It's not that kind of relationship. It's about sex and nothing more. Besides, at the point when we begin sleeping together, I doubt we'll have time for much pillow talk. Remember, no climax control. And I want to find out if multiple orgasms are real or something you porn stars just try to make look real."

Omega chuckled. "Oh, you're bad, and trust me, they are real…with the right man in control."

"We'll see. As far as being bad, I'm finally going to live a little, have some fun and enjoy myself. And I have a feeling Riley is just the person to make sure that I do so."

*"Brrr.* I can't believe the temperature has dropped five degrees already."

Riley smiled as he watched Alpha tighten her coat around

her when he escorted her to his truck and opened the door. "What are you complaining about, woman? It feels good out here."

She glared at him over her shoulder before easing into the truck's leather interior. "I can't help but wonder what kind of blood is running through your veins. Look at you."

He glanced down at himself. Okay, so he'd left his jacket in the truck. He looked fine. He felt fine. No sense reminding her he was hot-blooded. She would find the truth of that soon enough. He kept smiling as he closed the door and then rounded the front of the truck and opened the door to climb in on the driver's side. "I guess I've developed some sort of tolerance to Denver's cold weather."

After buckling up he smiled over at her and said, "My tolerance to Denver's cold weather drives everyone in my family crazy. They're convinced I'm going to die of pneumonia at an early age."

"I have to agree with them."

He tilted his head to look at her. "And you've been living in Denver for how long now?"

"It will be a year in April."

He grinned. "No wonder you're whining. You missed all the real good days."

"Lucky me. I'm not complaining," she said, chuckling. "If I had come any earlier I might have been tempted to head back south."

He glanced over at her. "You don't come across as a quitter, Alpha."

She chuckled. "I've thought of heading back south more than once, trust me."

As he was driving, he had to stop for a school bus. "I remember those days," he said thoughtfully.

"What days?" she asked.

He gestured with his head to somewhere outside the windshield. "When my brothers, cousin and I used to ride the bus to and from school. Either Aunt Susan or my mom would be there at the stop to get us. My parents had a van we all called Crazy Horse. It was blue and huge and could hold all of us."

"Sounds like a lot of good memories."

"They are."

"I admire you and your family, Riley," she said softly.

He looked over at Alpha. "Do you?"

"Yes. I heard about your parents and your uncle and aunt and how they died together in that plane crash. It must have been awful for all of you."

He stared straight ahead as his hand gripped the steering wheel and he watched the kids continue to unload from the bus. "It was, especially when there were so many of us still under sixteen. Seeing those kids reminds me of so many things. Kids think their parents are going to be around forever. I'll never forget the day I realized mine would not."

"How old were you?"

He glanced over at her. "Fifteen. Just a few months shy of my sixteenth birthday. Mom had promised me a party that year, and I was so looking forward to it. I had gotten my learner's permit, which meant I could start sharing Dillon's old truck with my brother, Jason. Life was good. Even Bane was good. He was my mom's baby. Spoiled rotten and a tattletale."

Riley was quiet for a second, remembering. "And then, suddenly all of it came to a crashing end, literally, when their plane went down. We lost them. Bane couldn't handle it and became a badass. He was hard for anyone to handle. Dillon was the oldest and then Ramsey. They had just finished college. Dillon was going pro in the NBA and Ramsey was on his way to Australia to learn about sheep ranching. They both gave up their dreams to keep our family together."

He felt her touch. Knew the moment she'd reached out and touched his arm. He needed the contact right then. Sad memories seldom came his way and when they did, they were too painful to dwell on. He'd been close to his mother, close to his father and aunt and uncle.

"Hey, you okay?"

He glanced over at Alpha. "Yes. Memories can be a bummer at times."

"Yes, I know."

He wondered if she was talking from experience. He had noted the indention on the third finger of her left hand where a ring used to be. Had she been married at one time? Deciding to change the subject, he said, "I thought about it and ran it over with the family. We're cool with the party being a black-tie affair. The reason I hesitated in making a decision was because I didn't want any of the employees to incur any unnecessary expenses if they didn't have to. But Dillon reminded me that this will be the company's fortieth holiday celebration so we need to be classy about it."

A huge smile touched her lips. "I was hoping that would be your decision. I like class and already have a lot of ideas on how to make the night special."

He nodded. "And they like the theme—One Winter's Night."

"That's great!"

When they came to a traffic light she opened her messenger bag to pull out several documents. "I have another presentation for you when we get to our destination. Now that you've decided on the attire, the menu can be planned accordingly. I'm working with Foods by Jerlon as the caterer."

"I've attended several parties he's catered, and everything he's prepared is delicious."

For the next half hour they covered more details about the party. It was only after discussing the budget that she lifted her gaze from her notes to look out the window. "We're a long way from town, aren't we?"

He glanced over at her. When had the sight of a woman with her hair in a ponytail ever turned him on? "Not too far."

He slowed the car to make a turn off the highway onto a two-lane road. A huge marker said Westmoreland Country.

She glanced over at him after reading the marker. "Westmoreland Country?"

He chuckled. "Yes. My great-great-grandfather settled here eighty-something years ago on over two thousand acres. Dillon, being the oldest, inherited the family home and the three-hundred acres it sat on. The rest of us got a hundred acres each once we turned twenty-five."

"So all of you stay around here, close together?"

"Close enough. Being on a hundred acres gives you privacy, at least most of the time, but there's still Bailey."

She raised a brow. "Bailey?"

"Bailey's my cousin and was the youngest Denver Westmoreland when my parents, uncle and aunt died. She likes to think she can boss all of us around. She hasn't reached twenty-five yet so she figures she can bum sleeping space wherever she wants. Usually she hangs out at Gemma's place since it's vacant now that Gemma is living in Australia."

"Is Gemma another cousin?"

"Yes." He decided it probably would be beneficial if he gave her a rundown of everyone. "On my parents' side there's Dillon. Then Micah, who works as a scientist for the federal government. He got married in June, and he and Kalina are expecting. Right now they're living in Alexandria, Virginia."

Riley slowed down when they reached another school zone. "Then there's Jason who's married to Bella." He chuckled. "She's from Savannah, and her first winter here was hard on her, too. Then there's me and my younger brothers, Canyon, Stern and Bane."

She lifted a brow. "No sisters?"

"Nope. I think my parents were hoping Bane was a girl, but it didn't turn out that way."

He then told her about his cousins, naming each one individually and the spouses of the married ones. Usually the last thing he talked about whenever he was on a date with a woman was his family. But he felt comfortable talking about them with Alpha.

He turned onto the road for his place and she glanced over at him and smiled. "Riley's Station?"

He chuckled. "Yes, Riley's Station."

Alpha was spellbound when they pulled into his yard. As far as the eye could see, she was surrounded by mountains and streams. Tucked away in the center of it all was a stately two-story house with a wraparound porch. Floor-to-ceiling windows covered the entire front of the house with a huge bay window facing the mountains on the side. A portion of the land close to the house had been cleared for a small waterfall and birdbath.

"All this is yours?" she asked, getting out of the car. He gripped her shoulders lightly when he placed his arms around her.

"Yes, one hundred acres. Isn't it beautiful?"

Beautiful? Words couldn't describe how soul-touchingly magnificent the view was. The one thing she had fallen in love with when she'd first visited Denver had been the mountains. Aside from the cold weather, Denver was a beautiful place.

"Now I understand about Riley's Station," she said, looking up at him.

"Do you?"

"Yes. On the way here I saw the markers—Ramsey's Web, Dillon's Den, Derringer's Dungeon, Zane's Hideout, Gemma's Gem…. Where on earth did those names come from?"

He threw his head back and laughed as he led her up the steps to the house. "Bailey. She figured all our places needed names and came up with them for us. She even designed the markers. At the time it was her pet project and we all gave in. We would have done anything to keep her out of trouble."

"I take it that she used to be a handful."

"If only you knew."

She stepped aside so he could open the door for her. "Welcome to my home, Alpha."

"Thanks," she said, passing him, stepping inside. For the second time that day her mouth almost dropped open. She moved from the foyer and glanced around at the open-concept room. His home was beautiful, the furnishings gorgeous and the decor breathtaking. The entire place was simply immaculate.

"Okay, although this is definitely a man's place, there's no way the decorating and coordinating of the furnishings was done by you. You hired an interior decorator, right?"

He moved away from the closed door. "Right. My cousin, Gemma. She owns an interior decorating company and insisted upon doing her thing in here."

Alpha continued to glance around. "Insisted."

"Yes, for the most part. I would have been satisfied just to have a kitchen table and a bed, but she'd made up her mind, after going into business for herself out of college, that her brothers and cousins would be her first clients. And none of us got discounts."

Alpha chuckled. "But I like that. Keeping it all in the family. Supporting one another."

"That's the Westmoreland Way." He moved across the room to open the blinds to a huge window that had a gorgeous, picturesque view of the mountains.

"And how do you keep it all clean and everything in place?" she asked, not seeing a speck of dirt or smidgen of dust anywhere.

His eyes glinted as if insulted. "Are you trying to insinuate I'm a slob?"

She waved off his pretended insult. "You're a man, Riley. Not too many tidy up after themselves. I'm impressed."

"Thank you, but I'll admit to having a weekly cleaning service. A woman drops by and takes care of the houses for all the single Westmorelands. It's an annual birthday gift from the ladies in the family for the single male Westmorelands."

He glanced at her messenger bag, which she was still carrying in her hand. "You can set up things in my office. I even have a pull-down screen in there." He glanced at his watch. "And while you're doing that, I'll start dinner."

She arched a brow. "You cook?"

He chuckled softly. "Yes, sweetheart, I learned how to fend for myself when I discovered the women inviting me over to their place to eat all had ulterior motives."

She tried ignoring the fluttering in the pit of her stomach caused by his term of endearment as she eyed him up and down. He had removed his jacket and tie and was standing in the middle of his humongous living room, looking at home and oh-so-sexy.

"Can you?"

"Can I what?"

"Cook," he said, opening blinds to another window.

"Yes."

"The kitchen is around that bend in the wall," he said. "After getting things set up, you can join me and we'll see how well you can cook."

When was the last time he'd whistled while cooking? Riley wondered as he pulled all the spices he needed out of the cabinets. He glanced to where Alpha stood at the island making dessert—sugar cookies. She had come up with the idea after discovering that he had all the ingredients she needed.

This wasn't the first time he'd ever invited a woman to his house by any means, and this wasn't the first time one had shared space in his kitchen. But he would admit, although he didn't want to do so, that she was the first whose presence felt totally right.

He pushed the thought to the back of his mind, not wanting to ponder why he felt that way. All he knew was that he enjoyed glancing across the way and seeing her there. She was wearing a pullover sweater and a pair of skimmer jeans, and he liked the short leather boots on her feet. He thought the outfit was perfect for what he had in mind later. They were going horseback riding around his property after dinner.

A thought then entered his mind. "You do ride, right?"

She glanced over at him. "Ride what?"

"A horse."

She chuckled and the sound echoed around his kitchen. "Yes. I went to school to become a vet, remember. One year I spent the entire summer on a horse ranch in Ocala, Florida, working as a ranch hand. It was definitely a learning experience. I'm no jockey, but I can hold my own."

He stopped what he was doing and turned around. "Glad you think so because we're going riding later."

"We are?"

"Yes."

She shrugged. "Okay." She then returned to what she was doing.

"How are you coming along over there?" he asked, curious. She had been quiet, concentrating on the task until he'd interrupted her just now.

"Fine. You did preset the oven to 350 degrees, right?"

"Yes."

"Good. I haven't made sugar cookies in a long time. What are the odds that you would have everything I need?"

"Only because Bailey likes my kitchen and keeps it equipped."

She glanced up and around. "I can certainly see why she likes this one. It's a cook's dream. Beautiful oak cabinets, granite countertops, stainless steel appliances and—"

"Hey, you have all those things in your kitchen, except your cabinets are maple instead of oak."

"Yes, but I can place my small kitchen in here three or four times over. Most men would see this much square footage in a kitchen as wasted space."

"I'm not most men."

She glanced over at him and moved her gaze up and down. "Yes, I can see that."

He smiled and shook his head. "You know those kinds of looks can get you into trouble."

An innocent smile touched her lips. "I'm not doing anything."

Instead of disagreeing with her, he turned back around to the sink to start peeling the potatoes that he planned to stew on top of the stove with pork chops and his special gravy. The dish wasn't as good as McKay's, but he didn't think it was all bad.

Out of the corner of his eye he watched as Alpha opened his oven door to slide the tray of cookies inside. "These are slow-baking, so an hour should do it."

"I can't wait," he said, turning toward her. "Once I get this started it will be on simmer for a while."

"All right. Do you want me to cover the rest of the info for the party before or after dinner? The only thing left to cover is the budget."

He nodded. On the drive over she had covered a lot, being detailed and precise and, not surprisingly, he had liked all of her ideas. "Let's do it before dinner."

"Okay, I'll go get things set up in your office."

He watched her walk off with his pulse hammering and his erection throbbing. She looked good all over but had such a curvaceous backside that seeing her in jeans was a total turn-on for him.

Riley drew in a deep breath as the rush of blood seemed to hit him right in the groin. At some point they would share a bed, but he had promised not to rush her and he wouldn't, even if it killed him. Alpha was not a one-night stand, nor would she be a one-and-done. She would have her six weeks.

More importantly, he would have his six weeks. He doubted he would want less than that. And he'd taken the time earlier that day, while in his office, to figure out the exact ending date, and wouldn't you know it, it would be the night of the holiday party.

So it would be one winter's night in more ways than one.

# Seven

"Well, what do you think about the pork chops?"

Alpha glanced across the table at Riley. It hadn't taken long to go over the budget and wrap up all the other minor details she needed to finalize in order to move ahead with her plans. All her people were ready and in place and now that he had approved her suggestions and the budget, it was full steam ahead. She'd be putting on a party that she knew would impress him and everyone attending.

She smiled ruefully. "I think if push comes to shove, you can quit your day job and become a chef. Everything tastes wonderful, Riley." And she meant it. The pork chops were so tender they all but melted in her mouth and the gravy and potatoes were better than any she'd ever eaten…even those at McKay's.

From his smile she knew her compliment pleased him. "Thanks. Wait until you taste my shrimp and lobster casserole. It's going to knock you off your feet."

Hmm, was that an invitation? Sounded like one to her. "I'll look forward to it."

"And I'm looking forward to eating your cookies. They smell good."

"Thanks."

She continued to eat and when she glanced up he was watching her with a strange look on his face. She tilted her head and arched a brow. "Something's wrong?"

"No," he said rather quickly and continued eating. Moments later, after taking a sip of his wine, he said, "I looked at a calendar earlier today and if we both agree to go the full six weeks for our affair, then it ends the night of the company party."

"Sounds good to me."

She saw something flash in his eyes. "So we understand each other?" he asked.

She smiled. "Perfectly." She then picked up her wineglass and took a sip, not sure why he was still sitting there staring at her. Had he expected her to request more time or something?

She glanced at her watch. It was getting late. She darted a look over at him. "Do you still want to go riding?"

"Yes.

"Then we need to get going if we want to take advantage of the daylight."

He stood. "I agree."

She stood, as well. "I'll help clear the table."

"You don't have to."

"I want to, and it's the least I can do for such a great meal. You outdid yourself."

He chuckled. "For you, any day."

She didn't say anything as she helped him clean off the table and load up the dishwasher. The heat was on, and it was getting to her already. And she had a feeling things would be getting hotter.

* * *

An hour later Riley stood at the window and looked out, waiting as Alpha used one of his guest bathrooms. He had enjoyed his time with her and now it was close to seven. It was hard to believe she had spent five hours with him today. And he had enjoyed every second of those hours. After dinner she had helped him clear the table and load the dishwasher. Then they had gone riding, and she'd pulled one over on him when she'd given the impression she wasn't good when it came to riding a horse. The woman was an excellent rider.

When they returned they had eaten the cookies she had baked and drunk cold glasses of milk. He shared more stories about his family and she had listened attentively, asking questions and laughing when he told her all about Bane's, Bailey's and the twins'—Aiden and Adrian's—escapades and how Family Services had threatened to separate the youngest Westmorelands from the family if their bad behaviors didn't improve.

But the one thing he noticed was that she hadn't talked a lot about herself or her family. He knew she was from Florida, that her parents owned a veterinary business and that she had a sister. But there was the issue of the missing ring on her finger. Had something other than a career move driven her to Denver?

"You even have a beautiful powder room, Riley. And it's so big. I probably could roll a bed in there and take a nap."

He turned around slowly. "Glad you—"

Whatever he was about to say died on his lips when their gazes connected. Suddenly, from across the room he held her in focus. His stomach tightened and his nerve endings sizzled. "Like it," he said, finishing his sentence.

She'd done something to her hair. It was no longer pulled back away from her face in a ponytail, but was now loose. A mass of brown curls were hanging around her shoulders. He'd seen her hair that way before, earlier today in his office.

But for some reason, at that moment, restyling her hair made her look incredibly beautiful.

His feet began moving toward her with a purpose ingrained in every part of his body. He met her gaze, held it, and when he came to a stop in front of her, he reached out and traced a finger across her chin. He then slowly moved his finger down the length of her neck before touching a lock of her hair. "You're wearing it differently," he said in a deep, husky voice, liking how the silky tresses felt flowing through his fingers.

She nodded slowly. "The clamp came loose while out riding and I thought I'd play it safe and take it off. The clamp was a gift from my sister and means a lot. I don't want to lose it."

"I like your hair this way. It's a stunning shade of brown. The color is perfect for your skin tone. It's beautiful. You're beautiful."

"Thank you."

He lifted her hands to his lips and kissed them while gazing up at her. "I promised not to rush you, but just so you know, I have no qualms about making love to you tonight. I'm tempted to do just that."

"Then I better move temptation out of your way by letting you take me home. Then you can concentrate on other things."

His lips curved in a smile. "Even if you weren't here, I would think about you, Alpha."

She chuckled softly. "I bet you say that to all the ladies."

Riley shook his head as he continued to kiss her hand. Now he was using the tip of his tongue to taste her skin. He liked hearing how her breathing sounded forced. "No, I don't say that to all the ladies."

And he meant that. He would admit to throwing out a convincing line or two when it served his purpose. That was to be expected when he was a man on the prowl. But that's not what he was doing here. With Alpha, he was being totally honest. He had thought about her over the past week more than he'd thought about any other woman. He had dreamed about her, waking up with a need and desire he'd never felt for any other woman.

Since he didn't know why his experience was so different with her, he intended to be cautious in whatever he did, whatever they shared. He had to be realistic enough to admit there had been something between him and Alpha from the first. She had been wearing gloves, yet when their hands touched he had felt the intense heat. He had felt the chemistry. An electrical charge had zinged through him. At first he'd thought it was a fluke, nothing more than an overreaction. But then, when he'd picked her up in his arms in McKay's parking lot to carry her into the restaurant, it was as if something had exploded between them, a connection he couldn't describe. And that was before he'd even seen what she was hiding under all those clothes.

He straightened and reached up to touch her chin again, coaxing her to meet his gaze. "Go out with me this weekend. We can do dinner and a movie or a play."

He studied the shape of her lips. Heat stirred his groin, making several ideas flow through his head and prompting him to add, "Or better yet, after dinner we can come here or go to your place and play a game."

Her brow arched. "What game?"

"The Pleasure Game. Have you ever played it before?"

He saw how her eyes darkened with desire when she shook her head. "Can't say that I have."

"Then let me assure you that you're going to enjoy it. It's easy to play, and there are not a whole lot of rules to follow. You can let me know that night if you want to play. How about if I pick you up for dinner around seven? There's this restaurant near the airport that I've heard nice things about, and I want to take you there."

"Okay," she said, smiling softly.

"And the Pleasure Game will require you staying overnight here or me staying overnight at your place. No pressure.

No rush. If you don't think you'll be ready to play Saturday night just let me know."

She nodded. "I will."

He leaned in close and slanted his mouth over hers, needing to taste her and leave her with something to think about. When she opened her mouth to return the kiss, he pulled her into his arms and deepened it, knowing he would be counting the days until he spent time with her again.

# Eight

"Wow, the invitations will be simply beautiful," Lindsey Hopkins said. The twenty-something stay-at-home mom assisted Alpha on a part-time basis. As she looked at the computer screen over Alpha's shoulder, she had a huge grin on her face. "And you're the one designing them?"

Alpha smiled, too, pleased that Lindsey liked them. "Yes, after coming up with what I thought would work for our theme, One Winter's Night, I thought the idea of a country house in a light snowstorm would be perfect."

And she knew just the house she would use as a model. Riley's home. It would be picture-perfect. She had mentioned using a picture of his home on the invitation when he brought her home the other night. He said he had no problem with it and had given her the green light to do it.

"Do you know whose house you're going to use?" Lindsey asked her.

She turned her chair around and met Lindsey's inquiring

gaze. "Yes, it belongs to one of the Westmorelands. Riley Westmoreland."

Lindsey's face lit up. "He's one of Bane's older brothers. I met him once, and I bet the house is as gorgeous as he is."

Alpha threw her head back and laughed. "Well, yes, I guess you could say that."

"Trust me, I do. Every woman in town knows how good-looking those Westmoreland men are. Some of us are married, but we aren't blind. Any woman can appreciate a good-looking man."

Alpha grinned. "True." She turned back to the computer. "So you think Riley's house might work as a backdrop?"

"I've never seen it, but I don't see why not. I've been to Westmoreland Country once or twice, years ago with my father when he did the landscaping for the main house. He took me and my brothers along to help. You know, free labor," she said, laughing. "The main house was huge and majestic. I heard all the siblings have built their own homes now."

Alpha switched her computer to another screen, one that showed an example of some of the decorations she contemplated using. "Yes, that's what I heard." None of Riley's rules had governed publicizing their affair, but she didn't feel comfortable broadcasting it to anyone.

An hour or so later, Lindsey had left to pick up her baby from her mom and Alpha was on her way to the kitchen to fix a sandwich—her favorite, peanut butter and jelly—when the doorbell rang. Wondering who could be calling on her, she crossed the living room to the door. A quick glance out of the peephole indicated a florist deliveryman.

Pursing her lips thoughtfully, she opened the door. Who would send her flowers? Perhaps the man was at the wrong house. "May I help you?"

The older man smiled. "Alpha Blake?"

"Yes."

"These are for you," he said, handing her the huge, beautiful ceramic vase of pink roses. A dozen of them.

"Thanks," she said, accepting the flowers.

"And the tip has been taken care of."

"Oh, thanks," she said, stepping back and using her toe to close the door. The roses filled her house with a sweet-smelling scent. As soon as she set the vase down on the table, she pulled off the card, eager to see who'd sent them.

*Two days left. Riley*

She threw her head back and laughed. She had thought about everything he had suggested for Saturday night, especially the Pleasure Game, and felt she was ready. There was no need to put off the inevitable. Besides, she'd never played games with a man in the bedroom. Eddie hadn't had an imaginative bone in his body. LeBron had been full of ideas but only with the pretense that his bed partner was Omega. Alpha shook her head at how he actually hadn't seen anything wrong with wanting to make love to her while pretending she was her sister.

Moments later, Alpha was still standing in front of the table and gazing at the roses when her cell phone rang. She pulled it out of her pocket and saw it was her father. She and her parents talked at least once a week, but usually at night. She was surprised he was calling her in the middle of the day.

"Dad?"

"Yes, Al, how's my girl?"

She couldn't help but smile. "I'm fine. What about you?"

"Great. Look, I just had to call you and tell you I saw Eddie today when he brought Cleo into the office."

She frowned. "Is Cleo okay?" she asked, inquiring about the beautiful Labrador retriever that Eddie owned. She had fallen in love with the dog and had begun considering Cleo as hers, too.

"Yes, Cleo's fine. He brought her in for her annual visit."

"Oh. You didn't have to call to tell me that, Dad."

"I know, but I figured you'd want to know that he asked about you."

Like she cared. "Did he?"

"Yes. He even asked if you've mentioned anything about moving back home." There was a pause. Alpha knew she wouldn't like what was coming next but decided to let her father have his say since he would do so anyway.

"Look, baby, I know Eddie was the one to call off the wedding and all, but understand it from a man's point of view. He didn't want your reputation tarnished."

Alpha gritted her teeth. "He wanted me to disown Omega."

"But your sister chose the life she wanted. None of us were happy with it. Even your mom and I haven't been able to forgive her for embarrassing us that way."

And to this day Alpha felt her parents were wrong. She'd told them so more times than she could count. Regardless, Omega was their child and her sister, and nothing should have slid a wedge between those relationships. But her parents had succumbed to their friends' gossip and whispers. "I know, Dad, and you know how I felt about that. No matter what, she's still your daughter and my sister."

"Well, one day you're going to face up to what she did to us, what she did to you. You had men looking at you funny, thinking you were her."

"It was only one man, Dad." She had heard all this before and wasn't in the mood to rehash this with her father. "Besides, that was three years ago. Omega is now a happily married woman."

"With a past."

She rolled her eyes. "We all have one. Some a little naughtier than others."

"Naughtier? What your sister did was a disgrace."

"What Omega did has nothing to do with Eddie."

"Had you and Eddie married, the two of you would have been one, so it did have something to do with him. And as far as I'm concerned, he's a good man. All he wanted was to protect you."

"No. He was trying to control me."

There was a pause on the other end. "So you're saying the chances of the two of you getting back together are slim to none?"

"I'm leaning heavily on none."

There was another pause. "I hope you're not making a mistake. What about the next man you meet who might find out what your sister used to do for a living?"

"Any man I become seriously involved with, Dad, is going to have to accept me as I am. Omega has nothing to do with it."

"You're wrong, Al. She's a part of your past that you can't get rid of."

"No, Dad. She's a part of my present, and I can't imagine it being any other way."

When he heard the brisk knock on his office door, Riley knew who it was without looking up. "Come in, Canyon."

His brother entered, letting off steam. "Keisha Ashford is not the same woman I was involved with three years ago. Do you hear me, Ry? She is not the same woman."

Riley leaned back in his chair. "Yes, I hear you. In fact, I'm sure everyone on this floor heard you. I take it the meeting didn't go well?"

"Go well? That woman deliberately tried to make me look as if I didn't know what the hell I was doing."

A smile touched the corners of Riley's lips. He seldom saw his brother hot under the collar and just to know a woman was responsible was somewhat amusing. Especially since the Canyon he knew would never let a woman get under his skin. "And did you?" he asked, watching his brother angrily pace back and forth in front of his desk.

Canyon stopped and glared. "Did I what?"

"Know what the hell you were doing?"

At first Canyon appeared to have been taken aback by the question. But then he lifted his shoulders in a defensive stance. "Hell, yes, I knew what I was doing, but she deliberately tried to make me look bad."

Riley forced the smile off his face. "And why would she do something like that? Was it because she found out you were seeing another woman behind her back, when the two of you were supposed to be dating exclusively? Hmm?"

Canyon glared. "I was not seeing that other woman and you know it. Bonita Simpkins set me up, and Keisha fell for it."

Riley opened his mouth to say something but the receptionist's voice on the intercom stopped him. "Mr. Westmoreland, Ms. Alpha Blake is on line two for you."

"Thanks." He then glanced over at his brother. "I need to take this call."

His brother shrugged. "Go ahead."

When Canyon just stood there, apparently still fuming over his encounter with Keisha, Riley cleared his throat and said, "It's a private call."

Canyon lifted a brow. "With the company's event planner? What could be so private about that?"

When Riley didn't respond but continued to sit and stare at his brother, waiting for him to leave, something flickered in the dark depths of Canyon's eyes. "Please don't tell me you've got the hots for the event planner."

"Okay, I won't tell you. Close the door behind you on the way out."

Canyon stood there and gaped at him. "I don't believe it."

Riley rolled his eyes. "What don't you believe?"

"What happened to your policy about never mixing business with pleasure?"

"It's still in place. I'm not mixing them. When we conduct business, we conduct business. And when we want pleasure, we'll have pleasure. Solely separate entities that aren't being mixed."

Canyon threw his head back and laughed. "You sound like a damn politician who's breaking the rule and then trying to find a way to make the situation work for you."

"Goodbye, Canyon. If I were you, I would focus on a way to make peace with Keisha Ashford."

The amusement on Canyon's face immediately vanished to be replaced with a glare. "You take care of your business, and I'll take care of mine."

It was on the tip of Riley's tongue to tell his brother that he was the one who sought him out and not the other way around. "Whatever."

It was only after Canyon had left and closed the door behind him that Riley clicked on the second line. "Alpha? Sorry for the wait."

"No problem. I'm just calling to thank you for the flowers. They are beautiful."

*So are you.* "I'm glad you like them."

"I do. I truly do."

He leaned back in his chair and did something he hadn't done in a long time—propped his feet up on his desk. "So, what have you been doing with yourself since I last saw you?" *Which was only two days ago.*

"Designing the invitations, picking up items for decorating and finalizing the menu with the chef. However, I did take time out for my dance classes."

He lifted a brow. "You're taking dance classes?"

She chuckled. "Yes, twice a week at the high school at night."

Why didn't he know that? And just as quickly as he thought it, he was reminded that their connection was about sex without commitment. There was no need for him to know what she did every hour of the day. "Sounds like fun."

"It is. Well, I don't want to hold you up. I just wanted to call and thank you for the flowers and to let you know how beautiful they are."

"You're welcome and have a good night." He paused a moment and then said in a low tone, "Think about me tonight."

"I will. We have two more days."

He drew in a long and deep breath, already feeling frustration settle within his bones. Two days was too long in his book. "Yes, we have two days."

It was hard not to suggest they shorten that time. He could drop by later. But he would hold fast and not give in to temptation. He had offered this time before their date on Saturday because he wanted it to be special for her. However, he decided to say, "I can't wait to see you again. I've thought of you often."

"And I've thought of you often, as well."

That was good to hear, but he doubted she had thought of him as much as he'd thought of her. It had been hard to concentrate on all the reports that had come across his desk and not on the memories of her and that night they'd dined together at his place. Whether it was the dinner they'd shared, the conversation between them or the horseback ride they'd taken, he had enjoyed his time with her, and there hadn't been anything sexual about it. Just sitting across from her, admiring the soft and smooth skin of her face, the stunning bone structure that made her such a gorgeous woman, the pair of lips he could get addicted to if not careful...

"Goodbye, Riley."

"Goodbye."

He eased his legs off his desk to stand and walk over to the window. He and Canyon had tossed for this office, mainly because of the view. There was snow on the top of the mountains and already he felt the urge to go skiing. He had a trip planned to Aspen in January and wondered if Alpha could ski.

He shook his head, chuckling at the foolish thought. She couldn't stand cold weather so chances were she would never venture anyplace where snow was waist-deep and you could feel the cold all the way to the bones.

But the most important thing he had to remember was that his affair with Alpha would be over by then.

For some reason that thought bothered him.

# Nine

Saturday night hadn't come quickly enough, Alpha thought, standing in front of the full-length mirror to give herself a final once-over. She had appreciated the good weather yesterday since it had given her the chance to go shopping. This was her first official date with Riley and she wanted to wear everything new—from the inside out.

This is when she missed Omega the most. As teens, and even while in college, they would go places and do things together, especially shopping. They'd shared some of the same taste in clothing and shoes, but when it came to undergarments, Omega was always more daring.

Alpha looked down at her legs. It would get colder later so she'd decided to wear a pair of boots, a new black suede pair she had bought yesterday. She liked the way they fit her legs, but more importantly, she liked how they looked with the outfit she was wearing—a printed kimono top with an elastic belt that emphasized her small waistline and a black sateen pencil skirt that highlighted her boots.

Her hair was styled slightly differently after her visit to a salon yesterday morning. She knew Riley liked seeing her hair around her shoulders, since he'd said as much that night at his place. So she had enhanced the look by making her hair appear fuller. She'd gotten it layered around her shoulders. A number of people had complimented the new style and said it was perfect for her face.

Riley had suggested that they either spend the night at his place or here, and either one was fine with her. She was so looking forward to tonight and a part of her felt giddy. Omega had called earlier that day and suggested she have an overnight bag packed just in case.

And because there was a chance this is where they would end the evening, her bedroom was ready. She had even bought silk sheets for her bed and scented candles had been placed all around. She liked the way her bedroom looked and although it wasn't nearly as large as Riley's, it would serve their purpose.

As she moved away from the mirror, she recalled the tour Riley had given her of his home. Why one person would need that much space she didn't know. But she had to admit there was something about every room that suited him.

Even his entertainment room suited him. Or should she say *rooms,* since there were two. There was a state-of-the-art theater with power-operated reclining seats. His music room held a white oak entertainment system with a sophisticated stereo, and a beautiful white Steinway baby grand piano sat in the middle of the floor. According to Riley, his mother, who had been a music major in college, had taught each of her seven sons how to play the piano. After she'd died, Dillon had made sure the lessons continued by hiring a private music instructor.

Alpha's heart kicked up a notch when she heard the ringing of the doorbell. A quick glance at her watch indicated Riley was fifteen minutes early.

She glanced around her bedroom one last time, liking what

she saw. Her queen-size bed was covered in a beautiful blue comforter and she'd added additional shams and decorative pillows. She'd changed the wattage of the lightbulbs in the lamps on both sides of her bed to soften the lighting in the room. Her bedroom had been transformed into a romantic haven.

She liked it. She liked it a lot. And she hoped that if Riley got the chance to see it, he would like it, as well.

"I hope I'm not too early, but I wasn't sure how traffic would be coming this way," Riley said, once he'd been able to regain control of his senses. He had almost lost them when Alpha opened the door. She looked absolutely stunning, from the new hairstyle she was sporting to the outfit she was wearing. Sexy enough to devour. She hadn't called to say she wasn't ready for the Pleasure Game later so he could only assume that she was.

Raw need, mingled with potent lust, consumed him. His body hadn't wasted time getting aroused. This was one time he was grateful for the long leather coat he was wearing. But his full concentration was on what *she* was wearing. Her outfit was designed to articulate every curve on her body and was doing a great job.

"No, you're not too early at all. It will only take a second to grab my coat," she said, stepping aside so he could enter her home.

"Take your time, Alpha."

"Thanks."

And then, with deep male appreciation, he watched her walk off, getting even more aroused by the sway of her hips with every step she took in that pencil skirt with the slit in the back. When she was no longer in sight, he drew in a deep breath, knowing it would be one of those kinds of nights. The only good thing about knowing it was being fully aware of how it would end.

He would let her decide whose bed they would sleep in tonight. It didn't matter to him since he didn't intend for them to get much sleep. That was why he intended to feed her well because she would definitely need all her energy for later.

"I'm ready, Riley."

That made two of them. He was ready, as well.

"I guess now is the time to ask whether I'll be coming back here tonight," she said. He saw the flash of color that appeared in her cheeks and knew the topic of what they intended to do later made her blush. He smiled thinking that she would be doing a whole hell of a lot of blushing later, if she had any shy bones in her body.

He shoved his hands into his coat pockets. "It's your decision. It doesn't matter to me where we make love."

His bluntness caused the color in her cheeks to deepen, but that did nothing for the heated look she gave him from beneath her silky long lashes. He knew it was unintentional, but nobody informed his erection, which was beginning to throb like hell. When she nervously licked her lips, he knew that if he didn't get her out of there now he would be initiating a roll on the floor in the next few minutes.

"I'd like to come back here," she said softly, holding his gaze.

"Then we shall. Ready?"

She nodded and led him to the door for them to leave. As far as he was concerned, it wasn't a moment too soon.


"Welcome tonight, Mr. Westmoreland. Your table is ready."

"Thanks, Pierre," Riley said, handing his coat to the manager of the restaurant.

While Riley assisted Alpha in removing her coat, she thanked the older man, who had a deep French accent, a Maurice Chevalier reincarnated. He gave her a brilliant smile, leaned in and lifted her hand to kiss the back of it. "Welcome to *Les' Amores, mademoiselle.* You are most beautiful."

She smiled at the compliment. "Thank you."

He straightened and then grabbed a couple of menus from a nearby rack. "Please follow me."

Alpha glanced at her surroundings as they followed their host. She had been quite taken with the French restaurant the moment Riley had turned into the courtyard of fine shops and boutiques. Since moving to Denver she had heard about *Les' Amores* but had never had the opportunity to dine at the plush brasserie.

As Pierre led them through the main dining area, she took note of the adobe brick walls lined with ornamental racks filled with fine wine and crystal glasses. The tables were adorned with red silk tablecloths and candle lanterns. Authentic French artwork hung on the walls and a large fireplace with a roaring blaze was in the middle of the room.

Instead of seating them at one of the vacant tables they passed, Pierre escorted them to a room in the back that had a table set for two. The room was quaint with wooden beam ceilings and a huge brick fireplace. Cozy and private.

Riley moved to pull out her chair before Pierre had a chance to do so and leaned close to her ear to whisper, "I love your outfit, but I can't wait to take it off you." She couldn't help the blush that crept into her features. She knew he was telling her that the seduction of Alpha Blake had begun.

He took his chair and Pierre handed them menus and proceeded to offer his recommendations for that night. That done, he asked about wine and Riley named a brand she'd never heard of. When she looked at him, he turned sensual dark eyes on her and said, "It's a magnificent blend. You'll like it."

She nodded, swallowing deeply and wondering if she would need something stronger to get her through the evening. "I'm sure I will."

"I'll give you time to look at the menu," he said, easing from the room and leaving them alone.

Alpha glanced down at the menu. "Everything looks good, Riley. What do you recommend?"

"About you or what's on the menu?" he asked with a flirty wink at her.

She gave him an admonishing smile, wondering if this was how it would be for the rest of the night. "The menu, Riley."

He smiled. "In that case I would recommend the…"

She listened while he rattled off a number of dishes, pronouncing each in a deep French accent that stirred her nerve endings. She gazed deep into the eyes staring back at her. In the depths of his dark gaze was a promise of what would come later. A hot, lusty night filled with pleasure. And heaven help her, she was looking forward to it.

"So what do you think, Alpha?"

She knew he was asking about the menu and the dishes he'd just told her about, but though she had heard, she hadn't listened. "I'll let you decide."

He nodded and gave her a smile, one that told her he knew why she was taking the easy way out. Pierre returned with the wine and poured some into their glasses and then took their orders. When he left, Alpha glanced around.

The room was small and intimate. They had been given a table with a view of Pikes Peak, and it was breathtaking. Music was flowing into the room through hidden speakers, and the tunes were romantic. She hadn't realized how secluded the room was until she recalled walking through the restaurant to get to it. Not only did the fire blazing in the fireplace provide warmth, but it also set an intimate tone. On the drive over, she'd tried bringing him up to date on the party plans, but Riley had reached out, touched her hand and said tonight was not about the party but about them.

"This is a nice room," she said.

"I'm glad you like it. So tell me, Alpha. Do you ski?"

* * *

Why was he asking her that? Riley immediately wondered. It had to be for the purpose of conversation, nothing more. The inquiry certainly couldn't have anything to do with his ski trip to Aspen in January since their affair would have ended by then.

"No, I don't ski."

He wasn't surprised. "Would you like to learn how?"

She shook her head. "That would mean being out in not just cold weather but super cold weather, so I'll pass."

He should let it go, but couldn't. "What if I promised to keep you warm?"

She chuckled. "I don't think you can keep me *that* warm, Riley."

"But if I could?" he inquired further, taking a sip of his wine.

"You can't."

He didn't say anything but, deep down, he saw it as a challenge. He held her gaze. "We'll see."

She tilted her head and looked at him. "Tell me. What do you get out of skiing? I heard it's not really a form of exercise."

He watched her take a sip of her wine. The way she closed her lips around the mouth of the glass sent flutters off in his stomach. "Not true. Any time you use muscles you don't normally use, you're exercising."

He took a sip of his wine as he told her about the first time he'd put on a pair of skis. "I was all but seven and my father and uncle took their sons on a ski trip for the sole purpose of providing us with professional ski lessons."

He chuckled. "I guess they knew their sons and figured if they didn't make sure we were taught by a professional then we would learn the wrong way and risk our lives. Being on the slopes with my family was special to me and I consider those memories some of the best ones of my childhood. Maybe that's why I enjoy skiing so much."

He saw the wistful look that shone in her eyes, so he added, "I'm sure you and your sister did things with your family that you hold as special memories, too."

She shifted her gaze from his to pick up her glass of wine. "Yes, of course."

Not for the first time, he thought she was deliberately not sharing information about her family. It shouldn't bother him, but it did, mainly because he didn't have any problem telling her about his family. The only thing he knew about her parents was that they had wanted her to go into veterinary medicine but had accepted her decision to change careers. She seldom mentioned anything about her sister, and he could only assume the two were not close. And he was still curious about the ring that used to be on her finger. He was about to question her on the topic when Pierre returned with their appetizers.

Pierre, efficient as ever, was in and out in no time, leaving them alone once again with a basket of hot buttered rolls, a platter of imported French escargots sautéed in a creamy, garlic butter sauce and steamed artichoke. He'd even taken the time to refill their wineglasses before breezing out.

Riley glanced over at Alpha. He should have used the time during Pierre's interruption to rethink pursuing his interest in the man who'd put a ring on her finger, as well as the reason she didn't talk much about her family, but he didn't. For some reason, he felt the need to address it. "Can I ask you something?"

She was reaching for an escargot and glanced over at him with a smile. "Just as long as what you want to ask has nothing to do with these. They look delicious."

He chuckled. "Not at all, please help yourself," he said, glad she was enjoying his choice in foods.

"Okay, then, ask away."

"I have two questions, really. I noticed you used to wear a ring. Were you married before?"

Her hands stilled. "Does it matter?"

He held her gaze and shook his head. "No. I'm just curious."

"No, I've never been married, but up until a year ago I was engaged."

"What happened?" he asked, as if he had every right to know.

She didn't say anything for a minute and then, "It was decided that marriage wasn't the right move for us after all."

She was being somewhat evasive so he couldn't help wondering who had made that decision. The guy? Her? Had it been mutual? Why did he care? It didn't matter, and he only cared if she'd gotten hurt by the decision. But, in a way, he was glad the marriage didn't take place because if it had she wouldn't be here with him tonight.

"And your second question?" she asked, returning to eating.

He smiled. She was letting him know there wouldn't be any further discussion on the first question. "Why don't you like talking about your family?" Her hands stilled again, and he could tell she was about to freeze up on him, but he refused to let her do that.

"I told you about my family, Riley."

"Not enough."

"I told you my parents were veterinarians in Daytona and that I have a sister."

"Is she still alive?"

She lifted a brow. "Who?"

"Your sister."

"Yes. Why do you ask?"

He shrugged. "Because you never talk about her. Where does she live? Is she married? Does she have any kids?"

Something, he wasn't sure what, flashed in her eyes before

she lowered her head to slowly bite into an escargot. "Omega lives in Paris. She's married to a wonderful man and they are trying real hard to start a family."

"Are the two of you close?"

"Yes, very close. As close as any two sisters can be."

His curiosity had been appeased. He decided that, in the future, the subjects of her ex-fiancé and her family were closed unless she brought them up. "You like that?" he asked, motioning to the escargot she had gone back to eating. He was getting turned on as he watched her chew a few times and then lick her lips.

"Yes, it's delicious."

A trickle of butter was running down her chin. "Come here and lean close," he told her, picking up his napkin to wipe away the butter. But when she leaned in toward him, he changed his mind and swiped the butter from her chin with the tip of his tongue.

"There," he said huskily. As he drew back, he met the surprised look in her eyes and smiled. "It's all gone now."

"Thanks," she murmured softly, drawing back in her chair.

"Anytime. I like the way you taste," he responded huskily.

She took a sip of her wine. "It was the butter."

A doubtful smile curved his lips. "Umm, the butter tasted good but you tasted better. Makes me anxious to taste you all over later."

Riley watched as a blush touched her cheeks and she took another sip of her wine. "Don't drink too much of that, baby. I want your mind completely functional for later."

"Will that be all, Mr. Westmoreland?" Pierre asked after he and another waiter finished clearing the table. He had already asked if either Riley or Alpha wanted dessert and they had both declined.

"No, Pierre, that will be all. Just make sure we aren't disturbed for the remainder of the evening."

"Yes, sir." The older man quickly left with the other waiter trailing behind him.

No sooner had the door closed than Alpha swore she heard the distinct sound of a lock clicking in place, and Riley turned his full attention to her. His dark, piercing eyes held her within their scope and she all but squirmed in her seat, feeling sexual currents flow from him. Suddenly, an electrical charge seemed to vibrate through the air causing blood to rush through her veins.

Blood was rushing through another area of her body, as well, the one located at the juncture of her thighs, which made her cross her legs. She drew in a slow breath when he stood and rounded the table. Holding out his hand, he said, in what sounded like a deep, husky growl, "Dance with me."

Alpha felt her stomach quiver with each word he said. Earlier, she had heard music flowing into the room but the sound had been rather faint. At that moment, as if on cue, the volume increased. She slipped her hand into his, feeling his heat immediately. Uncrossing her legs, she eased from her chair and he gently pulled her into his arms, right smack against his hard, masculine body.

The song being played was perfect, just the right tempo for the way their bodies melded together as they swayed to the lyrics and melody. With her hand on his shoulder and her head lying on his chest, she could feel the rapid beat of his heart, which was somehow keeping time with hers. Being this close to him, bodies locked as tightly as they could be, stirred something elemental in her blood and reminded her of just how potent the chemistry was between them.

Pressed against him, she felt every inch of his lean strength. And when his hips moved, so did hers, slowly, methodically, magnetically. Heat sizzled through all parts of her when she felt his hard erection against her middle. The pressure triggered her nipples to harden. An ache began in her loins and branched upward, filling her with an indescribable hunger, a sexual need she didn't know she was capable of feeling.

"You okay?"

The sound of his voice ignited rampant sensations within her. She raised her eyes to his and inwardly moaned when she connected to the dark depths. "Yes, I'm okay." *But barely,* she held off saying. Never before had dancing with a man caused this much havoc on her emotions. Never had it driven her to want things she'd never wanted before.

They continued to gaze into each other's eyes as they swayed to the music. When one song moved to another, they stood in the same spot, feet firmly planted, bodies barely moving while his hand spanned her backside, making a slow ache throb there. She reveled in the feel of him holding her in his arms.

When she couldn't take looking into his eyes any longer, she placed her head on his chest again. The heat from his gaze was unnerving her, making it hard for her to breathe. What was there about him that made her not want to fight the heat but to wallow in it? She wanted tonight. She needed tonight—and all the nights he wanted to give her…for six weeks. And when it was over, it would be over. Final, with no regrets, no worrying about a lost love that should last forever or a love that never was. She was going into this affair with her eyes wide open. She was not the naive woman who'd thought she was the luckiest female on earth when Edward Swisher, of the prestigious Daytona Swishers, had asked her out. She had learned her lesson. She should have learned it with LeBron. But it had taken Eddie to make her vow never to give her heart to another man.

The song melded into another and they continued dancing. He tightened his arms around her and held her closer. Her breath caught each and every time he would deliberately slide his leg between hers, letting her feel the length of him through his pants. She could feel her panties getting wet with each moment of contact.

Almost overwhelmed in desire, she tilted her head back, met the dark, penetrating gaze staring down at her and asked, "What are you doing to me?"

He didn't even pretend not to know what she was asking. "Prepping you for later."

Who needed to be prepped? She opened her mouth to ask him that very thing when he lowered his mouth to hers, slid his tongue inside and proceeded to kiss her in a way that sent powerful surges through her. He began toying with her tongue, feasting on it like a hungry man getting his last meal.

She was just as greedy when she tightened her arms around him while they devoured each other's mouths. Nothing else mattered at that moment. It meant nothing to her that they were in a public place and there were people on the other side of that door having dinner. Nor did it matter that Pierre and that other waiter probably had a good idea what she and Riley were doing in here. All that mattered at the moment was the way he was kissing her, stirring a need within her that was nearly making her lose it.

Riley pulled his mouth back, and she was able to draw in a much-needed breath. He was able to do the same and rested his forehead against hers.

"Baby, I should be the one asking what *you* are doing to me," he whispered softly against her lips that were still moist from their kiss. "All I want to do at this moment is put you on that table and spread you wide and take you like I've been dreaming of doing for the past couple of weeks."

Her heartbeat kicked up a notch, knowing he wanted her as much as she wanted him. She refused to play games about this. She wanted to experience it all, and she wanted to experience it with him. She wanted several nights of hot, mind-blowing sex with no strings attached and no guilty conscience to deal with afterward.

She would go into the affair as the consenting and mature adult she was. She was the one paying the bills on Noble Lane, and what she did there was nobody's business, certainly not her parents', who lived thousands of miles away. They would frown upon an affair between her and anyone. Her father was hoping that she and Eddie would get back together even if it meant she would have to cut ties with her twin sister to do so.

"Are you ready for me to take you home?"

His question gave her pause. Now would be the perfect time, if she wanted to change her mind about anything they planned to do later. But her mind was made up, and she wasn't changing it. "Yes, I'm ready."

He pulled back slightly and looked at her, those dark eyes locked with hers, refusing to look away, as if her very soul was laid out for him to read like a book. "Are you sure you're ready, Alpha? I intend for it to be one hell of a night."

And she was counting on just that. She nodded, deciding right then and there to shed her inhibitions once and for all. She countered his question with one of her own. "Maybe I should be asking you the same thing, Riley. Are you sure you're ready?"

He reached down, took her hand and led it to the crotch of his pants. "What does that tell you?"

Oh, he was ready all right. What he'd done by letting her touch him was a bold move, one Eddie would never have taken. Eddie would never have encouraged her to cop a feel. And since Riley put her hand there, she saw no reason to move it…at least not yet. She was simply amazed how large he felt behind his zipper. She moved her hand around to take in the length, shape and feel of him.

"If you keep it up, Alpha, I just might be tempted to take you here and now."

Something, she wasn't sure what, drove her to utter her next words. "Do it."

"What did you say?" he asked, his voice deep and throaty, his eyes steady, mesmerizing and hungry.

She could play it off and pretend she hadn't said anything. But she didn't want to do that. What would be the point? She wanted Riley, and she wanted him now.

Alpha leaned in close to him and whispered, "I said, do it. Do it now."

She could tell from the way his breathing changed that he got the message. "Then take it out," he whispered against her lips. "You want it, then go in and get it, baby."

Her heartbeat kicked up another notch. His gaze held hers as she slowly eased down his zipper and then reached inside the opening. She tried releasing him but found his briefs to be in the way.

After a few failed efforts, he asked, "Need help?"

She didn't see amusement in his gaze, just gut-wrenching need. "Yes. Please."

He took one step back, and she watched as he pulled himself out of his pants. She sucked in a deep breath when she saw him and her mouth nearly dropped open. He was huge and had a condom in hand.

"Don't tempt me with an open mouth, baby," he said, easing on protection.

She closed it, and before she could think about anything, he moved back toward her. "Now lift up your skirt for me, Alpha."

She slowly inched up her skirt, giving him a view of her silk thigh-high stockings and lacy black panties. She wasn't sure what he'd planned to do next, but she hadn't expected him to reach out and tug her panties past her knees and down her legs.

"That's what I want to see," he said, staring at the throbbing flesh her panties had been hiding. "It's just like I thought it would be. You look beautiful there, and your color is natural."

Alpha swallowed hard. "Yes, of course. I've never dyed my hair."

As if seeing that part of her bared wasn't enough, he reached out and touched her, trailed fingers through the curls and all around her feminine folds, slipping one finger inside as if to test her wetness. Her legs automatically parted to give him better access. And he took it, penetrating his finger farther inside of her.

She heard him draw in a deep breath before he said, "Your scent is killing me." And when he removed his finger from inside of her and inserted it between his lips to suck on it, she got weak in the knees.

"And you taste good, too. I'm having you for breakfast in the morning."

Before she could figure out if he was serious or teasing, his hands went to her waist and he lifted her off her feet. "Wrap your legs around me," he instructed huskily.

She did so and the moment he lifted her body, she felt the head of his erection touch her. Easing her legs apart a little more, she sucked in hard when he thrust inside of her, clutching tight to her hips until he was fully embedded within her. She wasn't aware a man could go that deep.

"Now we dance this way," he said against her moist lips.

And they did. While the music played, he held her in his arms with her legs wrapped around him, supporting her weight while he was fully planted inside of her. She tightened her arms around his neck, swiveling her hips against him in tiny circles, keeping a sensuous beat with the music. Never had she danced with a man like this before. Rocking his body hard against hers and reminding her of just how buried he was inside of her. The intense penetration combined with the moves of their bodies to stimulate her with searing intensity. She closed her eyes as her nerve endings became more and more charged. Electrified. Intensified.

And then there was the scent of him, clean and masculine.

Whatever cologne he was wearing was a fragrance meant to drive a woman over the edge, and it was definitely doing a number on her. His hold on her thighs tightened even more, and the next thing she knew there was a hard wall against her back. She hadn't been aware they had moved away from that spot in the center of the room.

"I can't take you slow anymore," he growled seconds before he began thrusting in and out of her hard and fast, working his hips back and forth and side to side. She tightened her legs around him, convinced he was trying to drive her insane.

When she felt her body about to explode, she moaned his name and was just about to scream when his mouth lowered and planted firmly on hers.

But that didn't stop her body from splintering into a thousand pieces. And she knew the moment his detonated, as well. He thrust deeper, harder and she felt him, all the way to her womb. Her muscles squeezed him, were driven to hold him hostage inside of her.

This was incredible. He was incredible.

She reveled in the feel of his body in hers, the hardness of his chest against hers and how his firm, muscled thighs felt while keeping her propped up against the wall. She fought not to scream again but couldn't retain it, and once again his mouth was there to silence her.

Moments later, when he pulled his mouth away, dark eyes stared into hers and she read what his eyes were saying. *I want more.*

She mouthed her response. *Get all you want.*

He remained inside of her, staring down at her, until they were both able to breathe normally again. It was only then that he lowered her feet to the floor and leaned down to pull up her panties before rearranging her skirt, smoothing it over her hips and thighs. She then watched as he proceeded to tuck himself back inside his pants.

After rezipping, he glanced over at her. "Ready to go play Pleasure Games?"

"I'm more than ready," she said, as a satisfied smile touched her lips, although she wasn't sure just where she would find the energy to do such a thing.

He returned her smile. "I'll instruct Pierre to bring our coats. The sooner I get you to your house, the better."

Funny, she'd been thinking the same thing.

# Ten

$R$iley had a tough time maintaining his self-control on the drive to Alpha's home mainly because she was deliberately making it hard for him. Instead of using his truck, he was driving his Lexus sports car. It was sleek and smooth and perfect for the classy woman sitting beside him. However, the car's intimacy was almost more than he could handle, especially since her scent was all over the place.

He glanced over at Alpha, knowing he should be keeping his eyes on the road. But he was finding it hard to do so when she was deliberately inching up her skirt to show a pair of luscious brown thighs. It didn't take much to remember how it felt being between those thighs, which made his erection hard with the anticipation of getting between them again.

He had enjoyed sharing dinner with her, had loved sitting across from her and watching her mouth move as she ate. Not for the first time, his head had been filled with thoughts of all the things he would love to see that mouth do to him.

But he would also admit he had enjoyed their conversation. Although he had pretty much gotten the hint that her past was not open for discussion, and he had told her early on that he didn't want them to discuss anything about the party, they had managed to find other things to talk about. Mainly movies they had seen, their thoughts about the ongoing war, the recent election and Hollywood scandals. He had been surprised to discover they had the same tastes and opinions about a number of things.

He'd also told her about his cousins in Atlanta, Texas and Montana, and how excited the family was about his cousin Megan's upcoming wedding in June, which meant the family would all be getting together again. And he shouldn't have been surprised when Alpha told him that Megan was considering her as a wedding planner and had interviewed her last week. Megan would be making her decision in a couple of weeks.

He told her about his great-grandfather, Raphel, and how Megan had hired a private investigator to find information about him, and how the two traveled to Texas to discover Raphel had a child before marrying Riley's great-grandmother, which meant the possibility of more Westmorelands somewhere.

He glanced around when traffic slowed down. He had decided to drive through town to hit the interstate, figuring there wouldn't be much traffic tonight. But that assumption had turned out to be wrong when he got caught up with people leaving a concert.

To get out of the mad rush he had taken another shortcut that carried him through another part of town known for its boutiques. Thanksgiving was just a few weeks away and already storefronts were all decked out for Christmas.

Riley glanced over at Alpha's thighs again. She had hiked up the hem of her skirt another inch or two. He loosened his tie when he brought the car to a traffic light and frowned over at her. "Be forewarned, Alpha. If tempted badly enough

I wouldn't hesitate to pull this car to the side of the road and take you again, here and now."

She threw her head back and laughed as if she couldn't imagine such a thing. The sound flowing from her throat stirred his blood and sent it straight to his groin.

"That should make interesting reading in the newspapers tomorrow morning if the sheriff or one of his deputies stumbles upon us," she replied smartly.

He held her gaze intensely. "Trust me, it won't make the papers. Dillon is best friends with Sheriff Harper and it wouldn't be the first Westmoreland he's come across on the side of the road."

She tilted her head. "Do tell. Is it something that runs in the family?"

He chuckled. "Only with Bane. I can't tell you the number of times Sheriff Harper brought Bane home after coming across him and Crystal parked somewhere."

"Crystal?"

Riley frowned. "Yes, Crystal Newsome, Bane's obsession. Maybe I should say they were equally obsessed with each other."

He decided to keep talking, figuring it would take his mind off getting under her skirt. "Crystal and Bane have been under each other's skin since they were kids. It would drive Mr. Newsome bonkers, not just because Bane was four years older than Crystal but because Crystal told anyone who wanted to listen—and even those who didn't—that she wanted Bane and vice versa, even when they were too young to think about wanting anyone. Mr. Newsome was totally against a union between his daughter and a Westmoreland."

"Why?"

He shrugged. "Something that happened years ago with our grandfathers, resulting in a grudge that ran deep. It was unfortunate for Crystal and Bane."

"What happened?" Alpha asked curiously.

"Carl Newsome got tired of Crystal climbing out of her bedroom window in the dead of night or cutting school just to be with Bane. Since Crystal was a minor, at fifteen, and Bane was nineteen, old man Newsome got a restraining order against Bane. If Bane came within a mile of Crystal he would go to jail. Well, Bane, being the hardheaded badass that he is, shrugged off the old man's threat and he and Crystal would sneak around. They did it for years, and then one night when Bane was twenty-two and Crystal not yet eighteen, they eloped."

"Eloped?"

"Yes, but they were found before they could tie the knot." At least that's the story Bane had told them. Riley often wondered if that was the case.

"Anyway," Riley continued, "they returned home and old man Newsome sent Crystal away to live with some relative, and Dillon talked to Bane about getting himself together by making something of himself instead of being a troublemaker."

Riley paused a moment and then said, "Losing Crystal almost destroyed Bane since he didn't have a clue where she'd gone. Her father made sure of that. We were able to talk Bane into not going after Crystal...at least until he made something of himself and both he and Crystal matured. Bane eventually joined the navy and is working toward being a SEAL."

"Do you think he'll eventually go after Crystal? Find her?"

Riley's frown deepened. "There's no doubt in my mind that he will."

She arched her brow. "You don't seem too happy with the thought of him doing that."

He thought she was very observant. "To be quite honest, I'm not. That whole Crystal thing, with her leaving Denver for parts unknown, nearly destroyed Bane. It's like Crystal is in his blood and he refuses to purge her out of it. She's a part of him that he can't let go of."

He didn't say anything for a long moment. "So yes, Bane will go looking for her one day and he *will* find her. What worries me is the possibility that he will get hurt all over again when he does. For all any of us know, Crystal might have moved on with her life and Bane is just a memory."

As he continued to drive, he decided not to talk anymore for a while. He didn't want anything to ruin his night and thinking of Bane and Crystal would do that for him.

But then maybe he should think about them and, more specifically, recall his brother's agony. Doing so would reinforce the reasons why he would never fall in love with a woman. He refused to ever go through that much pain.

He glanced back over at Alpha. She was quiet, as if she was thinking hard about something. He hoped like hell she wasn't having second thoughts about tonight. He eased out a deep breath when he turned on her street. His overnight bag was in the trunk. When he walked into her house, he intended to stay.

Thoughts of what she and Riley had done back at the restaurant filled Alpha's mind. That had been some dance. She doubted she would ever forget it. While in his arms and connected to him that way, it was as if nothing or no one else existed but the two of them. She'd felt as though the two of them were in their own little world. Never had she done anything so impulsive and spontaneous, so scandalous and wild.

And when they had made love, against the wall of all places, she'd felt sensations take over her body that she'd never felt before. Was this a sample of what she should come to expect from Riley? Anything but the norm? She had a feeling that with him there would never be a dull moment. He had promised her pleasure, and more pleasure, and so far he was right on point.

No man had ever made love to her that way, with such intensity and completeness. And just to think, there was more where that had come from. A lot more.

She blinked when she saw they had arrived at her house already and looked over at Riley when he brought the car to a stop in her driveway. She saw dark, penetrating eyes staring at her. She wondered if there would ever come a day when she would look into his eyes and not get turned on, not feel those incredible sensations flowing through her body.

Without saying anything, he leaned over, unbuckled her seat belt and then reached up and cupped her chin in his hand. "I enjoyed making love to you, Alpha. And I won't apologize for how it happened or where it happened."

She held his gaze. Did he assume the reason she had gotten quiet was because she'd begun having regrets? She held his gaze. "I don't want you to apologize. I asked for it." She chuckled. "You definitely gave me what I wanted, Riley." *What I needed,* she thought.

"Happy to please you, sweetheart."

She didn't have time to think about how easily that term of endearment had rolled off his lips before he was kissing her with an intensity that set her loins on fire. What was there about him that could arouse her so easily, to the point where he had her not only throwing caution to the wind, but also flying in the wind? He had her wanting to try things she'd never thought about doing before.

He slowly ended the kiss, pulled back and stared at her. She felt the intensity of his gaze all the way to the bone. "You had me worried for a minute, when you got quiet on me," he said.

She smiled. "I was merely relishing those moments."

He seemed pleased with what she'd said. "Then let me give you even more of them." He opened the car door and trotted around to her side of the car.

Alpha had a vague memory of him walking her to the front door. And then there was the moment when she'd found it difficult to insert her key into the lock until Riley had eased the key from her nervous hands.

He opened the door and moved aside for her to enter. When she crossed the foyer to the living room, she removed her coat and hung it on the rack before placing her purse on the coffee table. She glanced across the room and saw the fire still kindling in the fireplace, giving the room a warm, toasty feel. She was about to turn to ask Riley if he wanted something to drink when she felt his heat directly behind her. He wrapped his arms around her and pulled her back toward him. Immediately, she felt his aroused body pressed against her backside.

His heated breath touched the side of her face when he whispered, "I want to make love to you in front of the fireplace."

He eased his hold on her so she could turn around in his arms and she stared up into his face. "Sounds like a good plan to me." She leaned forward on tiptoes and slanted her mouth across his.

She wanted to initiate this kiss, master it the best way she knew how, and she figured if she let her tongue do the work that she would be fine. So she kissed him, trying to recall the ways his tongue had driven her crazy. She wanted him to see just how it felt to be on the receiving end this time.

So she feasted on his mouth and he stood there, rock solid, legs braced apart with his arms around her waist, and let her have her way with him. Never had a man's mouth tasted so good. She was enjoying herself so much that she couldn't help moaning in pleasure.

Then, suddenly, she found herself hauled against his hard chest as he took over the kiss, plundering her mouth with his demanding tongue. Desire took over her senses and sent fire through her, blazing hotter than the one in the fireplace.

After that, she couldn't recall how her clothes were removed. The only thing she recalled was being naked while watching in fervent anticipation as he removed his clothes.

When he had taken off the final stitch she couldn't do anything but simply stare. She had seen his erection at the restaurant, but now she was getting a view of the entire picture—the curly strands of dark hair covering his broad chest, rock-hard biceps, lean hips, sinewy thighs and muscled shoulders. But still, her gaze returned to his middle and she couldn't move her eyes away.

She could clearly see that he'd put on a new condom, and when he moved his powerfully built, masculine, naked body toward her, she couldn't help asking, "You do that often?"

"Do what?" he asked coming to a stop directly in front of her, easing his thigh between hers and wrapping his arms around her waist. His action caused her to lose her train of thought for a moment.

He leaned in close, brushed his lips across hers and asked again, "Do what often?"

"Carry a condom with you all the time."

Riley chuckled. "I don't carry one *all* the time, just when I know how the night's going to end. But in some cases, making love might very well be the beginning. I almost lost my head once and messed up and figured I would never come close to letting something like that happen again. It's better to be safe than sorry."

She could arrest his concerns and admit to being on birth control but she knew that with some men it wouldn't matter. They had to have their own form of protection as well, since pregnancy wasn't the only thing a person had to be concerned with.

He leaned in close and nuzzled his nose in her hair. "Mmm, you smell good all over."

His words reclaimed her attention and she lifted her head so she could meet his eyes. "Thanks. So do you."

Riley took a swipe across her lips with his tongue. "You taste good, as well…and I intend to taste you all over, starting now."

Then he claimed her mouth again, just as greedy as before, demolishing any and all of her coherent thoughts. Each and every kiss they shared was more powerful, commanding and potent than the one before it and this one was no different. His mouth ravaged hers, and she couldn't help the moans of pleasure coming from deep within her throat. The man was a great kisser, and he definitely knew how to use that tongue of his.

Being so enmeshed in sharing this heated kiss with Riley, she wasn't aware that they had sunk to their knees in front of the fireplace until he pulled his mouth away and she saw the room beyond his shoulders.

But that observation was short-lived. His mouth left hers to trail kisses along her lips and nibble the sensitive flesh around her mouth. She slid her hand up and down his chest, liking the feel of the curly hair beneath her fingers. She threw her head back when he began sucking her neck then moved slowly down to her shoulder blades. On instinct, she arched backward to rest on her elbows, which caused her breasts to rise upward and her hips to lift off the hearth rug.

His warm breath caressed the side of her face when he whispered, "I love you in this position, and I'm about to show you why."

Riley was convinced he had never wanted any woman this much. Everything about Alpha was perfect, from the smooth slope of her chest, which held two of the most beautiful breasts he'd ever seen, to her firm stomach, curvy hips and thighs and long, shapely legs with gorgeous calves.

Not holding back, he swooped a nipple into his mouth and began sucking on it intensely, hungrily, displaying the voracious sexual appetite that he had for her. With his mouth still clamped to her nipple, he began moving his hand, letting it roam everywhere, but definitely making a path toward the juncture of her thighs. His finger slid inside, finding her not just wet but drenched. Her hum of pleasure drove him to penetrate deeper and massage her clitoris with circular strokes.

"What are you doing to me, Riley?"

He figured he could ask her the same thing. The womanly scent emanating from her tempted him to eat her alive. It was such a luscious, feminine fragrance.

He released her nipple and before moving to latch on to the other, he glanced up at her and said, "I'm giving you pleasure. I also intend to pay you back for tempting me in the car."

"What did I do?"

"You deliberately flashed me some thigh. Not that I mind. But it was a hard drive back to your place. No pun intended."

Deciding he didn't want to talk any longer, he began giving her other breast the same ardent attention. He felt her hand on his head, rubbing gently. And she was shoving her breast deeper into his mouth. He didn't have a problem with either movement.

The more he devoured her breasts and inhaled her scent the more he was thrown into a sexual frenzy. He pulled back, smiled up at her flushed face, the heavy-lidded eyes staring back at him. Seeing her so stimulated plunged him into primitive desire, as raw as it could get.

He began licking his way down her body, liking the feel of his tongue on her skin. And when he dipped his head between her legs and replaced his fingers with his tongue, she cried out riotously while digging her nails into his back.

He ignored the pain as he lapped her up, using his tongue to pleasure her the way he'd done in his dreams. He held tight to her hips when she moved them from side to side, gyrating against his mouth. He heard her moans, and they were sensual music to his ears.

The trembling of her thighs was the first sign that an explosion was on the horizon, and when she released a deep, throaty groan followed by a hell-wrenching scream, his tongue penetrated deeper within her womanly folds. She pushed her hips upward even more, calling his name.

By the time she lay whimpering softly, he had stretched to settle between her legs. "Alpha?"

She slowly opened her eyes and gazed up at him. A shiver of some unknown force passed through him, gripped him within its clutches. The reflections from the blaze in the fireplace danced across her naked skin, making her even more beautiful. Desirable.

Alpha reached up and cradled his face in her hands. "That was incredible," she whispered.

He wanted to tell her no, that she was incredible. But instead, while still gazing into her eyes, he lifted her hips with his hands and entered her with one smooth thrust.

"Riley!"

"I'm here, baby, and tonight I intend to ride you hard all over the place."

And then he began moving, thrusting within her like the demented sexual maniac that he felt like tonight. The room was filled with the sound of flesh slapping against flesh, moans and groans, and with him whispering words to her that were erotic and wicked.

Then, for the third time that night, he felt her body explode as her inner muscles clenched him hard. He threw his head back and growled her name as he continued to plow her with deep, hard strokes.

He felt his own body shatter and fought to hold it together and couldn't. No orgasm should be this powerful, this mind-blowing, this dominating.

That's the one thing he couldn't let happen. He couldn't let any woman dominate him in any way. He refused to be another Bane. He forced the thought from his mind, deciding no domination would be taking place tonight. He was getting paranoid. He figured over-the-top sex could do that to a man. And this definitely had been over-the-top. She had blasted them off the Richter scale, hands down.

He continued to ride her hard while she wrapped her legs tightly around him. He took her mouth and kissed her with more hunger than he'd ever felt for a woman. His tongue was commanding and demanding as an orgasm continued to rip through him, flinging him to a universe unknown.

The fire roared in the fireplace when a short while later he settled on his back and pulled Alpha into his arms, trying to get their breathing and heartbeats back to normal. He wrapped his arms around her, needing to hold her this way. Not fully understanding why, but just knowing that he did.

She raised her head and looked over at him. "Riley?"

"Hmm?"

She opened her mouth to say something and then, as if she thought better of it, closed her eyes and shook her head. "Nothing."

He lifted a brow. "You sure?"

She nodded. "Yes." She then settled into his arms, snuggling close.

He entwined her legs with his and tightened his hold on her, wondering what she'd been about to say. He glanced down and saw she had dozed off already, breathing gently. Reaching up, he pulled the afghan off the sofa and draped it over their naked bodies.

They would sleep awhile and then wake up and make love some more.

# Eleven

"Hey, what did you do this weekend, Alpha? You can barely keep your eyes open. I don't ever recall you being so exhausted."

Alpha took a sip of her coffee as she looked across the table at Lindsey. Her assistant was right; she'd never been this exhausted. But then she'd never had to deal with the likes of Riley Westmoreland before, either.

It had been one heck of a weekend. He hadn't just spent the night with her on Saturday, but had stayed Sunday night, as well. To say it had been wild was an understatement. No matter how many hot baths she'd taken, she couldn't completely work the soreness out of muscles she hadn't used in a long time, if ever. And her hair—for crying out loud, ever since Riley had said he liked it down, that's how she'd worn it. It had been down all weekend, even when it had begun looking tousled and disheveled. When she had mentioned how crazy she must look, he'd said she didn't look crazy, just wildly sexy.

She was convinced Riley had a mental manual in his head

of every sexual position known to mankind and some he probably conjured up himself. He had names for all of them. There had been the Electric Slide, the Ball Game, London Bridge and Sweet Seat, just to name a few. And after kissing her, before leaving this morning, he had assured her with that sexy smile of his that there were plenty more where those had come from.

Needless to say, in one single weekend, the man had given her more orgasms than she'd gotten in her entire life. There had definitely been no climax control. How he stayed up she wasn't sure, but at no time did he go soft on her. He was always forever-ready.

"Alpha," Lindsey said, popping her finger in front of Alpha's face. "Come back down to earth. And why the heavy breathing? Are you all right?"

Alpha set her coffee cup down and smiled at Lindsey. "I'm fine but I admit to feeling tired."

Lindsey scooted back. "You might be coming down with something, so if you don't mind, I'd rather not catch it. With three little ones at home, that would be disastrous."

Alpha nodded, deciding not to tell Lindsey what she had wasn't contagious...unless your bedroom was invaded by the likes of Riley Westmoreland.

Besides, as much as they needed to go over the decorations they'd decided on for the party, she wasn't fully concentrating anyway. "Yes, maybe I need to go back to bed and get some rest after all."

"Sure, but just so you know, I think your decoration ideas are going to wow everyone that night. When do you meet up with Riley Westmoreland again to go over everything?"

Alpha drew in a deep breath. She hadn't a clue. Riley had decided that unless it was a scheduled business meeting, their time together was not about discussing business. Their time was strictly used for pleasure. "I'll probably meet with him in a week or so."

A half hour later Alpha was preparing to take a nap when her phone rang. Her heartbeat kicked up a notch at the thought that the caller might be Riley. She picked up the phone and tried to hide her disappointment when she saw the caller was not Riley, but was, of all people, Eddie. Why was he calling her? It had been more than a year since they had spoken last. She was certain he had gotten on with his life like she had gotten on with hers.

She started not to answer but curiosity had her clicking on the line. "Yes?"

"Alpha, this is Eddie."

"Yes, I know. Your name came up on Caller-ID. This is a surprise."

"Yes. I ran into your father the other day when I took Cleo in."

"Okay."

"I asked your dad about you. I'd heard you moved to Colorado."

"Yes, I'm living in Denver. I love it here."

He chuckled. "But I'm sure you hate the weather. You and I both know you don't like anything cold."

He was right. So why had she tolerated *him* for so long? It had taken spending time with Riley to realize Eddie had been as cold as a dead fish. "Yes, well, sometimes we learn to tolerate things that aren't good for us."

He didn't say anything for a moment and then, "I'll be in Denver on business next week and I'd like to see you while I'm out there."

She lifted a brow. "Why? Nothing has changed, Eddie. I didn't go along with your ultimatum, and there was nothing left to be said."

"I'm beginning to think that's not the case."

*Not the case?* She held the phone away from her ear and stared at it. Was she really talking to Eddie? The man who hadn't hesitated to dump her a week before their wedding because she wouldn't let him control her? "Well, I know that *is* the case. You made your decision."

"Yes, but since you and your twin aren't on speaking terms…"

*Not on speaking terms?* Where in the world did he get such erroneous information? "That's not true. Omega and I are closer than ever. Where did you hear such a ridiculous thing?"

He didn't say anything for a minute. "From your father. And even if it isn't true, I think that it should be."

Anger flared up within her when she heard the sharpness in his voice. "And what if I told you that I don't give a royal damn what you think? Now, goodbye and please don't bother calling me again."

She hung up the phone, furious with herself for answering Eddie's call in the first place. He hadn't changed. He still expected her to adhere to his wishes like a good little girl. The man just didn't get it.

As she crawled on top of the bed for her nap, she couldn't help but recall that the last time she'd been in it, Riley had been with her. Shifting, she pushed a wayward curl from her face as she lay on her side with her head resting on her hands, wondering how long it would take for the soreness to work itself out of her body. When she picked up Riley's scent, which was entrenched on the pillow, she closed her eyes, remembering the weekend. As desire gripped her… of all places…between her sore legs, she knew she couldn't wait to see him again.

After his meeting, Riley made it back to his office with both Canyon and Stern on his heels. He went straight to his desk, sat down and sent both brothers a questioning look. They were standing in the middle of his office with smirks on their faces.

"Okay, what's going on with you two?" he asked.

Stern crossed his arms over his chest and chuckled. "We

should be asking you what's going on. You could barely keep your eyes open during that meeting with Dillon. We expected him to call you out for dozing."

Riley rubbed a frustrated hand down his face. Had he really dozed off in one of Dillon's meetings? Especially one that Dillon had specifically come into the office to hold with them?

"You must have had one hell of a weekend, Ry," Canyon said, eyeing him curiously. "I dropped by Riley's Station a couple of times and it was apparent you weren't home. That means you were gone *all* weekend. Must be some hot number you're seeing."

Straightening in his seat, Riley picked up a file off his desk. Instead of responding to Canyon's comment, he said, "Don't you guys have other things to do? Because if you don't, I do."

"Will you be able to stay awake long enough to do any work?" Stern asked, grinning.

He was about to tell his brother where he could go…in not-so-nice words…when there was a quick knock at the door just before Dillon walked in. He smiled when he saw his three brothers. "Good, all three of you are here. I just got a call from Mack Owens. He's ready to sell that piece of land we've had our eyes on for a strip mall in Memphis. The trip will last until Sunday since Mack and his wife are hosting a dinner party Saturday night. Which one of you wants to go and close the deal with Mack?"

Riley could see both Stern and Canyon easing toward the door. Evidently they had hot dates for the weekend. But then so did he. He had invited Alpha to the movies Saturday night. He was about to tell Dillon he had plans but quickly changed his mind. Dillon was depending on them to keep things running smoothly while he was away from the office. And if Canyon and Stern had other plans that meant things fell on his shoulders. Going to Tennessee wouldn't be so bad if he could talk Alpha into going with him.

"I'll be able to go to Memphis, Dil. When do you need me to leave?"

"Thursday, if possible."

Riley nodded. "Okay, I don't see a problem." He glanced over at Canyon and Stern and took note of their relieved expressions. They owed him big-time.

"Good." Dillon headed for the door but then suddenly turned back around. "You're evidently keeping late hours someplace, Ry. I suggest that you get some rest."

Ignoring the "we told you so" grins on Stern's and Canyon's faces, he said, "I will."

When Dillon left, Riley glared at his brothers. "The only reason I decided to go to Tennessee is because the two of you evidently had important plans for this weekend."

Canyon waved off his words. "We do, and we appreciate you being the sacrificial lamb this time. Mack Owens has a tendency to bore you to tears."

"Whatever. Now will the two of you leave so I can get some work done?"

Moments later, after his brothers had cleared out of his office, Riley leaned back in his chair, finding it hard to believe he'd actually dozed off during one of Dillon's meetings. There was no excuse for that. However, he would be the first to admit he'd experienced one hell of a weekend. It had been simply incredible. He closed his eyes as erotic memories flowed through his mind.

First, he and Alpha had made love in front of the fireplace, then when they'd gotten hungry they went into the kitchen for a snack and ended up making love in there, as well. He had introduced her to the Courting Chair position. Never before had he enjoyed making love to a woman who was not only open to trying different things but was as exciting, energetic and beautiful as any woman could be.

He reached for the phone, but then hung it up before the first ring. He would wait until later tonight to call her when he could be assured there would not be any interruptions.

He opened the file in the middle of his desk, hoping that Alpha would agree to go with him to Tennessee. If she did, he would certainly make the trip worth her while. He would guarantee it.

Later that night, Alpha sat on the sofa going through her book of party favors. Since this would be the fortieth anniversary of Blue Ridge, the Westmorelands wanted each attendee to leave with a favor that would remind them not only of the significance of that night, but also of the party theme. She had marked a few items she thought would be perfect and still within the budget. The vendors she'd spoken with had pretty much guaranteed everything would arrive well in advance of the party date.

A log broke in the fireplace and the pop made her look up. It was then that she remembered making love to Riley, right there in front of the fireplace on the hearth rug. It had been simply amazing, and the memory caused flutters in her stomach. But then, she thought, every time they'd made love had been off the charts.

She stood and stretched, feeling well rested after her nap. She wasn't as sore as she'd been that morning, which she thought was a good thing. Tomorrow she had an eleven o'clock appointment with the granddaughter of a couple who would be celebrating their seventieth wedding anniversary on Valentine's Day. And on Wednesday she would be meeting with a woman who was giving herself a fiftieth birthday party in April.

Omega had called a few hours ago, wanting to know everything about her weekend with Riley. Of course Alpha hadn't told her sister every little detail, but she'd shared enough for Omega to draw her own conclusions about how well her weekend had gone. She hadn't mentioned Eddie's call, since she didn't want to upset her sister. But Alpha intended to talk to her father, who apparently had encouraged Eddie's call.

She was about to head to the kitchen for a cup of hot chocolate when her cell phone rang. She leaned down to pick it up off the table. "Hello."

"You've really done it this time, Alpha. The only reason Eddie called you was because I talked to him that day and told him you would love hearing from him."

Alpha drew in a deep breath upon hearing her father's voice. "You had no right to tell him Omega and I weren't speaking when you know that is not true, Dad. Things are over between Eddie and me. Why can't you accept that?"

"He'd take you back if you got your act together and did what he's asking. You shouldn't let your sister come between you and the man you love."

Alpha gritted her teeth, trying to hold back from telling her father just how wrong and unfair he was, and had always been, to his other child.

"I'll let you go so you can think about it, Al." She then heard a click in her ear. She shook her head. Not for the first time, her father had hung up on her.

Her phone rang. And not for the first time he would call her right back to give her more of an earful, but she had news for him. She clicked on the phone. "Listen, Dad. No matter what you want, Eddie and I are not getting back together. I'm seeing someone else now, and he's more of a man than Eddie will ever be."

There was a moment of silence and then a deep, husky voice said, "I'm glad you think so."

Alpha closed her eyes. *Ah, hell.*

"Alpha?"

She had gotten quiet on him, Riley thought. He didn't know what had prompted her to pick up the phone and say what she had, but evidently she and her father had been having quite an interesting conversation before he'd called. And evidently her father was a huge supporter of her ex-fiancé.

"Yes?"

"Are you okay?" he asked with concern in his voice.

"Yes. Sorry about that. I thought you were my father calling back."

"I see." He waited to see if she would expound on that. Instead, she changed the subject by saying, "I'm surprised you called. I hadn't expected to hear from you until the weekend."

"Yes, that had been my plan but something has come up. I'll be leaving town on Thursday for Memphis and won't be back until Sunday."

"Oh."

Was that disappointment he heard in her voice? "I was calling to let you know and to see if you wanted to go to Memphis with me."

There was a pause and then, "You want me to go out of town with you?"

"Yes. I have a meeting Friday morning and will be attending a social event Saturday night. I'd like you to be there with me. However, if you can't clear your calendar on such short notice, I understand."

"No, I'd love to go."

Riley released a breath he'd just realized he'd been holding. "That's great. We'll fly out around noon on Thursday. Have you ever been to Memphis before?"

"No."

"Then I'm going to enjoy showing you around. I've been there a number of times."

"Sounds like fun. I look forward to going."

There was another reason he had called. One that had concerned him since leaving her. "Are you okay? When I left you this morning you were quite sore." He, of all people, had been aware of the intensity of their lovemaking, but it was as if they hadn't been able to get enough of each other.

"Yes, I'm fine."

"Good." For some reason, he wasn't ready to end the call yet. "So what did you do today?"

He listened as she talked, liking the way she sounded. He had come home, showered and was sitting in his living room on the sofa with his legs stretched out in front of him, alone in the dark, talking to her. He had stopped by his brother Jason's place for dinner, and had enjoyed the time he spent with Jason's wife, Bella, and the twins.

"I'm glad you were able to take a long nap," he said, wishing he could have been there to take the nap with her. He had ended up leaving the office earlier than usual to go to the gym. It had taken a good workout to get his adrenaline flowing again. And talking to her now was a definite boost. There was nothing else he'd rather be doing. *Monday Night Football* couldn't even compete.

They talked for a while longer, and she did sneak in information about the favors she'd come across that she thought would be perfect for the party. They continued talking about some of everything, including which NFL team they thought would make it to the Super Bowl.

All too soon he glanced at the clock on the table and saw it was after midnight. "Sorry," he said, standing to stretch.

"What are you apologizing for?"

"For the third night straight I've kept you up late." He was certain he didn't have to remind her of what they'd been doing those other two nights around this time.

"No apology needed, Riley."

He liked the way she'd said his name just now. He liked it even better when she screamed it in the middle of an orgasm. And she'd done that a lot over the weekend. "Well, I'm not going to keep you. I enjoyed talking to you tonight. And I'm looking forward to our trip to Memphis."

"I enjoyed talking to you as well and can't wait until we leave on Thursday."

By the time he had ended the call, Riley knew the one thing was happening that he hadn't intended to happen.

Alpha Blake was getting under his skin.

# Twelve

"Welcome to the Peabody, Mr. and Mrs. Westmoreland."

Alpha tried to keep a straight face when she heard the hotel clerk's erroneous assumption. She glanced over at Riley, who was standing beside her, and wondered if he would correct the man. He didn't. Instead, he smiled and winked at her.

"Thank you," he said, accepting the passkey.

"I hope your stay here is a great one," the man added.

"I'm sure that it will be."

Taking Alpha's hand in his, Riley led her to the bank of elevators. As they waited, he leaned in close and whispered, "He made an honest mistake."

She nodded, not saying anything because she didn't see how the man could have made that mistake when neither she nor Riley had rings on their fingers. When the elevator arrived, they stepped inside along with several others. Every aspect of the hotel was gorgeous, even right down to the spacious and elegantly designed elevator car. She tried concentrating on the small television screen mounted above the door. Everyone's attention was glued to the commentary. Everyone's except hers and Riley's.

Their attention was on each other and had been since he'd picked her up to take her to the airport. He'd carried her luggage out to his truck, but not before kissing her in a way that had made her panties wet.

Now, the elevator stopped on the fifth floor and she moved aside to let a couple off. She immediately felt the warm rush of blood that flowed through her veins when Riley placed his arms around her waist and pulled her closer to his side.

When the elevator reached their floor, he led her out. Holding her hand, he walked beside her down the beautifully decorated corridor to their room. Although there hadn't been a discussion about it, she and Riley would be sharing a room. She hadn't thought of staying anywhere else.

They came to a stop and Riley let go of her hand to open the door. With an efficiency she wasn't surprised he had, he opened the door and then stood aside for her to enter.

She walked into the room and looked around. It was a beautiful suite, almost as large as her home. She was about to tell Riley just how beautiful the room was when strong arms encircled her waist and turned her around.

The eyes staring down at her were so full of need and desire that it sent a sensuous shudder through her. It didn't take much to recall all they'd done the last time they were together. A replay of those vivid erotic images had done a number on her mind all week.

"I missed you this week," he said huskily.

She couldn't help the smile that touched her lips. It was nice knowing she was missed. She had definitely missed him, as well. "You know where I live," she said teasingly.

He chuckled softly. "Yes, and trust me, not paying you a visit was one of the hardest things I've ever done. But your body needed a time-out. It had quite a workout last weekend."

"Now that's an understatement," she said, her smile widening.

He didn't say anything and she could have sworn she saw a guarded look in his eyes, but then he leaned in closer and asked, "Have I told you how much I like you?"

"No, I don't believe you have."

"Well, let me go on record by saying, I like you, Alpha Blake. Probably more so than I should."

She was about to ask what he meant by that when he quickly said, "Come on, we need to get out of this room. Let's do dinner and then a night of blues on Beale Street."

A few hours later, while walking down Beale Street, Riley couldn't help glancing over at the woman walking beside him, the woman whose hand was firmly held in his. When was the last time he and any woman had walked down a street holding hands?

Never.

So why was he doing so now? Sex with no commitment was just what it sounded like. No strings attached. No reason to lie and promise the moon, the stars or the sky. And no drama, since he'd laid out the rules. Why weren't they up in the hotel room making out since that's all their relationship was supposed to be?

He drew in a deep breath. And when was the last time he'd gone barhopping? Yet here he was, strolling down Beale Street, going from club to club, bar to bar, while holding hands with a woman he'd confessed to liking.

But what really riled him up was that he'd gotten angry when he'd seen a couple of guys checking her out at one of the clubs. He would be the first to admit she looked damn good in her jeans, but still. Why had he gotten jealous? It wasn't as if he had a serious relationship going on with Alpha. She was merely his sex partner for six weeks.

"This place is wonderful," she said, breaking into his

thoughts. Excitement and gaiety shone in her eyes. "I've really never appreciated the blues until now. Thanks."

His hand tightened around hers. "I should be thanking you. If you weren't here I would be up in my hotel room on my laptop getting a start on next week's work. You've turned what probably would have been a boring trip into a fun one."

She threw her head back and laughed before arching a perfect brow. "Truly you don't want me to believe that Riley Westmoreland would not have had fun without me?"

Yes, he wanted her to believe it because it was true. Yes, he would have had some degree of fun, but not like this. They had enjoyed some fabulous foods, had taken over the dance floor a few times and he'd even talked her into karaoke, a Billie Holiday number.

He stopped walking, reached out and lifted her chin with his fingertip. "I never say anything I don't mean, Alpha, and this is the most fun I've ever had with any woman."

She slid her hand up over his chest. "I'm glad."

He was tempted to kiss her but held back. There would be plenty of time for kisses when he got her back to their hotel room. Tightening her hand in his once more, he began walking again.

He glanced over at her. "So what are your plans tomorrow while I'm in my meetings?"

She leaned up on tiptoe, nuzzled her nose in the side of his face and whispered, "Depends on how well you wear me out tonight. If I'm up to it, I plan to go shopping. Christmas is next month, you know."

Yes, he knew, and they would have ended their affair by then. "You got a lot of people to buy for?" he asked.

"Umm, just the usual."

She was being evasive again. "You plan on going home for Christmas or staying in Denver?"

"Haven't decided yet."

"Does your family get together for the holidays?" he asked

her, holding tight to her hand and looking both ways before they crossed the street.

"No, not everyone." Then, as if she wanted to get a question of her own in, she quickly asked, "What about with your family? Will everyone be home for Christmas?"

"This Christmas, yes, mainly because of the holiday party, with it being the fortieth anniversary and all. I believe our parents, aunt and uncle would have wanted us all together, celebrating something that major. Bane won't be able to make it since he's on assignment someplace, but Gemma and her family are coming from Australia."

"Sounds like the Westmorelands will be having a fun time. And as the event planner for the holiday party, I intend to make it a night to remember." She smiled over at him.

He returned her smile. "I believe it." And he did. On the plane, she had gone over her decorating ideas with him and he could tell she was a person who was on top of every single detail.

"So what about it?"

He blinked, aware that Alpha had asked him something. "Sorry, what did you say?"

She smiled and the warmth of that smile filled him with something he couldn't name. She leaned closer to him. "I suggested that we call it a night and head back to our hotel. Are you okay with that?"

Instead of answering her, he stepped off the sidewalk and pulled her into the shadows where two buildings connected. They could still partially be seen but he didn't care. He pulled her body to his, lowered his mouth and kissed her—long, hard and deep, tangling his tongue with hers.

Moments later, he released her mouth and pressed his forehead to hers. "Did you get the answer you wanted just now?" he asked slowly, trying to catch his breath.

He felt the curve of her smile against his lips. "Most definitely."

* * *

There was no doubt in Alpha's mind, as she watched a
naked Riley stride out of the bathroom, that he was what any
woman would consider a hottie of mega proportions. And
speaking of proportions… Her gaze lowered to his middle.
He was aroused and had already sheathed his thick erection
in a condom. Her gaze stayed glued to that part of him as he
approached the bed.

He caressed the side of her face with his finger.

"Why are you staring at me like that? You don't think what
I'm packing is real?"

She looked up at him. "Oh, I know it's real. I'm just wondering how it tastes."

She saw the flash of intense desire fill his eyes, making
them dark orbs of heated lust and her heart started racing
wildly. She'd never been so bold with a man before. It was
almost unbelievable how comfortable she felt with Riley, to
the point where she would say just about anything.

He held her gaze and then said in a low tone, "Then I guess
I'll let you find out."

He moved his hand from her face, and she watched as he
slowly, methodically, removed the condom and dropped it in
the wastepaper basket near the bed. He then looked at her.
"Now what do you want me to do?" he asked.

She scooted over in the huge bed and patted a spot. "I want
you here. On your back."

The bed dipped beneath his weight as he joined her, lying
flat on his back as she'd instructed. She then eased between
his thighs, lifting them up so his knees braced both sides of
her head. On her knees, she smiled down at him. "I'm sure
there's a name for this position already, right?"

He swallowed deeply before nodding. "Heels Over Head."

Alpha nodded. "Sounds appropriate." She then eased her
head down to his aroused shaft. He was huge. Gigantic. And
the veins running along the engorged head were so eas-

ily visible that she swore she could see the blood rushing through them.

She touched him and appreciated the solid weight she held in her hand. He was so large it took both hands to hold him— definitely a handful—and she figured that he would be a mouthful, as well. She was about to find out.

Alpha opened her mouth over the head of his penis and her tongue swiped across it before fully taking him in. And once her lips locked down on him, she went to work, licking every inch of him, loving his taste. His masculine moans of sexual gratification made her feel totally feminine.

He gripped several locks of her hair but she felt no pain, only pleasure. He had a unique way of educating her and satisfying her needs at the same time. Describing what he would be doing to her in vivid detail was just as arousing as him actually doing it.

That was one of the reasons she wanted to make this special for him. He probably could tell she was a novice, but hopefully he would see that at least her heart was in it. And the thought that his heavy shaft was fully lodged in her mouth was a total turn-on for her. From the sounds he was making, he apparently liked everything she was doing. Encouraged by his response, she closed her eyes and turned up the heat, intent on satisfying her man.

Her man?

Where had that thought come from? But instead of dismissing it totally, she accepted that for all of six weeks, he would be her man. And then on the night of the holiday party, her fantasy fling would come to an end.

"Alpha…"

Her name, growled from deep within his throat, filled her with intense desire. She knew every long lick of her tongue, and the deep suction she was applying, was sending him over the edge just the way she wanted.

She opened her eyes when she felt a hard tug on her hair,

as he tried to get her mouth off him, but she held tight. He finally gave up and let go. She tasted the essence of him as he filled her mouth.

Moments later she released him and before she could say how tasty he was, he rolled over, pulled her down to her stomach and straddled her back. With his legs tucked between hers, he lifted her hips. In one smooth thrust, he entered her, going as deep as he could. He then leaned down close and whispered against the back of her neck, "This is called Inside Out."

She soon found out why when he began thrusting in and out of her hard, extending as far as her womb and then back again. She felt him in every stroke, and it was only then that she realized he wasn't wearing a condom.

"Riley, the condom!"

He went still. But she didn't. At least not on the inside where her muscles continued to clench him, milking him hard. His deep growl sent sensations through her pelvis, electrifying her spine. She expected him to pull out immediately but instead he leaned down so close that she felt his heated breath against her ear. "Please tell me you're on the pill or something, baby."

His plea was tortured and she was more than happy to erase his concerns. "Yes, I'm on the pill."

As if that was what he needed to hear, he began moving again, with even more urgency than before, stroking her deeply, growling like a primitive animal performing his last mating ritual. She felt him in every muscle of her body and shivers of pleasure rammed up and down her spine with every hard thrust. Then she felt him explode deep in her womb. His hand cupped tight to her bare bottom, tilted it at an angle that hit a spot that sent her screaming. She buried her head in the pillow to smother the sound, but it did nothing to the sensations ripping her apart. On top of everything, she felt his mouth on her back, nibbling her skin, licking it, nibbling some more. Branding her.

"Riley!"

Her body began quaking, all the way to her toes. Sensations overtook her. Pure feminine satisfaction tore through her, and she shivered with an intensity that shook the entire bed as pent-up passion was released from deep within her. When she collapsed, totally drained, he flipped her on her back and lifted her hips. Using the missionary position, he reentered her. She looked up at him, amazed, although, if the truth be known, she shouldn't be astonished. She had found out last weekend that Riley Westmoreland had the stamina of a bull.

And although she didn't think it was possible, a moment later he brought them both to yet another orgasm, and she knew this was only the beginning.

There would definitely be no climax control tonight.

# Thirteen

"I'm glad you're going to be my wedding planner, Alpha."

"And I'm glad you chose me for the job."

Alpha sipped her tea as she studied Megan Westmoreland—Megan Claiborne in six months. She thought Megan, who was a doctor of anesthesiology at one of the local hospitals, was a beautiful woman. And Alpha could see the Westmoreland similarities in the dark eyes, perfectly arched brows and cheekbones.

Other than Dillon and his wife, Pam, Alpha hadn't met any other family members. Due to the nature of her and Riley's relationship, there was no need for him to introduce her to his family and she was certain that none of them were aware they were having an affair.

Alpha's thoughts shifted back to the bride-to-be. Megan's engagement party had been held earlier in the month. With that out of the way, Megan was ready to plan her June wedding. Alpha had gotten the call on Monday, the day she had returned to Denver from spending four wonderful days in

Memphis with Riley. Goose bumps formed on her arms whenever she thought about just how fantastic those days had been.

"So you like the wedding colors I've selected?" Megan asked.

Alpha's attention was pulled back to the business at hand. "Yes, I think buttercup and lime are wonderful colors together. They give me a lot to work with."

Megan seemed pleased with that. "I'm glad."

They were in the middle of discussing the food items Megan wanted as part of her menu when Megan's front door opened and a man, who Alpha knew immediately had to be one of Riley's brothers or cousins, stalked in with a furious expression on his face.

A calm Megan glanced over at him and asked, "What has you so riled this morning, Zane?"

So this was Zane Westmoreland? Alpha thought, sipping her tea, trying not to let it be so obvious that she was checking him out. Since arriving in town, she'd heard a lot of feminine whispers about him. Women thought he was hot and she could see why. But then, Riley was hot, as well. Even hotter, in her book. But she would be the first to admit she was biased where Riley was concerned.

"This is Alpha Blake. She's helping me plan my wedding," Megan added, introducing them.

The man gave a quick tip of his Stetson in Alpha's direction before returning his full attention to Megan. "What's this I hear about Channing Hastings being on your invitation list?"

Megan smiled sweetly. "Yes, what of it?"

"I don't want her at your wedding."

Megan put her teacup down and gave her brother her full attention. "Why? No matter how your relationship with Channing ended, if you recall, she and I worked together at the hospital long before the two of you met. I've always liked her and still consider her a friend and—"

"I don't want her there, Megan."

Megan frowned. "It's my wedding, Zane, and she's invited, so if you have to get yourself together before seeing her again then I suggest—"

"That's not it," he snapped.

"Sounds like it is," Megan countered.

Instead of saying anything else, Zane Westmoreland turned and stormed out the door with the same turbulent gust of wind that had brought him in. When the door slammed shut behind him, Megan glanced over at Alpha with an apologetic smile on her face. "As you can see, not all the Westmorelands are civilized."

Alpha took another sip of her tea before asking, "Are you sure you don't want me to remove Ms. Hastings's name from the invitation list?"

Megan smiled. "I'm positive. It's time my brother comes to terms with his true feelings about some things."

An hour later, Alpha had wrapped up her meeting with Megan and stood, ready to go, when there was a knock at Megan's door. Alpha wondered if Zane had calmed down and was returning.

"Come in," Megan called out.

The door opened and Alpha's heart almost fell from her chest when Riley walked in.

Megan glanced over at her cousin. "Riley, if you're here on Zane's behalf to talk me out of inviting Channing to the—"

"No," he interrupted. "Channing is Zane's issue. He has to deal with it. You have the right to invite who you want."

His gaze shifted from Megan to Alpha. "But he did mention you had company, your wedding planner, so I thought I'd drop by to say hello."

Megan looked curiously from Alpha to Riley. "You two have met already?"

Riley nodded. "Yes, I'm working with Alpha on the holiday party at Blue Ridge next month."

Megan tapped her forehead. "That's right. How could I

forget you're coordinating that? Last time I heard you were doing it grudgingly, Riley. Evidently that has changed."

Megan would be surprised to learn just how much things had changed, Riley thought. "Yes, that has changed."

Megan smiled. "I'm glad to hear it."

When Riley didn't say anything but continued to look at Alpha, in a way that probably seemed like he could eat her alive, Megan cleared her throat. "Is that the only reason you dropped by?" she asked.

He shifted his gaze from Alpha back to Megan. "Not really. I wanted to ask Alpha something."

He glanced over at Alpha again. "My family is doing their monthly out-on-the-town dinner Wednesday night at McKay's. I wanted to know if you'd like to come? That way you can meet the rest of the family. I think they'd like to get acquainted with the person putting the party together."

Out of the corner of his eye, he saw Megan raise a brow, because in truth, there was no need for the family to get to know the person putting the party together. He knew it and she knew it, as well.

Luckily Alpha didn't know it. She smiled and said, "Yes, I'm available Wednesday night to meet the rest of your family."

"Good. I'll pick you up at six."

He glanced over at Megan, who was still staring at him. She was probably wondering why he offered to pick up Alpha when anyone living in Denver clearly knew the directions to McKay's.

"That will be fine and I'll be ready," Alpha said.

He began backing out of the house before Megan felt the need to ask him anything. "Great, I'll see you again later, then." And he meant that literally because he planned to drop by her place tonight.

"All right."

He turned and headed to the door in quick, powerful

strides. She'd looked good in her dark brown slacks and peach-colored pullover sweater. The coloring was perfect for her complexion. And her hair was loose and fanned around her shoulders, just the way he liked.

He told himself to keep walking to the door, to open it and not look back. But for some reason, he couldn't do that. When he opened the door and glanced back over his shoulder, he looked directly at Alpha. She was holding his gaze and he felt that sensual chemistry that had his body tingling with the same powerful awareness he felt whenever he was around her. He smiled at Alpha and she smiled back.

There was no way his perceptive cousin hadn't picked up on the exchange, which was probably the reason she kept looking back and forth between him and Alpha. She would have questions, he didn't doubt that, but he would deal with his cousin's nosiness later.

"Ry?"

He switched his gaze from Alpha to Megan, aware that Megan had said something. "Yes?"

"Either come in or go out. Holding the door open is letting out the heat," she said with an amused expression on her face.

"Oh. Okay, I'm leaving." He firmly closed the door behind him.

Riley smiled as he headed for his truck, but once he got inside, buckled his seat belt and saw his reflection in his rearview mirror, he frowned. What the hell was wrong with him? As soon as an angry Zane mentioned Alpha was at Megan's, he hadn't wasted time getting over there, leaving Zane staring at him like he'd lost his mind.

And, in a way, he was afraid that he had.

The first of the craziness had been making love to Alpha without a condom. Since the first time he'd made out with Emily Parker at the age of fourteen, he'd always used a condom. His father had had "the talk" with all his sons when they turned thirteen, and Dillon had reinforced those talks over the years. Since no form of birth control was 100 percent, it hadn't mattered one iota if the woman claimed to be on the pill or any other kind of birth control. His rule was to use a condom.

Why had he broken that rule for Alpha?

Granted, being inside her—skin-to-skin, flesh-to-flesh, feeling the way her inner muscles had clamped on him—had felt out of this world. Totally awesome. Even so, there was no reason for him to take chances, and he'd continued to take chances. He hadn't used a condom with her since they'd arrived back in Denver yesterday morning.

He leaned back in his seat. It didn't take much to remember the four days he and Alpha had spent together in Memphis. Words couldn't describe how much he had enjoyed the trip, and it had nothing to do with him signing off on that business deal. It had everything to do with Alpha being in Memphis with him.

He had finalized the contract early and had returned to the hotel room to find she'd gone shopping. He had paced the floor like an obsessed man, and the moment she had returned, he had swept her into his arms, making all her shopping bags go flying.

He'd never known he could undress a woman so quickly. Within moments they were both naked and back in the bed again. Saturday, they had done a tour of the city, including Graceland and the hotel where Martin Luther King Jr. had lost his life.

Then on Saturday night they had gone to Mack's dinner party. She had looked fantastic, and he'd known she would wow everyone just like she'd wowed him. He'd actually regretted packing up and leaving Memphis yesterday.

Drawing in a deep breath, he straightened and started the ignition. Now he'd done the unthinkable and invited her to share dinner with his family. He could just imagine what all of them would think when he arrived at McKay's with Alpha on Wednesday night.

He was beginning to act real crazy with her. That wasn't a good thing.

The best thing to do would be to put distance between them until the family dinner.

The last person Alpha expected to see when she opened her door later that evening was Riley. "Riley," she said, moving aside to let him come in. "I was just about to grab something to eat. Do you want to join me?"

"I'd love to."

She closed the door behind him. "You're not going to ask what's for dinner?"

"Doesn't matter. I came to see you. Dinner is an extra."

He'd come to see her, and she didn't have to guess why. The man had a ferocious sexual appetite that was contagious. But she had no complaints. He'd unleashed something within her. She would admit that she wanted him as much as he wanted her.

"And, if you're in the mood, after dinner I thought we'd grab a movie."

She glanced over at him. "A movie?"

"Yes."

"I'd love to but…"

He raised a brow. "But what?"

"I've already made plans for the evening."

"Oh," he said, and she could tell by his expression that he was surprised. "I apologize. I should have called first."

"No reason for you to do that. I figured it was time for me to organize my junk room and planned to spend the evening doing just that."

"Your junk room?"

She smiled. "Yes. Whenever I'm out and about and see anything that captures my interest, anything I feel just might work for a future party theme, I bring it home and stick it in my junk room. Needless to say, the room is pretty disorganized now."

He chuckled. "Need my help?"

She was surprised by his offer. "You want to help?"

"Yes."

She thought of all the other things he could be doing tonight. "Are you sure you want to do that?"

"Positive. Besides, it's the least I can do to thank you for inviting me to dine with you."

Alpha waved off his words with her hand. "No need to thank me. And if you're sure about helping, then thanks. I can certainly use it. It's been a while since I got things organized in that room, and I was determined that tonight would be when I started on it."

"Then count me in."

"Every time I eat a meal you prepare, I'm impressed," Riley said, leaning back in the chair as he used a napkin to wipe the corners of his mouth.

"You've only eaten two meals prepared by me," Alpha said, grinning.

"Then I've been impressed twice."

She threw her head back and laughed. He loved the sound. It was rich, feminine and genuine. It didn't matter at that moment that earlier that day he'd sworn to put distance between them. All it took was him being home alone with a deep craving to see her again. It was a craving that had him taking a shower, changing clothes and driving over to see her like a demented fool.

They sat and talked about her plans for Megan's wedding and then he helped her clear the table before assisting her in loading the dishes in the dishwasher. For no reason, other than he wanted to kiss her, he took her hand and pulled her to him. The feel of her hardened nipples pressing against his chest made him draw in a deep breath and fill his nostrils with her scent.

"I need to kiss you," he whispered against her lips before leaning in closer and claiming them. He maneuvered his arms around her waist to bring her closer to him. He enjoyed being inside her mouth, licking her from corner to corner, tasting her deeply as their tongues tangled passionately. And he definitely loved the sounds she made, those sensual moans of pleasure that made his mouth even hungrier for hers. He could lock lips with her for hours, days, weeks...well past six weeks.

He broke off the kiss but continued to hold her in his arms while inwardly chastising himself for even thinking such a thing. He would admit it was a novelty to want a woman this much, but he would eventually get over it. However, he would be the first to admit she wasn't making it easy. When she peered up at him, it was the most natural thing to brush his lips across hers.

A number of other women had been eager to say or do whatever was needed in the hope that he would extend his six-week rule. It hadn't happened. Yet he knew he would make Alpha the exception, if she was interested. But he had a feeling she wasn't. Why did it bother him that she wasn't interested in going beyond the six weeks like the others?

"Hey, don't think a few kisses will get you out of helping me," she said, placing her hands on his shoulders.

Tempted, and giving in to it, he leaned down again to trace a kiss along the nape of her neck. "Let me assure you, I'm not trying to get out of anything. Although I'll admit a few naughty thoughts have crossed my mind."

"There's always later," she whispered.

He wondered if she knew how much that promise made his erection throb. He went back to her lips, loving the feel of how they quivered beneath his. "Actually, I was hoping..."

She threw her head back. "Now, why doesn't that surprise me?" She took a step back. "Come on and let's tackle that room before we're tempted to get into something else."

He followed her from the kitchen to where her bedrooms were located. She passed her sleeping quarters and opened the door of another room.

He walked in behind her and glanced around. He'd seen junkier rooms, but her collection of items intrigued him. He walked across the room and picked up the For Sale sign and looked back at her. "Moving?"

She shook her head and smiled. "No, I kept that because you never know when I might have a moving party for someone."

He nodded and picked up another item. "Boxing gloves?"

She shrugged. "You never know when they might come in handy, as well, for one of my future events."

He picked up several other items, and she provided her reasons for grabbing them either from a store or a yard sale. "Okay, Ms. Blake. Tell me what we need to do to get this show on the road."

She rubbed her hands together as he rolled up his sleeves. "Okay. I've already named those huge plastic tubs over there by traditional party themes—birthday, wedding, anniversary, retirement and new baby. All we have to do is put them in the designated tub."

That sounded easy enough. "And if I'm not sure which one will fit?"

"Then remember the name of my business, Imagine, and let your imagination go to work. If you're still in doubt, then just drop it in the miscellaneous tub for me to sort through later."

"Okay."

He quickly went to work, knowing what was on the agenda for later. She had turned on a radio and, except for the music floating around the room, the only other sounds were those they made moving around while putting items in order. Using his imagination like she'd said, he put every item he picked up into what he felt was the appropriate tub. He tossed a few items in the miscellaneous tub when, for the life of him, he could not figure out what she'd had in mind when she'd bought it.

He thought they worked well together and within an hour he could definitely see them making progress. He glanced over at her. She had removed her pullover sweater to uncover a T-shirt that said Look at Me and Imagine. He smiled, thinking he could definitely do that.

At that moment, he could imagine her without a stitch of clothing, spread on top of the table where they'd eaten earlier. He could see her long legs dangling off the sides as he stepped between them after removing all his own clothes. He could further imagine taking his favorite jam—strawberry—and smearing it all over her body, then taking his time licking it off. He could imagine the tip of his tongue covering every inch of her and—

"Taking an unscheduled break, Riley?"

Her voice sliced into his daydream. He blinked, realizing he had been standing there staring at her, for no telling how long. Swearing under his breath, he shook his head. "No, I was just checking out your T-shirt."

"My T-shirt?" she asked, looking down at herself with a quizzical expression on her face. "Oh," she said, in a tone that let him know she'd forgotten about what was written on her shirt.

He couldn't hold back the smile that crept into his features. "Nice."

She shrugged. "It was a gift from my sister and meant to be funny."

He hadn't seen anything amusing about it. It had the opposite effect. Those had been some serious musings stirring his imagination. Pretty damn hot musings, in fact. "Really?"

"Yes, sometimes she has a warped sense of humor."

He would take her word for it since he'd noticed how she would change the subject when any discussion of her family came up. "Well, I think it's nice, and it's time to get back to work. We're almost finished."

She nodded and went back to folding up tablecloths of just about every color you could name. He latched his attention onto one of the last items he needed to put away, one of those bouncy exercise balls. It was bright yellow, reminding him of the sun. He wondered what she had in mind for it. He started to ask, but decided he would just use his imagination. The only problem was that the thoughts going through his mind were probably way off from what she'd intended.

He looked back over at her and saw she was pretty absorbed in what she was doing. He glanced back down at the ball, then back at her again. *Imagine.* He could see her naked, with her back on the ball. She'd be spread across it, facing him. Thighs open, her femininity wet and ready as he straddled her. And when she arched her body upward, he would lower his downward to connect. It would be a joining he would savor as he fought not to push too hard nor too fast inside of her. Sensations would take over and pleasure would seep into their pores, sink hard into their bones and—

"If the reason you're standing there staring at the ball is because you're trying to figure out where it goes, don't bother. It's not supposed to be in here. I use it to exercise."

He glanced over at her. "I was just imagining you working out on it." He shifted his gaze back to the ball and then returned it to her with a lazy smile. "So, what do you say, Alpha? Do you want to play ball?"

# Fourteen

Two days later, Alpha tried to downplay both her nerves and her excitement as Riley escorted her into McKay's to meet his family. Although she kept reminding herself that her purpose for being here was mainly to bring everyone up to date on the holiday party, she could barely contain her enthusiasm.

Riley had ended up spending Monday night with her and had dropped by for dinner last night, as well. She'd had that couple's seventieth anniversary party for Valentine's Day to work on, and while she sat at the kitchen table taking care of the details for that event, he had stretched out on her living room floor in front of the fireplace, watching a cop show on television.

He had pretty much left her alone to hammer out the details for the February party, but, from where she sat at the kitchen table, she could see him. She had been fully aware of each time he'd moved, whether it was to stand to stretch his legs or to shift his body into another position on the floor.

When she had finally finished her work, she had joined

him in front of the fireplace with glasses of wine. Later they'd stripped each other naked and made love before he left at midnight.

She was well aware that time was ticking. They had less than three weeks before their affair would end. Since the finale was the night of the party, she was reminded of it each time she worked on the holiday celebration.

"Well, hello, Riley. Welcome to McKay's," a feminine voice said. Alpha glanced up at their hostess and saw it was the same woman from before.

"Paula," Riley greeted. "I believe my family is here already."

"Yes, they are," the woman said, in a cheerful mood, deliberately not looking at Alpha. "Must be an important business meeting going on with your family."

"No, just our usual get-together," Riley said, handing Paula his leather jacket and then proceeding to help Alpha out of her coat to hand over to Paula, as well.

Alpha wondered why the woman blinked and stared at her so hard, roaming her gaze up and down Alpha's outfit. The ankle-length, formfitting dress Alpha was wearing had been one she'd purchased while shopping in Memphis. She could tell from the way Riley had looked her up and down when he'd picked her up, and the low whistle that had eased from his lips, that he liked the way she looked. So what was this woman's problem? Why was this Paula checking Alpha out with venom in her eyes? It wasn't hard to figure out there was history between Paula and Riley. Alpha had picked up on that the last time.

But then a part of her understood any woman giving Riley a second glance on any night. But especially tonight. The man looked so jaw-droppingly, potently sexy, so robustly masculine, in his Armani jeans, herringbone blazer and white shirt.

She was tempted to tell Paula to pull back her fangs. In a few more weeks, Riley would be on the eligibility list once again. That meant this woman might be the next woman in his bed.

As Alpha studied the woman's reaction further, she saw Paula turn her stunned expression to Riley, who merely smiled. Alpha couldn't help wondering if there was a private joke somewhere, and if there was, why it seemed to involve her.

She glanced over at Riley, who broke eye contact with the woman to glance over at her. A different smile touched his lips when he slid his hand in hers and asked, "Ready?"

She drew in a deep breath and tried dismissing from her mind the interaction she'd seen pass between Riley and Paula. She returned his smile. "Yes, I'm ready."

He then looked back at Paula. "Please show us to our table."

Alpha saw the stiffening of the woman's spine as she moved forward to do as Riley had asked. Paula might be ticked off, but that didn't stop her from deliberately swaying her hips in her short black waitress outfit as she led them toward the back of the restaurant. Alpha was sure Paula's saucy walk was for Riley's benefit.

When they reached the room, Paula opened the door and stepped aside. The look she slanted Alpha would have cut her to the core had she thought the situation was that serious. To her, it wasn't. Alpha thought it was simply pathetic for any woman to get pissed off at another woman over a man neither of them had any right to claim.

They stepped into the room and all the conversation between the people at the long table suddenly ceased as all eyes shifted toward her and Riley. The men stood and the women eyed her and Riley curiously. She knew Megan was expecting her, but she hoped her presence wasn't a surprise to everyone else. Surely Riley had told his family he had invited her. Therefore, Alpha could only assume the reason they were

staring with such intensity was because Riley was still holding her hand and didn't seem inclined to release it.

Seizing the moment when they had everyone's attention,
Riley said, "Hello, everyone. I'd like for you to meet Alpha
Blake."

Alpha waited for him to continue the introduction, expecting him to say something like "Alpha is the event planner handling our company's holiday party." But he provided
no further clarification as he tightened his hand on hers and
moved around the table, making individual introductions.
Because he had talked about his family so much, she felt like
she knew them already.

Everybody shifted places and she found herself sitting with
Riley on one side of her and his brother, Canyon, on the other.
To say the Westmoreland men favored was an understatement.
Because she knew Dillon and Pam already, she felt comfort-
able being included in the conversations. Other than being
asked where she was from—which led to a discussion about
Florida beaches—no one inquired about anything concern-
ing her family and she was grateful for that.

Riley helped tremendously by being so attentive. At some
points, she wondered if he was overdoing it, since more than
one of his brothers and cousins took note of it. When he
asked her to try what he'd ordered for dinner, he had fed it
to her with his fork and then used that same fork to finish
eating his meal.

"Are you excited about planning the party, Alpha?" Riley's
cousin Bailey asked from across the table.

Alpha smiled and nodded. "Yes, definitely, and I think all
of you will be pleased." Bailey had been making conversation
with Alpha off and on during the meal and it was hard to believe the young woman was the same one Riley had claimed
was once a holy terror in the Westmoreland family.

It was later that evening, when Riley was taking her back
home after dinner, that she decided to bring up that very thing

with him. Although he didn't take his eyes off the road, she saw the way his lips curved in a smile.

"Don't let the sweet act fool you. I would be the first to admit that Bailey has matured in a lot of ways, but if rubbed the wrong way, the old Bailey will resurface in a minute. I'm surprised she took to you so easily. Usually she's very stand-offish with those who aren't family."

"Then I guess I should feel special."

The car came to a stop at a traffic light and he turned his dark, piercing gaze toward her. The moment their eyes connected, she almost forgot to breathe. The kind of heat she was beginning to get accustomed to around him curled around in her stomach, making her nipples stiffen and her pulse rate increase.

"You are special, Alpha."

She had to draw in a deep breath, wondering why on earth he had to go and say something like that. Why had he spoken in that husky voice that could make her panties wet on impact? And why did she want to believe he actually thought she was someone special?

"Thank you," was the only response she could make. Her heart was beating a mile a minute. Riley had the ability to make her want things she shouldn't. Believe in things that she couldn't. Hadn't she learned her lesson with LeBron and Eddie? But still, she wished she could ask Riley to explain what he meant. Why he thought she was special. Heaven help her, she really didn't want to put too much stock into what he'd just said.

Riley turned his attention back to the road and she let out a deep sigh. No matter how many times he looked at her or touched her, her body responded in a way it had never responded to a man before. Her affair with him was supposed to be just a fling that meant nothing. Sex with no commitment.

She swallowed with difficulty. But she was beginning to

feel emotions that she shouldn't be feeling, especially when she knew the score.

That wasn't good.

Riley settled between Alpha's thighs and gazed down at her as he lifted her hips to ease unerringly into the essence of her. They stared at each other, looking deeply into each other's eyes, as he guided his throbbing erection right through her heat.

He released a low growl the moment her muscles began clenching him, pulling him deeper inside of her, sending frissons of pleasure rippling all through him. What was there about how she made him feel, the emotions making love to her evoked?

Riley closed his eyes as he began moving, slowly thrusting in and out of her. He didn't want to rush. He wanted to savor the moment. His body felt alive, free. Tension began flowing out of him, unwinding and easing away to allow sexual gratification to come in to such a degree that he flexed his toes in time with his strokes. This was what real lovemaking was about, the kind that made you realize what you'd been missing, and what you could only have when you loved a woman.

*What the...* He snatched his eyes open to look down at her and was grateful to find her eyes closed as a deep moan escaped from between her lips. Something made her open her eyes and her sultry gaze connected to his. He knew there was no way he could deny what he was feeling at that moment. Emotions he didn't want to feel. And he was certain they were the same kind of emotions that had torn Bane's heart in two.

But he was feeling them nonetheless.

There was no way he could deny that he had fallen in love with Alpha.

He had felt himself falling hard in Memphis, probably even before that. And each time he'd tried fighting it and denying it, he was drawn to her even more. He knew his family had questions since he'd never invited any woman to their little family gatherings before. By arriving with her tonight, he had made a statement. He was taking a chance with his heart.

A part of him wanted to believe Alpha was different. She would never hurt him the way Crystal had hurt Bane. But what about those family secrets she was obviously trying to keep? He brushed the thought aside. Whatever they were didn't matter. He loved her anyway.

His body kept moving inside of her, boldly claiming what he deemed, at that moment, would always belong to him. Starting tonight, he would be a Westmoreland in pursuit. He knew there were things she wasn't ready to share with him and that was fine; he would use his time to break down her defenses and prove to her that no matter what had happened in the past, he was a man worthy of her love.

Overcome with emotions he couldn't contain, he tightened his hold on her and leaned down to capture her mouth with his. It was either that or confess words she was not ready to hear.

She locked her legs tighter around him and he heard her deep groan at the same time as sensations burst within him, releasing spasms of pleasure that ripped all through him. Shot to every angle of his body.

He broke off the kiss to throw his head back. "Alpha!"

And then he exploded, spurting his release all through her as he encountered an out-of-body experience that connected him to her in a way that tested the bedsprings. He felt vibrant, alert, alive, and now he also knew how it felt to be a man in love.

As his tremors subsided, he eased off Alpha, lifted her in his arms and snuggled her head to his chest. Their bodies were wet with sweat and their limbs entwined as he gathered her closer. They were connected heart to heart, soul to soul. He knew that no matter how long it took to convince her, Alpha's place in his life was permanent.

# Fifteen

"Are you excited about the party this weekend?"

Alpha glanced up from her inventory list and smiled over at Lindsey. Her question was bittersweet. Yes, Alpha usually loved the day an event she'd worked on finally arrived, but since this event also meant the end of her affair with Riley, she was torn.

She decided to give Lindsey the answer her assistant probably expected to hear. "Yes, I'm excited."

She immediately glanced back down at her list so Lindsey wouldn't see the tears threatening to fall whenever she thought about what this weekend entailed. It was hard to believe it had been three weeks since her trip with Riley to Memphis. So much had happened since then. First, it had been his invitation to McKay's to meet his family. She was certain that is what had prompted Pam to call her two days later to invite her to the Westmorelands' Thanksgiving dinner.

Every one of the Denver Westmorelands had been there except for Bane and his cousin Gemma who lived in Australia. The twins, Aiden and Adrian, had schooled her on the family's after-Thanksgiving-dinner game of snow volleyball. Lucky for everyone, except for her, it had snowed that morning and a sufficient amount was still on the ground after dinner. After the players divided into the Reds and the Blues, she found her and Riley on opposite teams.

It had been the most fun she'd had in a long time, and she'd seen just how down-to-earth the Westmorelands were. For a little while, they had made her feel like she was a part of them. That was one of the reasons breaking up with Riley was going to be so hard.

Then there was also the fact that she had fallen in love with him.

As she continued to check items off her list, she couldn't help but feel the pain in her heart. Omega had warned her that such a thing could happen as soon as the flowers began arriving. The day after she'd had dinner with his family at McKay's, he had, for no reason at all, begun sending her flowers. The flowers would arrive practically every two to three days and when she asked why, he would merely smile and say it was because he was thinking about her.

Then there were those other habits they had started that would be hard to break—like sharing dinner practically every day, either at her place or his; his spending the nights with her more often than not; and their Friday date-nights. They would take in a movie or go to a play or roller-skating. More than once, he had mentioned something about her going skiing with him and she would change the subject, not having the heart to remind him that they wouldn't be together for the trip to Aspen that he had planned for January.

An hour or so later, after Lindsey had left, Alpha was busy making last-minute adjustments to the menu for this weekend's party when her phone rang. She smiled when she saw it was Riley.

"Hi. Thanks for the flowers. You are spoiling me."

"You deserve to be spoiled. I just want to make sure we're still on for tonight."

"Most certainly. I always enjoy any meals you cook." They would be dining at his place and, as usual, she would be spending the night.

"I have a special dish for you."

She chuckled. "What is it?"

"A surprise."

She liked his surprises. "All right."

"Good. I left work at noon today to come home to get things together, so I'll come and get you—"

"There's no need for you to do that, Riley. I can drive over to your place...unless you have a problem with my car being seen by anyone."

"Why would I have a problem with it?"

"I'm staying the night, remember. I wouldn't want your family to—"

"What I do is my business. Trust me, they know we're involved and have probably seen your car here overnight before. Do you have a problem with them knowing?"

"No, I don't have a problem with it, not at all," she said.

"Good. In that case, I'll see you when you get here."

She hung up the phone, thinking that even if she had a problem with it, it was too late. Time wasn't on her side and she wanted to spend as much of it with Riley as possible.

Riley had just finished everything and had put the stew on to simmer when he heard the sound of his doorbell. He glanced at his watch. He wasn't expecting Alpha for another hour or so and hoped it wasn't one of his relatives dropping in without calling first. Some of them could smell his stew from miles away and thought it was their God-given right to invite themselves over for a free meal.

As he walked out of the kitchen toward his front door, he couldn't help but smile. He was looking forward to Alpha coming over because, at some time before she left in the morning, he wanted to tell her just how he felt. The holiday party was in three days, and he needed to hear from her that although she might not have fallen in love with him yet, the idea was possible.

Without checking to see who his caller was, he snatched open his door. A deep frown settled on his face when he saw Paula standing on his porch. "Paula, what are you doing here?"

She smiled brightly. "I came to see you, of course. I have some information that I think you need to know."

Riley doubted it and was about to tell her so when she quickly slid by him to enter his house. Closing the door behind him, he crossed his arms over his chest and watched her look around like she'd never been here before, and then he remembered she hadn't. He had broken things off with her before the affair had gotten that far. "What information do I need to know?"

She turned to face him and threw her hair back from her face. She was wearing knee-high leather boots and a light blue mini sweater dress that was so tight it appeared glued to her body. "Mmm, something smells good. Don't you want to invite me to dinner?" she asked, placing her hands on her hips to draw attention to her small waistline.

At that moment, he admired Alpha even more. During the time they'd spent together, she'd never found any reason to flaunt her attributes. They were noticeable without her having to show them off. "Sorry, I'm expecting company in a few hours."

He saw the frown settle on her face. "I take it that you're still involved with that party planner," she said with a sneer.

He tried keeping his anger in check. "What of it?"

"You must like her a lot to include her in one of your family dinners. Not too many women get that privilege from Riley Westmoreland. I didn't. And I know how much you pride yourself on your reputation and the family's name and all that."

He wondered what she was getting at. "If you have something to say, Paula, just say it."

"All right, then." She paused a moment and then slid down to sit on his sofa uninvited, crossing her legs, deliberately showing plenty of thigh and said, "I'm sure you've heard I'm seeing Samuel Porter."

Not that he cared, but he wasn't surprised. Sam was and always had been a party animal, and Paula liked having a good time and getting wild and crazy. And he'd heard Sam was into over-the-top stuff in the bedroom, like group sex and all that. "And?"

"And I was going through Sam's collection of special videos one night to pick out one I thought we would enjoy watching together. Get my drift?"

Riley did get her drift and didn't have to ask what Sam's special videos were. He'd heard the rumor years ago that Sam had a cabinet filled with porn. He drew in a deep breath, still not sure where she was going with all of this. "And?"

"And…" she said, smiling, pulling something out of her purse, "I came across one, and the woman looked so familiar that I took a second look. You might want to take a look, as well. I'm sure you'll recognize her."

He took the DVD she offered and glanced at the picture of the couple, mainly the woman who was stretched out spread-eagle on a four-poster bed very naked. His heart nearly stopped beating, and he forced his hand to stop trembling. He looked at Paula, fighting to keep his teeth from gnashing together in anger. "What are you trying to insinuate?"

"That your girlfriend used to have a naughty past."

He tossed the DVD on the sofa next to her. "I think you're about to set yourself up for a lawsuit you can't afford. This is not my girlfriend on this DVD jacket, just someone who favors her."

Paula lifted her chin dubiously and smiled. "You sure of that?"

Riley's gaze narrowed. Yes, he was sure. The porn star on the DVD jacket was not Alpha.

"Positive. In fact I'm so positive that if I hear about this from anyone else, I'm going to assume you're the one spreading vicious lies and malicious gossip, and I will sue you myself for slandering her name."

The smile quickly disappeared from her face. "You wouldn't do that."

"Try me."

She drew in a deep breath. "I know what I see."

"And I know what I know, but if you want to play your hand, go ahead, I dare you. I won't stop until I make you not only a laughingstock but destitute. Now, I want you to leave and not come back. And remember what I said. If I get wind of any lies you're spreading, I will make sure you regret it."

She jerked up off the sofa and angrily headed for the door, opened it and slammed it shut behind her with enough force to make his windows shake. It was only then that he noticed she'd left the DVD behind, whether accidentally or intentionally he wasn't sure.

Picking up the DVD he headed for the bedroom to take a shower. His dinner guest would be arriving within the hour. And he knew just as sure as the forecasters had predicted snow for the weekend that at some point during the course of the evening, he and Alpha would have a long talk.

"We need to talk, Alpha."

Alpha glanced over at Riley. Something was wrong; she could feel it. Although dinner had been great and she enjoyed his company as usual, she was chilled by the feeling that something just wasn't right. More than once during dinner she had caught Riley staring at her only to quickly look away. What was going on?

A part of her didn't want to know, but still she couldn't stop the what-ifs from swimming through her head. What if he wanted to bring a date Saturday night and had decided he wanted to end his affair a few days early? He had been so adamant about her having dinner with him this evening and now she couldn't help wondering if it was one of those break-up meals. Men had a way of thinking a woman preferred to get dumped on a full stomach. Hadn't Eddie taken her to dinner the night before he'd given her the ultimatum about Omega?

"Alpha."

She took a sip of her wine before placing her glass down on the table. She was a big girl and could handle anything that came her way. But she didn't want to do it now. If he wanted to make this their last night together then she wanted it to be special.

Easing up off the sofa, she slowly crossed the room to where he sat in a leather wingback chair. With his legs stretched out in front of him, he was sipping his own wine while his dark, penetrating gaze watched her every move. And with good reason, she thought, since she was discarding her clothes, piece by piece. His attention was definitely being held the way she wanted it to be. They would have their talk but it would be later. Much later.

By the time she had reached his chair she was totally naked. He pulled her down in his lap and cradled her in his arms. "You like tempting me, don't you?" he asked huskily, leaning close to her lips.

"Umm, it wouldn't be any fun if I didn't." And she wanted him to remember all the times she had tempted him and he had tempted her. She wanted him to remember everything, especially when they were no longer involved. Because she would. Her memories would sustain her when she buried herself in her work to forget him.

It would be hard being involved with Megan's wedding.

She expected to run into him, but hopefully, she would have gotten over him by then.

Yet how could a woman get over a man she truly loved?

"Baby, we need to talk."

She leaned in close to him, and swiped the tip of her tongue across his lips. "And we will talk, Riley. Later. Now I want you to take off your clothes so we can have fun," she said, easing off his lap and pulling him up from the chair.

"Fun?" he asked her, reaching out and running his fingers across the tips of her breasts while letting his gaze roam all over her body.

"Yes," she said, looking up at him as she pulled his belt through the loops of his jeans and then began unbuttoning his shirt. "What do you say about that?"

He reached out and swept her off her feet and headed toward the stairs to his bedroom. "Then I'd say, let's get started."

Alpha stretched out her legs in bed the moment she opened her eyes. It was daylight, and through the window she saw it was lightly snowing. Just her luck, what with those last-minute details she had to handle to get ready for the party tomorrow night.

She turned over in the empty bed, wondering where Riley was. It was then that she saw the note pinned to the pillow where his head had lain the night before.

Didn't want to wake you, but I had an eight o'clock meeting at work. I know you probably have a ton of things to do today to get ready for tomorrow, but make yourself at home until you're ready to leave. Riley.

She held the note to her chest, thinking that at least he hadn't mentioned anything else about them talking. She flopped back down in bed as a smile touched her lips. She'd deliberately made him forget. All it took was for her to glance around at the rumpled bedcovers to know just where Riley Westmoreland's concentration had been last night and during the early hours of this morning. She hadn't gotten much sleep last night, which wouldn't be bad if she didn't have a million things to do.

She looked around the room for her clothes and then remembered she had removed them last night in the living room. The last thing she intended to do was parade around Riley's house naked. He mentioned that he never locked his doors and his brothers or cousins were known to just drop in. Easing out of the bed, she knew he had a robe around here someplace. When she didn't see one, she figured one of his T-shirts would have to do.

She recalled just where he kept them and opened the top drawer to his dresser. Her breath caught. Lying on top of his stack of T-shirts was a DVD, but not just any DVD. It was one of her sister's, titled *Time to Play*. Where did he get it? How long had he had it?

Alpha stood there staring at the DVD as a thousand questions flowed through her mind. Did Riley assume like LeBron had at first that it was her on the DVD and not Omega? Or did he figure like LeBron had later that if he couldn't have his ideal porn star then her twin sister would do?

She angrily shoved the drawer closed as fury ripped through her. No wonder he had wanted an affair with her.

But then why was she getting angry anyway? She'd known it was nothing but sex with no commitment all along. Nothing more.

Not caring anymore if anyone saw her naked, she raced downstairs and saw Riley had picked up her clothes off the floor and placed them on the sofa. She quickly dressed, grabbed her purse from the table and left. For the first time since moving to Denver, she didn't notice the cold.

What she noticed more than anything was how deep her heart was hurting.

# Sixteen

Riley walked into the ballroom of the Pavilion Hotel and stopped short. Wow! Alpha had miraculously transformed the room into one winter's night, just as the theme declared.

The color scheme was silver, blue and white. Large white columns had been erected, connected by swathes of white netting. The ceiling looked like a midnight sky with the moon and dots of stars. Miniature mounds of snow lay in one area and props of snow-covered mountains were strategically placed around the room.

"Welcome." A hostess dressed as a snow maiden greeted him. "And here's your gift from Blue Ridge Management," she said, handing him a snow globe with a replica of the Blue Ridge Management building inside.

"Thanks." He couldn't resist shaking it up and watching snow float all around. A huge smile touched his lips. His woman had definitely outdone herself. *Imagine*.

"Your girlfriend did a bang-up job, didn't she?"

He turned and looked into Bailey's smiling face. He could tell she was equally impressed. "Yes, she did."

Bailey tilted her head. "So, she is your girlfriend?"

He paused, thinking that Bailey was the second person in two days who had referred to Alpha as his girlfriend. He hadn't denied it then, and he wouldn't deny it now. "Yes, she's my girlfriend."

She stared at him. "Of all the women you've been involved with, I've never known you to claim any of them as anything other than a sleeping partner."

He grabbed a glass of wine from the tray of a passing waiter. Everything, including the outfits the waiters and waitresses wore, looked festive and right in keeping with the party's theme. "She's different."

"In that case, I hope you intend to treat her differently."

He already was, and would continue to do so. In fact, starting tonight, he intended for them to take their relationship to a whole new level, but first they needed to talk. He had left several messages, but she hadn't found time to return them. He knew how hard she had worked and planned for the party tonight, often staying up late and getting up early. But tonight she had to be proud of her accomplishments. He was, and was certain the rest of his family would be, as well.

"You look good, by the way," Bailey said, giving him a once-over. "You Westmoreland men clean up well."

He couldn't help but laugh. "So do Westmoreland women." He glanced around again. "Have you seen Alpha?"

"Yes. She's around here someplace, making sure everything is running smoothly. At some point, I hope you make sure she slows down to enjoy herself. She's worked hard for tonight and it shows."

It was a half hour later before he got a chance to see Alpha, and it was from across the room. He had been standing in a group talking to Morris Caper, one of the oldest employees at Blue Ridge, along with the man's wife, Canyon, Stern and two other couples, when Alpha came into his line of sight. His breath caught when he saw her. She was wearing blue, the same shade being used at the party.

He nodded a few times, trying to pretend to listen to the speaker, when in reality his attention was on Alpha. He began wondering why she wouldn't look his way. Surely she knew he'd arrived. However, he had to remind himself that tonight wasn't about him. She had a job to do. But he had a niggling discomfort that something wasn't right.

He was about to look back at Mr. Caper when Alpha finally glanced his way. He was about to give her a smile and a thumbs-up when the look she gave him made him go still. What was that glare all about? He lifted his brow, and she quickly turned to head toward the room where food was being prepared.

"Excuse me for a minute," he said to the group before walking off in the direction Alpha had gone. Something was going on, and he intended to find out what.

He walked through several rooms and was stopped by a number of people before he finally came within a few feet of her. She looked up, saw him and was about to walk away when he increased his pace and touched her arm. "Everything is above my expectations, Alpha, but I'd like to talk to you for a second."

He was very much aware that with others around, she couldn't deny his request. After all, his family was the one paying for this affair.

"All right."

To anyone else it would appear she was acknowledging his request, because, unless you were standing as close to her as he was, you couldn't see the sharp daggers in her eyes or the tightness of her lips. *What the hell?*

"Privately, please," he said, taking her arm and leading her to an empty room in the back, far away from her staff, his employees or his family members.

He closed the door behind them and then turned to her. She was looking at everything in the storage room but him. And he could feel her tension. Her anger. "Now. Would you like to tell me what's going on?"

Her brows furrowed, and she lifted her chin. "There's nothing going on, at least nothing you should be concerned about. This is our breakup night anyway, right? What did you say when we started out, that you didn't stay with any woman past six weeks? Well, your six weeks ended today, no sweat."

Riley gritted his teeth. "What's this about, Alpha?"

"Nothing, and if you don't mind, I have a party to run and—"

"Your assistant can handle things until you get back. And I intend to keep you here until you tell me what's wrong, even if it takes all night."

She placed her hands on her hips. "I don't owe you any explanations."

He crossed the room to where she stood in a furious stance with her gaze flaring, spine straight and head thrown back. "Yes, you do. When I left you in bed yesterday morning it was with a smile on your face, so what's with the venom tonight? Are you mad because I left without waking you?"

"Is that what you think?"

He rubbed his hand down his face. "I don't know what to think, so tell me."

Alpha tried not to give in to the plea she heard in his voice and turned her back to him. For two solid days she had tried putting thoughts of him out of her mind. She had tried to concentrate on what had to be done for this party. It hadn't been easy, but she had managed to get through it somehow, and every single Westmoreland here, including him, had complimented her on her work. Tonight should be a night of celebration and excitement for her. Instead it was one of heartbreak.

She heard him move and could feel his heat, breathe in his

masculine scent and knew he was standing directly behind her with little space between them. The thought of what he'd done and what he'd thought of her hit low and hard, and he had the nerve to act like nothing happened. In essence he had no idea what she'd found in his drawer. Maybe it was time for her to tell him.

She turned around and met his inquisitive gaze. "Yesterday morning after you left, I needed a T-shirt to put on before going downstairs to get my clothes."

"Go on."

"I thought you wouldn't mind if I looked in your drawer to get one."

Something in his gaze let her know that he knew what would come next and he spoke before she did. "And you found that DVD Paula gave me."

His words nearly sucked the breath from her lungs. "Paula?"

"Yes, Paula, from McKay's."

Her head began spinning. Now she understood the looks that had passed between him and Paula that night. "So that was the private joke between the two of you," she said, barely getting the words out, forcing them beyond the tears she refused to let fall.

"What are you talking about?"

"Nothing. The main thing right now is that you had that video and you thought it was me, didn't you? That's why you initiated an affair with me, isn't it? I played right into your hands—and into your bed."

Riley felt a sting to his cheek, thinking her words were like a slap to his face. He struggled against the need to lash out at her the way she was lashing out at him. How could she assume something like that? "What are you accusing me of, Alpha?"

"That you and your ex-girlfriend thought you had things

figured out. You both thought that I'm the woman on that porn DVD."

At that moment he felt angrier than he'd ever felt in his life because the woman he loved didn't trust him. She had a lot of nerve. He had been up-front with her about everything. She was the one keeping secrets yet he had fallen in love with her anyway, against his better judgment.

Risking the kind of pain he'd vowed never to feel.

"I knew you were not the woman on that jacket," he said through gritted teeth.

She took a step closer to him, got in his face. "How could you have known that when Omega is my identical twin? You wouldn't be the first man who thought I was her."

"I don't give a royal damn what other men thought. I knew it wasn't you the minute I looked at that DVD jacket. You might be identical twins but a man who has made love to you as often as I have, who has touched you, tasted you, got up close and personal with you, could tell the difference. I know every mole, crevice, indention and mark on your body. I knew that wasn't you and figured it had to be your twin...a twin you never told me you had."

He paused a moment and added, "And if you recall, I did mention we needed to talk and intended to bring it up on Thursday night, the same day Paula brought that DVD over for me to see. I told her then it wasn't you. So who's the victim here, Alpha? It seems pretty clear to me that I trusted you a whole hell of a lot more than you trusted me."

He then turned and walked out of the room.

Alpha drew in a deep breath the moment she heard the door close behind Riley. Was it really true? Had he known the woman on that DVD jacket wasn't her? If so, then she had done him a grave injustice, especially when she hadn't told him about Omega.

What had been lacking between them was trust and communication, more on her part than on his. He had told her about his family, introduced her to them, but she had told him hardly anything about hers. And he hadn't been quick to believe the worst about her like she had about him.

And he *had* wanted to talk Thursday night, but she'd assumed he wanted to break things off with her. Had she let him have his say, none of this would have happened, and if she hadn't jumped to conclusions and assumed the worst then she wouldn't be standing here filled with so much remorse. But after dealing with the likes of LeBron and Eddie, she had been too afraid to trust another man.

There was a gentle knock on the door. "Yes?"

Lindsey stuck her head in with a concerned look on her face. "Is everything all right?"

"Yes, why do you ask?"

She came into the room and shrugged. "I saw Mr. Westmoreland request to talk privately and wondered what could be wrong since everything seems to be going all right. Everyone I talked to thinks you outdid yourself. Everything is beautiful."

Alpha swallowed deeply. "I had a lot of help, and no, Mr. Westmoreland wasn't complaining about anything. He wanted to discuss another matter."

"Oh."

Deciding the best thing she could do now was to get back to work and stay busy, she said, "Come on. Let's make sure everything continues to stay impressive for everyone." She checked her watch. "It's almost time for the snow to start falling."

As part of the theme, she had decided to have fake snowflakes swirl from the ceiling, and with the special lightning she had installed, it would give the illusion that the entire ballroom had been transformed into a beautiful winter wonderland.

As Alpha left the room with Lindsey, she knew what she should do but had no idea how to go about it.

* * *

"You sure you don't want to come to dinner, Riley? With that huge snowstorm headed this way it might be the last good home-cooked meal you get for a while," Dillon said.

"Yes, it might be at that," Riley replied as he stood at the window and looked out. It hadn't started snowing yet but according to the forecasters a snowstorm was headed their way. "But I'll still pass. I wouldn't be much company anyway."

Dillon didn't say anything for a minute. "So Pam and Chloe were right. There's trouble in paradise."

Riley didn't have to figure out how they knew. He had found out a long time ago that the women in his family were too observant for their own good. "I guess you can say that."

"Then take it from someone who knows, people in love have spats sometimes."

Riley lifted his brow and said in a defensive tone, "Who said I was in love?"

"I did. And don't try denying it. I watched you and Alpha at the party trying to avoid each other. It's been over a week. Don't you think the two of you need to kiss and make up?"

Riley rolled his eyes. "Too complicated to kiss and make up, Dil."

"Not if you really love her. If I can forgive Pam for coming within seconds of marrying another man, then I'm certain you can forgive Alpha for whatever the transgression."

A short while later, after his conversation with his oldest brother had ended, Riley stood in the kitchen pouring a cup of coffee, replaying in his mind what Dillon had said. He appreciated the pep talk but there were times when it was better just to count your losses, move on and not look back. Instead, he was going to take the same advice he'd given to Bane— advice Bane had refused to follow. Now, his brother was *still* hurting and, more than ever, Riley refused to be another Bane.

He was about to walk over to the refrigerator to pull out a microwave dinner when he heard his doorbell. He didn't have to wonder who was probably at his door. Bailey. She'd called twice already and if Dillon had mentioned Riley planned on skipping a meal with the family, she wouldn't hesitate to come and grill him about things he'd rather not talk about.

He thought about not answering but decided if Bailey had braved the blistering cold to come to his place then he would see what she wanted. But he would not let her stay long. Although the snowstorm hadn't hit yet, it was cold as the dickens outside. He would send Bailey on her way, and he would eat his meal alone and get in bed early. The mayor had already predicted that most of Denver, including the airport, would be shut down tomorrow.

Riley opened the door to find this furry white thing standing in front of him. He leaned in the doorway, trying to make out just what or who it was when the person tilted her head and moved away all the fur. "Alpha?"

She nodded. "May I come in so we can talk? It's cold out here."

He quickly moved aside. "Get near the fireplace," he ordered, wondering what in the world she was doing out in this weather. It was in the low teens. He thought it was pretty damn cold and he was used to it. It would be murder on someone like her.

He stood back and watched as she peeled off a long white coat trimmed in fur with a matching hat and gloves. She then pulled a white knitted ski mask from her face before pulling off another coat and two sweaters. When she stood trembling in front of the fireplace in a pair of winter-white stretched slacks and a pretty winter-white pullover turtleneck sweater, he just stared. The outfit looked good on her. Too good.

And when she ran her fingers through her hair to fluff it out, he felt heat on his skin. He swallowed hard and said, "I'll pour you a cup of coffee while you warm up. And then you can tell me why you came here in all this bad weather."

He quickly walked away, to the kitchen, and tried to

breathe calmly while he poured her coffee. He hadn't seen her or talked to her since the party, but that didn't mean he hadn't thought about her, because he had—every waking minute as well as when he should have been sleeping. She hated cold weather, yet she had come here, on what would probably be the coldest day they'd had since last winter.

Trying to keep his hand steady, he walked back to the living room and found her standing with her back to him, in front of the fireplace, staring down at the flames as if she was in deep thought. He wondered what she was thinking about and knew he would soon find out.

"Here you are," he said, claiming her attention. She crossed the room to meet him. She took the cup from his hand and the minute their fingers touched, a frisson of warmth flowed through him. He took a step back and watched as she immediately took a sip.

She glanced up at him. "Thanks, I needed that."

"I'm sure you did. So why are you here, Alpha?"

"I was hoping we could talk. I considered calling but figured you would refuse."

She had figured right. "What more is there to say? I trusted you more than you trusted me."

"It's not just about trust, Riley."

He crossed his arms over his chest. "Then what else is there?"

"An understanding between us. And I would be the first to admit I didn't tell you everything, but I had a reason for keeping my family secrets to myself. All we were sharing was an affair."

She glanced over at the sofa. "May I sit down so we can talk? I think it's time that I tell you everything."

A part of him was tempted to tell her no. It was too late to tell him everything. He preferred that she leave.

But he knew he couldn't say any of that. She had come over in the cold weather, which meant whatever she had to say was important to her. So the least he could do was listen to what she had to say. "Yes, you may have a seat."

She sat down and he took the chair across from her and wondered why she hadn't been able to decipher when his feelings for her had changed and he'd wanted more than sex without a commitment. What had she thought those flowers were all about, the amount of time he had spent with her compared to all the others?

He watched her and knew she was trying to gather her thoughts. Why? Was he such a hard guy to talk to? He had shared more of himself with her than with any other woman. Too bad he couldn't say the same about her.

She looked over at him, met his gaze and he knew he had lied to himself.

He'd awakened that morning with a firm resolve that he no longer wanted her or loved her. But seeing her here at Riley's Station only confirmed that he still wanted her in a way he'd never wanted another woman. And, more than anything, he still loved her.

She finally began talking. "My identical twin sister, Omega, dropped out of college our first year when she met this older guy at some club near campus. The man convinced her she should be a model."

She paused a moment and took another sip of her coffee. "Omega was always the more outgoing of the two of us and always wanted that sort of thing—the limelight, recognition, stardom—so her decision didn't surprise me. And, in a way, I doubt that it surprised my parents. At least it shouldn't have, since she was the one who defied their every order while we were growing up.

"Anyway, my parents were livid about her dropping out of college. When she left they didn't hear from her for months, but because she and I are close, I knew her whereabouts. I knew before anyone when she discovered the man hadn't propositioned her for a real modeling job but for a job as a porn star. He didn't twist her arm or hold her hostage. Omega could have walked away at any time. It was a choice she made. She thought she had a beautiful body, and she didn't mind flaunting it. She considered what she was doing a job. She was a well-paid entertainer and nothing else."

He nodded. "Did your parents know what she was doing?"

She shook her head. "No, and Omega and I both figured that they wouldn't find out, either. She was living out in California and had become popular on the West Coast; whereas my parents lived in Florida, the Bible Belt. We thought good churchgoing people would never find out about stuff like that. But we were wrong. It seemed a few men who knew my parents were getting porn off the internet, so you can just imagine how they couldn't wait to spread the word. Soon it got back to my parents. Someone even sent them a DVD in the mail."

"That was kind of low," he said.

"Yes, it was, and it led to a full-blown scandal that embarrassed my parents. Some of their so-called friends stopped socializing with them and, for a while, they lost business at the vet clinic. Mom and Dad tried to talk to Omega. Of course they went about it the wrong way, by making demands, and that only made her defiant. In the end, they threatened to cut her off if she didn't quit what she was doing and return home. They also forbade me to have contact with Omega, which I refused to do."

"I'm sure they weren't happy about that."

She shook her head. "No, they weren't. They finally just left me alone and requested that I not ever mention anything about Omega to them. The embarrassment was too much, and in the end they made a decision to disown her until she came to her senses."

She took another sip of her coffee. "A few years later, I met this guy name LeBron, who moved to Daytona with his job from Ohio," she said softly. "LeBron and I dated for six

months, and I thought everything was going great until one
night he presented me with one of my sister's DVDs and said
he'd been a fan of hers for a couple of years. He even said
what had drawn him to me was that he assumed I was her.
And when he found out I wasn't, he figured he had the next
best thing. He wanted me to imitate what she did on the DVD.
He even wanted to call me Omega whenever we made love."

Riley tensed and anger flowed through his body. "He actually wanted you to pretend you were your sister?"

"Yes. I refused to do so and left. The next day he called,
breaking things off with me."

She didn't say anything for a long minute. "A year later, I
met Eddie when he brought his dog into the clinic. We hit it
off immediately. He had moved to Daytona from his family's
home in Palm Beach. They owned a slew of electronics shops,
and he'd moved to Daytona to open a new store there. It was
hard for me to trust anyone, and after we'd dated awhile, I
told him everything. I confided about Omega and told him
about LeBron. He was angry that LeBron could be such an
ass, and he said what Omega did for a living meant nothing
to him. It was her life and he could understand me wanting
to keep a relationship with my sister."

"Sounds like a nice guy."

"I thought so, and when he asked me to marry him, I
agreed. Everything was going along fine until someone, not
sure who, sent his parents a copy of Omega's DVD. They
were appalled and demanded that he end things with me. He
refused, but they put pressure on him to at least get me to
agree not to have anything to do with Omega."

She took another sip of coffee. "I refused, and he called
off the wedding a week before it was to take place."

She paused, as if remembering that time. "That was another embarrassment for my parents, especially when they
thought I should have given in to Eddie's request. I decided
to move as far away as I could, which brought me to Denver."

He leaned forward. "So when you saw that DVD in my drawer, you assumed I was another LeBron or that I could be another Eddie?"

She held his gaze. "Yes."

Her single answer gave him pause. "Is that the reason you didn't talk much about your family?"

"Yes. I know all families have issues but to this day my parents have not forgiven my sister. If they had their way I wouldn't have any contact with her. My mother is softening somewhat. She at least asks about Omega. But my father is still being hard-nosed."

"Is your sister still in the business?"

"No, she quit making porn movies a few years ago, but some people have long memories, especially since she was once very popular. I've been on business trips when men have approached me asking if I was Omega and could they have my autograph."

She paused again. "I still don't understand it. You say you knew immediately it wasn't me, but that's hard to believe when most people can't tell me and Omega apart."

He nodded. "The first thing I noticed was the dye job."

She lifted a brow. "The dye job?"

"Yes, you once mentioned you'd never dyed your hair and it was obvious the woman on the DVD jacket had. And then when I looked at it further, I noticed she had a mole on her inner right thigh. You don't. And you don't have a tattoo near your navel."

She nodded. "I'm sorry about jumping to conclusions, Riley, but we had agreed on a sex-only relationship because the last thing I wanted was to get seriously involved with someone. I had before—twice— and things didn't work out."

"What is your sister doing now?"

"Omega is living in Paris and is happily married to a wonderful guy who knows about her past and loves her regardless. Marlon is a successful businessman and the two of them travel a lot. With his encouragement, she returned to school and now has her graduate degree. But even with her marriage and her other accomplishments and achievements, my parents still haven't forgiven her."

"And I take it your father wants you and Eddie to get back together."

Her eyes widened. "How do you know that?"

"If you recall, I happened to call you one day and you thought I was your father. You said something that let me know he was trying to get you to reinstate your relationship with your ex-fiancé."

"Yes, but only because Eddie thinks he still has a chance to convince me not to have anything to do with Omega. But like I told him, my sister and I are closer than ever."

"I'm glad."

She looked surprised. "You are?"

"Yes, and I'm disappointed you would think that I wouldn't be. I love family, Alpha. I told you about Bane, the twins and Bailey and the reputation they had around town. Not once did any one of us think about disowning them. You don't disown family, and I think it's sad that your parents are doing that to your sister. Nobody is perfect."

"Yes, but having a bad reputation around town for things you did while growing up is one thing, Riley. Being a porn star is another, and Eddie's family let me know that families with good names wouldn't want to have theirs tarnished by such a scandal. Why would I even assume your family would be any different?"

"Because you met them. We aren't judgmental nor do we place ourselves on any type of pedestal. There are skeletons in every family closet. I told you all the stuff we're uncovering on my grandfather Raphel."

He paused a moment and then asked, "Have you ever heard of the Chamberlain gang?"

She nodded. "Yes. Father and two sons did a rash of bank

robberies across the country some years back. I was in high school, and one of my classmates brought in an article about them. We all found it fascinating how they were able to pull things off, zigzagging across state lines and evading the FBI for as long as they did before finally getting caught."

"What they did was pretty scandalous, wouldn't you say?"

"Yes, of course."

"Well, I happen to know one of their family members. Brooke Chamberlain. The Chamberlain gang consisted of her father and her two older brothers. They're still serving time, and I doubt they will be getting out anytime soon."

"You actually know someone related to them?"

"Yes, in fact I know her very well because she's married to my cousin Ian Westmoreland, who owns a casino near Lake Tahoe. All of us know about Brooke's family but none of us hold it against her. We're also aware she keeps in contact with them and find no fault in that, as well. Family is family, Alpha. I would never have judged you by what your sister did. Nor would I have pushed you not to have any contact with her."

"I see that now, but because I wasn't sure, I didn't want to take the chance."

"Do you believe me?" he asked, holding her gaze steadily, with single-minded focus. He knew at that moment how much he wanted her to believe him. To believe in him.

"Yes. I didn't know then," she said softly. "But I do now."

He nodded, satisfied with her answer. "Now that we've cleared up your issues, let's discuss mine."

Dread rippled down Alpha's spine. She wondered just what kind of issues he could have. "All right."

He slowly stood from the chair and paced a few times in front of the fireplace. The glow from the fire reflected on him. In jeans and a pullover sweater, he looked too sexy for her senses. She watched him move and her stomach tightened with each step he took. Moments later, he stopped and turned to face her. "I told you about Bane and Crystal, right?"

She nodded. "Yes."

"What I didn't tell you was how much their fiery relationship affected me. Bane loved Crystal with the passion and soul of a man beyond his years. I felt the love whenever he mentioned her or when he would look at her. We all did, and that worried us. In a way, I felt sorry for Mr. Newsome. The more he tried keeping them apart, the more they were determined to stay together at any cost."

He was silent for a moment. "I saw the pain Bane went through when he and Crystal were forced apart. I can still see that pain whenever he comes home and asks about her or mentions her name. A love that fierce scared the hell out of me. I never wanted that kind of love for myself. Our lives were shattered when we lost our parents and uncle and aunt in that plane crash. I could not imagine falling in love with a woman and going through that sort of pain due to death or any other kind of separation."

He went back and sat down. "So my issues were making it hard for me to ever consider a serious involvement with a woman. Until you. With you, it was hard to keep my emotions in check, and I found myself wanting things I felt I shouldn't have."

Alpha could barely breathe. Was he saying what she hoped he was saying? That at some point it had become more than just sex with no commitment? That he had been fighting his emotions for her like she had been fighting hers for him? "What are you saying?" she asked softly.

"I'm saying that as much as I wished otherwise, it stopped being just sex for me during our trip to Memphis. I wanted to tell you then but didn't want to push you into anything. So I decided to give you hints about where I wanted our relationship to go. That's why I started sending the flowers. Why I invited you to meet my family. They took the hint but you were slow. It angered me when Paula showed up at my place with that DVD. How could you have thought it had been a private joke between her and me?"

She tried to get her heart rate to slow down. Had he kind of said, in so many words, that he loved her? "I saw the exchange between you two that day at McKay's, when I took off my coat and she saw my outfit."

He smiled. "Oh, that. It wasn't a private joke. It was egg on her face. The last time she saw you, you were overdressed because of the cold weather. She made a comment about me dating a frumpy woman. She got to see just how *not* frumpy you were and was almost rendered speechless. I liked the fact that she had to eat crow."

"Oh."

"I think we both had misgivings about allowing our relationship to go beyond anything other than just sex. So now I want to make it clear what I want. I want you, Alpha, and not just in a physical way. I love you so damn much it scares me. But I'm willing to take a chance on love and believe it was meant for us to be together, no matter what."

Alpha tried to fight back the tears that filled her eyes. "Oh, Riley, I love you, too, but I had promised myself never to let anyone come between me and Omega. When I saw that DVD in your drawer, I thought the worst and I'm sorry."

He eased from the chair and crossed the room to sit down beside her on the sofa. Reaching out, he wiped away her tears and then took her hand in his and held it tight. "So what do you think we should do about our issues?"

She was filled with so many emotions, she almost couldn't speak. Then she said, "What do you suggest?"

"I think we need to communicate more when it comes to things that threaten the love we have for each other. The thought of losing you for any reason is my worst nightmare and something I won't let happen."

"Oh, Riley."

He leaned down and brushed a kiss across her lips. Then he pulled her into his arms and kissed her with all the intense emotion that he was feeling. When he finally released her mouth, he softly caressed her cheek. "Will you marry me?"

She reached up and caressed his chin. "Only if we can have a long engagement. We owe it to ourselves to build our relationship, develop open communication and trust. And besides, there's no way we can marry before Megan's big day in June."

He nodded in agreement. "Then you decide when and I shall be there. I love you, and I want to spend the rest of my life with you."

"I love you, too." She stood. "Now I need to get back home before the storm hits."

He stood, as well. "If you think for one minute I'm letting you go back out in that weather, then think again. It's hard to believe you even ventured out."

"We needed to talk and I wanted to do it face-to-face."

"Well, we did, face-to-face, and you know what I think?"

"No."

"That our very own one winter's night should start now," he said, standing and pulling her close to him. "What do you say to that?"

She wrapped her arms around his neck. "I would say start the party."

He swept her off her feet and headed upstairs toward the bedroom, intending on doing just that.

# Epilogue

*A beautiful day in June*

Riley grabbed Alpha's arm when she hurriedly walked by him and pulled her behind a huge planter to steal a quick kiss. "Hey, slow down. How long will I have to be without a date?"

Alpha wrapped her arms around Riley's neck. "Just long enough for Megan and Rico to cut the cake. Don't you think they made a beautiful bridal couple?"

"Yes, and thanks to Imagine, it was a storybook wedding. You truly outdid yourself. I thought everything was perfect."

"I think you're perfect." And she really meant that. Over the course of the past six months, she and Riley had continued to build an even stronger relationship. Somehow he had talked her into that ski trip to Aspen in January and, as promised, he had kept her warm…most of the time. She hadn't gotten the hang of being on skis but the evenings spent in his arms in front of the fireplace had given them plenty more winter nights to cherish.

He had flown home to Daytona Beach with her over Easter weekend to meet her parents. Before that, he had invited Omega and Marlon to a surprise party he'd given for Alpha at the end of February to celebrate her selection as Denver's Small Businesswoman of the Year. She could tell he liked Omega and was one of the few who could tell them apart. And Alpha knew Riley liked Marlon Farmer, Omega's husband. The two had hit it off immediately. Already plans were in the works for her and Riley to visit Omega and Marlon in Paris...especially since Omega was expecting. She had never seen her sister looking so happy and radiant.

She glanced down on the beautiful ring she wore. They had decided on an August wedding, and she was looking forward to becoming Mrs. Riley Westmoreland.

Alpha also knew that while in Daytona, Riley had talked with her parents and let them know that she had his full support in maintaining a close relationship with her twin. He further told them how much family meant to him and that he hoped one day they would be able to repair their relationship with Omega. She had fallen more in love with him at that moment.

The sound of loud laughter made Alpha look in the direction of the wedded couple. They had just cut the cake. After Megan fed Rico a slice it seemed he was still licking the icing off Megan's fingers.

Alpha then glanced around the huge ballroom and her gaze settled on Riley's cousin Zane. He was leaning against the wall and staring hard at Dr. Channing Hastings, the woman he hadn't wanted Megan to invite.

"What are you looking at, baby?" Riley asked her.

She smiled up at him. "Your cousin Zane and how he's staring at Channing Hastings. She's beautiful."

Riley nodded. "Yes, Channing is beautiful both in and out. She and Zane had an affair a couple of years back when she lived here in Denver."

"Now she's engaged to be married to the man with the roving eyes. I bet he's checked out every single woman here today, even a few married ones."

Riley nodded, looking over at the man at Channing's side. "You noticed that, as well? She deserves better, which has me wondering why Channing is marrying the guy. I bet Zane is wondering that, as well. But as far as I'm concerned, when you snooze, you lose, and Zane was definitely snoozing when it came to Channing. I would bet any amount of money that he's feeling the pain of his loss. We always warned him that his womanizing ways would cost him one day. So he won't get any pity from me."

Alpha couldn't help but grin. "How can you talk? You were just as much a womanizer."

Riley shook his head. "Nobody could top Zane when it came to women. And, as far as I'm concerned, you have to admit that when I met the woman I knew was for me, I had no problem making her mine and putting a ring on her finger," he said, reaching out and taking her ringed hand in his. "Zane was too stubborn to do that. And I hate to say it, but he probably has lost the only woman he is capable of loving."

"How sad." She truly meant it. Now that she had Riley, she couldn't imagine not having the person you loved in your life. But she had a feeling, from the way Zane was staring at Channing, that Zane would be changing that soon. Alpha couldn't help wondering why Dr. Hastings would marry a man with wandering eyes.

"I've got to get back," she whispered, before brushing a kiss across his cheeks. "My work isn't completed until I get Megan and Rico off on their honeymoon. I think it's wonderful that they're going to Dubai for two weeks."

"Yes, it is wonderful, isn't it?"

She glanced around at all the Atlanta, Montana and Texas Westmorelands she had met over the past couple of days. The men all favored and the women were ultrafriendly. She felt blessed that she was marrying into such a warm and loving family. She smiled when she glanced over and saw Pam and Dillon with their daughter, who'd been born on Christmas Day. She was definitely a beauty.

She then saw Riley's brother, Bane, whom she had just met earlier that day when he had arrived in town. He was such a handsome man she had to take a second look every time she saw him. Even though he was always smiling, she could detect sadness around his eyes. Now she understood Riley's reasons for not wanting to feel the pain his brother was enduring.

"Alpha?"

She glanced up at Riley. Immediately, he lowered his mouth to hers, swiping any thoughts from her mind and kissing her with a hunger that she couldn't help but reciprocate, capturing her tongue in his and doing all sorts of erotic and scandalous things to it.

Scandalous...

It seeped back into her brain just where they were and what she was supposed to be doing. Dislodging her mouth from his, which wasn't an easy feat, she took a step back and drew in a deep breath. "Has anyone ever told you that you shouldn't mess around with the hired help?" she said playfully.

"No, and I wouldn't listen to them anyway. I have tunnel vision when it comes to you, sweetheart."

He took a step closer to regain the distance she'd put between them, bringing his body to hers. She felt something else he had, an erection that was hard and thick. "I'm going now, and I think you need to stay behind this planter until you get yourself together."

He chuckled. "As long as you're close by, I'll never be together—unless you're sharing my bed. And I've been thinking."

"About what?"

"We've had our one winter's night so what about a summer one?" he asked, leaning down and nibbling her lips.

"Riley…" she whispered in a strained voice, "I do need to get back to the wedding."

"No, you don't," he said, wrapping his arms around her. "Lindsey is a great assistant and has everything under control."

"Megan is going to fire me."

"And I will hire you to plan my wedding," he said as his mouth moved lower to nibble her throat.

"Behave," she said, pulling out of his arms again.

"Only if you promise that as soon as this wedding is over you will meet me at Riley's Station for our own after-wedding party."

She gazed up at him. She had a million things to do, but he was right, Lindsey was a great assistant and Alpha had a fantastic staff. "Okay, I promise."

She quickly moved away but couldn't resist glancing back over her shoulder. She was one lucky woman, and later tonight, when she was through with Riley Westmoreland, he would be convinced he was one lucky man.

\* \* \* \* \*

# CAUGHT IN HIS
# GILDED WORLD

## LUCY ELLIS

Gigi is for you, Mum.

# CHAPTER ONE

'GIGI, GET DOWN from there. You're going to break your neck!'

Suspended two metres in the air, gripping the stage curtain between the tensed toes of her feet and using her slender muscled arms to propel herself upwards, Gigi ignored the commentary and made quick work of scaling the curtains alongside the four-metre-high fish tank. It was the same tank in which she would be swimming tonight, in nothing more than a G-string and a smile, with two soporific pythons: Jack and Edna. That was if she didn't get fired first.

The ladder, which would have made this easier, had been folded away, but she was used to shimmying up ropes. She'd been doing it from the age of nine in her father's circus. The velvet stage curtains were a doddle in comparison.

Now for the hard part. She grabbed hold of the side of the tank with one hand and swung a leg over, straddling the ledge and locking herself in place.

There was an audible sigh from below.

When Susie had yelled, 'Kitaev's in the building—front of house, stage left,' pandemonium had broken loose. While the other girls had reached for their lipstick and yanked up their bra straps, Gigi had eyed the tank and, remembering its superb view once you were up there, hadn't hesitated.

Susie had been right on the money, too. Down below, among the empty tables and chairs, deep in conversation with theatre management, was the man who held their future in his powerful hands, surrounded by an entourage of thugs.

Gigi's eyes narrowed on those thugs. She guessed when you were the most hated man in Paris it helped to have minders.

Not that he appeared to need them. His back was to the stage but she could tell his arms were folded because his dark blue shirt was plastered across a pair of wide, powerful shoulders and a long, equally sculpted torso.

The man looked as if he broke bricks with a mallet for a living, not cabarets.

'Gigi, Gigi, tell us what you can see? What does he look like?'

*Big, lean and built to break furniture.*

And that was when he turned around.

Gigi stilled. She'd seen pictures of him on the internet, but he hadn't looked like *that*. No, the photographs had left that part out… The *I've just stepped off a boat from a nineteenth-century polar expedition, during which I hauled boats and broke ice floes apart with my bare hands* part.

A beard as dark and wild as his hair partially obscured the lower portion of his face, but even at this distance the strong bone structure, high cheekbones, long straight nose and intense deep-set eyes made him classic-film-star gorgeous. His thick, glossy and wavy inky hair was so long he'd hooked some of it back behind his ears.

He looked lean and hungry and in need of civilising—and why that should translate into a shivery awareness of her own body wasn't something Gigi wanted to investigate right now as she wobbled, gripping the side of the tank.

Not when she had to talk to him and make him listen.

He wasn't going to listen. He looked as if he would *devour* her.

Self-preservation told Gigi that a smart girl would shimmy back down the curtain and mind her own business.

'What's happening?' called up Lulu, who clearly wasn't able to mind her own business either, because she had climbed onto an upturned speaker below and was tugging on Gigi's ankle.

'I don't know,' Gigi called back. 'Give me a minute—and stop pulling at me, Lulu Lachaille, or I really will fall.'

Chastened, Lulu let go, but there was an answering hum of protest from below.

'You're not a monkey, G. Get down!'

'She thinks she's made of rubber. If you fall, Gigi, you won't bounce!'

'Gigi, tell us what you can actually *see*! Is it really him?'

'Is he as gorgeous as he looks in all the photos?'

Gigi rolled her eyes. At least Lulu understood that this man was not going to take his winnings seriously. But the other girls—poor fools—didn't see it that way. They were all operating under the belief that a rich guy in want of entertainment would scoop up a lucky showgirl and whisk her away to a life of unlimited shopping.

Probably alerted by all the noise, Kitaev looked up.

His attention shot to the aquarium so fast she barely had time to think. Certainly it was too late to draw herself back behind the curtain.

His gaze fastened on her.

It was like being slammed into a moving object at force. There was a buzzing in Gigi's ears and suddenly her balance didn't seem as reliable as it had been a moment ago.

She made a little sound of dismay as her belly slipped a few notches from her holding place atop the aquarium.

He was looking up at her now, as if *she* was what he had come to see.

Gigi slipped another inch and grappled for purchase.

Then two things happened at once.

He frowned, and Lulu gave an extra-hard tug on her ankle.

Gigi knew the moment she lost her balance because there was nothing she could do to save herself other than prepare for the fall. And with a little gasp she came tumbling down.

# CHAPTER TWO

IT WAS POSSIBLE Khaled would never have known he owned this little piece of Montmartre if someone had not got hold of a list of Russian-owned properties in Paris and published them. Apparently it was fine to buy up significant real estate in the Marais and down south on the Riviera, but touch one of Paris's cabarets and lo and behold you were the most hated man in the city.

Not that Khaled paid attention to what other people thought of him. He'd learned that lesson many years ago, as the son of a Russian soldier who had destroyed his mother's life and brought shame on her family.

Growing up among people who shunned him had formed on him a tough hide, along with the ability to use his fists— although nowadays he was more likely to use his power and influence in a fight—and the wherewithal to take nothing personally.

'Emotional detachment' a woman he'd briefly dated had called it. All skill, but no heart.

Detachment had served him well. Wallowing in emotion probably would have got him killed before he was twenty in the part of the world he came from. He had grown up fast and hard and had survived because of it. Then he had flourished in the bear pit that was the Moscow business world. He knew how to get what he wanted and he didn't let sentiment cloud his reasoning.

What made him a bad bet for a woman looking to nest sent the stock prices of his companies regularly soaring. Not that he was uninterested in women. He had a healthy interest in the species—although the turnover had recently stopped. It wasn't down to emotional emptiness, or an absence of libido, but sheer boredom at the lack of challenge.

He was a hunter. It was intrinsic to his nature to take up a scent, to track, to chase, to make the kill.

Then he got bored.

He had been bored for a long time. Months now.

Then he looked up.

What in *hell* was that?

When a man stepped inside one of Paris's famous cabarets he was primarily looking to see that most legendary of creatures: a Parisian showgirl.

Long-legged, alluring, topless…

That wasn't what he was looking at.

Granted, he'd been living in tents, yurts and huts for the past six weeks, bathing in rivers, eating out of cans and off the carcasses of what they could kill. A hallucination involving a woman might well be the result—although he doubted this was what his mind would come up with. Because he'd swear he'd just got a glimpse of a knobby-kneed Tinker Bell in an animal print leotard, perched on top of the tank in which he'd been told a beautiful semi-naked showgirl would be swimming tonight—with pythons.

Almost before he could account for what he was seeing, the curious apparition vanished as suddenly as she'd appeared, followed by a thump and vague female shrieks.

'Do you want to check that out?' he asked of the two Danton brothers, both of whom were clearly sweating bullets over his unannounced appearance.

Neither man moved.

'The girls are in rehearsal,' said Martin Danton nervously, as if that explained everything.

His security detail looked around, clearly expecting all twenty-four luscious Bluebirds to come can-canning across the empty stage.

'Would you like to see a rehearsal?' Jacques Danton volunteered, catching hold of the shift in male attention eagerly. A little too eagerly.

The two Frenchmen who managed the place were nervous

as cats on a hot tin roof—as well they might be. Although Khaled suspected their nerves were nothing more than a natural response to having their shaky business practices put under the microscope.

'My lawyers will be in touch today,' he informed them calmly. 'I want to take a look at how the place is doing.'

'We're a Parisian institution, Mr Kitaev!' they chorused.

'So the French media have hammered home all week,' he replied, with the same measured calm. 'But it's a business, and I like to know how all my businesses are doing.'

Frankly, he wouldn't be here now if the press hadn't exploded last week with spurious accusations that he was the equivalent of the Russian Army—marching on Paris, ripping up its pretty boulevards and despoiling French culture. Turning their city into Moscow-by-the-Seine.

All because he'd won a cabaret in a card game.

Now, having pretty much run his eye over what was making it difficult for him to move around the city without security, he was ready to organise its disposal.

He had meetings lined up this afternoon, so L'Oiseau Bleu's time was almost up.

There was an interruption as a winsome girl with a mop of dark curls stuck her head through the curtain.

'Jacques…' she whispered.

The older man frowned. 'What is it, Lulu?'

'There's been an accident.'

'What sort of accident?'

'One of the girls has hit her head.'

With a Gallic gesture of acceptance, Jacques Danton muttered something that sounded like, 'Zhee-zhee,' and excused himself, pounding up onto the stage and into the wings.

Khaled's gaze flickered to the empty tank, towering over the stage. He still wasn't sure what it was he'd seen but he was interested in finding out.

He moved and his security team swarmed up onto the stage with him.

'I don't really think this is a good idea,' protested Martin Danton as he mobilised himself behind them, exhibiting the first bit of backbone Khaled had seen in either man.

He and his brother had been managing the cabaret for some fourteen years, according to the records. Managing it into the ground, Khaled suspected.

He made his way behind the curtains and through a jungle of stage props, stepping over various crates and boxes, and ducking overhanging cords and wires that probably constituted health and safety risks that would close the place down.

When he saw her she was lying sprawled on the stage floor.

Jacques Danton was ignoring her in favour of remonstrating with the little brunette. It had the effect on Khaled that all the mismanagement and blundering about hadn't yet delivered. He shouldered the Frenchman out of the way and went to her aid.

Hunkering down, he discovered that on closer inspection, despite her eyes remaining closed, he could see her delicate eyelids twitching.

His mouth firmed.

*Little faker.*

Looking up, he judged the height and recognised that although she'd fallen she couldn't have done much damage.

On cue, a clutch of other Lycra-clad, giggling, whispering twenty-something female dancers closed in around him. Khaled had had a similar experience only days ago, in the highlands of the Caucasus with a herd of jeyran gazelles. One minute he'd been naked, waist-deep in a clear stream, the next he'd been surrounded by knobby-kneed deer intent on drinking their fill.

He looked around to note that his security team appeared as bemused as he was feeling.

What were they going to do? Tackle them?

Obviously he'd been set up, and this was a stunt to get him backstage. But the girls appeared as harmless as the deer. He

looked down at the one gazelle who'd separated herself from
the herd. She lay there, unnaturally still, but those eyelids
gave her away, twitching at high speed as if she'd attached
a jump lead to them.

He pressed back one of the delicate folds. 'Can you hear
me, *mademoiselle*?'

'Her name is Gigi.' The curly-haired brunette had
crouched down opposite him and supplied the name help-
fully.

He was in Montmartre, in a shabby, past-its-use-by-date
cabaret, with a cast of showgirls whose cities of origin ranged
from Sydney to Helsinki to London—hardly any of them
were actually French. Of *course* her name was Gigi.

He didn't believe it for a second.

As if sensing his scepticism, she swept up her thick golden
lashes with astonishing effect. A pair of blue eyes full of
lively intelligence above angular cheekbones met his. Grew
round, startled, and bluer than blue.

*The colour of the water in the Pechora Sea.*

He should know—he'd just flown in from it.

He watched as the points in her face—a gorgeous Medi-
terranean nose, a wide pink mouth and a pointed chin, all
framed by wild red hair—seemed to coalesce around those
same eyes.

His chest felt tight, as if he'd been kicked under the ribs.

She sat up on her elbows and fixed him with those blue
eyes.

'Who are you? *Qui êtes-vous?*' Her accent happily butch-
ered the French with the sing-song cadence of Ireland blurred
with something a little more international.

*Qui êtes-vous?*

His question exactly.

He straightened up to assert a little dominance over her
and settled his hands lightly on his lean muscled hips.

'Khaled Kitaev,' he said simply.

There was a ripple of reaction.

'Ladies…' he added. But he didn't take his eyes off Red as he calmly offered her his hand, and when she hesitated he leaned in and took what he wanted.

Gigi had been falling professionally since she was nine years old, but that hadn't prevented her flailing backwards and striking her head and her tailbone on the stage boards. She was currently seeing two hands and was not sure which one to take.

'Get up!' Jacques was hissing at her like a goose.

The option was taken out of her hands by Kitaev, who plucked her effortlessly off the ground and deposited her on her feet in front of him. Only the room swayed and her legs weren't co-operating.

It didn't help either that she now found herself in the invidious position of having to tilt her head back even though she was five eleven—because he was *that* big—and he was standing far too close…looking at her.

*Boy, oh, boy, the way he was looking at her!*

Gigi blinked rapidly to clear her vision.

Sometimes men looked at you as if all they wanted was to see you naked. Gigi accepted this as an occupational hazard even if she hated it. Sometimes they made unwanted and sleazy advances, but she'd learned to combat those too.

This man wasn't doing any of those things. His eyes weren't desperate, greedy, pulling at her admittedly ratty leotard as if seeing her naked was all he cared about.

No, this man's eyes held intent. They said something else entirely. Something no man had ever promised her. He was going to strip her naked and pleasure her body as she'd never been pleasured before. And then he was going to take her job and bin it.

'You can't do that!' Gigi blurted out.

'Do what, *dushka*?' He spoke lazily, in a deep Russian accent, as if he had all the time in the world.

There was a titter among the other girls.

'Whatever it is you have planned…' Gigi's voice trailed off, because it didn't sound as if either of them were talking about the cabaret.

'At the moment,' he responded, with a flicker of something certainly beyond her experience in those dark and distant eyes, 'not much besides lunch.'

The laughter around them drowned out any response—which was just as well, because it didn't take much imagination to see that this man had absolutely no interest in anything here—and Gigi felt her initial frustration build once more.

He didn't care what happened to this place. The other girls didn't care. They *would* care, however, when they didn't have jobs.

But it wasn't just about losing a job. This was her *home*.

The anguish that pulled through Gigi like an undertow was real. It was the only place she had ever felt she really belonged since her mother's sudden death had upended her safe, secure world.

She'd served her time with her father until she'd been able to make her leap across the Channel onto the stage boards of what had seemed then to be a dream job.

Although, to be honest, if you'd asked her last week about her job she would have rolled her eyes and complained about the hours, the pay and the lousy chorie.

The Moulin Rouge, it wasn't.

But this wasn't an average day. This was the day everything she'd stitched together from her earliest life with her mother was threatening to come undone.

Gigi was not going to let that happen. She *couldn't* let it happen.

Besides, this wasn't any ordinary theatre. The most amazing women had danced here. Mistinguett, La Belle Otero, Josephine Baker—even Lena Horne had sung on this stage.

And then there was Emily Fitzgerald. Nobody remembered her—she'd never been famous…just a beautiful chorus girl among many who had danced on this stage for five short years. Her mother.

When she fell pregnant to smooth-talking Spanish show-man Carlos Valente she had been forced to return home to her family in Dublin, her Paris dream over. But from the moment she'd been able to stand Gigi had had her feet stuffed into *pointe* shoes, had been pushed in the direction of a stage and raised on stories of the Bluebird in its fabulous heyday.

Of course it hadn't been anything like those stories when she'd landed at its door aged nineteen, but unlike the other girls she knew how truly special L'Oiseau Bleu had once been…and could be again.

She'd been working on the Dantons. She'd been sure she was halfway to getting some improvements made to the routines…

Only now *he* was getting in the way.

At a loss as to where to start, it was then that she remembered she *did* have something that could speak for her. Folded up and stuck down her sports bra.

She tugged it out, sadly crumpled, and smoothed down the single page. It was a printout Lulu had made from a burlesque blog they both followed: *Parisian Showgirl*.

She looked up to find Kitaev was still watching her and had probably got an eyeful of her frayed purple bra. She knew this wasn't looking a whole lot professional, but she hadn't *meant* to come crashing down, she hadn't *meant* for him to come hunting around backstage, and right now all she had was…this. It just happened to be in her bra.

Something close to amusement shifted in those dark, watchful eyes. 'What else do you keep in there?'

His voice was pure Russian velvet, quiet and low-pitched, but a bit like a seismic shift in the earth's plates. You felt it in your bones…and other places.

Gigi experienced a whole body flush and drew herself up stiffly. 'Nothing,' she said uncertainly.

A couple of the girls tittered.

Ignoring them, she held out the page until he took it.

Gigi watched him run a cursory glance over the print. She knew it by heart.

*Paris is in revolt over the news that Russian oligarch Khaled Kitaev, one of Forbes' richest men under forty, got lucky in a game of poker.*

*Kitaev, whose fortune is in oil but who, like most Russian businessmen, seems to have branched out into property and entertainment until his holdings resemble nothing less than the behemoth nervous European business columnists fear will simply devour everything in its path—yes, that Kitaev—has taken possession of one of Paris's famous cabarets.*

*And this isn't just any theatre, people, it's one of Montmartre's oldest cabarets: L'Oiseau Bleu. Home of the Bluebirds. A charming, old-time cabaret—but for how long?*

*Judging from the media reaction, it appears the French aren't going to take this one lying down.*

His hand closed over the piece of paper and *crunch*—it was nothing more than a small ball in his large fist.

Gigi couldn't help feeling they were all a little like that ball of paper, and just as disposable.

'What do you want to know?'

He made it sound so easy, but she wasn't fooled. His dark eyes had hardened over the course of his cursory glance, and when he raised them there was a warning there.

Gigi told herself they weren't *her* words that she'd handed him. But she wanted him to know that this was the position they were operating from. A little information—even if it was misinformation. The sensible thing to do now would be to ask rationally and politely if he foresaw any major changes to the theatre that were going to affect their jobs.

Only then she noticed the subtle movement of his hard

gaze over her body. He wasn't being obvious but she felt it all the same—and, dammit, her nipples stiffened.

So instead of being reasonable she lost her temper and went for broke. 'We want to know if you've any plans to turn our cabaret into a full-on high-octane version of Le Crazy Horse?'

# CHAPTER THREE

MARTIN DANTON MADE a groaning sound.

His brother looked poised to take the little redhead out.

Red stood her ground.

'I wouldn't know,' responded Khaled, not taking his eyes off her, 'never having been inside the Crazy Horse.'

He caught the slight eye-roll and the tightening of her lips. His hand tightened around the crumpled ball of spurious invective this young woman had clearly swallowed whole.

'Gigi, *ça suffit,*' interrupted Jacques Danton. *That's enough.*

But she didn't back down. 'I think we have a right to know,' she protested. 'It's *our* jobs.'

He would have been more impressed if he hadn't suspected her boss had put her up to it.

'Your jobs are safe for the moment.' He threw it in because it was accurate—today. Tomorrow, possibly not.

*'Splendide!'* Jacques Danton beamed.

'That's not what I asked,' Red interrupted, and she lifted those lively blue eyes to his.

Not in appeal, he registered, but setting herself against him. Clearly not fooled one bit—unlike her boss.

For a moment he considered the alternative: that this *wasn't* some set-up and that the girl—a lot sharper than the Dantons and, unlike them, willing to take him on—was acting alone.

'We're not a strip club, Mr Kitaev, and it would ruin—'

She took a breath and something like anguish crumpled up her striking features. In the time it took her to compose herself Khaled became interested in what exactly she thought he was ruining for her.

But she shook her head and changed direction. 'Ruin the character of the theatre!'

'I wasn't told the theatre had a *character*.'

More laughter.

She looked around, as if thrown by the lack of support, and unexpectedly his conscience stirred.

'Nobody is going to be asked to take off their clothes,' he said, exasperated. Hell, he didn't know *what* would happen here. Go on as before, bleeding funds, because after the dose he'd had of French spleen over the place only a fool would touch it? He'd be lucky to give it away.

Red, however, seemed to be under the mistaken belief that there was something here worth saving.

*'Voulez-vous, filles?'*

Jacques Danton began clapping his hands at the other dancers and their audience began to break up.

'*Maintenant*, Gigi,' he snapped.

She was clearly torn between doing as she was told and continuing to question him about their jobs, but Khaled could already see she wouldn't stand up to her boss.

Just him.

Which was a first, given that men with a lot more where-withal than this girl—industrialists, Duma members, Moscow gangsters—stepped carefully around him. Then again, those men didn't have her lavender eyes or, frankly, her sexual pull.

She was by no means the most beautiful girl backstage, but she was the only one he couldn't take his eyes off.

Something to do with her bold features and lively eyes, and an innate sensuality she appeared to be entirely unaware of.

Pity she danced here…

Shame he was flying out tomorrow…

Another dancer—the frowning little brunette—had edged up to her. She took Red's hand with a furtive look of disapproval in his direction and tugged her away. Smart girl.

Red…*Gigi*…kept glancing over her shoulder at him before the rest of the dancers swallowed her up.

It was a slender shoulder, as finely designed as the rest of her, and it put him in mind of the Spanish painter Luis Ricardo Falero's amusing, graceful mythological girls. He knew he was done here, and yet he found his eyes following the red pigtails, bouncing amidst the crowd of other girls as the famous Bluebirds vanished into the rabbit warren of corridors.

That evening the dressing room was noisier and more lively than usual before the first performance.

Khaled Kitaev was the sole subject of discussion.

'The rumour is that the Russian supermodel Alexandra Dashkova had herself wrapped in a rug, Cleopatra-style, taken up to his hotel suite in Dubai last month and unrolled before him like war booty.'

This was greeted with various *ooh*s and *aah*s and had Gigi hesitating in the act of applying three-ounce lashes to her eyelids.

'No one's got a chance with him, then,' groaned Adele at Susie's announcement, and the cramped dressing room was filled with sighs and grumbles and more speculation.

'*C'est vrai.*' Solange regarded her breasts with satisfaction, adjusting her diamante-studded costume. 'He's asked for me by name. I'm having a drink with him after the show tomorrow.'

Gigi's hand slipped and the fake lashes ended up partway down her cheek.

'Great,' grumbled Lulu under her breath, leaning forward to pluck the feathered blob from Gigi's cheek and pass it to her. 'Ten to one she'll sleep with him and make the rest of us look easy.' Only being Lulu she didn't actually say *easy*—she mouthed it.

There was a neat little division down the centre of the Bluebirds. The dancers who accepted invitations from the visiting Hollywood A-listers and rock stars who came to the shows, and those who lined up each night after the last show for the courtesy bus.

It was something Gigi had organised when a couple of the girls had complained about not feeling safe leaving the venue at night, given that the theatre was bumped up against the red light district, and now the bus was a regular thing.

Gigi and Lulu never missed the bus. Solange took every invitation that came her way. Apparently she'd taken this one too.

Not that there was anything wrong with that, Gigi told herself. She only cared because it confirmed her worst suspicions about Kitaev's plans for them.

She slapped down the lid on her make-up case.

'Sorry G,' said Leah, obviously alerted by the bang of Gigi's case and not sounding sorry at all. 'You went to all that trouble for nothing.'

'Not for nothing,' Lulu rallied back loyally in her defence. 'We all got a good look.'

Too good, thought Gigi fiercely. Any hope that Khaled Kitaev was going to take ownership of the cabaret seriously was out of the window. As of now the Bluebird was in serious jeopardy.

And what was it with everyone thinking she'd done it on purpose? *Sheesh*.

No, she knew all about this man. She had scrolled through lists of his public holdings on the internet, chased them to various websites, and was still struggling to make sense of how he'd made his money.

Initially, it appeared, as an oil trader—but he seemed to have a finger in a lot of pies. *Shady*, she decided. She had learned from watching her dad at work that big money was probably amassed in the same way as her father's smaller cheats: through the exploitation of someone else.

'So what do you think he's going to do to us?' asked Trixie, one of the youngest dancers.

Given he'd already honed in on Solange, Gigi had a pretty good idea.

'Do you think he'll try to change things? Maybe fix things up?' Trixie sounded optimistic. 'It might not all be bad, Gigi.'

No, it was probably worse. Gigi hated to disillusion her, but facts had to be faced.

She stood up to face the room.

'Could I have everyone's attention?'

A couple of the girls glanced her way, but the noise level didn't drop.

She raised her voice. 'Can we just try to look at the big picture here—instead of getting into a lather about his sex life?'

The word 'sex' had a few more heads turning and the volume dropping.

'Kitaev owns a string of gambling venues around the world.' Gigi paused to let that sink in. 'Have you thought about what that might mean for us?'

'*Oui,*' said Ingrid, 'a pay-rise.'

There was a ripple of laughter.

'Loosen up, G,' advised another girl, giving her a friendly push.

'She can't—she hasn't been laid in so long I'm surprised she didn't squeak when she fell off that aquarium,' cackled Susie.

'Gigi's just smarting because her little stunt didn't make him single her out,' sang out Mia from across the room.

'Give it up, G,' said Adele. 'Oh, that's right—you never do!'

There was a howl of good-natured laughter.

Gigi knew she needed to get the discussion back on track, because now Susie was wanting to know what the point was of being a showgirl if you didn't take advantage of the perks: rich men.

'The point is no one should date Kitaev,' Gigi interrupted. 'He shouldn't be encouraged!'

The laughter only became more raucous. Even Lulu gave her a rueful look.

*He's going to win*, thought Gigi a little desperately.

The dressing room door banged open.

'Guess who's just arrived, ladies?' announced Daniela, sparkling in full costume.

There was a twitter of excitement.

'Not Kitaev.'

The twittering died down.

'Girls, its wall-to-wall security and every rich Russian in the city is here—and everyone from Fashion Week seems to have followed them. The media are ten-thick outside. I think I'm going to faint!'

Amidst the shrieks, Lulu adjusted her headdress and said brightly, 'There you go, Gigi. Maybe he's not so bad for business after all.'

'So he's sent his friends?' she grumbled. 'One night does not a week make. We're just a novelty act for a bored, spoilt-for-choice, testosterone-injected, arrogant—'

But now even her best friend had jumped ship and was on her way out, giggling with the other girls, trailing the six-foot feather tail they all had attached to their waists for the first number.

Troubled, Gigi finished attaching her own.

That many customers wasn't to be sneezed at, given they regularly performed to a half-empty theatre, and this had been their worst year yet.

Maybe the other girls saw something she didn't.

Yes, she thought cynically, they saw something, all right. They saw Solange draping her skinny arms around Khaled Kitaev's broad neck and a line of ambitious showgirls asking when was it *their* turn.

Solange was apparently going to have hers, and it firmed Gigi's chin.

The lowest common denominator was not going to save this theatre or their jobs.

Khaled Kitaev didn't care about the cabaret. He had no stake in it. He'd won the thing in a card game. All he cared about was the bottom line. Specifically at the moment that bottom being Solange's, but Gigi could well imagine him cutting a swathe through the other bottoms of the troupe. There were some very shapely bottoms.

Gigi swished her plumage-heavy tail like a haughty lyre-bird and took off after the other girls.

She would see about that.

'Mademoiselle…?'

'Valente.'

'*Mademoiselle*, I'm afraid I cannot give you the information you seek. At the Plaza Athénée we value our guests' right to privacy.'

The concierge gave her that bland smile peculiar to people in his job all over the world. Only somehow the Frenchman managed to add that extra little soupçon of superiority.

Gigi knew her bad accent wasn't helping. She should have brought Lulu along this morning. Lulu was half-French, and her big brown Audrey Hepburn eyes and air of delicate femininity made grown men trip over themselves to help her out. With her propensity to help herself and make a mess of it, Gigi found she was mostly sidelined and all too frequently laughed at.

Still, you could only work with what you'd got, and given she'd left her flat in such a hurry this morning she'd left off her make-up, and with her hair still damp and messy from being dunked in the sink, it wasn't exaggerating to say she currently had the sex appeal of an otter.

'But how am I supposed to reach him?' she tried again.

'*Mademoiselle* could try the telephone.'

'You'll give me his number?'

'*Non*, I would assume that as you are the *friend* you say you are, you will have it.'

'I'm not his friend, exactly,' Gigi prevaricated, and because she had a detestation of lies and subterfuge, having seen the chaos her father left in his wake, she opted for the truth. 'I'm his employee. I'm a showgirl at L'Oiseau Bleu.'

For the first time the concierge looked directly at her instead of addressing that distant spot beyond her shoulder.

*'Vous êtes une showgirl?'*

She relaxed. Everyone loved a showgirl. It was like carrying a great big shiny key to the city.

*'Oui, m'sieur.'*

The concierge leaned closer. 'Is it true, then? The barbarian is at the gate?'

What gate? It took Gigi a moment to catch on. She'd forgotten in the other girls' excitement that most of Paris shared her misgivings about the 'foreign usurper'. Giving it her best, *I'm as distressed as you are* look, she manufactured a theatrical sigh. 'I'm afraid so.'

*'Dieu sauver la France!'* He crossed himself.

Gigi tried not to let her surprise show. Given *she* was the one with her job at risk, it was odd how personally the Parisian in the street was taking the new ownership of L'Oiseau Bleu.

Perhaps if those same people transformed their outrage into actually coming to a show and pushing up box office receipts they'd have a chance of survival. Blaming the newcomer on the scene—even if he *was* a Russian oligarch with questionable intentions—didn't seem quite fair.

But she didn't hesitate to press her advantage—it was one of the few things she had learned from her father that she could use.

'Quite. Now, can I have that room number?'

The concierge looked most sympathetic. *'Non,'* he said.

Gigi didn't push it. She turned around, her shoulders sinking, and as she wondered if she should leave a message for him, which would probably go unread, everything changed.

Khaled Kitaev had just entered the lobby.

He was looking at his phone, which gave her the moment

she needed to pull herself together, although the aggression in his body language should have had her second-guessing her decision even to try this.

*Be brave, Gigi*, she lectured herself. *You've had more auditions than hot meals. It's just another audition...* Only this was possibly her last chance, and it could all go so horribly wrong.

As he strode towards her she took in the unruly dark hair, the beard that framed his beautiful face and enhanced that whole macho thing he was into.

It was working. Women's heads were turning as if they were EMF devices, picking up on his frequency, and not a few men were looking him up and down as they reconsidered the suits they'd so carefully dressed in this morning.

It took a lot of machismo and confidence to render a pair of trainers, sweat pants and a long grey T-shirt with some indecipherable Cyrillic lettering on it stylish against the luxury of the hotel's interior and its swish inhabitants, but Khaled Kitaev pulled it off. Everyone else just looked wrong.

He was coming right for her.

There was no hiding now.

*Think about what you're going to say. Be polite. Be professional.*

She took some deep calming breaths.

*Have some of your material ready. But don't shove it at him. Be friendly, but formal.*

She wasn't sure how she'd manage friendly but formal.

He looked up from his phone and at the concierge. All the nearby hotel staff had leapt to attention. He lowered the phone long enough to ask for two brand-new laptops to be sent up to his suite.

'Landslide?' he growled into the phone. 'There's one a day in that part of the world. Get a bulldozer in there and clear the damn thing.'

Gigi observed this exchange with pulse-raised interest, flinching a little as she watched his hand flatten to its full wingspan dimensions on the desk, so close to her she could have reached out and touched it. But she was glad she didn't when he fired some aggressive Russian into the ear of whoever was on the other end of his call. Maybe now wasn't a good time…

Khaled slammed his hand against the nearest solid surface. He couldn't believe it. *Another* meeting pushed back by the village council. *Another* surveyor's report held up because of a landslide.

He wouldn't put it past the clan elders to plant a stick of dynamite into the escarpment and bring down half the mountain onto the highway below just to damn well spite him. Two years and he was no closer to putting that road in.

No road—no resort.

How many people had he sent into the gorge to explain the benefits a new infrastructure would bring? *Any* infrastructure in a corner of the world where the men still herded sheep on horseback. Always there was the same response: initial agreement, new contracts drawn up and then at the last minute something would interfere.

When he had spoken with the clan council they had taken him to task about his Russian investors and the lack of consultation. Khaled had stood, arms folded, at the back of the low dark room that served as a community hall in the town and refused to react or engage.

All he had seen was the memory of his stepfather's eyes, narrow like slits, as he beat him with a piece of horse tack as if that would make him less another man's son.

Unable to withstand the brutality of the memory, without a word Khaled had walked out into the bright daylight, jumped into his truck and driven out of the valley. His last communication with the council was when he was much further north, flying over the Pechora Sea, inspecting a Kitaev oil platform, and a message had been sent to him via his lawyers.

*Where is your home? Where is your wife? Where are your children? When you have these things come to us in the proper way and we will talk.*

In other words, *Respect our customs and we'll see it your way.*

Customs… He was a modern man, and he had made his fortune in a modern world—he wasn't entering into that kind of old-world game-playing…

He turned away from the desk, snapping his phone closed, catching his elbow on someone's round, firm…

'Ow!'

He looked down and golden-lashed blue eyes turned up to his like searchlights, complete with a little scowl that brought her fine coppery brows together and formed a knot.

'You…' he said, clearing his throat.

'Yes, me!' Her low-pitched, softly accented voice was like Irish whisky—unexpected in a girl so slight and young. She had one hand clamped over her breast and was tenderly massaging the area, her expression pained.

'Forgive me.' His gaze dipped to what little he could see, given her hand was stashed under her jacket.

When she'd pulled out that bit of libel yesterday she'd flashed a purple bra cup and the swell of a firm milk-pale breast marked on the gentle upper slope by a single dark brown freckle. It was a freckle he'd had on his mind ever since.

Only today she appeared to be wearing some kind of pink T-shirt, high-necked, completely unrevealing, along with jeans and a blue wool jacket.

She'd also ditched the pigtails, and her hair hung heavily over her shoulders—coppery red, long, thick and wavy… messy, if you got down to it. Sexy.

*Sexy* he didn't need. For one thing, he was signing her pay cheques. Ostensibly. Although he'd seen how much those girls were paid. He'd laid down more on a tie than on her monthly wage.

All the more reason to keep moving...

Which he did.

Gigi watched him walk away from her without another word, as if their encounter had never happened. She tried not to be offended. She'd pretty much expected it would take some effort. After all, she wasn't sexy Solange, offering who knew what? She was woman-on-a-mission Gigi, offering flyers and a presentation.

Not that he knew that. But she guessed he only needed a glance to work out the difference between them.

Nevertheless, she hurried after him, swinging her backpack forward over one shoulder and rummaging inside for the vintage-style flyers she'd brought to show him—evidence of how classy the Bluebird had once been and could be again.

He'd see that she was serious and had done her research, and he might sit down and talk to her.

She was right behind him when there was a whoosh of movement in the air beside her—and for the second time in as many days Gigi found herself on the floor, the stuffing knocked out of her.

# CHAPTER FOUR

A MALE VOICE GRUNTED, 'Do not move.'

Gigi didn't think she'd be moving. No, not moving at all. She was too stunned to do anything other than lie there, even once the knee resting on the base of her spine was gone and her arms, which had been pinned to her sides, were once more her own.

She only began to react when she was being hauled—not ungently—to her feet. She swayed as blood rushed back into her head and an arm came around her waist to support her. She staggered, and her nose and forehead banged against a hard male chest. She inhaled faint spicy aftershave and heat.

Gigi edged up her chin and her gaze locked on eyes so lustrously dark it was like being dropped into a hot, dark night.

The world shrank down to his thick, steady heartbeat and her short, rapid breaths.

He was speaking to her, but it was like being underwater. All she could make out was that no one was attacking her and the big male arms clamped around her felt like protection.

Which was when she spotted a gorilla—the same one who had knocked her down—turning out her backpack.

It was a replay of her worst memory.

Her limbs exploded and she desperately tried to free herself.

"That's mine! Give me back my things! You have no right to touch my things!'

She made a hopeless grab for it, but Khaled Kitaev had hold of her elbow.

'Calm down, *dushka*.'

She wasn't going to calm down! The last time she'd had her belongings confiscated she'd had handcuffs slapped on her wrists and spent a night in the cells, thanks to her dad.

She struggled, but his strength was all over hers. Gigi lashed out with her elbow and struck him in the chest. Unlike her own chest there was nothing soft and tender about it—instead there was considerable muscle and definition and she only jarred her shoulder.

'That's enough!'

She stopped flailing long enough for him to release her. She pushed her hair out of her eyes with hands that were shaking uncontrollably. So much for being professional. Both of them.

'Mr Kitaev, do we have a problem?'

The discreet enquiry was made by the concierge she had spoken to earlier. He materialised at her side, every inch the gatekeeper for the wealthy and influential. Gigi's insides turned to liquid.

Khaled saw the effect on Red. She looked as if he was about to throw her to the lions.

'*Nichevo*. No problem. A slight misunderstanding.'

'Yes, sir, these things can happen. But the young lady—'

'Mademoiselle Valente,' said Khaled smoothly, and her name was right there, given he'd just happened to take a look at her file last night, 'is my guest.'

'I see, sir.'

'My security team didn't recognise her and were over-zealous. I apologise for the inconvenience to your other guests.'

'Not at all, Mr Kitaev.' But the concierge continued to regard Red with interest.

The look on her face had been comic in its alarm and indecision as she followed this exchange, but now as they both turned their attention her way she visibly pulled herself together.

'That's right,' she said gamely. 'I'm here to speak to him.'

*Him* being the hotel's highest paying guest.

Khaled fully expected the staff to evaporate, but to

his credit the concierge lingered. 'Are you certain, *mademoiselle*?'

The hectic look on her face was ebbing away as she appeared to realise that the hotel management was offering her real assistance and not showing her the door.

She nodded slowly, and added, '*Merci beaucoup,*' with an almost comically sincere look on her face, even as her eyes kept zoning in on her backpack.

Khaled gave it a light shake.

What did she have in there? The Crown Jewels? A nuclear weapon? After her little display, neither would have truly surprised him.

'You're not hurt?' he asked as the hotel staff evaporated back into the luxurious fittings.

'No,' she huffed, looking around as if expecting another attack. 'No thanks to your lunatic friends.'

'Bodyguards.'

She blinked, clearly not familiar with the concept.

'They are employed to look to my safety.'

'Why?'

*Why...?* Khaled wasn't often asked this question. Usually people were calling him sir and getting out of his way. 'It is common in my line of business.'

'Hmm.' She didn't sound convinced. 'Yes, well, you need to put them on a leash.'

Struggling manfully with a desire to throw back his head and laugh, Khaled murmured, 'I apologise unreservedly. It was an unforgivable breach of your human rights.'

She eyed him suspiciously. 'You don't sound particularly sincere.'

Was she going to argue with him about this too?

'I guess you're having some fun at my expense,' she allowed slowly.

Unexpectedly he remembered the lack of support given to her by the other dancers yesterday, and the laughter that greeted her pronouncements.

'My papa used to say all I needed was a curly wig and a red nose and I'd have a new job.'

He frowned. 'Most fathers think their daughters are princesses.'

Gigi wondered if being seventeen years old and dancing onstage in a costume made of balloons she'd strategically popped with five other girls, until she was virtually down to her little yellow bikini, while her father systematically fleeced the audience had an attendant fairy tale.

'My father raised me to live in the real world,' she said uncomfortably, darting another glance at her backpack. Was he *ever* going to give it back?

Following her gaze, he proffered it. 'I believe this belongs to you?'

She was obviously trying not to appear too eager but she still snatched at it, and clearly couldn't help plastering it to her chest.

'So, does this happen to you all the time? Bodyguards leaping out and knocking people over?'

'You were coming towards me and you'd reached into your bag.'

She frowned. 'Why is that a problem?'

He made a trigger gesture with his hand.

Her frown deepened.

'A gun,' he clarified.

'A *gun*?' Her voice rose. 'They thought I had a *gun*!' This notion was clearly as foreign to her as the French language she was so deliciously butchering with her accent.

A passing couple stared at them and she shut up.

Khaled tried not to smile.

'I really don't see that there's anything funny about this,' she said tightly.

'*Nyet*—nothing funny.'

'I didn't come to shoot you—obviously. I came to speak to you about the cabaret.'

There was an awkward silence as he just looked at her.

She tried again.

'I know it's unorthodox, but I figured as we'd met…'

He folded his arms. 'I remember you lying on the floor.'

Gigi wondered whether, if she'd been lying on the floor right now, he would have stepped over her and kept going. Probably.

She reviewed her options. She'd gone over it with Lulu last night and decided her best hope of success was to bring all the material she'd compiled on the cabaret's star-studded history and her ideas for its future and lay it before him.

Be confident. Make an appeal to his better nature and leave any mention of Solange out of it. The last had been Lulu's firm instruction.

*'Do not mention Solange.'*

Well, she hadn't. But maybe she hadn't been plain enough.

'It's handy that you remember me,' she said, overly bright. 'You see, I'm spokesperson for the troupe.

'You don't say?' He glanced at his watch.

She was already losing him.

For the first time Gigi noticed that he looked a bit more disreputable than she remembered him being yesterday, and it was only now she fully focussed on the T-shirt, running shoes and the pair of pricey sweats and what they represented.

'Are you on your way to do some exercise?' she asked, a little desperately.

*'Da,'* he said with enviable cool, his gaze flicking down her body. 'Are you here to help me out with that?'

'Well, I'm hardly dressed for it.' But she was talking to air, because he was gone, heading for the doors. He did that a lot.

Hitching her backpack, Gigi took off after him.

'The thing is,' she said, trying to keep up and not draw attention to herself, 'and I know this is completely out of order, and you have every right to tell me to get lost, Mr Kitaev, but we're all really concerned about our jobs. I thought if I could show you a few things you might understand where we're coming from.'

'What exactly have you got to show me?' He didn't break stride.

Well, the flyers and her presentation—but she needed a table for that and he was on the move.

Boy, was he on the move.

'Lots,' she said, mustering all the enthusiasm possible, given the situation. Only to bang straight into his back as he ground to a halt.

She looked up and swallowed. Hard. He was looking down at her in a way that made her want to pull a blanket around herself. A *thick* blanket. Possibly fire retardant.

*Oh, boy.*

'Tell you what, Red. Can I call you Red?'

*Red? Really?* 'Okay…sure.'

'You talk; I'll listen—if you can keep up.'

'Keep up with what?' she asked.

'Can you run in those?'

Gigi glanced at her feet, baffled. 'I guess so.'

But when she looked up he was already heading out.

She trailed him onto the pavement, only to watch him power off across the road framed by those two gorillas.

'But I don't *want* to run,' she called after him, even as she began to do just that.

It wasn't easy, with her backpack whacking her on the back like an uncomfortable metronome. The avenue was busy mid-morning. Gigi almost collided with a couple holding hands and her darting sideward leap to avoid disaster landed her in a puddle. Dirty water smeared her jeans.

Apparently he'd meant what he said—and, as much as it made her job harder, she could respect that. People who said what they meant and did what they said could be trusted. She hoped it would translate into a forthright exchange. If she could catch him.

She came close on the corner, just as he turned onto the Avenue des Champs-Élysées.

'Mr Kitaev?' she hollered.

To her relief he slowed his pace.

'Can you keep the shouting out of my name down to a low roar?' he asked as she came alongside him.

'Sure. Sorry.'

'So you're the rebel in the ranks?'

She cast him a worriedly baffled look. 'Not exactly.'

'Yesterday yours was an unusual approach.'

'What approach? I didn't approach you yesterday.'

'The dive from that tank?'

What was he on about? 'I did *not* throw myself off the tank to get your attention.'

'Right…'

'Honestly, I wouldn't endanger my spinal column—I'm not stupid.'

'*Horosho.*'

Gigi didn't speak a word of Russian, but she got the sub-text. He didn't believe her.

Her temper broke like a wave. 'Listen, I don't need to create silly diversions to get a man's attention!'

He thrust a staying arm in front of her as he checked the traffic.

'A word of advice,' he said, scanning the road. 'Don't squeeze your eyes shut. Just let them lie closed naturally, otherwise they twitch. It gave you away.'

What was he talking about now? Irritating man, with his dazzlingly dark brown eyes, the long, thick coal-black lashes sweeping over them above the sharp, deadly planes of his high cheekbones. If you liked that sort of thing…

'I wasn't twitching. *When* was I twitching?'

He meant her fall from the tank. He couldn't possibly think… Good grief, she'd been virtually concussed!

'You were twitching. And ditch the T-shirts while you're

at it,' he said as his arm dropped away and he moved forward. 'Play to your assets.'

'What do you mean, my *assets*?'

He headed across the road.

Gigi's gaze dropped to her chest. He didn't mean what she thought he meant, did he?

'Hey!' she called, taking off after him. 'I really don't think you should be saying those kind of things to me!'

Although men had said worse. You had to have a thick skin in this business. But, really, if he was going to force her to run through the streets of Paris he could at least be *polite* to her! It wasn't easy, even in her trainers. To make matters worse she had blisters upon blisters on the soles of her feet, from dancing in brand-new four-inch stilettos last night. Her feet were killing her!

*He* should try doing double performances six days a week, forty weeks of the year for five years—in heels—and see how he liked being made to run on hard pavement.

She stumbled and narrowly avoided a fire hydrant, and then dodged around a small dog on a leash.

*Stupid Parisians and their dogs...*

When she caught up with him she panted, 'I'm just trying to represent the troupe!'

'Why? What do the troupe want?'

Gigi stared at him. The man had barely broken a sweat. It was so unfair.

'An opportunity—a chance to prove themselves. A pay-rise!'

She tacked on the last because really, at this point, she might as well go for gold. She wanted to add, *And not to service you sexually!* But shouting that in the street was further than she was prepared to go.

She was really hoping she wouldn't have to bring Solange up—and not just because it was bound to antagonise him. Frankly, it was embarrassing. But, given he hadn't showed at the cabaret last night, she couldn't imagine him showing tonight and wondered how he'd manage to hook up with Solange after all. Not that he'd necessarily ever intended to.

It had already crossed her mind that Solange might be lying. It wouldn't be the first time.

A knot in her chest Gigi hadn't known was there loosened a bit.

Not that she'd spent a lot of time thinking about it... She'd just discussed it a little with Lulu last night over crêpes, as they'd walked home up the hill to their flat behind Sacré-Coeur.

The things other girls did to get ahead in the business... The things they would never do... The things they might be prepared to compromise on should they be pushed to the edge...

It had ended in Lulu posing the question, 'So, if your grandma needed a kidney transplant and the *only* way to get it was to sleep with him, would you do it?'

Gigi had pretended to consider it. 'I think I'd have to.'

Lulu had nodded. Then she'd looked at her with those big brown eyes and said solemnly, 'What if she *didn't* need a kidney transplant?'

Which was when they had both dissolved into giggles.

But in the light of day Gigi knew a better question was how would Solange approach this situation?

For one thing, she wouldn't be pounding the pavement after him, blisters bursting in her trainers. Not that Solange had the intelligence to understand that their jobs were at stake. No, all *she* saw was a sexy, famous man and she wanted her piece.

Had she *had* her piece?

Gigi eyed his long broad back, the muscles shifting as he kept up a powerful driving pace. It didn't take much imagination to envisage all that effortless masculine grace and power translating itself into something more intimate, something that required skill and rhythm, something—

Something she shouldn't even be thinking about!

What was wrong with her? His sex life wasn't her business, she told herself sternly, although she was fast losing sight of exactly what *was* her business with him.

Exhaling, she came to a stop. This was useless. He wasn't listening to her. He was amusing himself and she'd turned herself into the punchline of his joke. Nothing new there.

Her shoulders slumped. There didn't seem much point in pursuing this.

Which was when she realised he'd turned back. He moved like some predatory king of the beasts, deceptively at ease as he padded lightly but with a natural authority through the crowds towards her, and the female in her fluttered responsively.

The way he was looking at her as he approached, she could have been the only woman on the street.

Stupid female—she was going to get torn apart if she wasn't careful.

He circled her, forcing her to turn, and turn again, as he looked her up and down.

'What exactly are you going to do for this pay-rise, Red?'

'Dance,' she responded with a little frown.

'Right.' He winked at her and took off again, and she found herself hurrying after him.

This time he kept it to a slow lope, his attention on her. Maybe at last she could get him to listen.

'And when do you take your clothes off?'

'Pardon?' she squeaked.

'That's the bit I'm interested in, Red. I assume I get to see this private dance if I take you back to the hotel?'

Gigi almost hit a traffic sign. She put out her hands to grab the pole.

'What are you talking about?'

'Women throw themselves at me all the time. Why would you be any different?'

'I'm not here for *that*,' she said impatiently, trying to work out what he meant by 'private dance'.

'"That" is sex, and I can get it anywhere. You'll have to up the ante, Red.'

She almost stumbled over her feet. Sex? She wasn't offering him *sex*! Who had said anything about sex?

But he was getting away, and it shot through Gigi, hot and scalding, that this might be the last thing they ever discussed and he was going to go away thinking she was... well, *Solange*!

Her legs stopped working and she just stood there, watching his lean muscular form pound a little further into the distance. Frustrated beyond belief.

'I am *not* here to have sex with you!' she hollered after him.

# CHAPTER FIVE

PASSERS-BY ALMOST got whiplash, reacting to her announcement, but Gigi told herself it wasn't that bad. What stank was the fact that this awful, sexist, conceited man thought she had so little respect for herself she'd offer up her body... for what? A pay-rise?

He'd ground to a dangerously ominous halt and now came loping back towards her, his expression enough to send all her 'flee and survive' instincts into overdrive.

'What is this?' he growled.

'I could ask you the same question.' Her voice only shook a little bit. 'Is this how you got your—your grubby hands on L'Oiseau Bleu? By goading Ahmed el Hammoud until he buckled and...and put us in the pot?'

'Interesting turn of phrase.' His gaze narrowed, assessing. 'Know him well, do you, Red?'

*Do not rise to the bait*, she told herself. *He's doing this to work you up into a frenzy so you'll go away.*

'Even more interesting,' he continued conversationally— as if he *wasn't* crowding her and leaving only a hand span of space between them, as if the hot, hard reality of him *wasn't* pushing her on the back foot. 'Now that I've seen the place I know why it was "in the pot", as you put it. I should have folded.'

'Really?' Her voice came out all high and airless. 'I don't think you'd fold for anyone or anything. I think you like to win, Mr Kitaev, and that means someone has to lose. I don't intend for that to be our fate.'

He was looking at her as if she truly interested him for the first time.

'And what exactly are you going to do, Miss Valente?'

'Fight you.'

Khaled almost smiled.

'Go ahead.' He thought of the people lining up to do just that, half a world away. 'Take your best shot.'

'I will,' she volleyed back. 'Solange Delon!'

She said this as if they were magic words. Clearly it was meant to mean something to him.

'Solange Delon…' she said again, but this time with less confidence, given the lack of a response. 'You asked her to come for drinks. With you. Tonight.'

Nothing.

Gigi could feel the ground shifting under her feet. Somehow she'd got something wrong…

A faint smile began to tug at the firm, sensual line of his mouth.

Gigi's temper quivered. He had no right to smile like that. Not when he didn't even have the decency to own up to it. If there was anything to own up to…

'I just don't think it's right,' she proffered into his continuing silence. 'Picking up a showgirl like one of those plastic Eiffel Towers you buy at a kiosk outside the metro—a souvenir of your trip.'

'Is that what you think, Gigi?' His tone was deceptively soft. 'Or is that what you've read?'

Taken aback, Gigi hesitated.

Well, *everyone* had read it. The marauding Russian, grabbing whatever he could get—cultural artefacts, real estate, women.

She had an odd little visual of him as a cartoonish King Kong, pushing a fistful of showgirls into his open mouth, legs everywhere.

Despite everything, a little part of her wanted to smile.

'I suppose you're going to say it's not true?' she prompted into the tense silence.

He didn't respond.

'To be fair, I guess some of it is exaggeration,' she allowed tightly, knowing she was losing ground fast.

He gave her an unamused half-smile. 'Possibly.'

She reddened.

This wasn't where she'd intended to take things today—she was supposed to be professional.

'Like I said, women throw themselves at me all the time.'

'I guess you can't help being beautiful,' she said grudgingly, then closed her eyes briefly. *Don't tell him he's beautiful, eejit.*

'I was going to say that money has an odd effect on people.' He was watching her as if she fascinated him. 'But if you're going to throw compliments at me, Gigi, you could try aiming at something I might respond to.' His dark Russian accent had a lazy inflection, as if he was enjoying this. 'Most men aren't interested in being told they're beautiful.'

'I'm speaking objectively,' she said stiffly. 'Obviously you're good-looking…'

'Downgraded from beautiful? Keep going.'

She flushed. 'Look, I'm not going to stand here and discuss your looks.'

'You're attracted to me.'

Gigi went rigid. 'I am not! You're nothing like my type.'

'What *is* your type?'

'Sensitive, caring, an animal-lover, good to his mum…' Gigi wasn't sure how they'd got on to this topic, but she did have a list if he wanted to hear it.

'Gay?'

Gigi almost choked. She put her hands on her hips. 'You sound like the stereotype of a homophobic Russian he-man.'

He smiled. 'I'm not homophobic,' he said comfortably, 'and I'm fast revising my opinion of *you*, Red.

'Oh, and what opinion is that?'

'You're not here to have sex with me—you're going to pester me into giving you whatever it is you want.'

Gigi turned pink and told herself she'd rather be a pest than have him think she was trading sexual favours for… well, favours. Only she wasn't making a nuisance of herself, was she?

'You asked me what my type was,' she defended herself. 'And I'm sorry if I'm being a nuisance, but you asked me to run with you!'

'You need a new type.'

He was smiling openly at her now, but instead of feeling irritated she felt her heart pounding in her chest. She wished it would stop—it was most distracting. He should stop smiling too.

He was right. She did need a new type.

But it wasn't going to be him.

Not that he was offering. Apparently she was a pest. Gigi tried not to mind that too much. Besides, gorgeous Russian gazillionaires didn't date jobbing dancers.

Lead dancers at the Lido, maybe. Not chorus girls at L'Oiseau Bleu.

She worried at her lower lip. *Was* she being a pest? There was something so certain and old-fashioned about his masculinity that everything he said had weight to it.

She hadn't had much male certainty in her life. The men she knew were for the most part equivocal and slippery. Witness her dad—and more latterly the Danton brothers, who had effectively stuffed up the only home she'd truly ever had since her mother's death.

Gigi took a breath. Now was not the time to think about what made her want to howl. It was the time to do something about it.

'Look,' she said, instinctively reaching out to touch his arm. 'Let's just forget you said what you said, and you forget I said what I said, and we'll start again.'

Even to her own ears it sounded lame, but right now it was all she had.

He was looking at her hand and she moved to snatch it back, but he caught her fingers between his.

Her eyes jerked up to his, but before she could ask him what he thought he was doing a shower of gravel spattered at their feet, sending Gigi's confused thoughts flying as she followed its source to two boys who were old enough to know better.

A woman who was obviously their mother was on one of the culprits in an instant, clipping him behind the ear as she took hold of the smallest boy's arm none too gently.

*'Quittez notre cabaret tout seul!'* she said in a tense, tight voice with a sideward glare at Kitaev. *'Barbare!'* she spat.

*Leave our cabaret alone! Barbarian!*

A young couple had stopped, and the girl pulled out her phone to take a picture.

An older man said, 'Why don't you go back to London, where you belong?'

Gigi would have seen more, but Kitaev had stepped in front of her, effectively blocking her view.

For a moment Gigi was confused. Was he *shielding* her? She stared up at his broad back and felt quite odd, because no man had ever looked to her welfare before, and that it should be this man was, well…confusing.

He didn't even like her.

But she never could stand bullies.

*If you can't take the criticism, Gigi, you shouldn't be on the stage.*

Fair enough, but her two-faced bully of a father's critiques stayed with her to this day: too freckly, too red, too skinny, too stupid, too much trouble.

She'd learned to blank her expression and keep going. She hadn't had much choice.

Kitaev appeared to be doing the same.

Taking it.

Well, *she* didn't have to.

She scooted around him. 'Hey! Who do you think you are—talking to people you don't even know like that?'

In disbelief Khaled watched Gigi walk up to the woman clutching at the necks of her boys' T-shirts.

'No wonder your children have no manners if this is how *you* behave—and *you*, sir—' she gestured to the older gentleman '—you should get your facts right. He doesn't even live in London! None of you have seen what he's going to do with the cabaret. You're just condemning him out of hand. All of you!'

Given Red's opinion of him, this was interesting.

'Why don't you wait and see before passing judgement? He might just surprise you.'

On the contrary—he would be doing pretty much what they expected. Offloading it to the next buyer, charity or scrapheap. Because he wasn't invested in this heritage crap and this much aggravation wasn't worth the trouble.

'Besides, if people like you would buy a ticket to the show once in a while we wouldn't be in so much trouble in the first place!' Gigi put her hands on her hips, staring them all down.

She should have been funny to watch, and she was, but he also wanted to give her a shake. Why was she bothering? Why was she paying any attention to them? These people's opinions meant nothing. They could and would change with tomorrow's new headlines. Given what he'd said to her, he wasn't even worth her spirited defence.

'Who do you think you are?' demanded the woman accusingly.

It was the moment Gigi didn't know she had been waiting for. She drew herself up to her full five feet eleven inches and opened her mouth…

Khaled said something roughly in Russian.

'That's it,' he said in English. He grabbed her hand. 'Show's over.'

To Gigi's astonishment he began to drag her away.

'Gigi Valente,' she called a little desperately over her shoulder. 'I'm a showgirl at L'Oiseau Bleu. Best cabaret revue in town!'

He jerked her roughly to his side.

'Hey, what are you *doing*?' she snapped at him.

'I could ask you the same thing.'

'I'm trying to promote the cabaret.'

Khaled said a rude word. In English.

He scanned over his shoulder and his features tightened.

Gigi followed his example. People were taking more photographs of them with their phones.

'Do not turn around,' he instructed, 'and do not respond.'

'Fair enough,' Gigi replied, suddenly uncertain as to what was going on, and very aware that they were holding hands.

He glared down at her. 'I cannot *believe* you gave them your name.'

Gigi blinked, her thoughts still on their linked hands. 'Why wouldn't I?' Then the other shoe dropped. 'Oh, crap.'

He eyed her and Gigi frowned. 'What? You think I did it on purpose?'

*'Nyet,'* he shot back. 'I think you did it the same way you appear to do everything, Gigi—without a firm grasp on the reality of the situation.'

She firmed her mouth. He was referring to her accusations earlier. Accusations she still hadn't apologised for.

Someone else called out, *'Barbare!'*

Gigi shuddered at the viciousness of it. 'What is *wrong* with people?'

'Your cabaret has become a catalyst for public opinion, as you well know, and I'm newsworthy.'

Gigi hadn't been aware that public opinion could be this scary. She yelped as flashes went off in her face and instinctively turned away. Khaled tugged her into the shelter of his body.

'Paparazzi' was the only word she understood in the short volley of Russian invective he released. Although her ability to concentrate was somewhat impaired by being pressed up against him. He was incredibly hard and big and honed, and she was inhaling him like an addict. His scent was the faint spice of aftershave, the musk of his skin and fresh male sweat. It was a heady combination and, given his hand had settled solidly at the base of her spine, she guessed he wanted her to stay where she was.

As suddenly as they'd arrived the photographers were gone, but neither of them shifted.

He was making her very much aware that she was a woman.

'We need to move,' he informed her, his breath brushing her cheek, but he didn't.

Was he feeling it too? Gigi became excessively conscious of the hard muscles of his thighs against hers and how well their bodies fitted together. Warmth began to pool in her loins, her nipples tightened, and all of a sudden she became aware that she wasn't the only one with a problem.

As much as she tried to remind herself that he was a man, and their bodies were smushed together, and it might very well be an involuntary biological function, there was still a part of her that had been hammered by his comment about her being a pest, and her self-confidence staggered to its feet and bloomed a little at this rather impressive confirmation that he wasn't as immune to her as he pretended. *Not so much a nuisance now*, she wanted to say to him.

Which probably shouldn't be a woman's first reaction when she was cosied up in his arms.

She looked up. He was already looking down.

Gigi's breathing quickened. They were so close she could see the golden striations in his dark eyes and something of who he actually *was* as opposed to who she'd imagined him to be. A highly intelligent man who was perhaps insightful enough to see some worth in their cabaret. And perhaps if he recognised that he'd have second thoughts about throwing them to the wolves.

Only the longer they stood there the more uncomfortably aware she was that he could possibly be seeing a little more in her than she would be happy for him—or anyone—to know.

Instinctively she shied away and pulled back.

He unexpectedly took hold of her hand again, curling his fingers around hers. She tried to tug herself free, because it all felt far too intimate, but he had started walking, pulling her along with him.

'What are we doing? What's going on now?'

'We're moving,' he supplied gruffly.

She got that part. Where were they moving *to*?

He produced a mobile phone from his back pocket, thumbed a few buttons and released some Russian to whoever was on the other end.

'Thanks to your big mouth we're both going to be all over the internet,' he shared calmly as he re-pocketed the phone.

'What? What are you talking about?'

But she knew. It sank through her like a stone. She'd stuffed up.

From out of nowhere a group of men swarmed.

Kitaev's arm came around her again. 'It's all right—its Security,' he shared with that same masculine certainty that made her hold on to him as she was hustled in a phalanx towards a smoke-windowed limo that had also come out of nowhere and pulled to the kerb.

Without a word he pushed her forward into the car. She scrambled across the luxury seating, not really being given much choice in the matter.

'I've had some security issues since I arrived in Paris,' he informed her as the car shot forward.

'Issues?' she parroted weakly.

'The usual. Breaches of my privacy, photographers— as you've just seen—approaches from people with axes to grind.'

Gigi pursed her lips and remained silent on that one.

His attention returned to the traffic. 'The truth, if you're interested in it, is that I own some property in the South of France and several companies with holdings in and around Paris. There is no grand plan. L'Oiseau Bleu was an unexpected windfall that has turned into something of a catalyst for all the xenophobic feeling in this city.'

He was watching her broodingly.

'And, for your personal information, Gigi, Solange Delon was publicity. I have a PR team who thought a photograph of me with a French showgirl in full rig and the Danton brothers would put a cap on all the negative publicity doing the rounds.'

And just like that Gigi felt about an inch tall.

'Oh…' she said in a small voice.

He gave her an impatient look. 'Think about it—would I be prowling after showgirls with public opinion being what it is?'

'I guess not.'

The silence between them simmered with the unspoken question—given 'public opinion'—as to why he'd taken her with him on that run and courted the risk of exposure.

'Where are we going?' she voiced, not sure of her footing around him any more.

'My hotel,' he said.

# CHAPTER SIX

'I'M SORRY ABOUT all the trouble,' Gigi said awkwardly, struggling out of her seat belt. 'I misjudged everything.'

Yes, she had, Khaled thought, but so had he. The chemistry between them was very strong. It was going to complicate things.

Thankfully the rear entrance to the Plaza Athénée was the scene not of a paparazzi scrum but just a couple of vans making deliveries.

If they were discreet there shouldn't be a problem getting inside and upstairs.

He noticed she was out of the car at lightning speed but slow in approaching the service entrance. She clearly didn't want to go inside.

It raised his ire.

'Keep moving.' He put his hand in the centre of her back and gave her a gentle push forward, because hanging around out here was just inviting trouble.

They were in the middle of the busy lobby when she unexpectedly decided to drop down onto one knee.

He almost tripped over her.

'What the hell are you doing?'

She pushed back her unruly fringe and looked up a bit furtively. 'Don't worry about me—you go on, I'll find my own way home.'

Frustration warred with something else. He ignored the something else and very nearly hauled her to her feet—only they were once more in public, and he'd had enough scenes with this woman to sell tickets.

Mademoiselle Valente was going to sit down in the reception room of his suite while he dealt with this via telephone to his lawyer and Jacques Danton. He frowned down at her—only to encounter her behind as she crouched over, delineated in skin-tight denim like a perfect peach. His thoughts simmered… *Da*, either a phone call or he'd peel down those jeans and have her up against that wall over there. Whichever came first.

His attention slid from her peachy bottom to what it was holding them up—only to discover she had one heel wedged out of her trainer and appeared to be… Was she bleeding?

To Gigi's complete astonishment her new boss hunkered down beside her and had her laces loosened before she could react.

'Um…what are you doing?'

Although it was pretty clear what he was doing. He was lifting her left foot in his big capable hands and attempting to slide her shoe off.

She hissed at the dragging contact, and then realised he'd have her sock off in a moment.

*He'd have her sock off!*

'Hey—no, stop that!' She toppled back onto her backside and scuttled across the marble floor, one shoe on, one shoe off, aware that she was attracting attention, which was something neither of them wanted at this point, but he couldn't hang that one on her. *He* was the guy with the foot fetish!

He eyed her with a mixture of amusement and exasperation. 'I'm not attacking you, *zhenshchina*.'

'I didn't say you were.' She eyed him warily.

He stood up, all shoulders and amused appraisal as he looked her over.

'Just you stay there, and I'll stay here, and we'll keep our hands and feet to ourselves,' she said hastily.

There was no way she was showing this beautiful god of a man her *feet*!

No one saw her feet. Not even Lulu.

Other hotel patrons were stopping to stare at the one-shoed girl on the floor.

Gigi could feel heat creeping into her cheeks.

She tried to shove her foot back into her shoe, but it

had swelled up and it was like trying to shoehorn a balloon in there.

Giving up, she clambered to her feet, trainer in hand.

People were looking. Well, let them look.

She turned in the other direction and had limped a few paces to the doors when a big hand closed around her elbow and his breath brushed her ear.

'The lifts are this way, *kotyonok*.'

Confused, Gigi shivered at the unfamiliar word and the intimate contact.

He turned her in the direction of the lifts.

'The exit is over there,' she protested, not sure why he was prolonging the agony or why she didn't dig her heels in. Other than the fact that they hurt and two hundred plus pounds of arrogance and muscle was steering her into the lift. She gave it one last try. 'Mr Kitaev, I don't think this is such a hot idea.'

'Probably not—and we've established its Khaled.'

His hand slipped from her elbow to the small of her back and rested there, and she stopped struggling.

'Are those photos really going to end up on the internet?' she asked in a strangled voice as the lift doors closed.

'Undoubtedly.'

Gigi noticed he hadn't removed his hand from her back. She moistened her lower lip and tried to conjure up the will to tell him to take his hands off her. Her will was weak.

'Those pictures…will people put derogatory captions to them?'

'Possibly.'

She tried not to sag visibly.

'Could you ring me or something and let me know when they are up? I can give you my number.' *Subtle, Gisele.* She moistened her lips. 'Or I guess you could contact me at the cabaret,' she added awkwardly, wondering if he thought offering up her number smacked of a bit too much intimacy.

His hand shifted lightly on her back to curl around her waist.

Okay, maybe not. Intimacy apparently wasn't a problem…

'What time is tonight's performance?' he asked.

'Hmm?' Gigi wrenched her mind away from his hand on her waist. 'Eight o'clock.' Was he going to turn up? Her spirits lifted. She looked up at his ridiculously masculine profile. Had she actually got through to him?

'By the time you go onstage, Gigi, everyone in Paris will have seen them.'

Her hopes plummeted. 'Oh…'

'Precisely.'

The doors slid open and she waited, not sure what they were doing here. Khaled slid the rest of his arm around her waist and the other beneath her, lifting her effortlessly into his arms.

She was forced to grapple with his big, incredibly solid shoulders and hang on.

'What are you doing?' she thought she should ask.

'Looking after you.'

Gigi's mouth opened and shut. She was, after all, twenty-five years old and had been looking after herself for the past several years with some success. Still, she'd never actually been carried in a man's arms before, and like most women she'd harboured a bit of a fantasy about it…

He was moving, forcing her to hook her arms a bit more securely around his neck, effectively plastering her breasts to his chest. Gigi told herself it was purely a matter of necessity.

'You really don't have to do this,' she felt obliged to say.

'I am aware of that.'

He opened glass doors into the entrance room to his suite and luxury wrapped around them.

'Nice,' she said inadequately.

This earned her a brief, 'Not my taste.'

'Why are you staying here, then?'

'I needed an entire floor over the weekend for security reasons and this hotel provided that.'

He carried her through a very luxurious living area, down a hall and into a bedroom. It contained a very big bed.

Gigi wondered for the first time if she oughtn't to tell him he shouldn't confuse her with Solange?

Not that there had ever *been* anything with Solange…according to him. She was reserving judgement on that.

But still, she didn't bounce on beds with men she'd only just met.

'You could fit ten people on that mattress,' she pointed out in a high, airless voice not quite her own.

He didn't respond.

'I'm just imagining the troupe all laid out like sardines in a can,' she felt obliged to explain.

He looked at her as if she'd said something ridiculous, but she told herself he wasn't a woman in a man's hotel room, being carried around like luggage.

Maybe she should make it clear. 'I'm just saying…don't get any ideas.'

'About these other girls?'

Gigi bit her lip. She wanted to say, *About me*, but clearly he wasn't having any ideas. She was the one entertaining a fantasy.

'I'm just saying,' she mumbled, embarrassed. 'Anyway, in practice it wouldn't work. There'd be fights.'

He gave a gruff snort.

Gigi craned her head over his shoulder but, nope, he showed no interest in the bed. He didn't even break stride.

*He definitely hadn't confused her with Solange.*

He dumped her on the bathroom vanity.

Gigi was greeted with her reflection, which drove any thoughts of being confused with sexy girls who dated movie stars out of her head. She looked *awful*.

All of her freckles had become heat blotches and swarmed together like angry little ants at a picnic.

He looked—well, hot and sexy. Although all that brooding intensity and muscled capability was currently being channelled into running a tap.

Which was odd.

A sudden unreasoning panic gripped her. Had he brought her back here to punish her for the photographers? Was this some kind of set-up? If he wasn't bent on seduction why else would he bring her up here?

He took hold of her feet.

'Wow. Okay—stop there.' She clamped her hands over his, eyeing him warily. 'I'll deal with the wear and tear. There's nothing to see here.'

'What's the problem?' His dark eyes flickered over her face. 'I doubt you've got anything I haven't seen before.'

Had he just glanced at her chest when he said that?

Gigi felt her nipples tingle inside the soft cups of her sweater girl bra.

Uh-oh. This was *not* good.

Her relationships with men thus far had been of the duck and weave variety. As far as Khaled was concerned she was pretty much a sitting duck.

She was so distracted by her thoughts that she didn't immediately catch him working her socks off. As her cracked heels appeared she yelped, dragged back her feet like pulling up a drawbridge and wedged herself in hard against the mirror.

He said something in Russian and looked her up and down, as if she were a problem he had to solve.

But she didn't care. If there was anything seriously unsexy about her it was her feet. It was where all the damage and scarring almost twenty years of dance had wrought was so violently on display. It was like a confession. Nothing had been easy and she had paid a price, and right now she wasn't confessing to *him*!

'What is the problem now?'

His Russian accent was heavier, and that just upped the sexy quotient—which wasn't helping.

And what did he mean *now*? As if she'd been causing problems left right and centre…? He was a fully paid-up member of their trouble brigade. She wasn't wearing total responsibility for the disasters of this morning.

'There is no problem,' she grumbled. 'I just want to look after this myself.'

He looked sceptical.

'I didn't ask to be brought up here, you know. I didn't ask for all this attention.'

He gave her a long, searching look that implied she had. Which was so unfair!

Gigi wriggled uncomfortably. His gaze dropped lower and caught on something.

What now? Gigi looked down. She'd been aware that her midriff was bare, her T-shirt having worked its way up in all the manhandling, but she hadn't given any thought to the fact that because her jeans were low-riders she was showing off quite a lot of skin—nor to the fact that the indent of her belly button rose high above them, exposing her piercing.

Before she could even think to pull her T-shirt down he brushed his knuckles over her navel and set the miniature silver bell tinkling.

'It's a bell,' she said. Cringed. Could she sound more stupid?

He did it again, his touch unbearably gentle. Suggestive of how he would be in another even more intimate situation.

Gigi bit her lip.

Lifted her eyes to his.

He was smiling at her. 'I wondered what that sound was.' His accent had thickened.

Her breathing grew rapid and shallow in response.

She was now throbbing ever so subtly between her legs. All he had to do was touch her again for a little longer and that throbbing was going to detonate.

The problem was it also drew her attention to the way she was angled against him, thighs apart, virtually inviting him into heaven.

She could hear Lulu's lecture: *'There are really only two situations in a woman's life when she should be displayed at this angle to a man, and if that man isn't her significant other he should be her gynaecologist.'*

Denim or no, Gigi felt self-conscious, and she brought her knees down fast—only now he was standing between them and she was stuck...unless he moved.

He moved. Almost nonchalantly, but she wasn't fooled. And with the flats of his hands on the bench on either side of her she was trapped.

*This was his move. He was making a move on her.*

Gigi's heart began to flutter like crazy, because he was so close, and he smelt so good, and the energy pulsing between them was like jungle drums in her blood.

She swallowed, unable to break the clasp of his gaze.

Sweet heaven, she had to find a way off this bench. Because so much more than a full reveal of her manky feet was barrelling towards them, and she really didn't want to be the showgirl who gave it up on a bathroom vanity to the man who might or might not be instrumental in taking away the livelihoods of the Bluebirds.

And—oh, God—he was *smiling* at her.

'So what's the problem with your feet?'

This time his dark drawl sounded a lot less impatient, as if whatever the problem was he'd be willing to take the time to fix it.

Immediately her mind went to her other problem and how much time he might devote to *that...*

She cleared her strangled throat. 'There's no problem.'

He vibrated the bell with the tip of his thumb and she made a soft, inarticulate sound. He raised his knowing eyes to hers. The air between them pulled taut.

'Tinker Bell,' he said.

'Tinker Bell?' she echoed doubtfully.

'I read the book when I was a boy and I always had a thing for Tink—little nuisance that she was. Wendy didn't do it for me.'

Gigi narrowed her blue eyes at him and he wanted to laugh, because telling a woman she reminded you of a fairy from an old children's book was almost as crazy as what he was doing right now—sliding the pads of his middle and forefinger over the incredibly silken flesh just below her navel, stroking her there.

He only needed to slide his fingers a couple of inches south and he could snap the buttons on her jeans. Another couple of inches and he'd know exactly what she was wearing under the denim. Another couple and sweet, perfect nirvana.

'Stop that,' she croaked, nipping at her lower lip.

He drew back his hand into a tight fist and exhaled roughly.

She was right.

He exhaled. 'So what about these feet?'

Her mouth dropped open slightly but he had already slid his hands under her soles and brought them up onto the bench.

She didn't fight him this time, but drew up her knees, eyes squeezed shut, like a woman about to endure a root canal at the dentist. It would have been funny had he not been so deeply, unambiguously aroused. So hard it hurt.

He deftly and carefully eased off her socks and tossed them into the wastepaper basket, never to be heard from again. It was a hard shove to his unambiguous impulse to bury himself in her soft, agile beauty to discover how torn up her feet were. He thoughtfully stroked his thumb along the welts criss-crossing the top of her feet. This damage seemed to be from long ago, the scars faded to white.

She had narrow, knobby-toed feet, shaped by the years she'd used them to sculpt the exquisitely formed female body sitting before him. The raised white welts, however, didn't make a lot of sense.

When he was a boy, living in the mountains, he'd learned to fix the wings of birds and splint broken legs for all kinds of small mammals. His stepfather had patiently taught him, along with lessons in how to track and perform a clean kill. Before everything had gone wrong. Before he'd understood that with every year he grew more and more like his father in both feature and reputation.

And being bullied from the age of eight had nothing to do with him being good with his fists and quick to take offence.

He rubbed the pads of his thumbs over her calluses and she made a sound of despair.

He understood shame. He understood what it could do to you if you didn't fight it.

'Relax,' he said, looking up, but her eyes were squeezed shut again, as if that way she could hide.

Her very real dismay loosened the loop of memory that had momentarily tethered him to the past and the tightness in him lifted. Something softer fought for room. He knew how to make her forget her shame, her fear.

He took one of her long, narrow feet in his hands and pressed his thumbs into the sensitive cord of muscle where her foot arched. Avoiding her broken blisters, he dragged his thumbs along the soles of her feet.

She moaned, and her blue eyes shot wide to meet his in honest bewilderment.

A deep satisfaction stirred within him.

He knew how to handle her. Because under her shock, like a promise, was a sensuality as natural and unadorned as she was.

She was a beautiful wild thing he had caught, and he could see a pulse hammering at the base of her throat. But he knew how to handle a frightened wild creature...

# CHAPTER SEVEN

'GOOD?'

'Don't...' she groaned. When clearly she meant *more*.

He pushed again.

She gave a helpless moan and gave herself up to the relief. He kept working until the tension lifted off her and her head rolled back and she moaned again—a deep, utterly unself-conscious sound. Incredibly sexy. He felt it deep in his groin.

'Good?'

She made another approving sound.

*Too good.* He was dangerously close to losing control himself.

'This might hurt.'

Gigi hissed like a kettle as he slid her feet into the water.

Tender, exposed new skin didn't mix with water—even Plaza Athénée water.

Gigi cracked open one eye and then the other.

She hadn't been able to look at him while he worked on her ugly feet, and now she scanned his face anxiously for signs of disgust. Only she could find none.

He made quick work of the caked blood with the dexterous use of a flannel, before letting out the water and wrapping her feet in the sleek hand towel folded beside the basin.

His practicality saved her from real embarrassment.

'Thank you,' she said, a little at a loss as to what else to say.

She wasn't used to being looked after, she realised, and that it should be by this tough, intimidating man confused her.

He had handled her feet with a care and generosity that had once again made her mind wander to what else he could do with those large hands... She eyed him almost shyly.

'You're a funny girl' was all he said.

Gigi's warm feelings faded.

She'd heard that before. 'Gigi the Clown'. Her papa's fail-safe response to her falls, tumbles and general efforts to get him to pay attention to her.

'Funny ha-ha, or funny crazy?' she asked, her voice a little raw.

He glanced up at her, as if she'd said something odd, his dark eyes making her tummy flip.

'Funny sexy,' he said, as if it was obvious, and she believed him. He set the towel aside.

*Sexy?* Offstage sexy? Really?

He opened what was clearly a first aid kit and took out cotton wool, antiseptic and plasters.

She bit her lip. 'They're not pretty,' she said in a low voice.

She *hated* this—hated it that she felt obliged to point it out, hated laying herself bare. She'd rather just strip off all her clothes and distract him with what she knew worked for an audience of seven hundred every night.

'You're a dancer. You've got a dancer's feet.'

'I know, but the other girls don't have half my damage.'

He raised his eyes to hers and she saw a lot of questions, most of which Gigi really didn't want to answer. But at the same time she didn't want to make them too much of a big deal.

'When I was in my early teens I was in a highwire act and it involved twisting cords around my feet. My papa said the scarring would go away, but it never did.'

'Your father? How was he involved?'

'He managed the circus—Valente's International.' She couldn't help lifting her chin a little. In spite of everything she remained proud of that heritage. 'Valente's had been a family concern for almost a hundred years when my father was bankrupted.'

'You were an acrobat?'

'Not a very good one,' she admitted. 'But it cured me of any residual fear of heights.'

Being driven up a rope with your father yelling that you were holding up rehearsal had effectively removed that fear.

'This is criminal,' he said, running his thumb over a welt. 'What kind of a father allows this to happen to his daughter?'

Her heart was pounding. His questions were grazing too close to some painful truths in her past.

'That's not for you to judge,' she answered stiffly. 'You weren't there. It's a hard life—you have to be seasoned to perform every night. The pain is a part of it.' She could hear her father's voice, lecturing her on this.

'Yet you're ashamed?'

Gigi hesitated. 'I—'

'You have nothing to be ashamed of, Red.'

'I know that,' she said quickly.

She stared at her feet, wondering why she was even telling him all this. 'Do you think you could stop calling me Red?' She looked up. 'I'm Gigi…or Gisele—'

'Gisele.'

Gigi's breath caught at the way his dark Russian accent turned her name into something quite beguiling.

Feminine.

'It's beautiful.'

His sincerity was a lot to take in. She blinked. Looked down and flexed her toes. 'Unlike my feet.'

He looked at her seriously for a moment from those dark assessing eyes, and then straightened and whisked his T-shirt up and off.

Gigi was almost blinded by all that gorgeous golden skin suddenly on display, pulled taut over slabs of muscle and not an ounce of fat that she could see.

His physique wasn't fine and lightweight, like the boys she danced with. Although lean, it was heavy with broad bones and muscle, his chest covered in fine dark hair. Gigi's fingers stirred restlessly with the urge to tangle her fingers in it.

He was most definitely a different breed from the men she was used to. It wasn't quite fanciful to say looking at him half stripped was like being introduced to the male sex for the first time.

'Take a look at this,' he said, in that deep gruff voice.

He presented her with his gloriously defined back, reaching up to place his fingertips above a nasty scar on his left shoulder. 'This one was caused by a bullet—it lodged in bone, shattered my scapula—and here…' He took her much smaller hand and put it on his lean waist, where something had left a seven-inch incision that had healed badly and left a raised white scar. 'Knife wound.'

He turned around.

'The discolouration here…' He pulled his waistband away from the line of his lean muscled hip, revealing a taut pelvic cradle and dark hair arrowing down to his sex and a splash of darker pigmentation where some of the skin, obviously puckered, indicated burns. He spoke calmly but in a low voice. 'That was an explosion on a road that was supposed to have been cleared.'

Gigi stroked her fingers over the old wound, viscerally aware that she was touching his bare flesh and that he felt hot and hard and male. But on a more conscious level she was horrified by the kind of life he'd led to cause these injuries. The raised skin she had under her fingertips was testimony to the poor medical care he'd received. Bullets? Knives?

'How did you get these?'

'National Service. Hunting.'

He was looking down at her now with a faint smile, the nature of which would have made a more virtuous girl uneasy. Although Gigi guessed she *was* that virtuous girl.

'I've got more, but that would involve removing more clothing than you're probably comfortable with.'

Gigi had opened her mouth to tell him she felt pretty comfortable with clothing being removed when she caught the glint in his eyes.

Her breath caught.

*He wanted her.*

Before she could properly react his arm was going around her, his hand was at the back of her head, delving gently into her hair, and she only had a moment to look into his eyes before he lowered his mouth to hers.

He just *took* that kiss.

The confidence of his move left her with nowhere to go, and Gigi found herself going under with the sensuous slide of his mouth over hers. She parted her lips, the masculine taste of him invading every pore of her being. Her lashes drifted down. He didn't hurry it—he *enjoyed* it.

She clutched at him, giving way to his superior technique. No one had ever kissed her like this before. It was ravishing, and she never wanted him to stop.

But he did.

He released her after just one kiss, leaving her stunned and slightly panting.

'This is bad idea,' he said thickly in broken English, his fingers still sifting the soft hair at the nape of her neck, still staring at her mouth.

She didn't want it to be a bad idea—she didn't want him to stop. She *ached*.

She really wanted another kiss.

She was going to get one.

Gigi slapped her hand to his chest and spread her fingers like a starfish, using his chest hair to tug him back in the direction she wanted him.

'I don't think so,' she said, looking determinedly into his dark eyes.

Something clean and wild pierced through the guard she had become used to seeing in his eyes, as if everything else had been a cover for what lived inside him and she'd just woken it up.

Gigi had a flashback to that moment at the cabaret when

he'd turned around and she'd imagined he was going to devour her.

She just hadn't thought it would be literally.

A primitive thrill unlike any she'd ever known zinged along her spine to her brain, knocking out all the realities of their situation.

The paparazzi...who he was...who she was...the cabaret. Gone.

They were just a man and a woman.

Their mouths met, his fused hungrily to hers once more, and the scrape of his tongue was tasting her, his hand holding the back of her head the better to angle the kiss. It wasn't polite or gentle or coaxing. It was rough and raw and it sparked spot fires in her body Gigi couldn't reach to put out.

Instinctively she wrapped her arms around his neck and there was a clatter as the first aid gear went flying. She was caught by her legs and she clamped them around his lean, hard waist.

He swung her off the vanity, big hands cupping her behind, and with their mouths still fused he strode from the bathroom, carrying her with him.

It was all happening so fast, and Gigi wasn't sure why but she just knew that if they slowed down one of them would stop this.

He was stripping back her jacket and she was helping him, using her steely thigh muscles like grips to hold onto him. She wasn't sure what she really wanted here, but he'd freed something in her that had been caught, that she'd never known until now, and she felt a little wild with it.

Her breasts sang with sensation, squashed up against his chest as she fought free of her jacket.

Under the press of her pelvis he was formidably aroused, and it was a shot to her ego that she could do this to him. Then she was free to hold him tightly to her and kiss him back, a little drunk on the taste, aware that this was so out of character nobody who knew her would recognise her.

His knees hit the side of the bed and he lowered her on to her back in an economical move that spoke of much practice.

But not practice with L'Oiseau Bleu showgirls, and that was what counted.

He was pushing up her T-shirt, cupping her breasts, lifting himself so he could see her.

Her common sense was shouting. *This is not going to fix the cabaret. This is only going to get you into trouble.*

But still she ran her hands up his chest, revelling in his solidity and strength, looping her arms around his neck before he could get her bra off. She dragged his mouth down to hers again. His beard wasn't scratchy at all. It was soft. It felt delicious.

Her hands went shyly to his waistband, because she'd never been a girl to waste time, which was when she felt resistance shoot through his body. In the same instant his hand snapped like a handcuff around her wrist.

'No, you don't.'

His gruff words hit her like a bucket of cold water.

He released her wrist and what she saw in his dark eyes told her he was calling a halt to this—something *she* should have done minutes ago.

That he could pull back now, when she was still hot and bothered and clinging to him, was just horribly embarrassing.

As he moved away from her Gigi knew she should be getting upright fast, playing it just as cool and together as he appeared to be.

Only she discovered she wasn't that sophisticated. Or maybe it was that it had been so long since she'd been in a situation like this. With an actual. Live. Man.

Holy moly—when had she *ever* been in a situation like this?

*He's your boss.*

He was also a million years beyond her in sophistication, and she was proving that right now by squeezing her eyes shut, as if he might disappear, and she would wake in her own room, and all of this would be just one of those embarrassing being-caught-in-public-naked dreams.

When she found the wherewithal to crank up an eyelid she discovered he was standing over her, running his hands through his hair where only moments before her fingers had been. He was looking rueful, and because of it younger—more his twenty-nine years than the über-successful man of the world she'd spent the last hour or so with.

*An hour, Gigi, and you're flat on your back on his bed?*

She watched his biceps flex as he massaged the back of his neck and was distracted for a moment—until she realised what she was doing. She was acting like a sex-crazed rabbit!

'This isn't wise.'

His voice was rough and deep, and crushingly certain as his gaze ran over her, rumpled and prone and probably unattractively flushed, still lying on the bed.

No? Gigi struggled to prop herself up on her elbows.

She wondered what he meant to do. Was she supposed to say something?

'I need a shower.'

Did he?

She watched him go, uncertain of the etiquette. Still a little dazed and confused. What had she done wrong?

*Not what—who, you eejit. You're a Bluebird, and he's the boss, and this is not what you came for.*

She looked down at her breasts, which had been so happy beneath his hands, and at her nipples, which were still standing up like two little soldiers on parade.

*Not today, ladies.*

She watched the door close and she was left on her own in the middle of the glamorous bed. Her squeak firmly in place.

Khaled stepped out of the shower, his body under control after the effects of chill-level water, aware that this brief taste of Gigi had made her even more dangerous.

He knew now how she felt—soft, pliant, wild. How she

moved her mouth—sensuously. How she used her tongue, and the little sounds she made that were enough to tip him over the edge.

She was the sweetest, wildest thing.

He blew out a deep breath. Only not for him.

He'd caught himself a Bluebird—but with photographs of them together on the internet there was no way he could do what would clearly come far too naturally for both of them, it appeared.

It would not be conducive to a quick sale of the cabaret.

For now, he had to get her out of here.

He stepped into the bedroom and found—nothing.

The only sign of what had occurred was the rumpled coverlet and the scent of her—something like cinnamon and sugar baked hot. It made his mouth water.

'Gigi?'

Silence.

He'd dropped her backpack on the seat at the end of the bed and it was gone too.

Khaled stood with his hands resting lightly on his lean towel-wrapped hips and wondered at the disappointment dropping through him. He'd misjudged her. How in hell had he misjudged her? He'd been so wide of the mark he needed either a psychologist, to find out where his native intelligence had gone, or a sex therapist to work out at exactly what point what was between his legs had superseded his brain.

Thumping something suddenly appealed.

All that sweet, eccentric confusion she trailed—like breadcrumbs to the doorstep of that cabaret of hers. A con. How had he missed it?

He should have been analysing that the moment her thighs had locked decisively around his hips and her breasts, like the plump little weapons of male destruction they were, had hit his chest—not being concerned about her well-being and whether he was pushing this too quickly, and exactly how fast was too fast to peel her jeans off.

Yanking on his own pair of jeans and fighting into a fresh shirt, he wondered at his own credulity.

He'd been on the receiving end of women looking for a pay-off too many times to be this careless.

The problem was it had been her obvious distress and confusion when the paps had descended which had muddied his reactions.

She didn't act like a woman on the make—she came across instead as a lively, extroverted girl who incidentally had a cabaret to promote, and in the next breath as a vulnerable young woman with a past that sounded at best colourful and at worst abusive, given he'd seen her feet.

It had been instinct that had had him tugging off his T-shirt and showing her his own scars, wanting to take the sting out of her embarrassment about her own. He hadn't counted on how good her hands had felt on his body, and for a few minutes there she'd been utterly happy to accommodate him on the bathroom vanity. Seemingly *gratis*. No emotional fallout or extended lines of communication required.

It was a scenario that didn't happen in his life any more. Not since he'd made his first million. There was always a catch.

What he had discovered now wasn't unfamiliar, but somehow he'd let down his guard with her, and oddly her departure felt like a kick to the guts.

He snorted.

*Focus, man.*

She hadn't got what she wanted and she was gone—simple. Now he needed to make an overdue call to his personal legal advisor and find out what he could do about those photos.

# CHAPTER EIGHT

KHALED HAD HIS phone out as he wandered barefoot into the main living room, with its explosion of taffetas and velvets, but he never made that call.

Sitting on the sofa, with her impossibly long legs curled under her, her coppery head bent as she worked, was Gigi.

With a laptop.

He moved up silently behind her. A part of him was asking what the hell he was doing. What had he expected? To find her uploading photos of his hotel room? Possibly. Privacy was something nobody could take for granted any more.

He stopped behind the sofa. The screen in front of her was full of images of L'Oiseau Bleu.

'Gigi?'

She almost jumped off the sofa. 'Oh, Mary and Joseph, you scared me.'

After an initial moment of eye contact she guiltily returned her attention to the screen almost immediately.

His instincts prowled. He glanced at the screen—more in an attempt to work her out than out of any real interest in what she was doing. 'What is this?' he asked, more abruptly than he'd meant to.

'I'm just gathering some things I want to show you about the cabaret's history…its importance to Paris. I thought seeing as I'm up here…' Her voice ran away and she clicked on another image—one of the cabaret in its heyday.

Khaled was more interested in the laptop. Had she run with *that* in her backpack?

Come to think of it, the thing hadn't been light when he'd been carrying it around.

'Maybe this is a bad idea,' she said, still intent on avoiding eye contact. 'You probably don't have time to take a look. I should probably get out of your hair.'

She was putting down the lid on the laptop and unfolding her long legs.

He moved fast and dropped down onto the sofa beside her, reached for it.

'Show me what you've got.'

He'd jumped her in the bathroom—he could give her five minutes.

What she had was clusters of images, reviews, articles, all informatively cascading one after the other.

'This is our current show—we've been performing it for the last three years.'

The screen was filled with colour and movement and cheesy eighties dance music.

He was about to tell her she could skip this part when he zeroed in on Gigi, descending the stairs with a line of other showgirls.

She looked like a glittering peacock, dragging a shimmering tail. Her arms were gracefully outstretched, an elaborate neck-piece of glittering rhinestones falling from her throat to cover her chest, but doing nothing to hide the fact that all the girls who weren't wearing rhinestone bras were topless.

The warmth of Gigi's very real body beside him and the memory of the very real breasts he'd had his hands on was making a mockery of his decision to keep his hands off her.

One act succeeded the next—primarily *tableaux vivants* that involved the girls wearing as little as possible. In between there was a chanteuse, a performing dog, a barbershop quartet and some magic tricks. It was certainly different.

He folded his arms, switched off the male part of his brain that kept fixating on her breasts, and allowed himself to appreciate the very real charm of it.

Eventually she hit 'stop' and looked at him expectantly.

Until now he hadn't been convinced that it was anything more than a glorified strip joint. Frankly, he wasn't sure *what* it was. On the one hand there was all the charm and femininity of the over-the-top dance numbers. Even the male dancers looked as if they'd been neutered. On the other hand there were the boobs and the bottoms that gave it its risqué reputation. But that was very French. Gigi had been telling him the truth, and now he understood a little of why Paris was going slightly bonkers over the idea of him laying a hand on their precious L'Oiseau Bleu.

She was good. He hadn't expected her to be this good.

'What do you think?'

He thought that he was hard and aching, and it had nothing to do with what he'd just seen on this screen and everything to do with the sweet sexiness of the girl curled up beside him, who at every turn had proved herself to be not quite what he'd thought she was.

He looked into her hopeful, obviously secretly pleased expression and began to wonder exactly what was going on in that eccentric little head of hers.

Gigi congratulated herself on the professional way she was conducting herself. She'd kept her hands to herself and she was almost the whole way through her presentation. Really, nobody could find fault.

If you put aside the bodyguard incident in the lobby. The incident with the crowd on the Champs-Élysées. The incident with the paparazzi. The incident in the lobby with her shoes and—she closed her eyes briefly—the incident on the bathroom vanity, ending with her flat on her back in the bedroom, about which the less she thought the better.

No, all in all, putting those things aside, she'd handled this quite well.

Somehow she'd come through it all and had him where she'd wanted him hours ago, before all this began.

On a sofa, glued to her presentation.

It was time to fire some questions at him.

But first of all she made herself look him in the eye— the first time she'd done so since he'd sat down beside her.

After all, she wasn't ashamed of her perfectly healthy

sex drive. And she guessed she would have remembered soon after he did that this was a professional relationship and called a halt.

Only lifting her gaze to those velvet-lashed dark eyes she was instantly out of her depth again, and she knew to her embarrassment that whatever hadn't happened between them was all down to him.

She'd been the one kicking things and climbing over the poor man and forcing him to stroke her breasts.

'So what do you think?' she asked in a strangled voice.

'Impressive.'

*Impressive? Really?* She caught herself in time. *He doesn't mean your breasts, Gigi!*

Although, actually, stroking her breasts had been down to him…

*Stop thinking about your breasts!*

She cleared her throat. 'I was wondering if you'd given any thought to what road you might go down,' she ventured. 'We'd like to stay family-friendly.'

'Family-friendly?'

Gigi's optimism dwindled a little. Why did he have to say it as if it was a concept he wasn't entirely familiar with?

'We're sexy, but you can bring your mum. Family-friendly,' she explained. 'I mean obviously we'd have to keep our "Sixteen and Over" door rule…'

'Obviously.'

She resisted looking up at his dry tone, pretending instead to be interested in sorting through a few images of the current show as she wondered exactly how far she could push this without blurting out, *We don't want to become a nasty men's club.*

'It's a concern, given your other…um…holdings.'

'I own gambling venues, some nightclubs, hotels…'

She glanced up.

'No strip joints, Gigi,' he said with a faint smile.

She moistened her lips. 'It's just that when the girls took

off their pasties and started writhing unimaginatively round poles burlesque died.'

Khaled tried to imagine Gigi arching against a pole in nothing much. Curiously, it wasn't a salacious image. Instead it was one that made him feel like the morals police. In his mind he barricaded the stage and put up 'Nothing To See Here' signs, wrapped her in a robe and hustled her towards the exit.

He cleared his throat. 'Pasties?'

'Nipple shields—tassels sometimes.'

He frowned.

She gave a sigh, as if he were being deliberately obtuse, and spelt it out. 'Tit tape.'

'Does this mean you're not actually topless?'

He was speaking generally, but he suddenly wanted to know specifics. Specifically Gigi, and exactly how much of her was on show.

He'd seen a screen full of topless showgirls swathed in ropes of rhinestones falling from elaborate neck-pieces, nipples peeking through. It wasn't exactly salacious—you could see just as much flesh on most beaches in Europe—but he was a man…he knew how other men would be looking at it.

He'd got the distinct impression those were her nipples he was seeing on that screen. It took a manful effort not to let his gaze drift down to her chest, given that the real thing had been under his hands not long ago, and the memory of her nipples poking enthusiastically into his palms wasn't going away.

More blood rushed to his groin.

No, that wasn't going away either.

'Bare breasts are a traditional part of French cabaret,' Gigi said, looking blameless as sunlight. 'But a cabaret is not a strip joint. The emphasis in French cabaret is on fun, humour and glamour. There's no sleaze.'

'The entertainment division of the Kitaev Group is principally gaming and music venues.' He watched her teeth sink

into the lush promise of her lower lip and found his voice
had thickened again when he added, 'No poles.'

Gigi wasn't too sure if she believed him. Oh, she believed
him about the poles, but his plan for L'Oiseau Bleu was another thing.

Gaming and music venues?

*Don't frown*, she told herself.

'You don't look too happy about that, Gigi.'

She understood that he was humouring her, but she took
his question seriously all the same. 'I'm just concerned, given
you own some pretty outlandish venues.'

He gave her a smile. 'I admit the Oasis Pearl in Dubai is
fairly over the top, but it has to be to compete.'

Gigi made a mental note to look up the Oasis Pearl on
the internet.

'And what would make L'Oiseau Bleu…*compete*?' She
tested out the word and tried to sound as if she knew of
what she spoke.

'Why don't you tell me?'

*Drat.*

'I'm not really a businesswoman,' she mumbled, 'I'm a
dancer.'

'Why did you come to me, Gigi?'

It was a good question, and one she'd asked herself many
times over since she'd discovered L'Oiseau Bleu had passed
into new hands.

'I guess it's because the other girls needed a spokesperson and I kind of elected myself.' She met his eyes. 'And,
unlike them, I know what L'Oiseau Bleu once was, and I
have an idea of what it could be again. With the right person at the helm.'

There it was. The sincerity. Khaled couldn't deny that
she appeared to believe what she said. It went against his
grain to lie to her, but after her little performance on the
Champs-Élysées he couldn't risk handing over the sensitive

information that he was passing on the cabaret only to see it broadcast the length and breadth of Paris before nightfall.

Gigi had a mouth on her. She'd proved it.

He couldn't risk telling her the truth.

'The other girls are loyal to the theatre,' she said quickly, as if wanting to disabuse him of the notion she was a one-woman crusade, 'but I don't think they really understand how far downhill the cabaret has gone in the past few decades...' She trailed off. 'Sorry, I get carried away. You don't have to do anything. I mean, you could sell us on. It's not as if we saw anything of the last owner.'

'Ahmed el Hammoud?'

'We never met him. Do you know him?'

'I know he's useless at cards.' The oil sheikh's incompetence at poker meant Khaled now possessed some nice Arabian breeding stock and a tinpot cabaret that time forgot in Paris. And this girl.

No, she didn't come with ownership papers—more was the pity. Khaled smiled privately to himself.

'Is that really how you ended up with us?'

He glanced her way, almost literally tripping over that shy look she was so good at giving him.

It just muddied the waters—had him wanting to lecture her on coming up to a stranger's hotel room and at the same time wanting to drive her down backwards onto this sofa, scatter the cushions and reacquaint himself with the sweet, sensual response she'd given him in the bedroom.

He cleared his throat. 'I have a regular poker game with a group of guys I've known since my army days.'

'Where you got those terrible scars?'

'*Da*—some.'

It hadn't been a smart move showing her those scars. It had led to her hands on his body and his on hers.

Khaled slumped back on the sofa beside her and massaged the back of his neck, wondering what the hell he thought he was doing and knowing he had to wind this up.

'How long did you serve?' she wanted to know.

'Two years.'

'I guess you saw active service?'

'Chechnya, Afghanistan,' he said briefly, and a visual of heat and dust and sweat streaming between the bridge of his nose and a rifle sight bloomed in his mind. God, how he'd hated it.

'Was it your choice?'

Khaled gave a shrug, a little surprised by the question. Few people asked. 'It's difficult to escape conscription—but, yes, in many ways it was my choice. My father was a professional soldier.'

She sat forward and tucked one leg under her. Clearly interested.

'Did you want to follow him into the army?'

'Talkative little thing, aren't you?'

'I'm just curious.'

He could give her the truth, that military service had opened up his life in unexpected ways and had transformed his life. He'd learned that his father was a hero, that he came from a long line of professional soldiers, and that his own beliefs about who he was and where he came from had been false and fed to him as a youth by the only father he had ever known. Leaving him with the huge trust issues he carried to this day.

But he opted for the generic. 'It's something we must all do.'

Her world of feathers and stage make-up was so far from what he'd seen as to be another planet. And yet he couldn't help remembering those marks he'd seen on her feet, and the way she'd curled up like a snail on the vanity to hide them.

He frowned. Mostly it was his own fiercely protective reaction that continued to unsettle him, especially when he'd learned that some of that violence had been meted out by what sounded like a disgrace of a father.

'Military service is boredom punctuated by adrenalin,'

he found himself confessing. 'And a lot of poker. I got very good at it.' He angled a smile her way. 'When I was a kid I used to play cards for spent bullet cartridges.'

Hell, why had he told her *that*?

'Bullets, huh? I guess where you come from is a long way from the dressing rooms and trailers I was raised in.' She looked up at him through her lashes. 'You'd probably prefer them to a cabaret you don't want.'

'I don't know,' he mused, unable to resist the siren call of her eyes shyly meeting his. 'I wouldn't have met you.'

Her mouth trembled into a half-smile and then she pulled it tight again, looking away. He knew the feeling.

He rubbed his jaw, knowing he should be winding this up—only to encounter the beard he'd ignored for weeks now. Usually after a couple of months away on a trek he'd be freshly shaven and snapped back into his Italian suits, hunkering down in his offices in Moscow and hitting the ground running.

Diverting to Paris straight from the Arctic shelf meant he'd come without that symbolic shift between two worlds.

Maybe that was why he was tempting fate here. The wilderness of his previous environment was still running through his blood...

He cleared his throat. 'Gigi, in the bedroom—'

'I don't want to talk about it.' She cut him off hurriedly, looking cornered. She stumbled to her feet. 'I mean, it was just a stupid thing, right? Better we forget about it.'

A stupid thing? He didn't think so. His hunter's instinct kicked in.

Gigi set about clumsily gathering her things. 'I should get out of your hair.'

'I'm taking you home.'

The words formed and his certainty solidified around them.

'No, that's all right.' She was busily packing up her laptop.

'I'm taking you home.'

Gigi tried to ignore the little kick she got out of his assertiveness. Because, really, she shouldn't like being told what to do.

But she could literally hear her heart hammering in her ears, and more liquid heat was pooling between her thighs. It was embarrassing. It was also unprecedented in *The Romantic History of Gigi Valente*. So far officially two pages, along with today's Special Addition, and not much going on for the foreseeable future.

She couldn't understand the effect this man—of all men—had on her.

Obviously he had it all going on. He was gorgeous, he was powerful, and his fathoms-deep masculine voice with that accent was designed to be meltingly effective on a woman's hormones…

But if she had to pinpoint it she'd say it was in his eyes and the way he looked at her. As if he wanted to do all kinds of things with her that another woman would slap him for, and that instead made *her* feel beautiful and female and, yes, fluttery.

She just wasn't a fluttery kind of girl.

She zipped her finger into the backpack.

*Ouch!*

Shoving her middle finger in her mouth, she tried not to look at him. He was being so reasonable, which wasn't helping, and now he wanted to drive her home.

Didn't he understand that if she spent any more time with him she might very well push him down, climb on top of him and make him kiss her all over again?

Or, worse, make him stroke her breasts—because her nipples were like tight little marbles and they felt tingly, and she only had to close her eyes to remember how it had felt to be pressed up into his big hands…

She swallowed hard and kept her head down.

'You don't need to drive me home.' She slung the backpack over her shoulder. 'I can grab a taxi.'

Actually, she would find a *vélib* station and bike it home. Taxis were for rich people, or girls who danced at the Lido.

She adjusted the strap on her backpack to give herself something to do when he didn't reply. Raised her eyes. He was looking down at her as if she'd said something bizarre, and then he flashed her a scarily intimate look that told her he knew exactly how damp her knickers were.

'You're only saying that because you haven't seen my car.'

# CHAPTER NINE

'TAKE A LEFT up here and we're at the top of the street.'

Khaled didn't know what he'd expected. Something tight on space and utilitarian, given the area. Montmartre had come a long way from the fields and cheap lodgings of its artistic heyday. Apartment dwelling wasn't cheap in these parts. And he'd seen what the showgirls were paid—it wasn't a lucrative profession.

He hadn't expected the little dead-end cobbled street, the high grey stone walls or the four-storeyed *petit mansion* peering overhead.

He parked his yellow Spyder Lamborghini on the road-side between a couple of not inconsiderably priced cars and eased back to take a look at Gigi.

'This is it?'

She was taking off her belt. 'Sure.'

He watched her for a moment, running her hand over the door, trying to get out. She appeared to be in a hurry. He could have leaned across and done it for her. Instead he opened his own door and strolled around to her side of the car. He lifted the door and watched her get out, taking in those incredible legs and the pert roundness of her behind.

'Thanks.' She lugged her backpack over her shoulder. 'Are you coming up?'

'Do you usually let men you hardly know into your flat?'

She gave him a surprised look, as if it hadn't occurred to her before, and then reached into her jacket and brought out a small tube, brandishing it like a gunslinger.

'I'm packing heat.'

'What's that?' He took it from her, examining the simple pump-style device.

'A high-frequency alarm. All the girls at the cabaret have them.'

'I take it this was the Dantons' idea.'

She shook her head. 'Jacques considers what we do off the clock our own business—he's not big on the health and safety thing. But some of the girls have had problems with patrons following them when they leave the theatre, so I got Martin to introduce a courtesy bus system, which is great. Lulu and I use that all the time.'

'Who supplied the alarms?'

'Me. I got one for Lulu, after she was almost attacked one night, and grabbed one for myself too. The guy who sold them to me gave me a discount for a box of two dozen. So I got enough for the other girls.'

'Basically, you're doing the Dantons' job for them?'

Her expressive face gave her away. She obviously didn't want to down-talk the cabaret's management in front of him, but at the same time it was fairly clear what was going on.

'I guess if something needs to be done you do it, right? Besides, Lulu could have been in real trouble that night.'

'One of the dancers was attacked?' Khaled was frowning.

'Not "one of the dancers",' she said, with a little frown to match his. '*Lulu*. She went out with this guy a couple of times, and then she said thanks but no thanks, and he followed her home and wouldn't take no for an answer. If I hadn't been here I don't know what would have happened.'

Her natural animation had drained away and she folded her arms across her chest self-protectively. 'Plus we work at night, so personal security is pretty important. You can't be in this business without learning how to look out for yourself.'

'You carry a small alarm,' he said, struggling with primitive feelings that had no place here, with a girl who was certainly of a time and a place where she could look after herself, 'and you think this is security enough?'

'It's all I've got,' she replied simply.

He made a note to himself to beef up security at L'Oiseau Bleu. The cabaret he wouldn't be holding on to.

At the gate she keyed in the alarm code and pushed.

The courtyard was small and immaculate.

A black mop came hurtling across the stones to fling itself at Gigi's knees. She swept the ball up in her arms amidst much unhygienic kissing and cooing.

'This is Coco—he's Lulu's baby. Say hello, Coco.'

Khaled watched this interaction with a degree of mild male apprehension.

Normally women who treated defenceless animals as substitute children really didn't do it for him, and surely it was a warning sign that at some point this roving maternal instinct was going to be turned in a more natural direction.

But that was some other guy's problem. He could relax about the dog. It wasn't even her dog.

*Forget about the dog.*

'Here. You hold Coco while I let us in.' She shoved the fluff ball at his chest.

Khaled tensed. *It's a dog, not a baby*, he reiterated, and held the creature up, observing its shiny eyes, wet nose and glossy coat. Coco was clearly in good health and well looked after. He lifted the squirming ball a little higher and confirmed that Coco was indeed a he.

Gigi opened the front door and he put the dog down. It rushed forward and up the stairs.

'We're on the top floor,' she said, crossing the well-lit atrium and preceding him up the steps.

*We?* How the hell did she afford this on her wages? She barely made enough at that cabaret to live in a cardboard box in central Paris. He knew—he'd seen the books.

But his eyes were caught by Gigi's small round derrière, several steps in front of him and right on his eye level, and all the questions got pushed aside in favour of just appreciating the view. Her bottom should be illegal. In those jeans it was packaged for maximum impact. The soft denim wrapped around her as if it loved her body. He couldn't blame it.

He followed her into a brightly lit open-plan room with

windows looking out over the rooftops. It was a nice view. The floorboards shone. There was a loft bedroom above and circular metal stairs.

Gigi shrugged off her jacket and tossed it onto a chair.

His mouth dried up.

He hadn't got much of a look when she'd been under him on the bed, but now he could see the full effect of a tight pink T-shirt advertising the slogan 'Dancing Queen' in glittery dark pink letters across the high round curves of her breasts.

He'd had those breasts resting against his hands, felt the curve of her nipples rise to points under his thumbs.

She looked lovely and playful—and so sexy it hurt.

The blood zoomed so fast from his brain to his groin he could only be thankful he'd put his jacket on.

'Dancing Queen?' he said, a little stupidly.

Gigi glanced down at her chest, looked up, and beamed like a torch.

'I love Abba. Want a cup of tea?'

'*Chay*...tea?' he echoed. He never drank tea. '*Spasiba.*'

He knew he should be pounding down those stairs and driving away. Didn't he have meetings this afternoon? Instead he found himself moving around the room while she busied herself in the kitchenette, taking in the simple furnishings and girly throw cushions, the pile of books beside a small bookcase that had overflowed, a couple of framed prints that under closer inspection proved to be old numbers of *Le Petit Journal*, with illustrations of dancing girls—one from the Moulin Rouge, the other from a circus. No sign of male cohabitation.

She was saying something about the cabaret...about wanting to show him some memorabilia.

He drew closer to a twelve-by-twelve photographic portrait framed on the wall. For a moment he thought it was Gigi. The same sharp angular cheekbones were catching the light, the point of her chin, but the eyes were dark and sloe-shaped, the nose small. The face was more conventionally attractive, but lacking the energy which animated Gigi's striking features. Struck by the similarity to the woman with him, the last thing he noticed was that she appeared to be naked. Except for an ostrich feather fan.

'This is your mother?' he said.

Gigi put down the cups she was setting out and came over, settling her gaze on the picture with an oddly protective look on her face.

'That's right. Her name was Emily Fitzgerald. She danced at L'Oiseau Bleu for five years—same as me.'

'Your mother was a showgirl?' Khaled gave a soft laugh. 'Well, well…'

'She was amazing. A much better dancer than me. She had real presence. Those fans she's holding she had made for her. They were her signature. They weigh a ton. I know, because they were the only thing she took back to Dublin, the fans—oh, and her shoes. I used to waddle around in her shoes, trying to carry one of the fans. I couldn't have been more than five or six. She said if I practised I could grow up to be another Sally Rand.'

'Who was Sally Rand?'

'An American burlesque star—famous for dancing naked behind an ostrich feather fan. She started out in the circus too.'

She spoke so matter-of-factly that Khaled decided not to raise the subject of all this pointing towards a rather unusual upbringing.

'I gather your mother gave up the stage to have a family?'

Gigi's mouth tightened. 'You could say that. She fell pregnant to my father. Not the most reliable man in the world,' she added.

Khaled thought of the marks on her feet and decided this was Gigi's version of understatement.

'She decided to go home to her parents and I was born in Dublin. I didn't know my dad until I was eight or nine.' She reached out and straightened the picture, although it was already dead on. 'This photo was taken when she was pregnant with me. She had it done knowing her time was running out. She kept dancing right up until she started to show.'

'Do showgirls come back to work after pregnancy?' He had no real interest, but he wanted to hear her story—because it was clear that here on this wall was the reason Gigi was so anxious to protect the cabaret.

'If your body snaps back. A couple of the dancers have kids. The Dantons aren't great about childcare.' She folded her arms. 'That's something e    you might want to look into.'

In truth Khaled had forgotten this was the bone of contention between them. He'd been enjoying watching all the emotions crossing Gigi's face, like sunlight and cloud and little storms. She was so passionate.

He looked again at the photograph. Emily Fitzgerald looked serene as a sunset.

'She must be proud of you.'

'She doesn't know. She died.' A muscle jumped in Gigi's throat. 'She went into hospital for a day procedure, to fix some nodules that had formed on her larynx, and she never came out from under the anaesthetic. It was her heart—it was weak and no one knew, and it just gave up. It was sixteen years ago, but it's still hard to grapple with.'

She'd been just a child.

Khaled straightened. His voice was gravel. 'I'm sorry, Gigi.'

He had the unfamiliar sensation of not quite knowing his footing here. But this girl did that to him.

His own parents had been gone by the time he was thirteen, and it had given him a terrible freedom.

He frowned. 'What happened to you?'

'My dad turned up to collect me.' She put her hands on her hips, as if to counteract the wealth unsaid in that statement. 'That's when I went on the road with Valente's International Circus.'

'An itinerant life for a kid… Did you enjoy it?'

She shrugged. 'It was different. I threw myself into learning the life. I so wanted to please my dad, and it taught me lessons in discipline and the importance of practice.'

Khaled had a visual of the marks on her feet, and those words assumed a darker significance.

It wasn't hard to picture Gigi all those years ago, skinny instead of shapely, all freckles and bereft. They weren't so different. He knew all about trying to please the only person you had left. In Gigi's case it had involved climbing those ropes, her feet bearing the scars to this day.

Tough little thing.

Needing her mother and getting what…? The bastard who'd permitted that *thing* to happen to her growing feet.

Khaled was conscious of a tension in him he could have cut with a knife.

'Then Dad went bankrupt and we hit the vaudeville circuit,' she continued. 'I sang and danced and dad was MC. But it wasn't like this.'

She gestured towards the window and he surmised that she meant Parisian cabaret.

'As soon as I could I crossed the Channel.'

'You came to Paris to follow in her footsteps?'

'Something like that.'

She smiled at him, and it was that lack of self-pity coupled with her natural buoyancy that hit him the hardest. He was sure he could do something for her before he left Paris.

'Would you like that tea?' she asked.

'No, I don't want tea.' He stepped in front of her. 'I want to kiss you.'

She looked sweetly surprised, and then pleased, and it only made him want to power her back into that sofa over there and lose himself in her soft, sweet warmth. He took her in his arms and promised himself he'd only have a taste. But once her lips parted beneath his everything changed again, and his kiss became a fiercely possessive gesture that only intensified as her tongue tentatively slid against his. His blood roared and his restraint began to unravel fast.

The door behind him closed with a slam.

Gigi jerked in his arms, her head coming up. She made a sound of dismay that might have been funny if she hadn't then shoved him away from her and immediately begun smoothing down her hair and adjusting her T-shirt, looking guilty as hell and incredibly sexy because of it.

Which wasn't helping with the stone-cold kick he needed to give his erection.

Because the little brunette from yesterday was standing just inside the door, with a bunch of sunflowers and a bag of groceries. She dropped them on the floor.

It wasn't subtle. It wasn't meant to be.

'I'm interrupting,' she said stonily.

'No…' choked Gigi.

His personal phone vibrated inside his jacket for the hundredth time since he'd driven the Spyder out into the Paris afternoon. He thought he'd take this call. It had been a lot of years since he'd involved himself with a woman who had a *flatmate*.

Khaled palmed his phone and turned his back on the girls to give them a minute. *'Govorit,'* he breathed. *Talk*.

'What is *he* doing here?' hissed Lulu, stepping over the groceries.

Gigi opted for a casual shrug. She had no idea how she was going to explain two hundred plus pounds of Russian muscle in their flat, let alone her being welded to him. She had her own questions as to why she'd practically blurted out her entire family history to him.

Lulu looked very angry. She marched into her bedroom. Reluctantly Gigi trailed her.

'So you're replacing Solange?' she demanded as Gigi half shut the door behind her.

'No!' Gigi frowned. 'It's not like that. He was never interested in Solange.'

Lulu gave a very un-Lulu-like snort. '*Every* man's interested in Solange.'

Gigi's stomach curled uneasily. It was true. 'He told me
it was a publicity thing—to have his photograph taken with
a showgirl.'

Her best friend's face told her what she thought of that.

'So what are you doing here with him, Gigi? How did
this come about?'

She told Lulu about being tackled by his security team,
about running through the streets, being held up by aggressive strangers and swarmed by paparazzi. When she'd finished Lulu's mouth was slightly ajar. She shut it with a snap
when Gigi came to the part about going up to his hotel room.

'He took me up to fix my feet.'

'You let him see your *feet*?' Lulu's voice rose.

'Shh. He'll hear you. Don't make it such a big deal.' Although it *was* a big deal. Lulu knew that better than most.
'We happened to be in the bathroom.'

'How were you in the bathroom together?'

'He carried me there.'

Lulu's eyes narrowed suspiciously. 'What happened to
your ability to walk?'

'It was compromised by my blisters.'

Her best friend gave her a withering look.

Gigi decided there and then to omit the part about her
turning into a nympho on the vanity. Some things were private—and, besides, Lulu wouldn't understand. The only
time *she* got carried away by her hormones was when they
watched old Gregory Peck movies together, and Lulu would
hug a cushion and sigh and ask where all the real men had
gone.

Gigi suspected she had one, in the other room, but letting
Lulu know that wasn't going to help.

After all she'd said about him over the last couple of days, she couldn't blame Lulu for being suspicious.

'I gave him the presentation and he seemed interested. Then he ran me home because of the journalists.' Even as she said it, it sounded weak.

He'd brought her home and effectively diverted her from her task, which had been to show him the old memorabilia, by asking her about her mother.

Then he'd kissed her. Tenderly at first. She touched her lips.

Lulu's eyes zeroed in on the gesture and her expression turned mutinous. 'Has he even said anything about the cabaret? Or is this all just about getting in a showgirl's knickers?'

Lulu blushed as she said it, but she said it nonetheless.

'It's not like that!'

Lulu folded her arms. '"Nobody should date Kitaev"—quote, unquote.'

'I know…I know.'

Lulu's expression softened to its more natural lines. 'Gigi, just think for a minute. How are you going to explain any of this to the other girls?'

'The other girls won't know.'

The words just slipped out, and Gigi knew then that she was sunk.

'You want to do this behind everyone's backs? Really, Gigi?'

'No, of course not.'

Lulu knew about her past. Knew how fiercely she felt about deceit.

Her father had put her on the vaudeville circuit at the age of fourteen—a front for his petty crime spree as they travelled from town to town. And four years later, when she'd confronted him outside the court on that rainy day when he'd been convicted and she'd got a slap over the wrist, he'd told her that he hadn't thought it would matter as long as she didn't know…

Ignorance wasn't an excuse for culpability under the law—she knew that now, better than most.

She'd made a vow when she'd walked away from court that morning seven years ago that she was going to look life straight in the eye.

She looked Lulu in the eye now. 'It won't happen again.'

She couldn't promote the theatre and compromise her position.

The world could be a cold, hard place, but you didn't need to cheat and steal to survive in it. She had fought to make her own colourful, *honest* corner and she wasn't going to mess it up now.

Khaled was still talking on his phone when she re-emerged. Lulu followed her, arms folded. He indicated the door with a nod and headed out, clearly expecting her to follow him.

'Do *not* make any plans with him,' whispered Lulu.

No, no plans.

Outside on the stairs he pocketed his phone and said briefly, 'We've got a problem.'

'Yes, we do.'

She had a huge problem, given she still couldn't pull her eyes off him. But she was guessing it wasn't such a big problem for him, because she was looking at his back and he was taking the steps by threes, those big shoulders squared as he headed back out into the big, bad world.

'There are photographs of us in the lobby of the Plaza.'

That wasn't the problem she'd been thinking of, but… 'Okay…'

Because, really, what did he want her to say? She was sorry, but she had told him she was happy to go on her way. *He* was the one who'd gone all he-man over fixing up her feet. Her heart performed a little tumble and roll at the thought.

'No, it's *not* okay, Gigi.' He stopped at the bottom of the stairs and turned around. His expression was taut. 'They imply a sexual relationship.'

Gigi rocked back on her heels. Okay. She could deal with that. Just. The other girls were going to kill her, but it wasn't the end of the world. Was it?

She examined his fierce expression. Told herself she wasn't bothered that he seemed to think this was a disaster. I mean, some guys actually thought she was pretty hot stuff. She might not be beating them off with a stick, like most of the other girls, but she got asked out, a lot…and if she wasn't working most evenings she'd probably go…

'I suggest you don't step onstage for the next few nights.'

*What* had he just said?

'But that's impossible!'

'*Nyet*, it's very possible. You need to keep a low profile— although after today it's probably asking the impossible.'

'What's that supposed to mean?'

He leaned against the banister, effectively keeping her on the second to last step, which gave her a slight height advantage although he still made her feel tiny.

'*Dushka*, you're a walking headline right now.'

'Excuse me? There were *two* of us on the Champs-Élysées, and you were the one attracting all the attention. All I did was speak up for you.'

He looked at her with those unfathomable dark eyes. 'Yes, you did, and if you'd kept your mouth shut you'd just be the pretty, unidentified girl in some photographs of me out jogging. But you're a Bluebird, and you announced it to the whole world.'

He looked over her shoulder, up the flight of stairs, and Gigi turned around to see Lulu standing on the landing, arms folded.

Oh, honestly! Gigi jumped down the final two steps and headed confidently for the door. Lulu couldn't spy on them if they were outside.

Khaled's arm came down in front of her, effectively barring the door.

'Being seen in public together probably isn't our wisest step at this point,' he said, with calm certainty.

She looked up. 'But this isn't *public*. This is my street.'

'Nevertheless, there could be paps—stay put.'

She folded her arms, looking away. 'Fine.'

His mouth moved as if he were suppressing a smile and he picked up the ends of her hair and gave the silky weight a gentle tug, which felt oddly more intimate than that kiss upstairs.

'No more ambushing men in hotel lobbies, *dushka*.'

She bit her lip and gazed up at him, fighting the urge to move a little closer.

He dropped her hair as if he'd just realised what he was doing and cleared his throat. 'Next time you have a proposal to put forward pick up the phone and make an appointment.'

Gigi nodded, although she knew very well that if she *had* picked up the phone she never would have got anywhere near him.

Not the man who was solidifying to granite rock in front of her eyes.

This was the man she'd first seen yesterday—a monolith of inaccessibility. The open-necked shirt and jeans might as well have been a suit.

She guessed that if he'd been wearing a watch he'd be glancing at it.

A busy man, with places to be and people to do his bidding.

It was disconcerting to think she'd been kissing him upstairs not so long ago, but it helped her suddenly fragile ego to remind herself that there hadn't been anything inaccessible about the way he'd been acting then. It wasn't just her imagination. He'd been moulding his hands around her bottom and bringing her in tight against his erection. You couldn't fake that.

She hugged to herself the very female knowledge that he'd been putty in her hands for a few minutes there.

'So, will you keep in mind everything I've shown you?'

Her words prompted Khaled's attention to drop to her breasts. When he realised what he was doing he dragged his gaze away from her nipples, prominent against the T-shirt fabric between those glittery letters, and gritted his teeth.

He had to stop making this sexual—he *would* defeat it. Gigi was looking up at him as if she expected something from him. Only it wasn't sexual. She was still holding out hope for that damn cabaret.

He looked down into her anxious expression and almost told her the truth. He was selling up. She'd come to the wrong man. But the minute he did that all of Paris would know and the queue of prospective buyers would evaporate.

He did, however, want to do something for her before he walked out of her life. 'Have you thought about upscaling?'

'Upscaling?' She gave a nervous laugh. 'It sounds like a disease.'

'Paris is full of venues. Isn't the Lido still going strong?'

'Why are you talking about the Lido? I'd never get into the Lido.'

'I could pull a few strings...'

She pulled her generous mouth tight. He was beginning to recognise the gesture.

'That's not why I came to see you today. I don't need a handout. I came for the cabaret.'

'It's not a handout, Gigi, it's a word in someone's ear. It happens all the time.'

'Well, I don't want underhand things going on.'

Underhand? Khaled tried not to laugh, but she looked so indignant. 'Gigi, how did you get the job at L'Oiseau Bleu?'

'I tried out.'

'Did you mention your mother?'

'Yes.'

'Nepotism.'

She put her hands on her hips. 'I'll have you know I'm the best showgirl they've got. I earned my place on talent alone.'

He tried not to smile, given she'd unintentionally stuck her chest out. He was tempted to point out that a significant part of her job relied on the talent that filled out her bra, but their interaction could only go downhill from that point.

She clearly prided herself on her job.

'Then you should have no problem with the Lido.'

Gigi made an exasperated sound.

They were going round in circles and, he recognised, they were talking about different things. Her heart was in L'Oiseau Bleu.

But Gigi's loyalty was misplaced and she couldn't see it. He suspected she was blinded by that photograph on the wall upstairs.

She was trying to reclaim something that had never existed instead of looking at the facts.

He had always looked long and hard at the reality of things.

The fatherless boy who wasn't wanted had hardened into a man who understood that human relationships would always fail you. What you could rely upon was money in the bank and the things you built with your own hands.

But it was proving difficult to dwell on the harsh reality of things with Gigi standing in front of him, vibrating with passion and determination to have her way.

Khaled recognised that he was possibly behaving like every other man who'd crossed her path—being foolishly helpful towards her because he was slightly bowled over by her personality.

She *did* offer a powerful punch of sex appeal.

It was nicely packaged too, in tight jeans, and advertised with that glittery slogan stretched across her perky breasts.

He was tempted to give way to instinct and just take her. Throw her over his shoulder and get the hell out of Paris.

It was what his ancestors would have done.

It wouldn't be what she wanted. She was clearly happy where she was, but what she wanted was the impossible.

Even if he recharged the cabaret's batteries with money there were so many other variables to consider.

When he was younger he'd thought money and success would shift things, make life somehow easier. Naturally the little things, like domestic service—knowing that his clothes would always be pressed, a car waiting for him—made the wheels turn smoother, but the bigger tests in life remained. They just assumed larger and in some cases—as in this weekend in Paris—absurd proportions.

He was being attacked for being moneyed and successful and foreign.

But you couldn't change what people had decided to think about you.

He knew that better than most.

It was a fact he was fighting right now, in his efforts to get that road in down south.

He exhaled, the weight of the world shifting once more onto his shoulders and the weariness he'd been keeping at bay with work making itself known. Truth be told, he wouldn't mind just climbing into bed with Gigi for a week in this little flat in Montmartre. Ditch the friend and any reminders of the cabaret and work out this scorching lust until both of them were exhausted and he was bored and it was time to move on.

His gaze ran over her creamy freckle-dappled skin, the curve of her lower lip, noticed the faint blush of colour in her cheeks. He cleared his throat and said, 'Keep offstage tonight—do that for me.'

Gigi muttered something about pay being docked and Paris being an expensive city.

He wanted to shake her.

He wanted even more to slide his hand around her sinuous waist under the T-shirt and feel her body temperature rise, to have the points of her breasts brush against him and take her mouth and plunder it until she was making those sounds he suspected would rise tenfold when he was inside her.

Instead, what he said was, 'I'll put in a word. When you get an audition, take it.'

# CHAPTER TEN

KHALED MIGHT HAVE had a point about staying offstage, but for an entirely different reason, Gigi realised that evening as she faced twenty-two hostile dancers in the narrow confines of the dressing room.

'You sold us out, you cow,' said Leah.

They had just come offstage, and Gigi found herself surrounded by a lot of hot, riled-up girls who'd had to run the same gauntlet of media she had when they'd come in tonight. The atmosphere was slightly hysterical, to say the least.

'What happened to all that talk about him being the enemy?' demanded Trixie.

'You just wanted him for yourself,' said Adele.

'It's always the quiet ones,' said Solange, narrowing her green eyes, and there was a lot of murmuring in agreement.

Gigi folded her arms. 'Well, *that's* not true—I never shut up!'

Her attempt to lighten the mood went nowhere.

'Quiet, Valente. You're in trouble,' said Susie, levelling her with a look. 'We all know what's going on out front, and you can bet the headlines tomorrow aren't going to be about the show. It'll be wall-to-wall reports on how the Bluebirds are giving it up to the billionaire.'

'What did he promise you?' Inez wanted to know.

Gigi's mind flashed to the Lido and she reddened.

'After everything you said, Gigi!' cried Trixie reproachfully. 'I can't believe you'd sell us out.'

'I didn't! I tried to get him on side.'

'It's one rule for her, girls, and one for us,' said Leah contemptuously.

'I've got a bloody audition at the Moulin Rouge next week,' said Susie suddenly. 'If this stuffs it up for me I'm coming after you, Valente.'

'The *Moulin Rouge*?' chorused several of the girls, heads turning.

'Why?' piped up Adele.

'Why do you think?' Susie folded her arms. 'Gigi's right about one thing: this ship's going down fast. Probably a lot faster now, with half of the French media out front, zeroing in on what a hokey show we put on. Add in the hated Russian owner living it up in a hotel with one of the Bluebirds and we're the joke of Paris!'

'What's she talking about?' asked Trixie. 'We've got a full house tonight.'

'That's only tonight,' Susie scoffed. 'Kitaev isn't going to hang on to us. He'll hand this place over to the Conseil de Paris, it'll be heritage-listed and you know what *that* means—we'll all be out on our *derrières*.'

Gigi frowned. 'Who told you that?'

'What else is he going to do? He won't be able to sell the place now. We're a joke.'

The other girls were humming with consternation. A couple were glaring at Susie, but Gigi knew she wasn't off the hook.

Sensing the shift in hostility, Susie turned her way again and looked her up and down contemptuously. '*You*, Valente, have turned us into a joke. Why don't you ask your new boyfriend what he's got planned, Gigi? Or are you too busy dropping your knickers for him at the Plaza Athénée?'

Heads swivelled Gigi's way again, effectively pushing Susie's defection to the side—which had clearly been her intention.

Gigi almost told them that her knickers had stayed very firmly in place, only that wasn't entirely true. They'd slipped… But she didn't want to think about that right now.

Fed up, she picked up her things and shouldered her way out of the room. At least she'd tried!

Barricading herself in the second dressing room, she

checked her phone. She'd been too chicken until now. For good reason, it turned out. The girls were right. It was all over the internet. Photos of her and Khaled in the street, an 'eyewitness account' of them in the lobby of his hotel. Even a shot of him climbing into his car on her street.

*Kitaev and feathered friend!*

No wonder those journalists had been yelling her name out front.

Gigi said a bad word and shoved her phone into her change bag.

Wonderful. She was officially the Bluebird who'd sold out—not just in the eyes of her troupe mates but in the opinion of the rest of Paris!

It was all she could think about as she waited in the wings for her next cue.

Because right now she had to go out there and perform in front of people who believed she was some sort of Mata Hari. What on earth did people think? That she'd traded sexual favours for…what? Job security?

A sort of shock was stealing over her. She'd had such good intentions, and yet in the span of a single day she'd lost everyone's respect, probably her job, and risked any future jobs. And what happened to the cabaret was anyone's guess.

It wasn't Khaled's fault. Gigi knew she'd walked into this on her own two feet. But as she did her best not to fall apart so close to stage time she couldn't help feeling his exit this afternoon meant she'd been hung out to dry.

'I'm looking for Gigi Valente,' Khaled told the first stage-hand he found.

The kid just stared at him, bug-eyed. 'She's j-just gone onstage, Mr Kitaev,' he stammered.

His driver hadn't been able to get the SUV within a block

of the entrance to the theatre tonight. There were protesters picketing on the pavement, and the media presence spilling onto the road was causing traffic mayhem. He'd also seen that the billboard advertising the show out front had been defaced with graffiti.

The police had been throwing up a blockade as he'd arrived.

And Gigi had chosen to go onstage.

'What the hell are those idiot brothers thinking?' he snarled, and the kid jumped, but Khaled was already making his way out into the audience.

He'd fed Gigi's name into an internet search engine this afternoon. It turned out that Gisele Valente had a charlatan for a father—which wasn't surprising, given what she'd already told him. But what she had neglected to mention was her own role in his all-singing and all-dancing revue as the Valentes had travelled the English provinces, ripping off the punters.

A grainy photograph of Gigi aged eighteen outside court, with a physically imposing, defiant-looking middle-aged man sent mixed feelings through him. He'd seen her scars, and he knew enough of her story to know she hadn't had it easy, but she'd purposely left out the part about her being her father's accomplice.

It was a neat little con, and he had to wonder what she was up to now.

Although as he took in once more the faded glamour of the theatre he had to acknowledge that she'd achieved something this afternoon. The cabaret did look different to him after her presentation. She might not have sold him on the place, but her proposal had gone a lot further than all the media-manufactured ire of Paris and the bumbling excuses of the Danton brothers to bring him on side.

Speaking of which, the Danton brothers, alerted to his presence, were on his heels.

L'Oiseau Bleu had its first full house in months, according to an excitable Jacques Danton. They'd never seen anything like it.

'Mr Kitaev, we know members of the press are in the audience, but we can't do anything about it if they have tickets.'

Martin Danton was wringing his hands as Khaled shouldered his way along the perimeter of the auditorium.

'Who sold them tickets?'

There was an uncomfortable to-ing and fro-ing between the brothers.

*Buffoons.*

Onstage an act was in full swing, involving the tank he'd seen yesterday being put to a different use. Tonight it was full of bubbling water, like a cauldron, and inside two monstrous Burmese pythons glided to and fro.

There was also a girl in there, but he hadn't been paying it much attention, more interested in finding Gigi as unobtrusively as possible. Where the hell was she?

Impatiently he glanced at his watch. He didn't have time for this.

His attention was diverted when he noticed one of the monsters appeared to have wrapped itself around the swimming girl and was dragging her down to the base of the tank.

'Is that monitored?' he snarled.

'A handler is ready to intervene if there's a problem, Mr Kitaev,' Jacques Danton scrambled to assure him.

'It looks like they *are* having a problem. Those snakes—what size are they?'

'Almost three m-metres,' stuttered Martin Danton.

'Then they're capable of crushing the life out of a human being.'

'Only a *small* human being,' Jacques Danton countered, 'and Gigi is a robust girl—she's stronger than she looks.'

*Gigi?*

Khaled shoved the smaller man out of his path and made

his way to the stage. He was about to breach the safety rail when the swimmer broke free and shot through the water, breaking the surface to emerge gracefully from the tank, seemingly no worse for wear, dripping water.

It was Gigi, all right. Painted gold from neck to toes, with the lights strobing over her body and the music as seductive as any snake-charmer's medley.

She was also naked.

There was an appreciative intake of breath from the audience as she struck a pose and the lights slid over her gold-painted body in what was frankly an erotic tribute.

Only Gigi posed as if she was the star attraction that she was.

From the darkness of the audience came a shout. 'Kitaev's whore!'

He went cold, and then something hot and virulent licked up inside him.

Gigi, instead of vacating the stage, had climbed down from her perch and begun to search the darkness for the origin of the slur.

In a moment she had gone from glorious, sensual goddess, bewitching her audience, to the sturdily game girl who had chased him down the Champs-Élysées and stood up to his detractors like Liberté defending her people.

Khaled had already discovered he really liked that girl.

It galvanised him.

He vaulted up onto the stage, stepped over the footlights and strode towards her. Gigi's expression was one of total bewilderment as she saw him coming.

*That's right*, his id growled, *worrying about me is the first smart thing you've done all night.*

Such was her shock, she didn't so much as utter a squeak as he hoisted her up over his shoulder. She only began to struggle and scissor her legs as they came offstage, shouting something about him being a madman and telling him to put her down and that he'd ruined the act.

On the contrary—this felt like the sanest he'd been in years.

Gigi was quickly made aware that they were headed for the exit, with her riding his shoulder like a surfboard, through a sea of gaping showgirls, past gawping stagehands and their own security men, Jules and Jean, who made no attempt to stop him.

'Put me down!' she shouted. 'Are you crazy?'

*'Da.'*

'Where are you taking me?'

'Out of harm's way.' He said this as if it were obvious.

'Put me back onstage, Mr Kitaev. I have a show to do!'

'Mr Kitaev?' he growled.

'I think we should be professional at work.'

'Your work—not mine.'

'I refuse to go with you!'

'Bad luck. You're not climbing back in that tank.'

'It's my act!'

'Tonight Paris wants to drown you, and those idiot brothers thought it was a good idea to put you in a tank of water in front of them?'

'Nobody wants to drown me except the other girls, and now you've just made it worse!'

He kept going.

'You can't just carry me out of here. What are people going to say?'

'The same thing they're already saying,' he snarled, as if this was the last thing he wanted. 'That I can't keep my hands off you.'

There was shouting behind them, but Khaled was kicking open the exit door.

'You can't take me out of here—I'm naked!' she shrieked.

'Yes,' Khaled said, and he didn't sound happy about it, 'you *are*.'

The cold air and the night rushed at her, and then she was being lifted into a waiting SUV.

Khaled leapt in after her and the door slammed. They took off at speed.

Gigi scrunched herself up against the opposite door, arms plastered across her chest, legs crossed, horribly aware that she was practically naked, covered in gold paint and dripping wet. Humiliated.

'Are you *insane*?' she exploded.

He reached for her and she began kicking out at him with her feet.

'Don't you touch me, you pervert! You're a madman!'

One of her six-inch stilettos caught against the denim of his jeans and tipped the shoe off her foot. He grasped her other foot and yanked off the second glittery shoe, whisked down the window and threw both of them out into the passing night.

Gigi watched on in utter disbelief.

'Those shoes are the property of L'Oiseau Bleu! They're hand-made!'

'There are paparazzi crawling all over that theatre,' he snarled, as if this were *her* fault, and she retreated like a turtle who had stuck its neck out and almost had it cut off—before she realised he was holding a phone in one hand while warding off her pummelling feet with the other. 'I want to know how and why they got into the building.'

He pocketed his phone and sat forward, to shrug his big shoulders out of his wool coat.

'The paps will have photographs of us, but they can't do any more damage.'

'It was you they wanted!'

'Don't be so naïve,' he growled, 'and stop hammering me with your feet.'

'Then let me out of this car.' She gave him another inef-

fectual shove with the soles of her feet, but with no real conviction, only to have him throw his coat over her.

'What are you doing?' she demanded as he began to feed
one of her flailing arms into a sleeve.

'Keeping you warm,' he said impatiently. 'Hold still.'

'I don't want to be warm—I want to be back at the theatre, doing my job.'

But even as she protested she was quick to push her fists
through the armholes of the coat in an attempt to preserve
a little of her modesty.

It was one thing to be onstage, where the audience saw
her at a remove, under rose-coloured trick lighting. Quite
another to have the man she fancied being treated to this intimate view of her body before he'd even taken her to dinner!

She had a very clear progression programme on this:
meet, date, and then, if everything appeared to be going
somewhere meaningful—get naked. She didn't reverse that
order.

Khaled had bulldozed through it in the space of twenty-
four hours and gone straight for the naked.

Although he was keeping his gaze manfully above her
chin-line, which was making her feel marginally better.

'I've had threats, Gigi—stupid, puerile threats—a follow-
on from all this press coverage about your cabaret slipping
into dangerous Russian hands.'

Those hands were currently distracting her by drawing
the sides of the coat together to cover her properly.

'You'll have noticed, *dushka*, that you're not the only person in Paris who doesn't trust me.'

She did actually trust him—she just wasn't very happy
with him at the moment. But she wasn't letting on, because
clearly give him an inch and he'd take—well, take her offstage in the middle of a performance!

He was securing a couple of buttons on the coat. She
could have done it herself, but neither of them seemed about
to acknowledge this.

'The media aren't giving me much choice about how to handle your safety.'

'My safety is none of your business,' she grumbled.

A shiver of reaction shook her and he gave her arms a rub a little roughly, so that her teeth chattered.

'Stop manhandling me,' she snapped.

'You are cold,' he said, continuing to rub.

'And whose fault is *that*? Stop shaking me about! I'm not a chew toy for you to play with.'

He stopped rubbing. 'A what?'

She wasn't sure why she'd said that—only he'd gone all physical, and a bit of her was enjoying it, which wasn't right! 'Coco has one,' she mumbled, avoiding looking him in the eye. Then she ploughed on, 'Look, I won't go back onstage. Does that solve the problem?'

Gigi noticed that the lining of the coat still carried his body heat, and she was finding it unexpectedly comforting after her shock.

'This is a start,' he said, releasing her, and she could feel his gaze, dark and disturbing, on her skin. 'And now you're refraining from kicking me we can discuss this like rational human beings.'

'I *am* rational,' said Gigi promptly, pulling the folds of his coat up around her chin, teeth chattering, 'and if you'll take me home I would be most obliged.'

'Don't be naïve. Paparazzi are camped outside your flat.'

'My flat? How do you know that? How do they know my address?'

'You gave those people on the Champs-Élysées your name. I seem to remember you declaiming it like a town crier.'

Gigi instantly felt sick. He made it sound as if she was on the make.

She wasn't her father—always on the sell, always doing something for himself at the expense of other people. Including her. She tried always to do the opposite. All she'd wanted was to promote the theatre and build up their audience. She'd thought he understood that.

He cut through her muddled thoughts.

'You are going to need security for a few days.'

'I can't afford it.'

He looked at her as if she'd said something absurd. 'Naturally you will share my security.'

It was ridiculous, but she was sitting down and her legs still felt wobbly.

'How is *that* going to work?' As she spoke she drew her long wobbly legs up onto the seat and under her, so she was more securely covered, and noticed that he noticed them on their ascent.

She tucked the coat more modestly around her and his gaze cut to hers. She was surprised to see a bit of colour riding his cheekbones.

She'd been virtually naked in his arms and he'd covered her up like something in storage—but flash him some thigh and he zeroed in on it with all the subtlety of…well, a man.

Gigi wasn't sure how she felt about that, but she discovered she no longer felt so diminished.

'You will stay with me,' he said, as if there could be no question about it.

The tension in the car was changing from anger and confusion to something more charged.

Given her experience with men was more of the duck and weave variety, not the fly-to-the-Bahamas-with-me-baby, Gigi wasn't quite sure how to respond.

'Won't that just be playing up to this idea that we're in some kind of nasty beneficial relationship?'

She blushed as she said it.

'You're blushing,' he said, as if this were a wonder.

Gigi looked away. 'I am not. It's just hot in this coat.'

Which was when she noticed they seemed to have left the familiar *arrondissements*. There was less light and more lanes of traffic.

She tried to see out, but with the soft glow of light in the back of the SUV and the darkness outside she could really only see their reflections in the dark glass.

He was watching her as if she fascinated him. The feeling was mutual, but that didn't mean she was ready to go away with him. They hadn't even been on a *date*!

'I'm not going back to your hotel with you,' she said. 'My reputation may be shredded after today, but I'm not buttering it and putting jam on it.'

He gave her an arrested look. 'What is this jam?'

'Jam—you know, *jam*.'

'Sex,' he said coolly. 'No, I am not taking you back to the hotel.'

'Good.' Gigi tried not to let her disappointment show, because despite everything a part of her had leapt when she'd seen him striding across the stage towards her. Coming to collect her.

'We're going straight to the airport,' he informed her. 'I'm taking you with me out of the country—tonight.'

# CHAPTER ELEVEN

SHE LOOKED LIKE an angel. Her long, coppery red hair was snaking across the black leather of the seat, golden lashes lay recumbent on her high pointed cheekbones. Every last cinnamon-brown freckle stood out against the pallor of her scrubbed clean face. She had one slender hand cradling her cheek as she slept.

Against his better judgement Khaled reached across with one hand and lifted the blanket that had dropped from her shoulders to hang over her knees, and was now threatening to slide off completely. He draped it over her and returned to navigating the long stretch of highway taking them from the airport into central Moscow.

*What the hell was he doing?*

He'd been asking himself that question for the last three hours. The obvious answer was between his legs. The less obvious conclusion he'd come to was that he genuinely liked her. She might be a con artist and a stripper, but she had a way about her that had caught him unawares. And he could say this for her: he damn well wasn't bored.

Only now, when he looked at her sleeping, his suspicions seemed laboured and frankly untrue.

It was difficult to match up the wet, naked fantasy who had lied to him, furiously kicking her legs as he'd carried her offstage, with the soft-featured sleeping girl beside him, her face a study of the angelic, her impossibly long limbs curled up under her, her hair a swathe of burnished colour across the blue of the blanket.

A shower and a change of clothes had taken care of the gold-painted mess and the Gigi he'd spent the day with had been once more beside him. Khaled had been surprised by the level of his own satisfaction on that score.

He knew when she opened her eyes. He could feel them on him.

He glanced her way.

She blinked. Those eyes stayed on him. Very blue. She licked her lips. It should have been sexual. Instead what he felt was a warmth spreading through his chest.

She was safe. She was awake. He had no intention of letting her out of his sight.

It felt good.

She sat up, pushing back her fringe.

'Where are we?'

'Quarter of an hour outside Moscow.'

'What time is it?'

'Midnight. You lost three hours.'

'Where did I lose them?'

He tried not to smile. 'Back in Paris.'

'Along with my shoes,' she said. Then furrowed her brow at him. 'Why didn't you wake me up?'

'You were sound asleep—it was easier to carry you to the car.'

'You *carried* me?'

'It seemed the thing to do.'

She pulled on her sleeves, gave him an awkward sideward look. 'You've turned me into one of those showgirls who goes away with a wealthy man for the weekend.'

'Is that so?'

'I'm trying to work out how I feel about that.'

'Fill me in when you've decided.'

Gigi cast him another look. 'I guess I'm not here to sleep with you, so the nuts and bolts of that kind of thing don't apply, but nobody else knows that. It looks bad.'

It wasn't her imagination. He'd definitely tensed. Those capable hands, lightly sprinkled with dark hair at the broad wrists, flexed around the wheel and testosterone began to be pumped out into the atmosphere between them.

'Why do you care what other people think about you?'

'Twenty-two people, to be exact. The other dancers in the troupe. They already think… Well, never mind what they think. It's not true.'

Gigi thrust her hands into her lap and stared straight ahead. Khaled was silent. Apparently telling a man you weren't going to sleep with him after he'd gone out of his way to rescue you from a media scrum was a bit of a no-no.

Then it occurred to her that he might be tensing up because he had no intention of sleeping with her. In which case it made her sound desperate. Clearly she'd been on her own too long. She'd got cosy, living a charmed *Girls' Own* existence with Lulu, allowing her friend's anxieties about men to shelve her own fledgling sex life—until now, when you put her in the company of a gorgeous, testosterone-charged man and she began fantasising that he wanted her.

Gigi took another covert look at him. Most women would want him. He was built on a scale that made her think about that trip she'd taken to Florence, looking up at Michelangelo's *David*. Her attention dropped to the shift of his long, powerfully muscled thigh as he accelerated.

'I can hear you thinking,' he said, in that low, strongly accented voice, and Gigi jumped, her gaze yanked back to his.

Oh, God, he'd caught her looking at his groin. She wasn't doing that—honestly. She *wasn't* thinking about what she'd had pressed against her yesterday. Even if it *had* been memorable and she *had* been very flattered it had been to do with her…

Was she speaking this all out loud?

He glanced at her again. 'Don't worry, Gigi. I'm not listening in to your thoughts.'

Her face felt hot. 'It wouldn't matter if you were, I've got nothing to hide.'

'*Da*, I saw that onstage.'

Gigi straightened up. Reviewing her performance was fine by her. She could take criticism. 'I was on fire tonight,' she declared.

'Is that what you call it?'

She made a face. *Everyone's a critic.* 'Pity you had to spoil the act.'

'You were naked.'

Gigi bristled. 'I was not! I was in costume.'

'A piece of string.'

'Plus gold body paint and pasties. *And* shoes.' Her eyes narrowed. She wasn't going to forget what had happened to her shoes.

'That's not a costume—it's an incitement.'

'To what?'

He made a derisive sound. 'Are you serious?'

'Excuse me? I was *not* naked.'

'I saw *everything.*'

'You did not!'

'Maybe not everything,' he responded, and it was his turn to drop his gaze to *her* lap, 'but I saw enough.'

Flustered, Gigi crossed her legs. 'You saw what you wanted to see,' she snapped back, feeling ridiculously self-conscious. 'Lulu's right. Men have lurid and depraved imaginations.'

'Lurid and depraved?'

She could hear the disbelief in his voice and it had her sitting up straighter. 'You make things sexual that aren't.'

'You were swimming in a spotlit tank, on a stage, with two pythons wrapping themselves around your naked body,' he growled. 'How is *that* not sexual?'

She looked at him blankly. 'You mean Jack and Edna?'

'Who?'

'The snakes. Edna's an old softie. Jack's the one you've got to look out for—he can slap you around with that tail. Mind you, they're both way past retirement age, but Jacques wants to see this season out. The "Snakes in the Amazon" act is one of our most popular.'

'This would be because it's dangerous and because you are naked.'

Gigi smoothed her hands over the long, beautifully tailored pants he'd provided for her aboard the jet, entirely grateful that she wasn't virtually naked now. He was making it all sound grubby.

'Wow, you are *such* a prude,' she said uncomfortably. 'Who'd have thought it?'

'After your presentation, Gigi, I was under the impression that the place was a bit more classy. My mistake.'

What exactly was he implying? That *she* wasn't classy?

A hot feeling at his unjustified criticism shot through her, but what was sharper was the needling sensation that she had something to be ashamed of.

She didn't.

She did the best she could with the material she was given—act *and* costume. She should tell him there was nothing sexy about breath control underwater and managing two temperamental reptiles while keeping a big smile on your face for the patrons. It was hard work!

Besides, she wasn't keen on the pythons act herself, and she was fairly sure it was her complaints that meant Jacques would be phasing it out at the end of the season, but Khaled had no right to imply that there was anything tawdry about it or her participation in it.

She was already feeling humiliated enough after being trussed up and thrown over his shoulder like a naked turkey.

Better to say nothing.

She folded her arms. She really didn't want him to know just how utterly out of her depth she was feeling. The most excitement she ever got was pedalling a bicycle down the hills of Montmartre. She might play at being Gigi, Queen of the Amazon, onstage, but frankly she was Gigi, Queen of the Ordinary, in her everyday life. Tearing down a Moscow highway at midnight in a supercharged sports car with a man who dated supermodels wasn't exactly the usual end to a night onstage for her.

The problem was it seemed to be turning into one of those

episodes with her father, where she'd been forced to keep
her opinions and fears to herself because he hadn't wanted
to hear them—and even if he had it would just have been
something he'd expected her to get over.

'You've grown soft, Gisele Valente,' she could hear him
saying. 'Life's tough—you need to toughen up.'

'Gigi?'

She sniffed.

Which was when something landed in her lap.

It was a phone. An elaborate little device.

'Eight-ten-thirty-three.'

'Pardon?'

'The international code to phone Paris. I thought you
might want to ring someone,' he said gruffly. 'Your friends
might be concerned.'

The fact that it hadn't even occurred to her until now
startled Gigi.

Of course Lulu would be frantic! She hadn't been at the
theatre tonight, but no doubt some of the other girls had
spread the news of her being carried out in his arms.

Lulu probably had her stepfather pulling all kinds of
strings at the Ministry of Foreign Affairs, where he pretty
much ran the show.

She made the call. Lulu picked up immediately and
shrieked her name, confirming her fears and forcing her to
hold the device away from her ear.

It was even more awkward explaining herself with Khaled
right beside her.

'I'm fine. He's not a murderer.'

She glanced at him, wondering what he was making of
this, but Khaled's expression gave nothing away. She might
have been talking about her shopping list.

'No, it's okay—I'll be back in a few days.' She turned
towards the door and tried to keep her voice down. 'No, it's
not a stunt. I'm in Moscow.'

'We're on Kashirskoe Shosse.' Khaled's deep voice cut

through the shrill sounds of disbelief in her other ear. 'Your friend can find it on a map.'

'Did you hear that, Lu? Yes, that's him. Yes, he is.' She lowered her voice. 'No, he hasn't.'

Khaled shifted beside her and Gigi wished the seat would swallow her up.

Lulu's description of the protesters' arrests and the media's interest was alarming. None of it had apparently been an over-exaggeration on Khaled's part. Then again, he had not yet struck her as a man given to anything but the stripped-down facts. It was something, given her murky past with her shyster father, she really liked about him.

*Had* liked about him…before he'd started going on about her act.

She listened as Lulu described how she'd had to wade through paparazzi to get into the apartment building and how she and Coco were staying with her parents tonight.

Khaled had told her the truth.

She glanced at him, feeling a little stupid for all the fuss she had made.

'People at the cabaret are talking about it like it's the romance of the century,' Lulu went on. 'I think some of the girls have even talked to the press.'

'Romance?' She said it out loud, before she could censor herself. 'I don't think—'

Khaled plucked the phone out of her hand. 'She'll talk to you tomorrow.'

Lulu must have said something cutting, because Khaled's expression was cool as he ended the call.

'She does not like me.'

*What on earth had Lulu said?*

'You might want to rein her in on making threats. They'll get her into trouble.'

Gigi blinked. 'It's *Lulu*,' she said faintly. 'She's not a threat to anyone.'

'Nor are you to feed stories to her while you are here.'

'Stories?'

'"Romance of the century…"' he drawled.

Gigi went hot. He'd heard Lulu's end of the conversation. He must have ears like a cat. A big, predatory cat—the kind who brought down the unwary.

She was beginning to feel distinctly savaged herself by this line of discussion.

'It's not me or Lulu—it's the other girls,' she defended herself.

'Who won't be receiving any bulletins from *you*, Gisele.'

'You can't possibly think I *want* people to be speculating about us—' She broke off awkwardly, not wanting him to think she thought there was an 'us'. 'I mean me.'

'Why wouldn't I think that? This is what you wanted, wasn't it? To revive interest in the cabaret? As I remember it you put together an entire presentation with that in mind.'

'For *you*,' she said, thrown by what he was intimating. 'I showed that to you—not the rest of Paris!'

She felt stupidly hurt, because she had been holding on to that interlude as one of the nicer interactions between them—something genuine, when she'd been allowed to show him what she could do. Weirdly, it had felt more personal than when he'd been expertly gliding her under him on the bed.

'You invited the rest of Paris in with that neat little speech on the Champs-Élysées.' He drummed the wheel with his fingers. 'Then there was your performance in the lobby of the Plaza.'

'I did *not* want to go up to your hotel room. You were the one who was so all-fire keen.'

For the first time it looked as if she'd scored a hit, because he didn't appear to have anything superior to say.

'You had an injury,' he said finally.

She'd had an…

Gigi pressed her lips together, aware that if she kept this up she was going to say something unwise.

Something that might see her standing at a bus stop at one in the morning on the side of a Moscow road.

Did they even *have* bus stops?

Light was smearing the windscreen and her gaze was drawn to neon advertisements, the glowing façades of sky-scrapers. The tension in her body increased.

This was the way she'd used to feel with her dad—that airless, suffocating feeling when she couldn't say the wrong word, do the wrong thing, because then she'd be out. On her own. Carlos's way or the highway. The only problem was she'd never quite been sure what the wrong thing *was*.

A feeling a little like panic began to spiral through her. It was bringing back her dependent teenage years with a thump. No say in where she went, what she did. *You're not powerless any more*, she reminded herself. *Those days are gone—you have options.*

She had her passport. She could take a taxi back to the airport. She could book a flight and have Lulu pay for it, using her credit card, and pay her back when she got home. She didn't *have* to stay with this man.

By the time they pulled up she had several speeches ready for him. But when she climbed out and looked up, took in the imposing building with caryatids on the stone columns either side of the entrance, and the doorman in uniform, she discovered her overriding feeling was one of nerves.

She wouldn't be intimidated. *She wouldn't.*

'Come.'

He took hold of her elbow none too gently and something inside Gigi tugged and tore.

She yanked her elbow out of his grasp. 'Stop being so horrible to me!'

'Horrible?' He stood over her, keeping the wind out of her face with those broad shoulders of his.

Gigi stepped a little closer, because it was cold, and he was big and warm, and even if he was being a horrible she trusted him.

'I want you to be nicer to me.'

'*Nicer* to you?'

He made it sound like a word in a foreign language, and maybe it was. Maybe she'd got this all wrong and she was just a nuisance in his world.

'I just think you could make an effort to be nicer to me,' she grumbled. 'After all, I've had a rough day too.'

He didn't respond, but he was looking down at her as if she had said something weird.

'Don't worry—forget about it.' She shrugged her shoulders and looked up at the building. 'Is this where I'm staying?'

He said something in Russian, but this time he didn't touch her or hurry her inside.

She tried not to feel self-conscious as she stood beside him in the lift taking them from the ground to the sixth floor.

She'd worked out that he wasn't very happy with her. She guessed she couldn't blame him. It wouldn't matter so much, but all the running about with him yesterday, the confidential talks, the amazing way he'd been with her insecurities over her feet, not to mention what had happened afterwards, had…well, had aroused feelings in her.

She didn't often have these feelings, and if she'd had a choice in the matter she wouldn't have picked him as the ideal target for them, but it wasn't as if she had any say in it. They were her *feelings*.

In contrast, Khaled didn't seem to think she had any—or was it just that he was so used to women falling into his lap?

She guessed he kissed women as if he was lost in the desert and the woman in question was water every day of the week.

It wasn't the same for her.

Before Khaled had taken her unawares on the bathroom vanity yesterday she actually hadn't kissed anyone since New Year's Eve—although that was something she'd be keeping to herself. He didn't need to know that her private life was the equivalent of a mill pond. She'd be holding on to her out-every-night-showgirl status, thank you very much.

Then the lift doors opened and she stepped out into what had to be the most glamorous lobby, fitted out in black and white marble and granite.

'Wow…' she breathed.

Movement-activated sensors shed low light through the hall ahead of them. It all looked very welcoming and expensive and intimate.

'Will I be staying *here*?'

He closed the doors behind them and his hand caught hers. Not a snatch, but a tangling of his clever fingers with hers.

Gigi's arm tingled. Her breath caught as he turned her around and she found herself looking up into beautiful dark eyes so thickly lashed it was a wonder he didn't need splints to keep the lids up. This inconsequential thought flew away with all the other butterfly thoughts about what she was doing here and why she felt so nervous.

She would never be too sure if she stepped towards him or he to her, only suddenly there was no space between them at all and she was in his arms.

This was her answer, she thought fleetingly, This was him being nice to her.

*Very nice to her.*

The need swelled up in her like a symphony as she lifted on her toes and wound her arms around his neck and held on.

She didn't know why, but when he kissed her she always felt as if she was on the deck of a ship. Everything was heaving up and down in the most delightful manner and she would lose her footing if she let go.

He re-angled the kiss, going deeper, moving against her, backing her against the wall. She moaned softly and kissed him back, her heart beating like a drum. She instinctively moved her hips, pressing her pelvis into his groin, feeling the length of him so impossibly hard against her.

At first all Gigi allowed in was a feeling of relief that finally the torturous suspension of this powerful feeling between them was over.

But then she discovered she couldn't shut down her thoughts, even though her body was going crazy with wanting him.

What was she *doing* here? Did she *really* think she could just give in to her feelings and forget about the consequences? She didn't even know what was in Khaled's mind. Would he think she was making up to him just for what he could do for her?

*Stop thinking!* she shouted at her busy little brain.

No. She couldn't give in to this physical longing, because that was all it was, when her motives must appear extremely ambiguous to him.

She broke the kiss.

It was the hardest thing to do in that moment.

'I don't want to be accused of using sex for leverage,' she panted.

*'Ch'to?'* His eyes were heavy-lidded and he was breathing hard.

'All the girls think I slept with you to further my career.'

'This is not a problem for me,' he responded, and his mouth moved over hers again, making it impossible to do anything but absorb the sensation, the fierce push of his lean, hard body against hers.

Still her mind kept beating, like the sea against a tethered boat. No…yes…oh, help. It was so unbearably exciting, and so unfair. He was being no help at all with her moral quandary! He branded her with that mouth of his and for a few incredibly exciting seconds she gave way.

It was even better than before because she just let herself *feel*. Her thighs literally felt as if a landslide was going on. She could barely hold herself up. But he was there, hard and powerful, doing all the supporting work a girl could need.

No, there was nothing to stop them…nothing but her conscience. Nosy, interfering thing that it was.

'Khaled?'

She wedged her elbows in between them to give herself some wiggle room.

'This can't happen,' she told him, even as she melted with pleasure over each hot, knicker-elastic-snapping kiss he laid down her neck.

*If the other girls could see me now.*

They'd kill her.

No, Susie would tell her to go for it—get that squeak fixed. Solange would scoff, because Gigi hadn't got a promise of *anything* out of him and she was just offering up the goods without a contract. Lulu would be horrified.

*Forty-eight hours?*

Gigi strained against him as he stroked a searching hand up under her sweater, under the completely unsexy thermal vest, and found a very happy to see him breast.

Oh, yes, her nipples remembered him.

Bad, *bad* nipples.

He circled one with the broad pad of his thumb and she whimpered, because she felt it directly between her legs.

He did it again and her knees buckled.

'This isn't fair…' she whimpered.

'Life isn't fair,' he responded against her mouth, as if he were telling her something she didn't already know.

The phone he'd gifted her began to vibrate in her hip pocket. At first it was difficult to tell, given that she was doing some serious vibrating herself in that area—but, no, it was a lozenge-shaped vibration, coming from the general vicinity of where she'd shoved the phone.

She broke the kiss and reached down between them. Khaled watched her actions as if riveted, and for a moment she wondered if he thought she was going in another direction.

No—she could have told him she wasn't that bold. She left that kind of forthright sexual move to girls with a lot more know-how than her. She was more of a wait-and-see-what-he-wants-to-do-with-it kind of girl.

She held up the phone like a red flag.

'What are you doing?' he growled.

'Answering my phone,' she breathed, because he still had one hand cradling her breast. 'Excuse me.'

She pushed 'talk'.

'Hello, Lulu?'

Khaled stared at her as if she'd developed a second head, and as Lulu's voice complained at being hung up on she supposed she had. Khaled looked at the phone, and for a breathless moment Gigi wondered if he was going to smash it on the floor.

The part of her that had been anticipating that was to be severely disappointed.

He said something in Russian, his hand slid away from her, and she found herself on her own, slumped against the doorframe. Lulu was wanting to know if she was safe and telling her she didn't sound like herself.

'We've just arrived—barely got in the door,' she breathed, watching him stride away from her down the hall.

'You sound like you've been running a race,' Lulu countered suspiciously.

Gigi swallowed hard. 'No, no…just a flight of stairs.' It was only a little lie, and there was no way she was going into what had just happened. She wasn't even *sure* what had just happened. 'Look, Lu, I'm beat. I'll talk to you tomorrow. What time is it there?'

'Dawn,' said Lulu. 'I'm in bed with Coco, watching all the repeat coverage of what happened last night. They're saying Kitaev bought the cabaret so he could have you.'

'Have *me*?' Gigi knew she was red as a beetroot. 'I'm not a prop. And besides, he won the cabaret in a card game!'

'Maman says you have a pretty good case for slander.'

A court case? No, thanks.

Gigi began to make her way down the hall. Where had he gone?

Lulu was recounting several cases in which people had been defamed in the press and won huge payouts, but Gigi wasn't able to concentrate on a word. She needed to go in search of Khaled. Because right about now she was feeling she'd behaved like a rabbit, and she owed him an explanation—besides which, she didn't even have a bed to sleep in.

# CHAPTER TWELVE

SHE PEERED AROUND the corner into one dark room, and then another. Honestly, it was a bit rude, leaving her on her own.

Which was when he appeared unexpectedly at the end of the hall, shirt unbuttoned.

'I'm not driving you back to the airport tonight.'

His deep, dark voice startled her, given she still had Lulu's high, melodious French accent in her other ear.

Gigi made her choice. She pushed 'end'.

'I think we should clear something up,' she said, trying to firm her voice.

'I agree. I know what you're going to say: I shouldn't have touched you.' He headed off around the corner.

Gigi almost broke into a sprint. No, no—that wasn't what she was going to say at all. 'Listen,' she said, following him down a flight of stairs, 'what I wanted to say was I know you're probably going to sell L'Oiseau Bleu.'

'Is that so?'

'Yes, and also everything that happened today is my fault and I'm willing to take it on the chin,' she said in a rush.

For such a big man he was incredibly light on his feet as he padded down the steps. He'd removed his shoes, and in jeans and an unbuttoned fresh shirt open across his chest he looked incredibly sexy, and for some reason younger, but also entirely beyond her reach.

'You didn't have to bring me here, but you did. And I guess you know something about press intrusion and I should be grateful—and I am. But I don't want you thinking I want something from you.'

Khaled stopped so suddenly she rammed into his back. Gigi was aware she'd been in this position before.

'Gigi,' he said patiently, turning around slowly, 'the only

reason we got into all of this was because you want something from me.'

'That's not true!'

She took a step back, because frankly she didn't trust herself within bumping distance of him. It took every ounce of her concentration to rip her eyes off his bare chest.

'Look, I know your cynical viewpoint was probably earned the hard way, but my life hasn't exactly been storybook either. I know well enough how mercenary and self-serving people can be, but that doesn't mean you have to abandon your best instincts. You've certainly spent enough time with me now to form some idea of my character and to know I'm not on the make.'

He shook his head. 'Gigi, at the moment I'm too achingly hard to laugh, but your indignation is rich, given the events of the last forty-eight hours.'

He was…? She tried to ignore the melting response of her body to the news that he still wanted her. God knew she wanted him. They just had things to discuss first.

Only he kept going down the stairs.

'I guess it suits you to think I want stuff from you!' she called after him. 'It means you can keep treating me like luggage and not talk to me about what happened between us in my flat and at the hotel.'

She shut her eyes briefly. She hadn't meant to say that.

'Why would I want to talk to you about it?'

'Oh, I don't know—because you kissed me?'

He looked up at her. The way his eyes ran over her body made her shiver.

'It was a mistake.'

*Was it?*

Which was when her stomach decided to yawn open and a noisy, unambiguous rumble made itself known.

*Kill me now.*

He frowned. 'When did you last eat?'

'Four o'clock. Yesterday.'

He said something clearly uncomplimentary in Russian.

'What did you just say to me?'

'Stupid girl,' he said in English, but his tone was almost warm. 'Come on, I'll feed you.'

'Stupid being here with *you*,' she muttered. But she trotted after him.

He took her downstairs to the kitchen. He dug out fresh bread, ham, cheese, salad stuff, and went to work on sandwiches.

He did everything he could to get his mind off her soft-as-rose-petals lips, the pointy curve of her breast that fitted perfectly into the palm of his hand, her sweet enthusiasm even as she pushed him away and twittered nonsense at him about it not happening.

'You cook for yourself?'

He looked up. She was sliding her pretty little behind onto a stool at the bench, her blue eyes on him.

'Why not?' he growled, feeling like a bear with a sore head. Because she was right—it *shouldn't* happen. 'Every man should be self-sufficient.'

'Yeah, I'm getting that vibe off you.'

She fell quiet. He didn't trust her when she was quiet. Gigi's mind didn't stop whirring.

'When I first saw you I thought, *Now there's a man who's been somewhere*,' she said suddenly.

'I *have* been somewhere. Central Asia and the Arctic Circle, with a band of scientists and geologists.'

'To do with your oil?'

She was a quick study—he'd give that to her.

'To do with my oil. There's nothing like being on the ground, seeing the erosion for yourself, experiencing it, watching the visible proof of changing migration patterns, the changes to the soil. Stops me from getting comfortable or lazy about my responsibilities to the planet.'

'You sound like a bit of a green.'

Khaled shrugged. 'I grew up in the mountains—it's difficult not to be ecologically aware.'

'Do you miss it, now you're living in cities?'

'I head back into the mountains when I can. I also have shares in alternative energy source companies, and I'm moving away from petroleum.'

'What's it like, running the world?'

'Is that what I do?'

'All that money—do you ever count it? Or do you stop thinking about it at a certain point? I mean, I live from month to month, and my budget is always blown by week two.'

Khaled frowned. She was nervous—was that why she was talking so much nonsense?

He wasn't accustomed to sexual nervousness in a woman. The women in his life were bold, mostly self-serving, conscious of the desirability which they put such a value on.

Gigi's actions upstairs began to make a bit of sense to him.

'You need a good accountant, *dushka*.'

'I don't earn enough to warrant one. Not all of us own oil fields.'

'Money isn't always the answer, Gigi. I've got a project in the Caucasus Mountains facing local objection and I think a good deal of it is connected to my billions in the bank.'

'Why's that?'

He laid down the knife and leaned forward on his hands. 'I'm the local boy made good—it doesn't go down well there.'

'I just assumed you were from Moscow.'

'The first time I saw Moscow I was fresh out of the army and I'd washed up with a duffle bag and some ambition. Until then all I'd known was the mountains.'

Gigi settled her elbows on the bench, her chin in her hands, and fixed her beautiful blue eyes on him.

'Were you born there?'

'I was. My father was a career soldier stationed in Chechnya.'

He began piling the sandwich filling high, slapping thick crusty bread on top. His housekeeper was an angel.

'Isn't that a dangerous place?'

'My father took a bullet from a sniper when I was four,' he confirmed, eyeing her when she sat back, clearly perturbed. 'After that my mother struggled. She was forced back to her family in the mountains further west and remarried a sheep farmer. We never had any money—we just had sheep.'

'I'm sorry about your dad,' she said. 'It must have been awful for you and your mum.'

'Difficult for my mother. She was in her early twenties, had little education, and not much chance of supporting me on her own.'

'But she remarried?'

'He had land, a home—respect in the village. He rose to be head man. She believed it was better than what she'd had.'

'She had *you*,' said Gigi.

'She had a corner in her parents' home, where she was the disgraced daughter who'd married a Russian soldier.'

'Disgraced? Why?'

'She was pregnant before she married him—and where I come from, Gigi, Russian soldiers aren't exactly welcomed with open arms. There's a long history of guerrilla warfare in the mountains between Russia and the peoples of the Caucasus. Nobody was happy with their marriage.'

'Were your parents happy?'

Khaled suddenly became aware that he'd just told Gigi more about himself than he'd ever revealed—to anyone.

He didn't talk about this. *Ever.* He didn't need reminding of that part of his life. Why was it at the forefront of his mind now? Probably because at the moment the building of that road down south was swinging over him like an axe.

'How did we get on to this topic?'

His tone was one that had made grown men fall silent in his presence. He hadn't meant to use it on her, but he couldn't stem the tide of anger when it came to his parents.

Gigi blinked. 'I just wanted to find out a little about you.'

Yeah—her and a lot of busy journalists.

Then he remembered that photograph of her mother and her own sentiments regarding her father. *He wasn't a reliable man.* He guessed Gigi knew enough about broken families for him to give her a little of what she wanted to hear.

'My parents loved one another very much.'

Gigi raised an eyebrow. 'You don't seem over the moon about it.'

'"Love" is a word that's used to cover a lot of ground,' he replied. 'I'm not a big fan.'

'I don't think we have too much say in who we love.'

He pulled a chilled jug of cold *chay* from the fridge.

'Love didn't save my father from a stray bullet, and it didn't feed and clothe my mother, or shield her from criticism when she was forced to come home. In fact love only made it a lot harder for her.'

'But how do you *know* that? Why couldn't it have been the opposite? She'd known love and it was a wonderful memory for her, something she might find again.'

The *chay* sloshed as he lifted the jug towards the bench. 'I'll tell you why, Gigi. My stepfather couldn't forgive her for being in love with my father. It didn't matter what she did—it was never enough to assuage his jealousy.' Khaled banged the jug down with force. 'There was nothing wonderful about the way he treated us.'

He realised he was breathing hard.

Gigi sat back, her brow pulled in that knot he remembered from their first encounter, but she wasn't backing away from him.

'I think Carlos was in love with my mother even after she refused to have him in her life. I'm sure that was why he came for me after she died. But it didn't translate into love for *me*. He pretty much resented me from the start.'

'You were his blood—why would he resent you?'

'Because she loved me,' Gigi said, with devastating simplicity, 'but she didn't love *him*.'

Khaled stilled.

'You see,' she said quietly, 'we have more in common than either of us realised.'

His chest wall tightened. She was looking at him with those bright, hopeful blue eyes and all he could think was that it was like putting a little field hare in a cage with a grey wolf to compare their lives in any way. He could so easily tear her apart.

Gigi didn't seem to understand this. She didn't understand who he was.

Right now he was relieved that he'd turned down the stairs and not up—because if he took her to bed she was bound to read more into it than there was.

He would put her in a guest room tonight and a hotel tomorrow. It was time to reassert the barriers between them.

Instead he heard himself ask her gruffly, 'Your father is no longer in your life?'

'He's in Barcelona. We talk on the phone. I'm not good at holding grudges. You don't seem to be either.'

He tried to ignore the fact that she was telegraphing something else with her eyes—something about what had happened upstairs. She was biting her lower lip.

'You'd be surprised,' he murmured. 'Tell me about your dad.'

She gave a rueful little shrug that held a great deal. 'He tries to make amends, but he's very old-school traditional—he thinks the way he raised me was right: being strict, withholding praise…'

'Winding cords around your young feet?'

'Oh, no, I did that myself, trying to please him. It was being lifted and lowered on the ropes every day that did it. Carlos is many things, but he's not a sadist.'

'Those marks on your feet make me want to meet your father in a quiet place,' he said with intent.

'It's not necessary.' She looked up at him through her lashes. 'Although the cavewoman in me appreciates the gesture.'

Shoving aside his very real desire to clear the table and haul her into his arms, he pushed a plate towards her and poured cold *chay* into glasses.

She needed food in her stomach—that was the only reason they were down here together—and then he would do the right thing and send her to bed alone.

If it killed him.

Gigi bit into her sandwich with gusto and moaned.

He was a dead man.

'Good, this is so good,' she mumbled. 'You're like the King of Sandwiches.'

'I'll mention that to my investors,' he murmured, watching her eat. 'You really *are* hungry.'

'This is normal for me. I eat like a horse. It's all the dancing.' She swiped at her mouth unselfconsciously.

Many women had gone to great lengths to seduce him. Not one of them had ever thought just to eat a sandwich.

He noticed he hadn't touched his own. Food wasn't a priority for him right now.

His skin felt tight, hot, and he couldn't help looking at the wondrous architecture of her dancer's body and the soft female curves of her breasts and bottom beneath her clothes. He'd had his hands on her, and he wasn't going to forget that any time soon.

To take his mind off it he concentrated on what she needed. He knew she must still be hungry and dug out some kirsch-flavoured dessert from the fridge.

While he was fossicking around Gigi was collecting the

two plates and wiping up where she'd splattered bits from
her sandwich. He paused with the fridge door open, taking
in the sight of Gigi pottering around his kitchen. Rinsing the
dishes. It all felt weirdly domestic.

He slammed the fridge door behind him.

'You don't have to do that,' he said, more harshly than
he'd meant it to sound.

She finished wiping the plates and gave him a self-conscious smile. 'I'm much messier at home.'

'But you're not at home.'

The smile faltered. 'No.'

*Send her upstairs now.* His conscience was drumming it
into him, but something primitive and a lot more persuasive
was rushing hot and insistent through his veins. Knocking
out the more civilised switches and allowing everything that
was natural and male in him to take over.

His resolve was gone.

She was so lovely, in every way, and he knew how the
night was going to unfold.

There would be no guest room.

'Come here. I've got something for you.'

Pink colour zoomed up into her cheeks, which told him
he wasn't the only one feeling this, but she approached him,
and Khaled was well aware that the hunter in him was responding to the fact she was a little skittish around him.

Her eyes fell on the bowl of dessert and then she lifted
them with an almost guilty expression on her face.

Sex and food.

How was he going to resist this?

Without even thinking about it, he spooned some straight
into Gigi's lips.

She held it in her mouth and her lashes drifted down as
she savoured it.

He felt it in his groin.

She swallowed.

He groaned silently.

'Feeling better?' he asked in a thickened voice, offering her another spoonful.

Those golden lashes came up. 'Yes.'

He cleared his throat. 'Still hungry?'

She nodded and reached for the spoon, but he held on to it. 'Let me.'

She licked her lips and a coil of heat thrummed in his belly. But there was nothing salacious about her actions—she was just enjoying her food. And strangely enough he was enjoying feeding her, looking after her, making her happy.

'No more.' She refused her sixth spoonful, shaking her head, all that heavy auburn hair tumbling forward to frame her narrow face.

*Bozhe moy*, she was lovely.

He was playing with fire.

She leaned forward unexpectedly and reached out, caught the sway of his silver chain and cross, tangled it around her fingers.

It reminded him of how she'd tangled her fingers in his chest hair to drag him into their first kiss. She was doing it again.

His libido growled.

'What's this?'

'My baptismal cross.' His voice had deepened with arousal but also with pride in something he hadn't always been proud of. 'I was christened Aleksandr, after my father and the saint in the Russian Orthodox Church.'

'Where did Khaled come from?'

'My mother. When she came back to the village she thought it was politic that I be known by the name of her father, and his father before him. It was the only name I knew after the age of four.'

Strange how after all this time it still weighed on him.

'I'm Catholic,' she said, tracing the cross. 'I don't have anything so beautiful.'

'I disagree.' He brushed the line of her jaw with his fingertips.

Her expression was a speaking look of welcome. It would have been easy to lean down and capture her mouth with his.

It had been his intention.

But upstairs he'd had an intention, and Gigi's little performance was still there in the forefront of his mind. If she needed seducing *he* shouldn't be messing with her.

Gigi knew before Khaled moved that he wasn't going to kiss her. She saw the decision in his eyes, in the way his jaw tightened, and although the air between them was thrumming she knew this man had a whole lot more self-control than she did—and if he'd made up his mind he wouldn't be changing it.

Her heart sank as he turned away and said something about showing her to her room.

*Right. Okay.*

She probably wouldn't see very much more of him after this. Tomorrow he would go back to being the guy in charge and she'd have to start thinking about her future, because the writing was on the wall.

Only right now they were alone together. His barriers were down and, although it might have been lack of sleep and all the excitement of the long day, she felt as if she might die a little if this was going to be it.

She already knew she was going to miss him when she went home, and that whatever happened with L'Oiseau Bleu she would never forget him. He was the sort of guy a girl would look back on a little wistfully and wonder *What if?* for ever.

Did it really matter at this late stage if she made the rumours true?

It was just between the two of them. It didn't have anything to do with the cabaret, or the other girls, or the Paris press. It was private—and couldn't what happened behind closed doors remain private?

Lulu had a hundred rules about men and dating, and all of them came down to the same thing. *Respect yourself.*

But Gigi rather thought the better thing was to be true to yourself.

It was the reason she'd climbed up on that tank two days ago, risking if not her limbs then her dignity. Despite that, she didn't regret it—and she wasn't going to regret this. Because sometimes a girl just had to do what a girl had to do…

# CHAPTER THIRTEEN

THEY NEEDED TO SEPARATE.

Khaled reached into the fridge and grabbed a bottle of chilled water to take upstairs. He'd put Gigi in the guest room and book a flight home for her in a few days. He'd hardly have to see her.

'You'll probably be happier in a hotel,' he said, closing the fridge. 'I'm not going to be here and you might get lonely on your own.'

He turned around, bottle in hand, expecting her compliance.

Only Gigi was in the process of peeling her sweater off.

She was wearing a thin thermal vest underneath.

He'd wondered what that extra layer was upstairs.

No bra and visibly erect nipples.

That would account for why a thermal vest suddenly became the sexiest item of clothing he'd ever seen on a woman.

That was until she stripped it off and everything sensible stopped working inside his head.

Milky freckled skin…delicate, gracile build…and small, high breasts tipped with—surprise, surprise—cinnamon-pink nipples.

It crashed through him. He'd thought he'd seen her naked onstage. He'd seen *nothing*.

She'd been telling him the truth.

This was Gigi as she was. Not some kitsch cabaret fantasy of a woman, but real, warm, not entirely sure of herself and incredibly sexy because of it.

He wasn't an audience member, or even her boss. He was the man she'd chosen.

She gave him an uncertain smile. 'Do you want to get naked with me?'

*Yes.* Yes, he did.

It was as if everything that had come before had fallen away. There was just this.

And if this was Gigi seducing him it was working.

It was also entirely unnecessary, because the first time she'd looked up at him from her vantage point on the dusty floor of that stage he'd been hers.

'I take it that's a yes?' she said, and she closed the distance between them and began sliding his shirt down over his shoulders, not hurrying anything.

He felt the tips of her breasts brush against his chest and desire stabbed him as deeply as anything had in his life. He put his hands around her shoulders and felt the quiver through her delicate body.

Although she'd initiated this, he had the oddest feeling of having something not quite tame under his hands, and that any sudden move might change the trajectory of this encounter and see her scooting off into the underbrush—or running for her phone.

It was all beginning to make some sort of sense.

Her skin was like cool silk as he explored the narrow breadth of her back. Her whole body was trembling as she wound her arms around his neck, and now he felt the dancer's tensile strength in her grip, and when she looked into his eyes hers were bluer than blue.

'Khaled,' she said seriously, 'please don't stop now.'

'*Nyet*—no stopping,' he assured her, and lifted her in a single movement up onto the bench.

'Here?'

She blinked, and he wrenched his attention from her quivering breasts, alluringly close to eye level.

'Not here?'

'Maybe not…'

'Where? Anywhere you want.'

'You're a man—you're hardly going to argue with me right now.'

'This is true.'

Only he'd been arguing with himself since he'd set eyes on her, but right now he couldn't think of one damn reason why they shouldn't have this night.

He couldn't resist, and took one small cinnamon nipple into his mouth. She whimpered.

She tasted like heaven. She *was* heaven.

Her fingers tangled in his hair.

He used his tongue. He sucked. She made sounds of approval that invited him to move to her other breast and went wild against him.

Khaled knew he wasn't even going to get his jeans unbuttoned at this rate. He was going to disgrace himself like a fifteen-year-old boy with his first girl.

He had to slow this down. He wanted to take his time.

But he *had* to have her.

But not in the damn kitchen. Gigi deserved a bed.

He carried her up two flights of stairs and into his room. Khaled realised his mistake, but it was too late. Gigi was looking around his bedroom with a rapt look on her face.

'Holy Mary, it's the Arabian Nights.'

He'd forgotten the impression it made.

The keyhole doorway…the vast bed low to the ground… the gallery above where he kept his books. It had been copied from an etching of an old Muscovite *terem*. He supposed to a non-Russian it *did* look like an eastern fantasy.

For him it was an excellent use of space and the existing architecture.

He couldn't say she was the first woman he'd brought here, but she was one of only a few. This was his private realm, and he guarded that privacy, but his usual sense of needing to distract and create distance didn't come.

Gigi could sense a little tension in him as he lowered her feet to the floor. Her hair swung around her shoulders. He framed her face and kissed her. It was a deep, soul-stirring, come-and-let-me-show-you-things kind of kiss—the sort Gigi imagined she wasn't ever going to get enough of.

To her surprise he turned her in his arms and said her name against her throat—a rough whisper that shimmered down her spine as his hands skimmed over her unbearably sensitised breasts to curve round her jutting hips and spread across her belly, only to move up again and cup her breasts.

His breathing was gratifyingly heavy, his mouth hot against the back of her neck, and Gigi thought the backs of her knees weren't going to hold her.

'Khaled…?' She needed to say his name.

'*Vechno*—that's how long I've been waiting for you.'

'*Vechno*?' she breathed.

'For ever. I thought you were a hallucination,' he said into her hair, his voice rough as sandpaper. 'Tell me I'm not still in the desert.'

Her heart lifted.

'No—thank goodness! Imagine where the sand might go.'

Laughter rumbled in his chest, and it felt so good against her that she wanted to stay there for ever. Sparks and sensations were cascading through her like the most beautiful waterfall as he continued to circle her nipples with his thumbs, teasing them into points of unbearable sensitivity. He fondled her breasts and stroked her body as if touching her like this was all he wanted, and Gigi thought she might die of it.

But what a way to go.

She made a soft sound of relief as his mouth slid over the sensitive nape of her neck, and then she felt his kiss on the tip of her spine right down the centre of her to her molten core, where she simply combusted.

'Is this what you want, Gigi?'

She felt her heart spike at the thickly worded question, thrilled that he would still ask.

She turned in his arms and sought his mouth, and kissed him with all the sensuous passion he drew out of her.

*This, this, this.*

'Oh, yes,' she said against his mouth.

It was his turn to make a deep, gratified groan as he

cupped her bottom and brought her up against him. She wrapped her long legs around him and he feasted on her mouth.

He carried her over to the bed, lowering her onto her back. He knelt over her and undid the button at the top of her trousers, deftly rolled them down the length of her legs, taking his time to enjoy the milky, satin-smooth limbs he was uncovering, smoothing the way with his hands.

'Don't stop now,' she warned.

'*Dorogaya*, Hannibal's army couldn't stop me now.'

She was still wearing the tiny glittery G-string she'd worn onstage, and he ran his thumb under the string that held it around her hips, all the way to the heart-shaped piece of satin that preserved her modesty.

'This,' he said, 'is indecent.'

Gigi's breath hitched as he stroked beneath it, his thumb finding her clitoris all plump with need.

Kneeling over her, he looked as wild and untamed as he had when he'd come for her across the stage, his shoulders massively broad. Only this time he was stripped. His bare chest was covered in dark hair, arrowing down to an abdomen as taut as a drum and a deeply cut pelvis where the hair grew thicker.

Gigi's eyes were drawn to the thrust of his heavily erect penis. It was beautiful—like the rest of him.

She began to explore him with her hands, but Khaled was soon moving out of her reach, and any further attempts to pleasure him as he was pleasuring her exploded into a thousand inconsequential pieces as he snapped the string and bared her to his gaze.

She had a slender strip of golden-red curls. A lot of the girls had everything off—it was just easier, given their revealing costumes—but she'd wanted something to remind her she was a woman. Khaled seemed to appreciate it as he touched her there, his expression a little blurry with lust.

He slid down between her thighs, gently but inexorably

pushing them apart. He coaxed open the petals at the heart of her and found her hot and wet and very ready.

Gigi made a startled sound as he used the flat of his tongue to lap at her, and clutched at whatever she could get her hand on—the sheets, a pillow—tangling the fingers of her other hand in his thick hair. She felt shameless in her need as pleasure rocked her body like a little boat in a storm. She whimpered and keened, and when he lifted his head the boat was in pieces. She felt like a tiny piece of flotsam in the midst of a cyclonic tempest, poised for a moment on a high wave.

Through the blur of her own pleasure she saw muscle definition on him that she'd never seen on another man, and she couldn't help but run her hands over it, feeling those muscles contract under her touch.

He bent his head to her breasts, no longer tugging but feasting on her nipples until she could barely stand it.

'No more, Khaled,' she whimpered, yanking not gently on his hair. 'Please, I just want—'

He raised his head, those heavily lidded eyes and the most carnal of smiles sending her core body temperature through the roof.

'Just think about how achingly aroused I've been for forty-eight hours, Gigi. This is payback.'

Gigi tried to do the mathematical calculation, but it wasn't easy with her body on fire and with Khaled licking her nipples with the flat of his tongue like a big, wild cat.

He couldn't mean from the first time he saw her?

'But… '

'*Da*, you've worked it out—I'm *that* basic,' he growled, rising up over her and rolling on a condom with brutal efficiency.

The hard heat of him sinking into the wet heart of her was so welcome she almost wept. Maybe she did, because everything suddenly looked blurry.

He didn't rush, and he held himself still for her, waiting

for her muscles to relax and get used to the invasion, his eyes soldered on her expressive face.

Then he began to seduce her mouth with his and she melted around him, lifted her hips. He sank further.

'Oh…'

She could feel him so deep inside her. Too much.

He brushed the nub of her clitoris. Tiny nerves sang.

'Khaled…' she sobbed.

'That's my girl,' he crooned.

He drove into her and they both groaned. He built and built the gorgeous ache in her body and she met every stroke. They moved together, as if their bodies were made for this dance, and she knew she would die, she would just die, if she didn't reach that peak soon. And he took her there, holding himself in check with a gritted jaw as she pulsed around him.

Then he was moving again—harder, deeper. Her hands clutched at his shoulders as he licked her breasts and over she went again, gripping him, crying out. Thighs trembling, skin gilded with perspiration. This time he came with her, his deep groan speaking to her own bliss before he crushed her to the mattress.

Gigi wrapped her arms around him. *This* was what she needed—skin on skin, the weight of him anchoring her after the gorgeous devastation.

When he stirred she thought he would move away, but instead he took his weight on his forearms and his mouth sought hers so sweetly she felt astonishment. She clung.

His eyes met hers, heavy-lidded, still drugged with the pleasure they'd given one another.

Gigi rolled onto her side as he got up to dispose of the condom and watched him through her lashes.

She felt replete, but she wasn't sure what to expect next.

She simply didn't have the heart to say anything that might shatter what felt to her so intimate and new.

So she waited for him to say something as he came back to

the bed, lowered himself beside her. And then he did the most perfect thing—without a word he pulled her into his arms.

Gigi went to him. It was absolutely where she wanted to be.

Her heart was beating so fast.

She mustn't read too much into it.

This was animal warmth, she told herself. It was natural to cling together after their bodies had come to know each other so well, so fast. Natural to take what was on offer— body heat, a fleeting sense of security—to take comfort.

She closed her eyes and took the comfort. Told herself this elated feeling was merely part of the natural high after great sex. Told herself so many silly things. But in the end, with her cheek pressed against his shoulder, the warmth and solidity of him against her, she felt like staying there all night. Longer. Eternally.

*Vechno.* She knew the word now.

Khaled didn't say anything, merely grunted as if satisfied that he had her where she was.

It was the nicest sound in the world, she thought before sleep claimed her.

Well, she'd had her night with him. Now what?

Gigi eased her deliciously aching body into a sitting position, slid her long legs off the bed and, with a slightly *triste* glance backwards at Khaled's much larger, uninhibited body taking up most of the mattress, tiptoed off in the direction of the bathroom.

Under the bright lights she looked as if she'd been dropped head first into a spin-dryer. Her hair was sticking up, her eyes were sleepy, and she had a cockeyed smile on her face that just wouldn't go away.

She was also covered in the scent of him, and washing it off wasn't her first priority. She leaned into the mirror and eyed her reflection curiously.

'So, what exactly do you think you're doing, Gisele?' she asked aloud.

Apart from the obvious.

She giggled, and made a face at herself.

Her mouth was swollen, and she had beard rash in all kinds of places, but as she ran her fingers through her crazy hair she felt insanely good. There had been nothing awkward about last night, and although she could put that down to Khaled's experience, she rather thought there was something about the way they were together that just *worked*.

She'd never had casual sex before, so she couldn't compare it, but a deep female instinct told her that this wasn't how 'casual' felt.

She had never felt so connected to someone or so secure as she had in Khaled's arms.

It had her smile fading.

She'd grown up through her vulnerable teenage years with a father who'd put her through hoops—literally—to secure his attention. Nothing she'd ever done had pleased him. But it hadn't stopped her trying over and over, and she didn't need a psychologist to tell her that she feared sending herself down the same unsatisfactory path in an adult relationship with a man.

Which probably explained why she had never taken any of her previous romantic brushes with men very seriously. Better to be sure you wouldn't tumble into love when love, as far as she knew it, was akin to falling down a flight of stairs. However, she had *never* just tumbled into bed with a man after forty-eight hours.

She was frowning at herself, and at this development in her life, when Khaled appeared in the doorway, leaning there with that extraordinary muscular grace he'd applied so breathtakingly to making love to her. Naked, rubbing his chest as he yawned, he was looking incredibly gorgeous, with a lock of dark hair falling over his eyes.

*Mine.*

Gigi bit her lip. *No, not mine—borrowed.*

She tried not to cover herself. She had no problem with nudity—she'd lost a lot of her self-consciousness in those first months at L'Oiseau Bleu. You couldn't be too hung up about your body when you danced in the equivalent of a bikini every night. Still, it felt different with Khaled's gaze hot and heavy on her and her nipples visibly budding in the mirror.

*No place to hide.*

Given his penis was behaving the same way, she shouldn't be embarrassed.

Gigi dropped her chin and smiled as he came up behind her and put his arms around her shoulders.

'Do you do this a lot? Talk to yourself in the mirror?'

'Only when the person I want to talk to is passed out on the bed.'

He smiled then—a slow, incredibly sexy spread of his mouth in alignment with his dark eyes as they creased with appreciation.

'Last night was incredible,' he said against her ear, sincerely, kissing her neck, lifting his face so that his dark gaze met hers in the reflection.

They looked good together. Complemented one another. Him so dark and male, her so tawny and female, her lithe frame bracketed by his powerful body.

Gigi even thought she looked a little beautiful this morning, as if all the happy exercise had given her a glow.

Which didn't explain the glow inside her.

She felt as if she'd swallowed sunshine.

'But, Gigi…' he said, and he looked very serious. 'I'm not a good bet if you're looking for any more than this.'

Gigi had the quick wits to respond before hurt got a hold. 'Why is it men never say those words *before* sex—only afterwards?'

Colour actually scored his high cheekbones and Gigi, despite the way her stomach was hollowing out, almost smiled.

What worked in his favour, aside from his obvious discomfort, was the fact that he kept his arms around her—as if he had no intention of letting her go.

Still, it was a bit rich, his assuming she would have 'catch and contain' plans for him. She had a very nice life, thank you very much, and she didn't intend to swap it for hot nights in Moscow with him.

So she let him have it. 'I should probably let you know I've got a ten-kilometre rule. I only date men who live within ten kilometres of Montmartre, otherwise it just gets too difficult. If it got serious he might want me to move, and I won't be doing that.' She raised a brow. 'So *I'm* not a good bet if you're looking for any more than this.'

Khaled lifted his head away from hers. 'Ten kilometres?'

'Don't worry,' she said with a little smile, 'we'll just consider this a weekend fling—that way we have the back-to-the-real-world clause open to us. You can go back to your normal, and I'll go back to mine. Deal?'

Khaled's arms tightened around her and there was a frown in his eyes. 'This is what you want?'

Gigi didn't have a clue what she wanted. She knew what she *liked*. She liked his arms around her, the closeness physical intimacy had brought them, but she already knew this was probably the biggest mistake of her life.

If she let it be.

She wasn't going to do that.

But her fighting words were already beginning to topple, because he might be saying one thing but his body surrounding hers was saying another—and she was fairly susceptible to his body.

She'd have to watch out for those mixed signals. She didn't want to get confused. She really didn't want to find herself jumping through hoops to make him pay attention to her. She'd been there, got the T-shirt.

No, she needed to hold on to her independence even if it

choked her. She was perfectly capable of meeting his sophistication with some of her own. Yes, she'd definitely do that.

She lifted her chin. 'Sure.'

He let her go. Only to slide his hands over her hips and
delve down between her thighs. Heat followed those hands
and Gigi arched her body helplessly back against him.

He cupped one breast and plucked at her nipple as his
other hand teased and pleasured her. She turned her head to
try and kiss him but he was controlling their movements,
and when he gruffly told her to put her hands forward on the
bench she did as she was told and he entered her.

The eroticism of the movement took her unawares, and
then he was moving inside her, guiding her hips with his big
hands, and she couldn't think—only feel. Her body had become a vessel for their mutual pleasure, until she splintered
into a thousand pieces and he followed her.

Gigi turned, clumsy and off-centre, not sure what had just
happened, wanting connection and touch and to be kissed.

Khaled curved his hand around her cheek and she strained
upwards to kiss him. For a moment she thought he was holding back, but something flashed in the back of his eyes and
with a groan he lowered his head and kissed her with all the
lush romanticism she could have wished for.

Then he scooped her up and carried her back to bed and
began all over again.

# CHAPTER FOURTEEN

'HAVE YOU GONE *LOCO*?'

Khaled pictured the long-legged, red-haired beauty he'd left less than an hour ago, sleeping like a Burne-Jones pre-Raphaelite maiden wrapped in white sheets, and thought maybe he had.

This raging possessive feeling inside him *was* a form of madness.

Which was why he'd needed to go for a run. Clear his head. Get some space between him and the woman he'd left in his bed.

Now he was loping back through the park across the road from his apartment building, his phone against his ear, his old friend's amusement putting some perspective back into the picture.

Alejandro du Crozier had experienced his own share of media attention. He was one of the world's highest-paid polo players, and the paparazzi had a love affair with the Argentinian's private life.

'The press are calling it a kidnapping. I hope she's worth it, my friend.'

Khaled frowned. He wasn't discussing Gigi. Even if her actions *had* brought much of this upon herself, the woman he'd come to know did not deserve to be the target of spurious stories in the media. And after last night he didn't want to discuss her even with Alejandro, and they had shared a lot over the years.

The Argentinian had rolled up in the gorge below Mount Elbrus several years ago, looking for Kabardian breeding stock, and a business relationship had turned into a strong friendship. Khaled was not a man who had many friends, but he took those he had seriously.

Still, he would not discuss Gigi with him.

She would be distressed to know he was even talking about her.

She wasn't as sturdy as she tried to appear. There was a gentleness inside her that brought out instincts in him he had made a life's work of repressing.

The fact that he knew this about her wasn't what bothered him. It was that he cared.

She didn't guard herself or put on a pretence of sophistication—she was simply herself.

Which was when it struck him that she couldn't possibly have been a knowing participant in her father's petty crimes. If he'd ever really believed it.

She had a redoubtable quality in her that probably made her a good and loyal friend, and that explained why her little flatmate had been ringing the phone off the hook—she was clearly concerned for her well-being.

Khaled wasn't unaware that if something happened to him the only people to weep and wail would be his shareholders.

He liked it that way. He didn't want people feeling responsible for him.

His mother had given up any chance of a real life to make sure he was raised in her home village. He hated that knowledge. It had haunted him all his life. So he'd been careful not to form relationships where sacrifice was involved. Of any kind.

He was generous in his sexual relationships with women. He made sure the women concerned were happy, and usually his money took care of that. Just as he was using his wealth and his influence to shield Gigi from the media. But emotionally he didn't risk anything—which was why his unease about Gigi was like taking a step into the dark.

Shaking it off, he turned the conversation back to sport and to horse stock before he finished his call with Alejandro and headed across the road. He was anticipating finding Gigi awake and dressed and off-limits.

He was just going upstairs when a call showed up from his

lawyer in Nalchik. He tore his attention away from a mental image of Gigi naked, with that little half-moon smile tilting her expressive mouth.

'They want to talk.'

Everything but Gigi's little smile fell away as he stopped in his tracks, unable to credit what he'd just heard.

'Talk next year or talk in the foreseeable future?'

'Tomorrow.'

Even as he listened to his lawyer lay it all out he called up the internet sites of Moscow's major papers. It was all there.

*Kitaev conducts Tartar raid on Bluebird in Paris.*
*Bride-stealing gets an update as Russian oligarch*
*plucks his bird of paradise.*

'The elders believe you've shown respect for tradition. It seems they believe the "romance of the century" story. It's done the trick.'

*Two years.*

Two years and *this* was what shifted the balance?

Khaled didn't know whether to laugh or curse.

'I'll fly down tonight.'

'Not just you,' said his lawyer. 'You need to bring this woman.'

For a moment something sharp and hot and entirely violent passed through him.

*'This woman,'* he growled, 'has a name.'

'Miss Valente.' He literally heard his lawyer swallow. 'It is advisable, given she appears to have swung the vote.'

Which meant, effectively, that Gigi wasn't going home. Not yet.

Khaled exhaled, shoved his phone into his back pocket and strode energetically down the hall, pushing open the door, struck by how good he felt. He put it down to finally getting his hands on the road.

Gigi wasn't in bed. She was sitting on its edge, rolling a

pair of tights up her legs. Her incredibly long, dance-honed legs. His eyes followed all the way up to a pair of white cotton panties that somehow did more for him than last night's teeny-tiny bit of gold dental floss.

She looked up as the door reverberated on its hinges.

He whipped his T-shirt up over his head, tugged his sweats and briefs down and powered her back onto the mattress.

'Khaled!' she shrieked, giggling.

'Gigi.'

He fastened his mouth to hers and her body leapt under his. He dragged her top up over her head and her hair sprayed everywhere.

'Do you *ever* wear a bra?' he groaned, as if it were a complaint—or a prayer.

Gigi parted her lips to speak but his mouth was there first, and then he began to make love to her until she was wrapping her long legs with those dangling tights around him, making happy cries.

She was still panting when he collapsed and buried his face in her lovely silky hair, inhaled the scent of her. He could do it all over again.

But he'd had a purpose before he'd been distracted.

He sat up and looked around.

Gigi watched him with slightly glazed eyes. Waking up alone had not been the best of feelings, but she'd tried to be pragmatic about it, given their conversation in the bathroom. This pragmatism was going to be a little hard to hold on to if Khaled insisted on doing *this* to her every time the mood struck him.

To her astonishment he vaulted over her and began rummaging in the bedside drawer.

More condoms? Again?

Gigi was a little amazed to discover that her blissfully aching body was on board with that.

But after a few moments he wrenched the drawer loose and emptied it onto the bed.

She sat up. 'What on earth are you doing?'

'I'm looking for your passport.'

Gigi went cold.

She didn't think—she acted. She grabbed a pillow and whacked him hard across the back with it.

It was like using a feather to swat a water buffalo. 'Hey,' he said, giving her an almost boyishly baffled grin, 'what's that for?'

'Timing!' she hurled at him, and leapt off the bed and marched into the bathroom, slamming shut the door. Then throwing the lock for good measure.

He thumped on the door.

'Not. Coming. Out.'

'Gigi…'

He didn't sound angry. He didn't even try the lock. She waited a few minutes. Nothing.

Cautiously she opened the door and found him throwing clothes into an overnight bag.

She picked up her new grey trousers, which he'd left in a puddle on the floor last night, and threw them at him. *Hard.* 'Check the pockets.'

He retrieved her passport and tossed it to her. 'There'll be a border check—you'll need this.'

Gigi just stood there, her heart pounding. *He wasn't sending her home?*

'You'll need to pack a bag, Gigi.'

She folded her arms. 'I didn't agree to go anywhere further than this with you. Khaled, I have to go home—my job's at stake.'

'Your job's fine. I'm the boss, remember?'

'For how long?' She hadn't meant to ask, but now they were having this conversation she intended to find out.

'Long enough for you to pack a bag and come with me now. Listen, I'll look after it for you—you don't need to worry about your job, *malenki*. Come with me now, and when we get back we'll work something out.'

'Don't *do* that,' she blurted out. 'Don't make out that I'm with you because of what you can do for me. I've not asked you for one thing to do with the cabaret since we left Paris. That's not what this is about. I won't let you make it into something it's not.'

Khaled stilled. 'What is it, then, Gigi?'

'Great sex,' she whispered, her chest hurting. 'I thought that was what we'd agreed—you can't change the rules now.'

She waited for him to say that he hadn't, that he wasn't looking any further ahead, that he didn't want to try for something a little more committed. Then *she* would say, well, she didn't want that, she was quite happy with what they had. Only maybe one night was enough—because she wasn't sure her heart could survive any more nights and days knowing there was no future between them.

But she wouldn't say the last part, because it made her sound like an unsophisticated ninny.

'So I am no longer great sex?' His tone was surprisingly gentle.

Her heart lurched, because he was trying to make her smile, trying to wind this back a notch. And that was a relief—because they were entering territory it was probably best they didn't.

'Well, you *are*...'

*He didn't mean for you to answer, eejit, he meant it rhetorically.*

'But I guess you know you are.' She frowned. She was stuffing this up. 'What I mean to say is that I didn't mean to reduce you to something physical. I mean, it's not like I'm out there every night with men drinking champagne from my shoes or something.'

*Way to go—impress him with your showgirl lifestyle, Gisele. Tell him about your knitting project—that'll put an end to this.*

'You surprise me,' he said, in that dangerously quiet way of his that made her think he might be laughing at her again. Only when she took a peek he looked a million miles away from laughing.

It suddenly occurred to her.

'You don't want me to go? Home, I mean?'

He said something soft and exasperated in Russian and she stayed where she was as he walked up to her, took her face between his hands and looked at her.

*Really* looked at her.

Gigi got lost in his dark eyes.

'Gigi, I've got to go south for business.'

Then he kissed her. And although she'd thought he had already kissed her and she had kissed him last night in all the ways imaginable, this was so lushly romantic, with his hands in her hair, and her hands curled trustingly between them, it felt new. It felt like the first time. Not just between them, but like her first kiss.

Gigi opened her eyes to find him gazing down at her, as if the kiss had astonished him too.

'My mother's people are indigenous to the region of Kabardino-Balkaria in the mountains of the North Caucasus.'

He spoke with a quiet sincerity that moved through her like a promise.

'I tell you this because I have a place down there, at the foot of Mount Elbrus. We can be alone for a couple of days. No work, no interruptions...' he gave her a smile '...great sex.'

Then he sobered.

'I want to show you where I come from. What matters to me. Give me that time.'

More time to stumble deeper into this. To lose a little more of her ability to find her way out.

His next words didn't make her heart lift as they should.

'Then I promise to return you to Paris.'

* * *

He hadn't told her it would be like this.

Gigi lay in a cot of marmot fur in Khaled's strong arms and watched the moon and stars through their own private observatory.

'Why did people stare at me in the village today?'

'You're the exotic creature I've snared in my net. If I'd hunted and skinned you they couldn't have been more surprised.'

Gigi frowned. 'Because of what was printed in the Moscow papers about me being a showgirl? I guess this is a pretty conservative place.' She raised her head to look at him anxiously. 'It won't get you into trouble, will it?'

He was quiet, and then he said in that low, sleep-gravelled voice Gigi liked to pretend no other woman in the world had ever been privy to and belonged only to her, 'Other men may try to lure you away…that's about the extent of it.'

'If they use cake I can't promise not to go.'

'That's my girl.'

She looked up archly. 'I think you could have left me in Paris.'

'Do you?'

'Yes, I do. I don't think I was in much danger at all. I think it's perfectly clear you wanted an excuse to act like a Russian he-man—'

This earned her a squeeze around her waist.

'—to sling me over your shoulder like a kill and bring me with you without the chance that I might turn you down!'

Khaled put his mouth to the shell of her ear. 'You've found me out.'

Gigi beamed.

It had been this way since they'd left Moscow and flown into Nalchik two days ago, and then driven for miles along a highway that could be described at best as bumpy in a landscape that had taken her breath away.

Deep valleys, high mountains peaked with snow… At

one point huge mountain deer had forced them to a stop as they crossed the road.

He'd brought her in the gathering dusk to a gorge littered with tall stone fortresses. Khaled had told her he'd refurbished this one, all six storeys of it, and they were now on the top floor, with its glass ceiling and panoramic views.

He had tossed her into this cot filled with marmot furs, pulling off her clothes and some of his own like a man possessed, and had made love to her with such fierceness and tenderness Gigi couldn't help feeling a little way in over her head.

After all, he'd made this amazing romantic gesture—bringing her here.

'I've never brought a woman here before.'

Okay. He had her attention.

'Why is that?' She tried to sound casual.

'Hmm?'

She frowned at him and wondered if she acted like one of those female mountain goats they'd seen yesterday trying to get a male's attention, bucking and sending clods of earth into the air so he'd get the message.

'Why have you never brought a girlfriend here?'

'I haven't had one to bring.'

She rolled her eyes. 'Right. So what was Alexandra Dashkova?'

'Who?'

'She had herself wrapped in a rug and rolled out before you.'

'Did she?'

'The other dancers were talking about her,' Gigi persisted, because *Didn't she?* wasn't going to cut it.

'I've met her several times socially—we've never been intimate.'

Gigi didn't know why, but something very heavy that she hadn't even known was pressing down on her chest suddenly wasn't there any more.

'I guess people write all sorts of nonsense about you. I should know.'

'Some of the nonsense I don't mind. The truth is none of the women I've been involved with are the kind of people I'd bring here.'

There was a lot to unpack there, so Gigi went with, 'Too glamorous?'

He grunted noncommittally, which made Gigi think she'd got it right.

'So I'm the mountaineering kind?'

'You don't strike me as particularly outdoorsy, Gigi.'

'Oh, I am. I've just never climbed a mountain before.'

'There's a first time for everything.'

# CHAPTER FIFTEEN

HE SHOWED HER waterfalls where the water was crystalline and made love to her in a hot stream where the minerals were said to cure everything from aches and pains to old age—neither of which were on Gigi's mind as her wet, naked body cleaved to his against a slippery boulder, where they were afforded the smallest privacy from anyone else trekking in the area.

They climbed high enough to find wild mountain goats grazing on meadow grass and he told her about his youth, working as a shepherd with his stepfather's flock. About his dog, his knife and the wild animals he'd encountered.

He told her about the threat from poachers who had nearly wiped out the entire mountain bison population here. He took her up to the top of Mount Elbrus by chopper and pointed out the area where his company was putting in a resort using prefabricated eco-friendly modules from Denmark.

'The more eco-tourism we encourage into the region the further we can push the poachers out.'

Gigi understood his commitment to the natural world. How he kept it in tandem with the oil holdings that had made his fortune. And it made sense that he was diversifying as he moved further away from an industry known to be aggressive against the planet. How could you grow up in this place and *not* care about keeping it alive?

She knew now that he was an extraordinary man— nothing like the one-dimensional, showgirl-eating beast the whole of Paris believed was going to devour their candy-coloured theatre. He was her lover, and she thought her friend, and really she'd do better with the latter.

Maybe when this was all over she could keep him as a friend.

But that wasn't likely, was it? Her pain when this was

over was going to be intense. They were sexually involved now and there was no going back from that.

Nobody lived in that world.

Nor would she want to.

They headed for the truck. It was the middle of the afternoon and everything was bathed in sparkling sunlight.

It was difficult to believe this had ever been a place of darkness for Khaled.

But it had, and she didn't want to ignore that. *He* hadn't ignored her poor, damaged feet.

She angled a look up at his beautiful broad features. 'How old were you when you left here?'

He stopped, and the look on his face had her heart pounding like a drum. He looked…surprised, then thoughtful. She'd expected him to clam up.

'Do you remember the highway we came in on? When I was fifteen I filled a duffel bag and hiked up it all the way to Nalchik.'

'For a job?'

'You could say that. I was working for the local crime boss.'

'Oh,' said Gigi.

'Welcome to twenty-first century Russia, *malenki*.'

'I take it you did well out of it?'

'Well enough to start selling black market imports at a local market.'

'I guess you did well out of that too?'

'Enough to invest with a friend in a company. Then I did national service. After that I made the move to Moscow.'

He folded his arms, his sleeves rolled up to the elbows. He looked so inherently masculine as he surveyed the valley around them that he took her breath away.

'It doesn't say any of this on the internet.'

He gave her a bemused look, but there was affection in it. 'I don't broadcast it, Gisele.'

No, but he'd told *her*.

'Why did you leave when you were fifteen, Khaled, when you clearly have this place in your blood?'

The remnants of his smile reconfigured into something she had seen in his face before when he talked about his past but hadn't understood.

'I would have killed him if I'd stayed.'

'Your stepfather?'

'I was big enough then—and angry enough. I also had the skill. There was just the two of us. He taught me how to track and make a clean kill, and how to cover my traces.'

Gigi said nothing, because now she understood.

'He taught me everything I knew at that age about being a man—and that's the catch. He was a man without honour, and yet he taught me our code the same way the army taught me how to assemble and disassemble a rifle in the dark—and because of that he got to live a little longer before liver cancer dragged him off, and I got to live with the question I ask myself every day. Did I make the right choice?'

'Of course you did.' Gigi turned up her face, wet with tears. 'You were just a child. You did the right thing and you survived.'

'I haven't shocked you?' he asked, and she could see the strain behind his eyes.

*He cared what she thought of him.*

'The only thing in that story that shocks me is how you became this man. This good, kind, decent man.'

He blinked, as if her words made no sense to him.

'I've never seen you cry,' he said, as if this were the wonder, and not the fact that he'd survived as he had.

'I only cry when there's something to cry about,' she said, wiping at her eyes.

He took her face between his hands and kissed her. Sweetly at first, then fiercely, and then they just stood wrapped around each other by the truck.

He stroked her hair. 'What am I going to do with you, Gisele?'

'I don't know,' she murmured against his neck, aware that he'd probably told her much more than he'd meant to over the last few days and later would be uncomfortable about it and withdraw back into that place where she couldn't follow him. But right now she had him out here in the sunlight and she was going to do what she could to keep him there.

She looked up and gave his beard a gentle tug. 'I do think it's time to take this off.'

But even as she spoke her phone vibrated in her back pocket.

'Your friend is doing me a favour,' said Khaled as she took it out.

Sure enough, it was a text from Lulu.

It had been sent yesterday, but the WiFi in the tower was sporadic at best.

Dantons out. Theatre shut. Thought you should know.

For a moment Gigi did nothing. Then Khaled's hand closed over hers and he took the phone. He didn't even look at the message. He just looked into her eyes.

She stumbled back.

'Why did you fire the Dantons as managers?

Khaled rested his hands on his lean hips. 'The Dantons couldn't manage their way out of a paper bag.'

'That's it? That's all you've got to say?'

He shrugged.

Gigi shook her head, utterly confused by his refusal to see this as important. Didn't he care about her feelings at all?

He was watching her closely, and bizarrely Gigi wondered if this was a test.

'I have shut the theatre down for renovations, not for sale. This is what you wanted.'

The wind in the trees was the only sound.

Gigi ventured a little closer. 'You're not selling?'

'I have heard nothing but how important this place is to you—why would I sell?'

Gigi put her hands against her sides, because there was a sudden feeling like a stitch under her ribs.

'It will reopen in six months. I want you to manage it.'

'What?'

'You heard me.'

The stitch stabbed at her. She was suddenly utterly terrified. She turned and wrenched open the truck door and climbed inside, slamming it shut after her.

In the warm quiet of the cabin she tried to make sense of what had just happened.

Khaled took his time coming round, swinging his larger frame inside. He wound down a window, propped an elbow on the ledge and said, so reasonably and so authoritatively that she could only stare at him, 'You've got the passion, the vision—you've even got the skills. With the right people behind you I can't see why you won't make a success of it.'

'What skills? I'm a *dancer*, Khaled, I'm not a businesswoman. I thought that would have been obvious when I turned up at your hotel like a crazed stalker and chased you through the streets of Paris and thrust a laptop at you.'

'Imagination, guts, determination. *I'd* hire you, Gigi, if we weren't in a relationship.'

'You *are* hiring me!' Gigi's whirling thought processes ground to a halt. *Hang on. Rewind.* 'Did you just say we're in a relationship?'

'It makes things—what was your word?—*murky*. It smacks a bit of nepotism, and I know you're touchy about that.' He drummed his left hand on the window frame, looking out across the gorge below. 'But sometimes, Gigi, great things grow out of the most unlikely seeds.'

Gigi was busily sorting through everything he was throwing at her. It was a bit like being tied to a circular board—as she had been as a fourteen-year-old—and being spun while someone threw knives at her. Only some of the knives had turned into bouquets of flowers.

'But what if I fail?'

'I'll replace you.' His dark eyes settled on her now and his expression was serious. 'This is a genuine business decision, Gigi. It has nothing to do with how beautiful you are, or how incredible you are in bed.'

*Was* she? Beautiful? Incredible in bed?

'This is all about what you showed me on that first day. Best job interview I've taken.'

'What usually happens in your job interviews?' she asked unnecessarily.

'I grill people.'

'You didn't grill *me*.'

'What do you think that run down the Champs-Élysées was about?'

'Now you're funning me.'

'The bathroom vanity was all about the fringe benefits, and back at your place I was checking out the facilities.'

Gigi wanted to laugh, but she also felt sick—because he didn't know the one thing about her that made all of this impossible.

He'd find out soon enough—someone would object to her elevation and then all the old stories would emerge. It wouldn't take much digging at all.

Carlos Valente, small-time con artist and his dancing daughter.

She didn't know what was on the internet—she'd never wanted to look. But she could guess that there would be some record from past English newspapers.

She'd been lucky it hadn't come up in the current coverage of 'The Showgirl and the Oligarch'. She guessed the main thing exercising people's minds was her showgirl feathers tickling Khaled's chin…and other parts. The story of a teenage girl travelling round England's provincial theatres several years ago with her sleight-of-hand father was less sensational than a sex scandal with a rich man.

It *would*, however, be of interest to Khaled when he discovered the truth.

He would look at her differently.

He would know of her less than savoury background and he would judge her.

And she couldn't blame him.

You couldn't let someone like *her* undertake this kind of job.

It was a position of trust. The first thing that went wrong and the finger of blame would be pointed at her.

Gigi panicked. Her heart went into overdrive.

She wanted out of this car.

Only even as she looked at the door handle she knew she wasn't going to run from this.

'Khaled, there's something you need to know.'

She clutched her hands together in her lap and began in a low voice to tell him about her father, his petty thefts up and down the country, and how it had all caught up with him one night in a Soho nightclub.

Khaled said nothing and allowed her to spill it all out.

She told him how she'd been arrested, put in a cell, interviewed, bailed. She told him about being acquitted nine months later, and that her father had been given a suspended sentence.

She told him how one of the reasons she'd gone to Paris was because no English club or theatre owner would employ her.

'I like the other story better—about my mum being a showgirl.' She bit her lip. 'But it didn't really start out that way. I don't know if I ever would have had the guts to try out for the Bluebirds if it hadn't been impossible for me to get a job in London. Not even Lulu knows the real story. I'm not really as brave as you seem to think I am.'

Khaled was looking out across the gorge, his profile un-readable.

'I won't make a fuss if you've changed your mind now,' she said huskily, her tongue sticking to the top of her mouth.

In response Khaled started the engine.

'I won't be changing my mind,' he said.

Gigi released a huge, shaky breath.

'Do you trust me?'

'A woman who has a blade poised at my carotid artery? Why not live a little dangerously?'

Gigi gave a nervous laugh, but she was sincerely wor-ried about this first stroke of the blade. Trust Khaled to in-sist that an electric version wouldn't do the job and produce this cutthroat razor. After they'd returned from the moun-tain he'd stropped it for her and spent half an hour taking her through the procedure.

They nestled in the grassland that lay beyond the tower, Khaled perched on a fisherman's stool and Gigi standing with a towel over her shoulder, a bucket of warm water and the cutthroat razor in hand.

'You've never shaved a man before?' he queried as she practised using the blade on a small section of her forearm, where fluffy golden hairs grew.

'The opportunity has never arisen.'

She'd never actually lived with a man, and her former boyfriend had used an electric razor as far as she knew. Frankly, none of the boys she'd dated had been as *hairy* as Khaled. The male dancers she performed with had almost as little hair on their body as she did, and she had a regular appointment with the Bluebird's beautician and her little pot of pink wax.

'This makes me your first,' he said, with a great deal of satisfaction in that deep, dark Russian voice that made her hand shake.

'Yes, Khaled…' she'd give him that '…you're my first.'

He chuckled.

'Thirty degrees to the skin…perpendicular to the edge,' she muttered under her breath, and then she took the first stroke, running the blade up his throat.

Gratifyingly, only soapy hair fell away and no blood. *Yet.*

'I still think you should have gone to a barber,' she murmured.

His dark eyes flashed to hers and held them. 'If you want the kill, your honour is the head.'

Gigi made a humming noise. 'I'm going to leave that one alone. It sounds too weird.'

He chuckled. 'I'm doing it for you—you should have the privilege.'

He was being incredibly patient with her, watching her face as she concentrated on the task, telling her he'd never seen a woman make so many grimaces in his life.

Finally she was done and he got up and thrust his face into the bucket of cold water, bringing his wet head up like a wild animal and shaking off the beaded residue.

Gigi stared at him in astonishment.

She was looking at a man she only half recognised. It unnerved her for a few seconds—perhaps because of the dream she'd been having since arriving in this strange place. In the dream she'd woken to an empty tower room. She called and called and when Khaled finally came up the steps he was a different man.

Silly. She gave a self-conscious laugh and reached up to stroke the clean sweep of his jaw. He grinned back at her. It really was Khaled. Just not as she'd ever seen him before.

The beard was gone, but so was something else—the weight in his eyes. And he was breathtaking.

If she'd thought it would render him more vulnerable she'd been wrong. The sweeping planes of his cheekbones and jaw lay fully visible; the clean, subtle lines of his lips and the strength of his chin gave him solidity. Sure, he was bleeding a little here and there, from her nicks and cuts, but it only added to his rugged appeal.

Now she knew why she'd clung to that idea of 'just sex'. Thrust it at him constantly like a shield and a sword to keep him from getting too close to the truth. Or maybe to keep her own feelings at bay. She'd tried so hard to 'be a guy' about it, but in the end she was just a woman, with not a lot of relationship history, trying to make sense of how to be with this man. This big, tough, complicated man. The kind of man older, wiser women would probably reconsider before scaling.

She hadn't hesitated.

'What is it, Gigi?'

He wasn't slow on the uptake. Any minute now he'd work it out.

She could feel his concern and it focussed her. 'I missed a bit on your upper lip,' she said huskily.

Trying to steady her hand, because she really didn't want to end the life of the only man she could see herself spending the rest of *her* life with, Gigi scraped carefully along his lip-line.

Then she was done. He was clean-shaven, and she was suddenly aware that he was looking at her as if he knew what he was about to say was going to hurt her.

Gigi wanted to stopper up his mouth, but she couldn't.

She couldn't do anything but look at him as he said, 'Gigi, there's something you need to know.'

It had been her confession earlier this afternoon that had landed a hammer-blow to his decision to keep the facts from her.

If he didn't tell her, and she found out from someone else, she might just start to hate him—and he didn't want that to happen with Gigi. Not with Gigi.

He looked down at her. 'Do you remember the resort my

company's building on Mt Elbrus? It needs a road and there's been some difficulty with permission.'

'Oh?'

'People aren't happy about it.'

'The local people seem relatively friendly.'

'The road traverses traditional grazing land. Nothing new gets built without clan approval.'

'And you need clan approval for the road?'

'Smart girl.'

'How will you get it?'

'That's where you come in.'

'You want me to help?'

And that was when Khaled knew he was going to hurt her.

'The day I brought you here I'd received a phone call that morning, letting me know the clan elders were willing to talk.'

She kept wiping the blade, nodding as he spoke.

'A few weeks before that I spoke to the head man here. He wanted to know why I didn't have a home here, why I wasn't married, where my children were—'

Gigi looked up with interest.

'And he told me if I respected their customs they would see it my way.'

She gave a nervous laugh. 'So when do I meet your wife and children?'

'It's you, Gigi. You're the custom I've respected.'

She went very still.

'The Moscow papers were reporting that I'd stolen you off the stage in Paris. The elders approved. I was given this meeting.'

A sudden gust of wind scythed the grass around them and the towel over Gigi's shoulder flapped away.

She didn't move an inch.

'You brought me here to win permission for your road?' Her voice sounded very small, hollow.

'I brought you here because I wanted to be with you,'

he said with passionate conviction because he knew now it was true, only to add slowly, 'and because it was politic for the road.'

Gigi stared past him.

'I had no idea this was going to be the result.' His voice was slightly hoarse as emotions he didn't recognise began to push up through his body.

'But once it was, you went ahead and did it anyway? Without asking me?'

'I didn't think it mattered that much, Gigi.'

Her eyes shot to his.

'I was wrong to do it.' He made a gesture towards taking hold of her but she backed away. 'I should never have brought you here.'

But Gigi wasn't listening. She was running.

She ran up the slope, the breath coming short and sharp from her lungs. She would have kept running if she'd had a choice, but there was nowhere to go.

She was stuck—in a strange, wild country with a stranger, wilder man.

Whom she was in love with.

She had waited on the hillside until she'd seen Khaled leave before she returned. It was only when she was inside, packing her few belongings, that her hand began to sting and she unfisted it to discover a nasty red welt across her palm from where she'd tightly held on to the razor.

She'd been so worried about cutting him, but in the end he'd been the one with the blade to her throat. She'd just been blinded by her own feelings and what she'd thought were the genuine feelings of the man sitting before her to notice.

He'd been the one to draw her blood.

Khaled had gone no further than halfway down to the village when he knew he couldn't do it.

He shut off the engine and sat in the truck, looking down

at the flat roofs and winding roads of the mountain pass where he'd been raised.

If he went down to that community hall there would be some macho posturing, the scratching of pens, and then he would get the signatures he needed. But for the rest of his life he would see Gigi's trust being shattered in front of him.

He'd have to find another way.

He started the engine, turned the truck and tore back up the hill.

He didn't know what he wanted with Gigi, but he knew it wasn't this.

Which was when he swung out of the truck and looked up.

The top of the tower caught the late-afternoon sun.

Unease settled on him.

He looked across the yard and his belly went cold.

The Jeep was gone.

Khaled's head was pounding. His stepfather had used the claim of love as his weapon of choice. He'd used it like a gun, and like any weapon it made a man weak, prey to the worst of his nature when things went wrong. As a grown man Khaled only carried a rifle when he went hunting, a situation in which he had a purpose, and he never fired without the knowledge of every available variable. He did not inflict needless suffering on an animal. Everything he did in life had a moral centre and was a choice.

He'd told himself he was not his stepfather.

He didn't deal in cruelty, and nor did he fashion weapons to turn upon others or himself.

He made the right choices.

Only then Gigi had come along. Gigi had burrowed under his skin. Nothing with Gigi had ever felt like a choice. It was inexplicable to him—this feeling—because it had never happened to him before.

He had no idea what to do about that.

And as he strode through Nalchik's airport, knocking over a plastic chair that got in his way, cutting through security as he forced his way into the passenger lounge, he was aware that he wasn't entirely in control any more.

Gigi was huddled in her oversized cardigan in the airport lounge, staring out at the blinking lights of a plane that wouldn't take off.

An hour. She wasn't sure how she would get through the wait so she took it minute by minute.

If she'd felt vulnerable alone in that tower of Balkar stone in the gorge, it was nothing to how she felt now—the only woman as far as she could see, with no luggage, no money, just her passport and the ticket Lulu had organised for her.

It was a far cry from the way she'd come here, wrapped in the luxury of Khaled's world, trusting as a lemming heading for the proverbial cliff.

She drew her knees up to her chin, thankful for the denim keeping her legs warm.

She glanced around and caught the gaze of two men sitting nearby. They hadn't been nearby five minutes ago. They'd shifted closer.

Gigi told herself not to be paranoid, but she wrapped her arms a little tighter around her knees.

She was perfectly safe.

An announcement was made in Russian.

Would she even know when her plane was going to take off?

She buried her face against her knees.

Heavy footsteps came ominously close and then stopped. Forcing herself to take a look, she lifted her head slowly.

Khaled was standing over her, in jacket and jeans, twice the size of the men who had been eyeing her up.

He was a wall no one was coming through.

That must be why relief was pounding through her. Now Khaled was here nothing bad would happen to her.

Even as the thought formed a fatal crack appeared in her logic.

Khaled *was* the bad thing.

'Gigi,' he said, and the urge to leap out of her seat and fling herself into his arms was almost overwhelming.

But she couldn't—not any more.

He was a liar. He'd lied to her. He'd used her. He cared only about his business interests. What had he said to her about the cabaret? *I'll replace you.* He'd only keep her in the role as long as she made it pay.

She held her ground.

'I've been out of my mind,' he said. 'I came home and found the Jeep gone. Then I got a call from the French Embassy, asking me to report to their consulate in Moscow tomorrow concerning my activities with an Irish national currently resident in France. That would be *you*, Gigi.'

He seemed angry, but it was anger held in restraint, and Gigi was also getting something else from him. A fierce sort of bewilderment. Crazily, a part of her wanted to take his hand and hold on.

It was what she'd been doing for the last couple of weeks.

But that wasn't possible any more.

She was so tired and cold, and just worn out from thinking in circles—no wonder she was fantasising like this…she just didn't know what to do.

'Lulu,' she said hoarsely. 'I rang her for my ticket. Her stepfather—'

'Is a French government official—so I have learned. So now I must take you home and restore you to your friends.'

'No, that's not what I want,' she began, leaping up. 'I can go home on my own two feet. I don't need you organising things for me any more.'

'But it is what I want.'

'What *you* want?' Gigi could barely look at him she was

so angry. 'That's all it is to you—what *you* want. What about *me*? What *I* want?'

'You got what you wanted, Gigi. L'Oiseau Bleu.'

If he'd punched her she couldn't have been more winded.

But suddenly she could look him in the eye. And she lifted her chin—because she'd learned in the hard school of Carlos Valente that you didn't stop taking the knocks until you couldn't get up any more.

'You knew I was falling in love with you. You can't have been blind to it. You used my feelings against me, for your own ends, and the joke is I would have helped you had you just *asked* me. You didn't. You chose instead to make a fool of me.'

'You don't love me, Gigi. Love is just another word for fear.'

'You think I'm *afraid*? You think I'm—what?—hiding behind the cabaret?'

'You won't try out for the Lido, Gigi, and as far as I'm aware that's the most prestigious joint in town. Why is that?'

'Because I'm loyal!' she hollered. 'Something *you* seem to have missed!'

'Loyal? You're scared.'

'No.'

She was shaking her head vigorously but she knew he could see she was weakening. She was backing away now. He'd almost pushed her backwards entirely.

He gave her another shove.

'And you're lying to yourself. This has always been about what I could do for you.'

'No.'

'Prove it,' he said. 'Make the choice. Me or the job.'

Suddenly Gigi wanted him to be that billionaire bastard he'd been written about as being.

But she knew better. She knew so much more about him.

She knew enough that she could feel her legs almost breaking under her with the weight of what he was doing to her.

Because if he cared for her he wouldn't put her love to a test.

She hadn't asked him to love her. She hadn't asked anything of him.

She looked at him sadly and shook her head.

'I want the job,' she said, swallowing hard on the fierce craving pushing up her throat, and she saw the flash of hard satisfaction cross his face and knew at last that what her instincts had been warning her of was true.

'Because there *is* no choice,' she said, almost to herself. 'You haven't given me a choice.'

As she turned away he tried to take her bag from her. For a moment she was thrown, almost thought he was going to stop her.

She wished in that moment that he would. A terrible, terrible wish.

But then she saw that he only wanted to hand it to his bodyguard, who had been hovering there the whole time.

She'd been so upset she hadn't even noticed.

'Grisha is flying with you to Moscow. End of discussion.'

She didn't argue because what was the point? He was always going to win.

And suddenly it was as if she was twelve years old again, and finally able to do that double somersault.

Carlos would be so proud of her—he'd have to love her. Or so she'd thought.

*'My daughter,'* he'd kept saying. *'My daughter is going to be the star attraction in this show.'*

But when she'd broken her collarbone and hadn't been able to perform it hadn't been Carlos who'd sat by her as she lay frightened and tearful in hospital.

*The show has to go on.*

She'd been all alone. Just as she was now.

She didn't let herself feel again until the plane was in

the air. By that time the aerial silks were cut and she was tumbling, tumbling…all her pretty tricks and turns lost to her now. All she could do was try to fall without breaking any bones.

Khaled boarded a helicopter and flew back to Moscow that same night.

He stormed into his apartment and the first thing he spotted was her shoe. Her little caramel boot, lying on its side beside his bed. He spent twenty full minutes hunting for its twin.

He never found it, but he did pull out a bottle of rot-gut vodka and proceed to get very, *very* drunk.

It was easier than facing what he'd done.

He'd seen what love did to people. How it failed you— when his father had died on his mother. How it twisted you—his stepfather's cruel jealousy. And how it weakened you—his own longing for comfort as a boy which had been beaten and kicked out of him, and then enabled him to make all of the tough decisions that had brought him to where he stood today: bloody but victorious in the Russian business bear pit.

Yes, he thought he had seen what love did to people— until he'd seen what he had done last night.

To Gigi.

To the woman he loved.

Because he *did* love her. How the hell could he *not* love her?

Yet even to imagine undoing those knots he'd tied tore at the weft and weave of the life he had put together. He had no idea what his life would look like if he undid them all. He suspected it wouldn't be pretty.

But Gigi had given him a glimpse of a *different* life. One which wasn't his, or hers, but *theirs*, and he was still under the influence of how strange and utterly beguiling it had looked.

On that last afternoon, as Gigi had run up the slope, her long back straight and her bare legs flashing through the grass, he had tried to imagine...

How it would feel to lose her.

How it would feel not to have her in his life any more.

He hadn't been able to get it out of his head.

And now he knew how bleak it actually was.

No light—just sounds. Even his Moscow apartment felt empty.

He'd literally built a fortress inside him. It was like the one he had taken Gigi to, but there was no illumination at the top of the tower that was his life. There was no moon and stars to gaze up at from their bed.

There was only fear and paranoia and the sound of his stepfather's fist banging on the door.

Two years ago Khaled had built up the interior of his real fortress in tandem with an architect and a designer. Made of Balkar stone, it had been standing for eight centuries against the immensity of the mountain. He'd known what he needed—space and light and warmth—two years before he had first laid eyes on Gigi Valente.

Khaled suspected that from the moment he'd looked up and caught his first glimpse of a bright-haired alluring fairy he'd known he'd been laying the ground for her. He'd won her cabaret in a lucky hand of poker. If that wasn't fate he didn't know what was.

She'd tumbled into his life and he should have caught her.

The next morning brought him the mother of all headaches— a sort of drilling in his skull that he endured stoically because he deserved every bit of suffering he could visit upon himself.

He showered and shaved and put on a suit.

He had to get her back. But first he needed a plan.

# CHAPTER SIXTEEN

GIGI'S SKIN FELT CLAMMY, her limbs weak, as she stumbled into Arrivals at Orly after several hours in the air.

Probably the flu, she decided dully.

She saw Lulu coming towards her. She looked like a snowman in a white puffy jacket. Only Lulu could look attractive in that much puff. Pink fur framed her face and her dark curls were frothing about merrily. Her smile faded as she took in Gigi's appearance.

*I must look awful*, thought Gigi tiredly.

'Oh, God,' said Lulu, stopping a few feet in front of her, 'what have I done?'

'I don't know,' she whispered hoarsely, 'but can we save it for later?'

Her best friend took charge as only Lulu could, nabbing them a cab immediately as several drivers swarmed Lulu's barely raised hand.

Gigi laid her head in Lulu's lap as the taxi took off.

'Are you sure it's flu?' Lulu was asking anxiously.

'That or travel sickness. Let me sleep, Lu. I feel so tired.'

She stirred some time after they'd hit the stop-start traffic of inner Paris.

As the taxi climbed the hill Gigi wound down the window.

'Stop here,' she told the driver.

'What are you doing?' Lulu called after her.

Gigi staggered from the cab and made her way to the central strip. She stood there staring up at L'Oiseau Bleu. Sure enough, it was boarded up.

A top-tier architectural restoration firm responsible for many sites around the city had its signage plastered everywhere.

Lulu reached her side and hovered.

'Don't hate me, Gigi. I didn't tell you that part because I

wanted you to come home. I know I was wrong. But I was scared something would happen to you.'

When Gigi didn't answer Lulu sniffled.

'The rumour is he's put up fifteen million euros.'

Gigi shook her head.

'Please forgive me, Gigi.' Lulu began to sob. 'I didn't realise.'

Struggling out of the grip of her depression, Gigi turned to her friend. '*What* didn't you realise?'

'That you love him.'

It moved through her like sunlight.

'Well, of *course* I love him, you eejit—I loved him from the moment he washed my feet!'

Lulu was still crying in earnest, and Gigi wrapped her arms around her best friend's shoulders.

'I didn't come home because he shut the Bluebird down, Lu. I came home because he's given me a job.'

Lulu gave a sniff. 'What sort of job?' she asked suspiciously.

'You're talking to the new manager of L'Oiseau Bleu.'

Lulu dropped her handbag. 'You're the *what*?'

Despite everything. Gigi found it in herself to laugh—even if it was a watery one. She bent down and handed Lulu's bag to her.

'Oh, Lord, if even *you* don't believe it I haven't got a chance with anyone else.'

Lulu dabbed at her nose with her wrist. 'It's not that I don't believe you, but of all things… You must be so happy, Gigi!'

'I—I am.'

Only she wasn't happy, and from the way Lulu was looking at her—had been looking at her since her arrival—her misery was plain to see.

She hadn't known how miserable she was until this moment. It was like being drenched with a bucket of cold water.

She wasn't happy, and no amount of telling herself that this was her dream come true was going to change the fact that what mattered more to her than the realisation of her dreams for the theatre, more than the knowledge that the jobs of her friends were safe—more even than doing something to preserve the memory of her mother—was telling Khaled that she loved him. She loved him in all the ways a woman could love a man.

Only all that mattered to him in the end was himself. His comfort, his financial success, having all of it *his* way.

That night as she lay alone in her bed, rendered cold and narrow and not like hers at all, she couldn't sleep. She climbed out of bed and went to her window. She could see the corner of the theatre's peaked roof further down the hill. That old theatre held so many of her childhood dreams, but it didn't hold her attention as it once had.

She looked up into the sky, unmarked by pollution on this cold winter's night, and wondered if Khaled was looking up at the same wedge of moon and sprinkling of stars in that fearsomely clean sky over the gorge. Was he thinking of her? Was he remembering how it had felt to lie in that cot of marmot furs, sharing body heat and stories? Was he thinking about how good it had felt to fall asleep like that? Was he thinking about her at all?

'He thought you were Rita when we all *know* you're Katharine Hepburn. So you got burned.'

Susie said this so pragmatically Gigi couldn't be offended. But then, she'd made an art form of not being offended. Until Khaled had torn the blinders off her eyes.

'Rita?' Adele frowned.

'Hayworth. Married all those larger-than-life men who disappointed her one way or the other.'

'Khaled virtually *gave* her the cabaret to manage—that's not a disappointment,' said Leah, but everyone stared at her until she hung her head.

The girls had turned up at the theatre this afternoon to

stick their noses in. As long as they wore hard hats that wasn't a problem on-site.

But as Gigi walked away with Lulu she said, 'He *did* give this cabaret to me, and that makes me the lowest common denominator.'

Lulu screwed up her nose. 'The what?'

'I'm the lowest common denominator,' Gigi said desultorily. 'He gave it to me because I slept with him.'

'I don't think anyone makes a fortune with bad business decisions, Gigi. He clearly thinks you're capable.'

That was the nicest thing Lulu had ever said about Khaled, and it had a ring of truth.

Gigi stood in her hard hat as the carpenters swung hammers overhead and dust rose from the curtains every time something got shifted on the stage.

This wasn't her usual environment, although in the past four weeks she had learned to read the builder's plans—well, she could make sense of where they were putting the toilets. Her real role was organising the talent. She'd already lined up a choreographer and costumier for the new show, which was far more up her alley than chip dust and power saws.

Only today she'd got a message to say they were bringing in the flooring and wanted her to approve the colour.

'He's doing this for *you*,' Lulu insisted, looking around.

Gigi flinched. 'Do you mind if we don't talk about him any more?'

Lulu eyed her nervously. 'Sure. Only he's standing over there.'

For a few beats it had sounded as if Lulu had said, *He's standing over there...* Which was when she turned around and...

Gigi almost dropped her clipboard.

Lulu evaporated like smoke—along with the workmen, the noise, the past few weeks.

He filled all her available vision and everything else was reduced to the horizon.

She took a step towards him. Stopped. He looked different. He'd cut his hair, and although he remained clean shaven there was stubble. He wore a suit.

She hated suits. But maybe it was better to see him like this. *As he was.* A ruthless businessman with his own agenda.

Only the eyes that met hers were not those of a businessman.

They were hot—and starved.

He stepped out of the gloom and into the light and the dust motes.

She wouldn't be surprised if he was just a figment of her imagination.

Then, 'Gigi…' he said. His voice was low and rough… and so familiar.

She pulled herself together. There would be no fainting at his feet on *her* watch.

Gigi was highly aware that this was approximately the spot where she'd landed at his feet just a few weeks ago.

Given the cabaret was now a shell around them, and the place looked as if a bomb had gone off, it was somehow appropriate.

He'd hit her life like a meteor, and if L'Oiseau Bleu was in the process of transformation she could be said to be too.

Only Gigi didn't hold by all that hokum. She had always been capable—she just hadn't been given the means by which to bring things off.

'You're cutting it fine,' he said, in that dark, roughened voice, stepping towards her.

Six weeks and that was what he said to her?

'On the contrary,' she said, and her voice only shook a little bit, 'we're ahead of schedule.'

'The press conference, Gigi. It's in an hour.'

'I'm not going to that.'

'I'm afraid it's in your contract. You *did* read your contract, didn't you?'

'I read enough.' He was so close now she had to tilt back her head.

Actually, she hadn't read anything—but she had used a lawyer, and she knew there was something about media appearances in it, but until now hadn't made that link.

Why on earth would anyone want to hear from *her*?

'You should have had a closer look at what you signed on for.'

She didn't respond.

He was looking at her with the strangest look in his eyes and giving her all the wrong messages again.

'I'll drive you over.'

Every kind of refusal was on her lips, but what came out was an exasperated, 'All right.'

He didn't touch her as he walked her out into the street but she could feel him—and it was a special kind of wonderful torture.

In the bright daylight she could see there was a grey tinge to his skin. He didn't look well.

'Have you been ill?' She had to ask.

'Flu,' he said, and shrugged, all the while holding her with his eyes.

'Me too,' she mumbled, and then noticed the limo hovering.

'Not the Spyder today,' he said, as if reading her mind. 'I wanted to talk to you.'

'About my job?'

'No, Gigi, about us.'

She began to shake. She couldn't look at him.

She shook her head. 'No, no, no…' And kept walking.

'Gigi! Be fair!'

Somewhere she found it in herself to shout, 'Life's not fair, Khaled! I'm going home to change. I guess I'll see you at the press conference.'

* * *

There was no way she was climbing into the back of that car with him.

Everyone would talk.

She couldn't bear it—not when she'd made a little progress over the last month or so. She might not have everyone's respect, but she had their co-operation and that was a start. She told herself she wasn't risking that by hopping in and out of limos with their billionaire boss.

Gigi went home and took a quick shower, and she almost put on her version of a suit she wore to most meetings when her eye was caught by the white and scarlet frock she'd picked up on a whim under Lulu's influence in a vintage clothing sale.

She had it on and her hair swept up when Lulu walked in.

'You are *so* not wearing that to the press conference?'

But Lulu sounded thrilled.

'Yes, I am,' said Gigi, knowing now what Lulu meant when she said that some days the right frock was the only thing that stood between you and despair.

Well, only vintage Givenchy was going to hold her together this afternoon.

'In that case,' said Lulu resolutely, 'we all will.'


The press conference was being held in a reception room on the ground floor of a luxury hotel.

Half of Paris seemed to have turned up, and the audience had spilled over into the lobby. The hum of preparation and the sound of chairs being shifted ceased as the doors swept open and the Bluebirds arrived *en masse*.

Gigi led them, in their showy old-time frocks: twenty-four glamour girls lined up in a row.

Clicking cameras responded.

'It's like something straight out of Fashion Week,' said one journalist.

'No, it's called making an old-time entrance,' said another.

Gigi indicated the need for chairs for the other twenty-three dancers and as she took her own identified where Khaled was in the room.

She sat with her girls and glared at him.

'Ladies and gentlemen…'

One of the suits launched into the press release.

Questions erupted.

Gigi listened to Khaled answer all the questions in that same deep voice that had haunted her dreams for six awful weeks.

She tried not to stare too long at him, but he was magnetic, charming the pants off all the females in the room with that quiet Russian drawl.

Although she knew now he wouldn't be taking advantage of that particular skill. He wasn't that man at all.

He was *her* man.

Only he didn't want to be.

'Why have you chosen to do this, Mr Kitaev?'

'Some people have called this your love letter to Paris. Is there any truth in that?'

Khaled leaned forward, his eyes focussed on her, and said in that low, deeply accented voice, 'It's my love letter to a particular woman.'

He had clearly gone off-script, because the suits looked alarmed and there was a flurry of hands raised as everyone vied to ask the next question, given the answer to that one wasn't in the information sheet.

'What's her name?'

'Is she French?'

'Is she a Bluebird?'

Gigi struggled to understand his meaning. She wanted to leap to her feet and demand to know exactly who he was sending love letters to when he'd told her love didn't even exist!

There was a low murmur among the girls, and a rustle of

skirts, and Gigi suddenly became aware that twenty-three mascara-laden pairs of eyes were glued to her.

Khaled gave the cameras the half-smile that had caused all this trouble to begin with and said directly, 'She's Irish. She *is* a Bluebird. She's the reason I've moved heaven and earth to have you all here today. Exactly six weeks from the day she first dropped so fatefully into my life. She's the person two million Parisians have to thank for saving their cabaret.'

Adele drummed her feet enthusiastically. Susie gave a thumbs-up, and Leah looked so sour her drooping mouth might drop off.

Gigi only knew this afterwards—when Lulu filled her in—because at that very moment she couldn't take her eyes off the man telling the world—well, what *was* he telling the world?

'My last visit to Paris was the most memorable of my life, because I met the woman I want to spend the rest of my life with.'

The cameras exploded in a flurry that sounded like applause.

Gigi didn't know she was on her feet until she was halfway out through the side door.

'Gigi!'

She heard him call her name, but didn't wait to find out why.

Khaled scraped back his chair.

There was another flurry of questions, but he didn't hear a word as he shouldered his way out of the reception room.

Gigi was exiting through the entrance doors when he exploded out into the lobby.

She was on the avenue outside, getting into a taxi, when he hit the pavement. He saw the flash of her skirts and began to run.

He grabbed the door as she went to shut it and jumped in alongside her.

'Get out of my taxi!'

He gave the driver an address in Montmartre.

Gigi folded her arms. 'I'm *not* sharing this taxi with you.'

She was, he thought, the most amazing girl, with her hands balled into fists, looking ready to belt him one. But her eyes gave her away, and they made him feel…made him feel…

Khaled gave a groan of sheer frustrated happiness and pulled her forward into his arms.

She went. But she was rigid, and she fought against him a little, and dipped her head so he couldn't kiss her. He understood, because she needed words, and he was struggling to find the ones that would make sense of the enormous reservoir of feeling he had stored up these last weeks without her.

Because there had never been any doubt for him: from first sight she had been the one.

After all, she'd thrown herself off a tank, turned up at his hotel, had herself papped as if they were Jagger and Faithfull back in the day *and* let him lock her up in a tower.

They were stories to tell their grandchildren. Because there *would* be grandchildren, after a tribe of children—a family he would build with her. A home…

But all he wanted right now was to be where he was: in the back of this taxi, holding her in his arms and knowing she was safe and sound and would be his, as he was hers. *If* he could find those damn words.

'Bastard,' she said.

That wasn't the right word, but from Gigi's soft lips it was a kiss.

'I love you,' he said, holding her strong yet fragile body against him. 'I've loved you from the moment I saw you on that stage floor. I've missed you every moment of every day. I should never have let you go. And if I want to give you a cabaret as a gift I damn well will and Paris can go hang.'

They might have been the words she wanted, but she gave him a hard shove in the chest all the same. 'You made me choose between you and the theatre.'

'Have them both—have it all.' He kissed her in between promises. Her temples, her eyelids, her nose, her mouth. 'Never again, *malenki*. You do not leave me ever again.'

Given she was kissing him back, with damp, tear-salty lips, the ground beneath his feet began to feel more solid.

They sailed up the hill without either of them really noticing, until the driver was tapping on the window. Khaled got out and gave her his hand.

'Where are we?'

It was a pretty narrow street at the top of the hill. There was a house with cream walls and square windows behind a high stone wall.

He drew her by the hand into the rambling garden behind the wall.

'The ten-kilometre rule,' he said, locking the gate behind them.

'What…?' she choked.

'You once told me you had a rule about the men you dated—they couldn't live outside a ten-kilometre radius of Montmartre. So I bought a house within your exclusion zone.'

'A house? But you live in Moscow.'

'Here…there. I can run everything from my phone—or so you tell me. It's a little smaller than the cabaret, but it's big enough. For us. For any children we have.'

A slow smile began to blossom on her lips.

Which was when he knew those were the words they both wanted.

Gigi looked up at him. Something wonderful was happening inside her. Everything was opening up and she felt love pouring through her like an elixir.

Khaled stood four-square in front of her, a wall that nothing was getting over, through or around. *Her wall.*

He framed her face.

'Marry me, Gigi. Have children with me. Grow old with me.'

In response Gigi wrapped her arms around his neck, and he pulled her against him and proceeded to kiss her passionately, thoroughly, and without much respect for the garden and its bed of long, soft grasses.

Several of which Gigi was plucking out of her hair as they ambled, arms entwined, down the road at twilight back to her flat. Below the rooftops of Montmartre glittered and deep shadows sprang up to cast everything in a mysterious heady glow.

\* \* \* \* \*

# BILLIONAIRE'S
# BABY BIND

## KATHERINE GARBERA

Thank you to all of the Mills & Boon Desire
authors, editors and readers who have welcomed
me as part of this wonderful reading family.

# One

Amberley Holbrook wasn't too keen on meeting new people; she preferred the company of her horses and keeping an eye on the stables where she worked. Normally her boss, Clay Everett of the Flying E, was happy to let her do what she wanted. But they had a guest on the property who had told Clay that he liked to ride. So as a courtesy Clay had suggested she stop by and introduce herself and offer to take the guest for a ride.

This held little appeal for Amberley. First of all, the dude was from Seattle, and the last time she checked there weren't any real cowboys from there, so that meant he was some kind of city slicker. Second…she and city slickers didn't get along. She would be the first to admit that was all down to her and her lousy attitude, which was something her father had advised her to keep in check if she wanted to keep this job.

Third…well, there wasn't any third. Digging in her heels and refusing to do as Clay had asked certainly wasn't an option. Amberley had packed more into her twenty-four years than most of her peers. She knew she needed to keep her job because she loved the horses she took care of and she certainly didn't want to go back to her family's ranch in Tyler, Texas.

That was something her daddy had been sure to remind her of when she'd called him earlier and told him about Clay's guest. She and her father were close. Her mom had died when Amberley was thirteen and she'd had four younger siblings to watch over. She and her dad had worked as a team to make sure everything on the ranch got done and her younger siblings, ranging in ages from four to ten, were taken care of. Sometimes her dad would say he cheated her out of a childhood, but Amberley never felt that way. She had her horse, Montgomery, and her family, and until she'd turned eighteen, that was all that had mattered.

Amberley understood why she was nervous about this new guest. The city guy had rented a danged Ford Mustang to drive around in this rugged Texas landscape. She could see the sports car parked next to the guest house that Clay had assigned him.

The Flying E was a sprawling ranch built in the heyday of Clay Everett's Professional Bull Riding career. He'd been at the top of his game until a bull named Iron Heart had thrown him. Clay had had a few ups and downs, but landed back on his feet and started a new career as CEO of Everest, a company that provided ironclad cloud infrastructure to companies. Amberley was the first to admit she had no idea what that really was, but it made Clay a nice fortune and enabled him to employ her as his full-time horse master.

She took care of the stables on the Flying E, provided lessons to locals from Royal and the surrounding county and made sure any guest of the Everetts had access to horses. The ranch itself was sprawling, with a large mansion for the main house and several smaller guest houses. Amberley lived in a cottage that suited her to a T. She'd always wanted her own place and lots of ranch land, something that was beyond the budget of a simple barrel racer like herself. So living on the Flying E and working for Clay gave her the best of both worlds.

She took another look at the sports car.

City guy.

As a teen, she'd watched shows like *Gossip Girl* and longed to be in Manhattan, though she'd have stuck out like…well, a sore thumb, but she had liked the fantasy of it.

So perhaps it wasn't quite so surprising that this man was making her curious before she'd even met him.

"Are you going to knock or just stand here all day?" Cara asked as she stood in front of the guest cabin that had been assigned to Will. The cabin itself was really a sprawling three-bedroom cottage that was all natural wood and glass.

Cara was seventeen and also worked on the ranch with Amberley, as her apprentice. She'd brought the teenager with her to meet Clay's new guest to be sure Amberley didn't do anything…well, stupid.

"Yeah. I was just waiting for the music to die down a little."

"I don't think it's going to," Cara said. "I thought he had a baby. You'd think the old dude would put on some headphones."

"You think he's old?"

Cara raised both eyebrows at Amberley. "Most def. He's got a kid, right? So, I'm guessing he must be old—"

"Geez, kid, back in my day we had to boot up a big old DOS machine and wait half a day for our computers to start working."

The voice was deep and rich, like the faux bass line in White Stripes' "Seven Nation Army," and Amberley felt a blush starting at her chest and working up over her cheeks as she turned to look at him. Their eyes met. His were forest green and made her think of the meadow she rode past each morning on her dawn ride on Montgomery.

There was a sardonic note in his voice that she totally got.

He wasn't old.

He wasn't old at all.

He wore a faded MIT T-shirt that clung to his shoulders and lean stomach. He had on a pair of faded jeans that hung low on his hips, and as she glanced down at his feet she noticed he had on Converse sneakers.

He was exactly what she'd been fearing and, if she was honest, secretly hoping he would be.

"You don't look too bad for your age," Amberley said. "I'm Amberley Holbrook, horse master, and this is my apprentice, Cara. Clay asked me to introduce myself and let you know that the stables are available for your use."

"Thanks," he said, holding out his hand to Cara. "Will Brady. Ancient one."

"Geez, dude, I'm sorry. I was just being mouthy. My mom has been warning me about that forever," Cara said.

"It's all right. I probably do seem ancient to a high schooler."

Cara shook his hand. Amberley wiped her hands on the sides of her jeans and took a deep breath and then their hands met. His skin wasn't dry and rough, the way so many of the hands of the men on the ranch were. They were soft, and as she looked down she noticed that his nails were neat and intact, not split from accidentally smashing one with a hammer.

She rubbed her thumb over his knuckles and then realized what she was doing and dropped his hand.

"Anyway… Come over to the stables anytime. I'll have to observe you riding before I can clear you to ride alone."

"No problem. I'll probably stop by this afternoon," he said. "I have a conference call with the sheriff this morning."

"Is this about Maverick?" Cara asked. "I heard you were in town to stop him."

Will shrugged and gave her a self-deprecating smile. "Just going to see what I can find on the internet to track that SOB down."

"I know we will all be glad for that," Amberley said. "I'm pretty much always at the stables, so stop by anytime."

Cara arched one eyebrow at Amberley but kept

her mouth shut, and they turned and walked back toward the stables. She tried to tell herself that he was just a guy...but she knew that he was so much more than that.

Amberley wasn't the kind of woman who had time for gossip or staring at hot guys. Yet she'd found herself riding by his place for the last two mornings hoping for a glimpse of him. Instead she'd had a conversation with Erin Sinclair, Will's nanny, and she'd even cuddled his cute daughter, eleven-month-old Faye.

Will had called down to the stables earlier to say he was going to come by for a ride, but he wasn't sure when the computer program he'd been running would be done. So it could be anytime between now and sunset. She was trying to focus on the work she had to do. There were horses to tame to the saddle, and she liked it that way. She'd always preferred animals over people. They were easy to predict, she thought. She'd grown up in a very large family, and the thought of having her own, well... She liked kids and men, but having to take care of her own brood made her break out in hives.

"You have to admit he's hot," Cara said. "Not old at all."

"He's a city slicker who probably can't tell a horse from steer. Who has time for that?" Amberley asked.

She and Cara were both grooming horses for the newcomers so they'd be able to take a ride around Clay Everett's ranch and get the lay of the land. When Cara had asked Amberley if she could help her out at the ranch, her gut instinct had been to say no. After all, what exactly did she have to teach the high school girl, but Cara had been insistent and one thing had led to another, and now she was in the barn grooming horses with a chatty seventeen-year-old.

"I'm just saying if a guy like that looked at me—"

"Your boyfriend would be jealous," Amberley said. Cara was dating one of the varsity football players.

"Yeah, he would be. For now. Next year he'll be gone and I'll be…I don't know where I'll be. Did you ever wish you'd gone to college?" Cara asked.

Amberley thought about it. At seventeen she'd wanted to get as far away from Texas, her siblings and the ranching life as she could. She'd wanted a chance to be on her own. But her family hadn't had the money for college and, to be honest, Amberley had only been an okay student. No one had been offering her any money for school and this job with Clay had come along at the right time. She'd met his foreman when she'd been rodeoing during her early teens and he'd offered the job.

It hadn't been her dream, but it had meant she'd be out of her dad's house and away from the siblings she'd had to babysit, and that had seemed like a dream.

At times, it was easy to forget she'd once wanted something else from life. She wasn't a whiner and didn't have time to listen to herself think of things that might have been. It was what it was.

"Not really. I have my horses and Clay pretty much lets me have the freedom to run the barn the way I want to. What more could a gal ask for?" Amberley said, hoping that some of her ennui wasn't obvious to Cara.

"I hope I feel like that someday."

"You will. You're seventeen, you're not supposed to have it all figured out," she said.

"I hope so," Cara said. Her phone pinged.

"Go on and chat with your friends. I can finish up the other horse. You know he mentioned he didn't know when he'd be down here."

"Here I am," a masculine voice said. "I hope I'm not interrupting."

Amberley felt the heat on her face and knew she was blushing. She could blame it on her redhead complexion, but she knew it was embarrassment. She could only be glad he hadn't arrived any earlier.

"Not disappointed at all," she said, reaching for her straw cowboy hat before stepping out of the stall and into the main aisle of the barn.

She'd sort of hoped that he wouldn't be as good-looking as she remembered. But that wasn't the case. In fact, his thick blond-brown hair looked even thicker today and his jaw was strong and clean-shaven. His green eyes were intense and she couldn't look away from him.

She told herself her interest in him was just because he was so different than the other men around the ranch.

If he had a pair of Wrangler jeans and some worn ranch boots she wouldn't be interested in him at all. But the fact that he had a Pearl Jam T-shirt on and a pair of faded jeans that clung to all the right spots was the only reason she was even vaguely attracted to him.

She noticed his mouth was moving and she thought she wouldn't mind it moving against hers. But then she realized he was speaking when Cara, who'd come out of her stall as well, looked at her oddly.

"Sorry about that. What did you say?"

"I was just saying that I'm sorry if just showing up messed up your schedule. I do appreciate you being available on my timetable," he said. "If you need more time to get ready I can wait over there."

She shook her head. He was being so reasonable. But she just had a bee in her bonnet when it came to this guy. Well, to all men who came from the city. She wished he wasn't so darn appealing. That maybe his voice would be soft or odd, but of course, he didn't have some silly city voice. Instead, his words were like a deep timbre brushing over her ears and her senses like a warm breeze on a summer's day. Since it was Texas, October wasn't too cool, but it was fall and she missed summer.

But with him… Dammit. She had to stop this.

"I'm ready. Cara, will you show Mr. Brady to his horse?" she asked her apprentice, who was watching her with one of those smirks only a teenager could manage.

"Sure thing, Ms. Holbrook," Cara said sarcastically.

"You can call me Will," he told Cara.

"Ms. Holbrook, can Will call you Amberley?"

That girl. She was pushing Amberley because she knew she could. "Of course."

"Thanks, Amberley," he said.

She told herself that there was nothing special about the way he said her name, but it sent shivers—the good kind—down her spine. She had to nip this attraction in the bud. Will was going to be here for a while helping Max St. Cloud investigate the cyber-bully and blackmailer Maverick, who'd been wreaking havoc on the local residents, particularly the members of the Texas Cattleman's Club, releasing videos and other damning stories on the internet. Will was the CTO of the company, so he was more of a partner to Max than an employee, and rumor had it they were old friends.

"No prob," she said. "How'd you end up here in Royal?" Amberley asked Will while Cara went to get his horse.

"Chelsea Hunt and Max go way back. So she asked for our help to try to find the identity of Maverick."

Maverick had been doing his best to make life hell for the members of the Texas Cattleman's Club. He'd been revealing secrets gleaned from hacking into smartphones and other internet connected devices. He'd made things uncomfortable for everyone in Royal.

"I like Chelsea. She's smart as a whip," Amberley said. And she seemed to really have her stuff together. No shrinking violet, Chelsea was one of the women that Amberley looked up to in Royal. She lived her life on her own terms, and Amberley was pretty sure that if Chelsea liked a guy she didn't have to come up with reasons to avoid him…the way that Amberley herself had been doing.

Cara came back with Will's mount and Amberley went back into the stall and saw her faithful horse, Montgomery, waiting for her. She went to the animal and rested her forehead against the horse's neck. Montgomery curved her head around Amberley's and she felt a little bit better. She had always been better with horses than people.

And normally that wouldn't bother her. But it would be nice not to screw up around men as much as she just had with Will. She didn't enjoy feeling like an awkward country bumpkin.

Will hadn't expected to feel so out of place in Texas. He'd been to Dallas before and thought that the stereotype of boots, cowboy hats and horses was something from the past or in the imagination of television producers. But being here on the Flying E had shown him otherwise.

Amberley was cute and a distraction. Something— hell, someone—to take his mind off Seattle and all that he'd left behind there. All that he'd lost. To be honest, coming out here might have been what he needed. His baby girl was sleeping with her nanny watching over her, and he was someplace new.

Max hadn't batted an eye when Will had told him he needed to bring his daughter and her nanny along with him to Royal. His friend had known that Will was a dedicated single dad.

He had work to do, of course, but he'd ridden a long time ago and thought getting back on a horse might be the first step to moving on. From his wife's death.

It was funny, but after Lucy's death everyone had been comforting and left him to process his grief. But now that so many months had gone by and he was still in the same routine, they were starting to talk, and his mom and Lucy's mom weren't as subtle as they both liked to think they were, with their encouragement to "live again" and reminders that he still had a long life ahead of him.

Lucy had had a brain hemorrhage a few weeks before she was due. The doctors had kept her alive until she gave birth to Faye. Then they took her off the machines that had been keeping her alive and she'd faded away. He'd asked them to wait a week after Faye's birth because he hadn't wanted his daughter's birthday to also be the day she'd lost her mom.

"You okay?"

"Yeah. Sorry. Just distracted," he said.

"It happens," she said. She spoke with a distinctive Texan drawl. It was so different from Lucy's Northwestern accent that he… Hell, he needed to stop thinking about her. He was getting away for a while, helping out a friend and having a ride to clear his head. He knew he should let that be enough.

"It does. Sorry, I'm really bad company right now. I thought…"

"Hey. You don't have to entertain me. Whenever I'm in a bad place mentally—not saying you are—but when I am, I love to get out of the barn, take Montgomery here for a run. There's no time to think about anything except the terrain and my horse—it clears away the cobwebs in my mind."

He had just noticed how pretty her lips were. A shell-pink color. And when she smiled at him her entire face seemed to light up. "Just what I need. Let's do this."

"Well, before we get started I need to know what your horsemanship level is," she said. "We'll pick our route based on that."

"Summer camp and college polo team," he said.

"I stopped playing about three years ago. I'm a pretty decent rider and keep a horse at a stable near my home. But haven't been riding much since my daughter was born."

"Sounds like you might be a bit rusty but you've got some skills," she said. "I'll start ya out easy and see how it goes."

"I'm yours to command," he said.

"Mine to command? Not sure I've ever had anything with two legs under my command."

He threw his head back and laughed. She was funny, this one. He wasn't sure if she'd meant that to be a come-on, but there was something sort of innocent about her so he guessed not. She was very different from Lucy, his late wife. That twinge he always experienced at the thought of her colored the moment.

"Let's start with a ride," he said.

She nodded. "There's a mounting block over there if you need a leg up. I'll let you go first."

"Thanks," he said, leading his horse to the block and mounting easily. He shifted around in the saddle until he was comfortable. The horse she had him on was easily controlled and led and seemed comfortable with him as a rider.

"So why are you here?" she asked as she mounted her own horse.

He told himself to look away but didn't. Her jeans hugged the curve of her butt and as she climbed on the horse there was something very natural about how she moved. As she put both feet in the stirrups and sat up, he realized she looked more at home on horseback than she had talking to him.

"Ah, I'm here to investigate all the trouble that Maverick is causing. I'm really good at tracking someone's cyber footprint."

She shook her head and then gently brushed her heels against her horse and made a clicking sound. "I don't even know what a cyber footprint is."

He laughed a little at her comment. "Most people don't think about it, but with smartphones and social media apps, we all are leaving a trail that can be followed."

"That makes sense," she said. "You ready for a run or do you just want to take it slow and steady?" she asked as they left the barn area and reached the open plains.

The land stretched out as far as he could see. It was October, so in Seattle it was rainy and growing colder, but the sun was shining down on them today in Texas and the weather was warm. He lifted his face to the sun, taking a deep breath. It was a good day to be alive.

As the thought crossed his mind, he remembered Lucy again and shook his head. He wasn't going to cry for the wife he'd lost or the family that had been broken. Not now and not in front of this strong, sunny cowgirl.

"Run," he said.

"Just the answer I was hoping for. Follow me. I'm going to start slow and then build. This part of the ranch is safe enough for a run."

She took off and he sat there for a moment stuck in the past until she glanced over her shoulder, her long braid flying out to the side, and smiled at him.

"You coming?"

This ride was just the thing he needed to draw him out of the gloom of the past.

"Hell, yes."

Riding had always been Amberley's escape. But with Will riding by her side, she felt more fenced-in than free. Clay had asked everyone at the Flying E to make Will feel welcome and she tried to tell herself that was all she was doing now. He was just another guest, a city boy, at that. He was here temporarily. She didn't like to think about her past or about the guy she'd fallen too hard and too quickly for. But there was something about Will that brought that all up.

Mostly, she realized it was superficial. They were both outsiders to her way of life. But where Sam Pascal had been looking for some sort of Western fantasy, it seemed to her that Will was looking…well, for a cyberbully but also for some sort of escape. There was a sadness that lingered in his eyes and when he thought no one was looking she could see that he was battling with his own demons.

Something she battled herself.

She heard him thundering along behind her and glanced over her shoulder. He sat in the saddle well and moved like he'd been born to ride. It was hard to keep him shoved in the city-slicker box when she saw him on horseback. She turned to face the field in front of them, taking a moment just to be glad for this sunny October day.

It was good to be alive.

The air had the nip of fall to it and the sky was so

big it seemed to stretch forever. She slowed her horse and waited for Will to catch up to her.

He did in a moment and she glanced over to see a big smile on his face.

"I needed this."

# Two

"Not bad for a city boy," Amberley told him as they allowed their horses to walk and cool down after their run. "I'm sorry I was judgmental about your skills."

Will couldn't help but like his riding guide. She was blunt and honest and it was refreshing. At work everyone treated him like he was the walking wounded and, of course, at home his nanny only discussed Faye. Rightly so. But Amberley didn't. She'd been treating him like a regular guy.

He hadn't realized how much he needed to get away and be with people who didn't know the personal details of his life. There was something freeing about being with Amberley on this sunny October afternoon. He felt for a moment like his old self. Before Lucy.

He felt a pang. Shook his head to shove the feeling from his mind.

"I didn't realize you were judging me," he said.

She tipped her cowboy hat back on her head and turned to gaze at him with a sardonic look. Her face was in shadows beneath the straw cowboy hat, but he could read her body language. She was sassy and funny, this cowgirl.

Distracting.

"I was judging you and it wasn't fair. It's just the last time I was around city folk was when I worked on this dude ranch in Tyler and a lot of them were… well, not very good riders. So I lumped you in with them. I should have known Clay wouldn't have told me to give you free rein if you didn't know what you were doing," she said. She held the reins loosely in one hand, and pushed the brim of her hat back on her forehead with the other.

Her eyes were a deep brown that reminded him of the color of his mocha in the morning. They were pretty and direct and he was almost certain when she was angry they'd show her temper. Will wondered how they'd look when she made love.

Then he shook his head.

This was the first time lust had come on so strongly since Lucy's death. And it took him by surprise.

He shook his head again. "To be fair, I'm not sure he knew my skill level. I think Max asked him to make sure I get the full Texas experience."

"The full Texas? That's funny. Well, this might be about it," she said, gesturing to the pastures.

He skimmed his gaze over the landscape and then settled back in the saddle. It reminded him of some of the places he'd visited growing up. His family had some property in Montana and there was a similar feeling of freedom from the real world here.

"I'm sure riding across the open plain isn't the only thing that's unique to Texas," he said. "You mentioned Tyler—did you just visit that dude ranch?"

"Nah," she said, looking away from him. But before she did he noticed a hint of sadness in her eyes.

"I worked there when I was in high school in the summers. Clay offered me this job after…well, when I was ready to leave my family's ranch. My daddy said I was losing myself by mothering my brothers and sisters and he wanted me to have a chance to have my own life. I'm pretty good with horses. My daddy has a nice-sized ranch in Tyler. What about you? Where are you from? The Northwest, right?"

"Yes. Seattle area. Bellevue, actually. It's a suburb," he said. He'd never wanted to live anywhere else growing up. He loved the mountains and his waterfront property, but after Lucy…well, he'd been struggling to make Bellevue feel like home again.

"I've heard of it. I think Bill Gates lives there."

"We're not neighbors," Will said with a laugh.

She shook her head and laughed. "I'll jot that down. You ready for a ride back or you want to see some more?"

"What's left to see?"

She rocked back in her saddle, shifting to extend her arm. "Out that way is the south pasture—there's a creek that runs through it. Down that way is the—"

"Let me guess—north pasture."

"Ha. I was going to say castration shed. We do that in the spring," she said.

He shook his head. "I'll skip that."

"Guys always say that."

She was teasing him and he observed that her entire countenance had changed. Her relaxed smile made him realize how full and lush her mouth was, and the way she tipped her head to the side, waiting for his response, made him want to do something impulsive.

Like lean over and kiss her.

He slammed the door on that idea and sat back in his saddle to be a little farther away from her. There was just something about her easy smile and the wind stirring around them. And he was on horseback in Texas, so far away from his normal world, that he wanted to pretend he was someone different. A man who wasn't so tired from not sleeping and hoping he was making the right choices all the time.

He knew that nothing would come of kissing Amberley. He wasn't here to hook up. He was here to do a job. Besides that, he wasn't ready for anything else. He knew that. But for a moment, he wished he were.

"Back to the ranch."

She didn't move, but just stared at him—there was a closed expression on her face now. "Sorry, sir, didn't mean to be inappropriate. Follow me. You want to run back or walk?"

"Amberley—"

"I was out of line. I guess I forgot you were a guest for a second."

"Who did you think I was?" he asked.

"Just a guy," she said, turning her horse and making a clicking sound. Then she took off back the way they'd come.

* * *

He galloped after her and reached over to take her reins, drawing both of their rides to a stop.

She took back her reins and gave him a good hard glare. "Don't do that again."

"Well, I couldn't figure out another way to stop you," he yelled. He wasn't sure what he'd stepped into, but he could tell something had changed and he was pretty damn sure he was the cause.

"Why would you want to?" she asked. "I'm pretty sure you want to get back to the ranch and I'm taking you there."

"Don't act that way," he said. "I'm sorry. My life is complicated."

She nodded and then looked away. "Everyone's life is complicated. We're not simple hicks out here on the ranch."

He hadn't meant to hurt or offend her.

And all of a sudden he felt ancient. Not twenty-eight. Not like a new father should feel, but like Methuselah. And he hated that. He'd always been…a different man. His father had said he was lucky and someday his luck would wear thin. But he knew his father wouldn't rejoice in the way his luck had run out. Losing Lucy had changed him, and some people would say not for the better.

"I'm sorry," he said. The words sounded rusty and forced but they weren't. She didn't deserve to be treated the way he'd treated her, because he wanted her and he knew he wasn't going to do anything about it. He wasn't about to invite another person into the chaos that his life was right now.

"What for?"

"That sounded…jerky, didn't it? Like I'm trying to imply that your life isn't complicated," he said. "That's not at all what I meant. I just meant I'm a mess and this ride was nice and you are wonderful…"

He trailed off. What else could he say? He thought she was cute. Maybe he'd like to kiss her, if he wasn't so stuck in that morass of guilt and grief. And then more guilt because his grief was starting to wane. And it's not like Lucy would have expected him to grieve forever, but moving on was like saying goodbye again.

"I wouldn't go that far," she said.

"What?"

"Saying I'm wonderful. I mean, I have faults like everyone else," she said. Her words were light and obviously meant to give him a way back from the dark place he'd wondered into. But in her eyes he saw weariness and he knew that she wasn't as…well, un-damaged as he had believed she was.

"You seem like it from here," he said at last.

"Then I better keep up the illusion."

But now that she'd brought it up he was trying to see what there was to the young horsewoman. She seemed uncomplicated. He thought about how when he was her age, life had been pretty damned sweet.

"Tell me," he prompted.

"Tell you what?" she asked.

"Something that isn't wonderful about you," he said.

"Ah, well, I think that would be easy enough. I have a short temper. I believe I gave you a glimpse of that a moment ago."

"You sure did," he said with a laugh. "But that could also be called spunk. I like feisty women."

"You do?" she asked, then shook her head. "What about you? What's one of your faults?"

"Hell, I'm not even sure where to begin," he said. And he knew that he didn't want to open that can of worms. His life was littered with regrets lately. Only spending time with Faye or sitting in the dark working on the computer tracking down code seemed to get him out of his own head space.

"I'm not as clever as I once believed I was."

She started laughing. "Well, I think that's the same for all of us. Race you back to the barn?"

"Sure, but since I haven't ridden in a while I think I deserve a handicap."

"Really?" she asked. "That is such a load of crap. If I hadn't seen you ride out here I might have fallen for it."

"It was worth a try," he said.

The fall breeze blew, stirring the air, and a strand of her red hair slipped from her braid and brushed against her cheek. He leaned forward in his saddle and gripped the reins to keep from reaching out and touching her.

He'd just shoved a big wedge between them. A smart man would leave it in place. A smart man would remember that Amberley wasn't a woman to mess with and he had never been the kind of man who screwed around with anyone.

But he didn't feel smart.

He felt lonely and like it had been too long since he'd been able to breathe and not catch the faint scent of hospital disinfectant. He wanted to sit here until night fell and then maybe he'd think about heading back to the life he had. He wanted...

Something he wasn't in a position to take.

He knew that.

"Hey, Will?"

He looked up, realizing that she'd been staring at him the entire time.

"Yeah?"

"Don't sweat it. I've got a beef with city dudes and it's clear that you have something with your baby's mama to deal with. You're hot and the way you ride a horse makes me feel things I'd rather not admit to, but that's it. You're on the Flying E to work and as a guest and I'm going to treat you like that. So don't think…"

"What do you feel?" he asked.

Will knew he felt reckless and dangerous and he wasn't going to stop now. He wanted to kiss her. He wanted to pull her off the horse and into his arms and see where that led.

"Like I said, I'm not going there."

He shifted in the saddle and dismounted his horse, dropping the reins on the ground to check that the horse would stay, and it did.

Will walked over to her and stood there next to her horse, looking up at her. He was closer now, and he could see her eyes, and he wasn't sure what he read in her expression. He was going to tell himself it was desire and need. The same things he was feeling, but he was afraid he might be projecting.

"Come on down here," he said. "Just for this afternoon let's pretend we aren't those people. I'm not a guest and you're not a ranch hand. We're just a guy and his girl and we've got this beautiful afternoon to spend together."

\* \* \*

Never in her life had Amberley wanted to get off a horse more. But her gut said no. That this wasn't going to be sweet or uncomplicated. And the last time she'd been sweet-talked by a guy it hadn't ended well. It didn't matter that she was older and wiser now. She didn't feel as if she was either.

Riding hadn't helped to chase away her demons back then, when she'd found herself pregnant and alone at eighteen, and it wasn't helping now. He stood there in his clothes, not fake-cowboy duded up the way some city guys dressed when they came to Texas, and to be fair he looked like he fit in. He wasn't chasing a Wild West fantasy, he was here to do a job.

And her job was to make him feel comfortable.

What could be more comfortable than hanging out together?

Dumb.

Stupid.

His hair was thick and wavy and he wasn't wearing a hat, so she could see the way he'd tousled it when he'd run his fingers through it. She wasn't getting off her horse. She was going to be sensible.

*Please, Amberley, be sensible.*

But she never had been.

She suspected it was because she'd had to be so responsible so young. She'd always had to take care of her younger brothers and sisters. But that was in Tyler, and she was away from there now, with no one to worry about but herself.

And this was safe. He just wanted to spend the afternoon together.

One afternoon.

Surely even she could manage that without having it go to hell.

She shifted and started to turn to swing her leg over the saddle and dismount, then she saw the smile on his face and the look of relief.

He was unsure.

Just like her.

Except he wasn't like her. He had ties. And she hadn't asked about them earlier. There was so much she didn't know. Where was his baby's mother? That baby was pretty damn young to be living with a nanny and her father. Was there any way this could be just an afternoon?

If it was...then the mom didn't matter... Unless they were still together. That would be—

"Hey, before we do this. Where is your baby's mother? I don't want to pry but you're not still with her, right?" she asked.

He stepped back—stumbled was more like it—and she suddenly wished she'd kept her mouth shut.

There was no denying the way all the color left his face, or how he turned away from her and cursed under his breath.

"No," he said, walking back over to his horse and taking his saddle with much skill and finesse.

"We're not still together. She's dead." He made a clicking sound and took off across the field as if the hounds of hell were chasing him, and Amberley guessed maybe they were.

She stood there, a wave of sadness rolling over her. A part of her had died when she'd miscarried. Seeing Will...had made her realize that they were two sides of the same coin. She had no baby and no family and he had a baby and no wife or mother for the child. He was trying to deal with the loss the same way she had been.

She knew that riding helped at times but she'd never been able to outrun the pain. Those memories and the truth of her life were always waiting when she'd gotten off the horse.

She clicked her mare and followed Will close enough to call out if he took a path that wasn't safe, but he had watched their trail on the way out and he made no mistakes on the way back.

She slowed her own horse to a walk as Will entered the stable area and decided that maybe she should just let him go. Give him some space to dismount and leave before she entered the barn again.

She saw the ring that she'd set up earlier to practice barrel racing and rode over that way. Montgomery and she had been partners for the last year or so. And when the Flying E could spare her she took the horse and went and competed in rodeos.

# Three

Will had just spent the last ten minutes in the barn trying to avoid a confrontation with Amberley—the woman he'd practically run away from. But he had no doubt she would be avoiding him after his foolish reaction to her harmless question about Faye's mother.

It was hard to think that at twenty-eight he was turning into his father, but it seemed that way more and more. And it wasn't Faye who was forcing the change. It was him. It was as if he'd lost that spark that had always driven him. And the therapist he'd seen for two sessions at his mom's insistence had said that grief took time.

But as he left the barn and spotted Amberley exercising her horse in the ring, he felt that stirring again.

It was lust, because even though he was grieving he wasn't dead, and the feeling was laced with something more. Something much more. She was one with the horse as she raced around the barrels, her braid flying out behind her as she leaned into the curves and got low over the horse's neck, whispering encouragement, he imagined.

He watched her and wanted her.

She stopped at the end of her run and looked over toward the barn. Their eyes met and he felt stupid just standing there.

He clapped.

But that felt dumb, too.

It seemed that he'd left his smarts behind in Seattle, he thought. Everything was different here. He tried to justify his feelings—like he needed an excuse to find a woman pretty or be turned on by her. Yet in a way he felt he did.

But that was his issue, not Amberley's. And it wasn't fair to her to bring her into the swirling whirlpool that his emotions were at this moment.

She nodded and then turned away from him.

Dismissing him.

He'd had his chance and he'd ruined it.

Maybe it was for the best. He had Faye to take care of and a criminal to catch. In fact, he needed to get back to work. Without another glance at her he turned and walked to the golf cart that had been allocated for his use during his stay on the Flying E. He put it in gear and drove to the house that Clay Everett had been generous enough to provide. To be honest, he knew that Clay had a stake in Will finding Maverick, as did most of Royal.

He shifted gears as he drove farther and farther away from the barn and the cowgirl that he'd left there, but a part of his mind was still fantasizing about the way his afternoon could have gone.

His nanny, Erin Sinclair, was waiting for him at the door when he got back.

"Faye's asleep and I need to run to town to pick up some more baby food and formula. Are you okay if I go now?" she asked.

He had hired Erin to help with the baby even before Lucy's untimely death. His late wife had been a product rep for a large pharmaceutical company and traveled a lot for work. Though Will spent a lot of time in his home office, he tended to have a single-minded focus, so he knew that by the time Faye was born, both he and Lucy would have needed help with the baby.

"Yes, go," he said.

He went into the bedroom they used as a nursery and looked down at Faye's sleeping face. He tried to see Lucy in her features but he was starting to forget what she looked like. Of course he had pictures of her but he was starting to lose that feeling of what she'd looked like as she smiled at him. The different feeling she'd stirred in him with one of her expressions that a mere photo couldn't capture.

Dammit.

He turned away from the crib and walked out of the room. He had a monitor app on his phone and had a window that he could keep open on one of the many monitors in his office so he could keep an eye on her.

He walked into the darkened large bedroom that he'd turned into his office for the duration of his stay in Royal. He had four large computer monitors that were hooked up to different hard drives and were all running multiple programs that would determine where Maverick was basing himself online.

Almost all of the attacks had been cyber-based, so Chelsea was working on the theory that he was very internet savvy. In a way that worked in their favor because there weren't many top computer experts in Royal. But then hackers wouldn't be known to many.

One of Will's skills was the ability to look at code and see a digital fingerprint in it. Maverick had habits just like everyone and Will was searching for those, looking for a trail back to the creep's identity.

He opened his laptop after he checked the progress on the different computers and made sure all of his scripts were still running.

He launched his internet browser and searched for information on Amberley Holbrook. He wasn't surprised to see her listed in a bunch of small-town rodeos, stretching from Texas to Oklahoma to Arkansas, as a winner or a top-three finisher in barrel-racing competitions. There was a photo of her winning run in a recent event and he clicked to open it larger in his photo application so he could zoom in on her face. There was concentration but also the biggest damn grin he'd ever seen.

That girl was happiest on the back of a horse.

Why?

He noticed how she was when she was off her horse. On her guard and waiting to see how everyone around her reacted. Given that he was starting to behave that way, he wondered what had happened to force her to build those kinds of walls. She definitely had them.

Why?

And why the hell did he care?

Because she intrigued him. She was different. Funny, sexy, sassy. She made him think of things he hadn't in a really long time.

And he'd just walked away from her. He'd decided he had too much baggage to dally with a woman who was tied to Texas and this ranch. He wasn't here for longer than it took to find the cyber coward Maverick, then he was out of here. And back in the Pacific Northwest, where he could slowly rot from guilt and grief.

That sounded damn pitiful. He had never been that kind of man and he wasn't too sure that Faye was going to want a father who was like that.

He knew he had to move on.

Will had come here in part because Max had asked and also because he knew he had to get away from the memories, get away from the guilt and the grief. But he was in no position to move on. He had to keep moving forward until he figured out what he wanted next. Amberley had been a distraction but also something more. She was honest and forthright. He liked that.

He liked her.

If he were in a different place in his life then the zing of attraction that had arced between them...well, he would feel better about acting on it.

But he wasn't.

And that wasn't fair to her.

*Who said life was fair...* The words of his therapist drifted through his mind. He'd been lamenting the fact that Faye would never know Lucy and that it wasn't fair.

Well, life might not be, but he knew he couldn't just use Amberley for himself and then leave. That wasn't right.

And he hadn't changed at his core.

But she intrigued him…

Amberley blasted My Chemical Romance as she got ready to go out. It was Friday night and two days had passed since…whatever the hell that had been with Will. She tried to remind herself he was a city dude and she should have known better than to be attracted to him, but that hadn't kept him out of her dreams for the last two nights.

So when her cousin from Midland had called and said she'd be driving through Royal on Friday and did Amberley want to go out, she'd said yes. Normally she was all for comfy jammies and binge-watching one of her favorite TV shows on Netflix, but tonight she needed to get out of her own head.

She was ready to dance to some rowdy country music, drink too much tequila and flirt with some small-town boys who wouldn't walk away from her without a word. It had been a long time since she had blown off steam and it was the weekend. Even though she sometimes acted like she was ready for the retirement home, she was still young.

But she didn't feel it.

There was a weight in her heart that made her feel older than her years. And when Will had said his life was complicated she'd…well, she'd ached because she knew complicated.

She knew what it was like to be a big, fat, red-hot mess masquerading as normal. She'd done that for a year after she'd lost the baby and then gotten the devastating news that she'd never be able to have a child. A part of her should have rejoiced that he'd only seen what she had wanted him to—a cowgirl who was damn good with horses.

But that connection she'd felt with him had made her want him to see more.

And he hadn't.

*He hadn't.*

She was wearing her good jeans—a dark wash that fit like a second skin—and a pair of hand-tooled boots that her brothers and sisters had given her for Christmas. They had a fancy design featuring turquoise and she'd completed her outfit with a flirty peasant top. She'd taken the time to blow-dry her hair and not just pull it back in a braid, so it fell around her shoulders.

She finished her makeup and put a dash of lip gloss on before grabbing her purse and heading out. She was halfway to her truck when she realized someone was in her yard. Not that it was really her yard, since Clay owned all the property, but that little area in front of her place.

Amberley glanced over and realized the someone was a dog. A ragged stray that was making mewling sounds that she couldn't ignore. He was a rather sad-looking animal with a matted coat. She tossed her purse on the hood of her truck and turned toward the dog, careful not to spook it as she walked toward it. She crouched low and held out her hand for it to sniff once she was close enough.

The animal whimpered and then slowly moved closer to her. She held her ground, noticing that it limped. One of his legs was injured. Just the distraction she needed. Animals were the one thing on this planet that she was actually good with.

She waited until the dog came closer and noticed that there were some briars wrapped around his hind leg, and when she reached for the leg he moaned and moved away from her.

"All right, boy. I'll let it be. But we are going to have to take you to get that looked at," she said. She stood up, pulled her phone from her back pocket and texted her cousin that she'd be a little late. Then she went back into her place, got a blanket, a bowl and bottle of water. Then she grabbed a carrot from the fridge and went back outside.

The dog was exactly where she'd left him. Waiting for her.

"Good boy. You're a boy, right?" she asked.

The dog didn't answer—not that she expected him to. She put the bowl down in front of him and gave him some water and stood to watch him as he drank, then texted the small animal vet that Clay used to let him know she'd be bringing in an injured dog. Though it was after hours, Clay had an agreement for the ranch that included 24/7 coverage.

She spent the next hour getting the dog settled at the vet. He had a chip and the vet contacted his owners, who were very glad to find him. Amberley waited until they arrived before leaving to meet her cousin. But the truth was she no longer wanted to go out.

The dog—Barney—reminded her of how alone she was. Even the stray had someone to go home to. His owners had been really nice and so happy she'd found him and Amberley was gracious to them, but a part of her had wanted the stray to be a loner. To maybe need her.

She hated that she was feeling down about her life. She'd finally gotten past everything that had happened when she was eighteen and now some dude was making her question her situation. She'd never been this knocked on her butt for some guy. Yet there was something about him that had made her want to be more. Want to be someone she hadn't thought about being in a long time.

But there it was.

She wanted to see him again.

Her cousin was waiting in the parking lot of the Wild Boar, a roadhouse that served food and drinks and had a small dance floor with live music on the weekends. There were pool tables in the back and a mechanical bull. If you weren't in the upper echelon of Royal and weren't a member of the Texas Cattleman's Club, then this was the place to hang out.

"Hey, girl. You ready to blow off some steam?"

She nodded. Maybe a night out with Royal's rowdy crowd was what she needed to remind her of where she belonged and whom she belonged with…and it wasn't a hot guy from Seattle.

Midnight was his favorite time of night and when he found the most clarity when he was working—tonight wasn't any different. Faye was a little night owl like he was, so the baby was playing on the floor at his feet while he watched the scripts that were running and tracking down Maverick on the monitor nearest to him.

She'd woken up crying. Erin was worn out from

a long day of dealing with Faye teething, and since Will was up at night working anyway, they'd established that he would take the night shift.

Maverick wasn't the cleverest hacker, but whoever he was, the man was running his internet through a few connections. It would have fooled someone who didn't have Will's experience, but he'd been a pirate hunter in high school for a large software company that his dad had helped found and he'd spent a lot of years learning how to follow and find people who didn't want to be found.

"Dada."

"Yes?" He looked down at Faye. Her face was so sweet and she was holding a large round plastic toy up to him.

He took it from her.

She immediately reached for one a size smaller and held it up to him. This was one of her favorite new games. She gave him all the toys around her and then he had to sit still while she took them back and put them in a seemingly random order in front of him.

But this time she was done handing them all to him, so she crawled over to where he sat on the floor next to her and crawled onto his lap. He scooped her up and hugged her close.

His heart was so full when he held his daughter. She smelled of baby powder and sweetness. He knew sweetness wasn't a scent, but when he held Faye it was what he always felt.

He stood up and walked around the house with her while she babbled at him. He set a notification on the computers to alert his phone when the scripts were finished running and then put Faye's jacket on her so they could go for a walk. He'd grown up in Bellevue, near the water, and some of his earliest memories were of being outside with his mom at night looking at the sky.

He knew that many people would expect Faye to be in bed at midnight, but she wasn't looking sleepy at all. It was probably his fault for having a long nap with her in the afternoon. He'd been keeping odd hours since they had arrived in Royal.

He walked toward the barn, telling Faye the stories his mom had told him. Will's mom's people had been sailors and the sky and the water were a big part of their history.

He heard the rumble of a truck engine and turned as a large pickup rounded the corner. He stepped off the dirt track to make sure he wasn't in the path of the vehicle.

The truck slowed and the passenger-side window rolled down. He walked over and was pretty sure it was Clay Everett. But Will knew if he had a woman like Sophie waiting for him at home, he'd have a better way to spend his night than patrolling his ranch.

"Hey, Will. You okay?" Amberley asked.

He was surprised to see her. She had obviously been out, as she smelled faintly of smoke. Her hair was thick and fell around her shoulders. The tousled tresses, so different from her neat braid, made his fingers tingle with the need to touch her hair.

He regretted leaving her the other afternoon. One kiss. Would that have been so bad? Even Lucy wouldn't begrudge him that. But he hadn't taken it.

So instead a need was growing in him fast and large. Each day it seemed to expand and he knew he was losing control.

"Yeah. Faye's a night owl like me so I thought I'd take her for a walk."

Faye heard her name and started babbling again.

"Want some company?" Amberley asked.

"Sure," he said.

She turned off the engine of her truck and climbed out, coming around by him. Her perfume hit him then—it was sweet like spring flowers. There was a slight breeze tonight and Amberley tipped her head back and looked up at the sky.

"When I was little, my dad told us that if we were really good we'd see a special angel in the sky."

"Did you ever see one?"

"Yeah," Amberley said. She stretched out her arm and pointed to Venus. "There she is."

"That's Venus."

"Show some imagination, Brady. That's my special angel. She watches over me at night."

"Does she?"

Amberley nodded. But she wasn't looking up anymore—she was staring at Faye. "She'll watch over you, too, little lady."

Faye answered with one of her babbles. And Amberley listened until Faye was done and then she nodded. "I know. It's hard to believe that someone up there is looking out for you, but she is."

Faye babbled some more.

"Your mama?" Amberley asked when she was done.

Faye babbled and then ended with "Mamamam."

"Mine, too. They are probably friends," Amberley said.

Faye shifted toward Amberley and Amberley looked over at him for permission before reaching for the baby. Will let Faye go to Amberley and watched the two of them talking to each other. She was good with the baby. He was surprised that Faye had wanted to go to her. She was usually pretty shy with strangers.

He noticed that both of the girls were looking at him.

"She's usually not so eager to go to strangers."

"Well, we're not strangers," Amberley said. "We chatted up a storm while you were holding her."

"You sure did," Will said.

Something shifted and settled inside of him. It was a tightness he wasn't even aware of until that moment. And then he realized that he wanted Faye to like Amberley because it didn't matter how guilty he may feel afterward, he wanted to get to know her better.

# Four

The night sky was clear, filled with stars and the waning moon. Amberley tipped her head back, feeling the emotions of the week fall away. The baby in her arms was sweet and soft. She had been cooing and pointing to things as they walked and Amberley fought against the pain in her heart she'd thought she'd finally gotten over.

She loved babies. Loved their smiles and their laughter. The way that they communicated if you just took the time to listen to them.

Her dad had told her that she shouldn't give up on a family, but the hysterectomy she'd had at eighteen had pretty much put paid to that. She couldn't have a baby of her own. So she tended to spoil any kiddos she met.

"You're awfully quiet over there," she said, realizing that Will hadn't said much in the last few minutes. She'd suggested they lie in the bed of her pickup truck and watch the night sky. Will had agreed but only, he'd said, until Faye got sleepy.

"Just trying to get this app to work," he said.

He'd mentioned having an app that could show meteor and comet activity in the night sky and was trying to get it to work. Amberley had spread a blanket she kept for picnics on the bed of the truck and she and Faye had been playing together while he tried.

"If it doesn't work we can just make up stories," she said.

"Like what?" he asked.

"That star over there is Lucky."

"As in it brings luck?" he asked.

"No, its name is Lucky. Sometimes the star falls to earth and takes on the persona of a rock superstar during the day, and at dusk it's drawn back up into the night sky, where she stays steady and true so that little cowgirls and cowboys who are out late on the range can find their way home," Amberley said.

She'd been a huge Britney Spears fan when she'd been about ten and her dad had made up that story about one of the pop star's songs.

"Okay, let me give it a try," Will said. He shifted his shoulders and leaned back against the cab of her truck. Faye crawled over to him and he lifted her onto his lap. The baby shifted around and settled with her back against his chest.

They were so cute together, Amberley thought. She ached for little Faye because even though she had her daddy's love and attention, Amberley knew that one day Faye was going to need her momma.

She just felt close to them because she saw herself in the two of them.

"See that constellation?" he asked, pointing to Sirius.

"Yes."

"That's Lobo and he is really good at catching the people who skunk around in the shadows. Every night he looks down on the earth for clues and then during the day he turns into computer code and helps track down the bad guys."

She smiled. "Like you."

"Yeah. Like me."

"How's that going? Is it okay to ask?"

Faye turned in his arms and he rubbed his hand over her back. He lifted her higher on his chest and she settled into the crook of his neck.

"It's going pretty well," he said, his voice pitched low so as not to disturb his daughter.

"I'm glad. Will you be here for long?" she asked.

"Probably a month."

A month…not enough time for anything serious.

"I'd love to know more about what you do," she said. Sometime between the dancing and talking with her cousin tonight she'd realized that no cowboy or Royal guy could make her stop thinking about Will. Probably not her wisest idea, but she had decided she wasn't going to just walk away unless he pushed her to.

"Stop by anytime and I'll show you. It sounds more exciting than it is. Usually it's me in a dark room with my computers running programs or tracking scripts."

"That is so foreign to me. I spend all my time outside and with animals. I mean, I have my phone, which keeps me connected, but I don't even own a computer."

"I don't see why you should need one," Will said. "Smartphones can do just about everything you'd need a computer for."

"Want me to drive you guys back home?" she asked.

"I don't have a car seat so we probably shouldn't," he said.

She felt silly because she'd been used to riding in the back of the truck from the time she'd been a child. She guessed it wasn't that safe, but there wasn't much out here to cause an accident. It underscored to her the many ways they were different.

But he was only here for a month.

Why was she trying to make it acceptable to get involved with him?

She knew why.

She was lonely. It had been a year since her last boyfriend and she was using that term loosely. She and Pete had hooked up at a rodeo and then gone their separate ways. But she felt something stirring inside of her.

Maybe it was just lust.

She sighed and then realized that he'd been staring at her.

Crap.

"Sorry. I guess I'm getting tired. What did you say?"

He shook his head and shifted around, setting Faye on the blanket next to him. The little girl curled onto her side and cooed contentedly as she drifted to sleep.

"I didn't say anything. I was only watching you,

regretting that I didn't kiss you when we were on our ride," he said.

Kiss her.

"Uh…"

Great. He'd rendered her speechless.

No. He hadn't. She wouldn't let him.

"I thought we both decided that was a bad idea."

"I like bad ideas," he said, leaning in closer. He wasn't touching her at all, but he'd tipped his head and she knew he was going to kiss her.

She licked her lips, tilted her head to the side and met him halfway. His lips were firm but soft and he tasted…good. There was something right in the way he tasted as his tongue brushed over hers. She closed her eyes and forgot about everything except this moment.

Will had tried avoiding kissing her, but with the certainty that the moon would rise every night, he knew he really couldn't keep from falling for Amberley. Tonight, sitting in the back of her pickup truck with Faye, had been one of the first times he'd been able to just enjoy being with his daughter and not think of all she'd lost.

He hadn't felt that gnawing guilt-and-grief combination. And now, when his lips met Amberley's, he'd stopped thinking altogether.

God, he'd needed this.

Just to feel and not think of anything but the way her lips had softened under his.

He lifted his head and looked down at her. By the light of the moon he could tell that her lips were wet from their kiss and her eyes were heavy-lidded. She lifted her hand and rubbed her finger over her mouth.

"Damn. I wish you didn't kiss like that," she said.

Surprised, he tilted his head to the side.

She shrugged. "Just would have been easier to write you off as a city slicker if you didn't know what you were doing."

He threw his head back and laughed at that statement. "Glad to know I didn't disappoint."

Faye stirred at the sound of his laughter and he realized it was getting late, even for two night owls.

"You didn't disappoint... Did I?"

The woman who'd fiercely ridden her horse around the barrels and who walked with a confidence that made him think she could conquer mountains was asking him if he liked her kiss. He patted Faye on the back and she settled down before he looked back over at Amberley.

Her hair was tousled, her lips swollen from his kiss, and he knew that later tonight, when he was alone in his bed, he was probably going to fantasize about doing much more with her.

"You were fantastic," he said. "If we were alone one kiss wouldn't be enough."

She nodded.

"For me, either."

"Good," he said. "Now I hate to do this but I really should be getting Faye back home. But maybe I can see you tomorrow?"

She nibbled her lower lip and he moaned.

"What?" she asked.

"You are making it damn hard for me to resist kissing you again," he said, but Faye had begun to wake up. He needed to get her back and into her comfortable crib.

"Sorry. It's just I like the taste of you."

He groaned.

"I could do with a little less honesty from you, cowgirl," he said.

"I'm not made that way," she admitted.

"I'm glad. I'll see you tomorrow afternoon."

"Okay. I'm giving a riding lesson from one until three, so after that, okay?"

"Perfect," he said. He leaned over and stole a quick kiss because he liked the way she tasted, too, and then he stood up with Faye in his arms and hopped down from the bed of the truck. He glanced back over his shoulder and noticed that Amberley had moved to the tailgate and sat there watching him walk away. It was pretty dark, but he was using the flashlight on his phone. And the moon was full, a big harvest moon that lit up the land around them.

He waved at her and she waved back.

"Good night, Will," she said, and there was a smile in her voice.

"'Night," he returned and then cuddled his daughter closer as he walked back to the guest house.

He kept the image of Amberley watching him walk away until he entered the house and saw the photo of Lucy on the hall table.

He took Faye to her room. He removed her coat and then changed her diaper before laying her in the bed. He turned on the mobile that Lucy had picked out for her and that guilt that he'd thought he'd shaken free of was back.

When Will first came to the guest house on the

Flying E, he'd asked if Clay would allow him to set up Faye's room as it had been in Seattle. He wanted her to feel at home and little things like the mobile and her crib and her toys were important. Clay hadn't minded at all and told Will to make the guest house into his home, which he had. And Erin had been instrumental in making sure everything was set up the way they liked it.

Lucy had been so excited when she'd seen it in a magazine. It was a version of the cow jumping over the moon, similar to one that Lucy remembered from her own childhood. They'd had to search all over to find it. Will had scoured the internet—exhausting every avenue—to find it. He remembered how thrilled Lucy had been when she'd opened the package.

He touched the cow as it spun and instead of thinking of Lucy he remembered Amberley and the way she'd played with Faye while he'd been on his phone trying to get technology to work in the middle of the night.

She hadn't gotten impatient with him the way the nanny sometimes did. He liked how easily Amberley got along with his daughter, but a part of him also knew that Lucy should have been the one holding her daughter.

But she was gone.

This job out here in Texas was supposed to give him perspective and help him finally realize that Faye needed him. It was easier here in Texas to shake off the gloom of the last year. And he was moving forward. Slowly. He hadn't realized how isolated he'd let himself become. His world had shrunk to just his work, and then Faye and Erin.

It had been a while since he'd just had a normal conversation. He and Erin mainly just talked about the baby and her eating habits or how teething was going.

He'd never felt like he would be raising his daughter alone.

He had no idea how to do it.

As much as he enjoyed being with Amberley, she wasn't his forever woman. Will had had that. Faye drifted off to sleep and Will went to his own room to shower away the scent of Amberley and then he brushed his teeth and used mouthwash to try to forget the way her kiss had tasted.

But he remembered.

And he still wanted her. His arms felt empty through the night and when he dreamed he was making love to a woman and he looked at her face, it was Amberley's and not Lucy's.

And the dream left him wide-awake, tortured with lust and need and the kind of guilt that felt like he was never going to be normal again.

When Will had been a no-show for their afternoon ride, Amberley chalked it up to him needing to do his job. Clay had told her that Maverick had struck again. Clay had even been a victim of Maverick. The hacker had made it seem as if Everest's cloud encryption software had been compromised, causing clients to panic. But luckily that had all been cleared up.

So Will was probably deep into his investigation. At least that's what she told herself.

Except he hadn't come around the next day, or the day after. A week later she was beginning to believe he might be more like Sam, the guy she'd hooked up with nearly six years ago, than she'd wanted to believe.

Amberley finally went by Will's place one afternoon only to be met at the door by Erin, holding Faye on her hip.

"Hi, there, Amberley," Will's nanny said.

"Hey. Sorry to bother you. I was stopping by to see if Will wanted to go for a ride," she said.

Erin stepped out onto the porch. "He's not here. He had to go into town to meet with Max and Chelsea. Something about Maverick."

"Clay told me he might have struck again," Amberley said. "I've never really had much patience for bullies. Especially ones like Maverick. If I have beef with someone I take it to them. I don't attack from a hiding place in the bushes, you know?"

Erin laughed. "I do know."

Erin's phone beeped. "That's my timer. I was making some teething biscuits for little Miss Faye here. Want to come in and chat? It's kind of lonely out here."

"It is. I'm used to it, though," Amberley said as she stood up. She glanced at her watch, that old battered Timex she'd been wearing for as long as she could remember. "I could stay for about thirty minutes."

"Good. Come on in," Erin said.

As soon as they stepped into the kitchen, Erin put Faye in her bouncy chair on the counter and went to the oven to check on her biscuits. Amberley went over to play with the baby, who was making her nonsensical sounds again.

She looked into the little girl's eyes and wondered what had happened to her mother. Without really thinking about what she was doing, she turned to Erin, who was putting the biscuits on a wire rack.

"What happened to Will's wife?" she asked.

Erin finished moving all the biscuits to the rack before she took off her pot holder and turned to face Amberley. "She had a brain hemorrhage before Faye was born. They kept her alive until about a week after Faye was delivered. It was heartbreaking."

"I can imagine. Is that when he hired you?" she asked.

"No. Lucy was planning to go back to work so I'd already been hired. They wanted the baby to be familiar with the nanny so the thought was Lucy, Will and I would all be in place from the moment Faye was born," Erin said.

That just broke her heart a little bit more. It sounded like Lucy had been ready for motherhood. That their family was getting settled and then bam, the unexpected. Her daddy had always said that change was inevitable, but Amberley thought it would be nice once in a while if things just stayed on course. Like they should have for Faye's family.

Erin offered her a glass of iced tea. She accepted and stayed to chat with her about the Fall Festival, but she felt uncomfortable in the house now that she knew a little bit more about Will's wife. Lucy. She had a name now, and when Amberley left a few minutes later, she saw the photo on the hall table. Lucy had been beautiful.

It was the kind of classic beauty that Amberley, with her tomboyish looks, could never pull off. She wasn't down on herself; it was simply that Lucy was really different from her. And Amberley wondered if she'd been fooling herself to think the man she'd sat under the stars with could see her as anything other than a distraction from his real life.

She wasn't sure she could see herself as anything other than that.

Determined to remember what she was good at and how great her life was, she spent the next few days with the horses and deliberately tried to shove Will Brady out of her mind.

The following weekend, Amberley went into town for the Fall Festival at the Royal elementary school. It was way past time for her to start decorating for the season. She pulled into the parking lot at the elementary school and realized the mistake she'd made.

There were families everywhere. Why wouldn't there be? This was a family event. Perfect for a Saturday.

She'd come after she'd finished her morning routine with the horses and now she wished she'd stayed on the Flying E with her animals. Instead she was watching everything that she would never have and she hated that.

She'd been devastated when she'd had the hysterectomy. But as her father had pointed out in his sanguine way it was better than the alternative, which in her case would have been death.

But she'd never expected to feel this alone.

She'd always thought when she'd been growing up that she'd one day have a family of her own. And holding Faye a week ago had just reminded her of all that she was missing.

She was twenty-four—too young to feel like this.

She got out of the truck because she felt silly just sitting there. She needed pumpkins. Some to carve, some for making pies and muffins, and some just to use as decorations that she'd keep out until Thanksgiving.

She walked through the playground, which had been turned into the Fall Festival, and tried to make a beeline to the pumpkin patch, but Cara was working at the caramel-apple booth and waved her over.

"Hey, Amberley! I'm glad you showed up."

"You know I need a pumpkin," Amberley said. The booth Cara was using was staffed by high school kids from the Future Farmers of America. They still wore the same jackets they had when Amberley had been a member in high school. She'd also done 4-H. She bought a couple of caramel apples and met Cara's boyfriend, who was clearly smitten. They were cute. It seemed easy for them to be together.

Unlike Amberley, who always seemed to find the rockiest path to happiness with a man. Whatever that was about.

"See you on Monday, Cara," Amberley said leaving the booth and carrying her bag of goodies with her.

The pumpkin patch had an area at the front set up for pictures and she saw the kids lined up for photos. She walked past them, head down and focused on getting what she needed and getting home. She was going to give herself the rest of the day off. Maybe stop at the diner in town and grab some junk food and then go home, sit on the couch and binge-watch something on Netflix. Anything that would take her mind off the place where she kept going back to.

The missing family that she craved.

Will.

Screw Will.

He was clearly messed up from his wife's death. She got that. She could even understand what he must be going through. She was pretty damn sure he hadn't married a woman and had a kid with her if he didn't love her. That just didn't strike her as the kind of man he was. It was going to take him time to get over it. Obviously more than a year and she didn't begrudge him that.

She was angry at herself. She'd spent way too much time thinking about him. She should be thinking about one of the guys she'd met at the Wild Boar, or maybe one of the guys she'd met at the rodeo. Or no guy.

Maybe she'd just start collecting cats and build herself a nice life surrounded by animals and friends. Sure she'd miss having a man in her bed, but she could deal with that. Eventually.

She picked out five pumpkins to decorate her porch and two for the house—she had two windows that would look good with jack-o'-lanterns in them. And then she paid for a large bag of mini gourds and accepted the help of a pumpkin-patch employee to carry them all to her truck.

She carried the last pumpkin herself after three trips to the truck and was feeling much better about her day as she pulled into the diner. She'd phoned in her order so all she had to do was go in and grab it. She hopped out of her truck and walked straight to the counter to pick up her order when she heard someone call her name.

Will.

She turned to see him sitting at a corner table with Max St. Cloud. Though she'd only seen him in town, she knew Max on sight. And she tried to smile and wave, but she was just still so pissed.

She hadn't realized how much she'd been counting on him to be different from every other city guy she'd ever met. She settled for a little wave as the girl at the register called her name. She walked over and paid for her patty melt, fries and onion rings and then turned to walk out of the diner without looking over at Will.

One of them had to be smart and no matter how country she was, she knew it was up to her.

# Five

"What was that about?" Max asked Will as they watched Amberley walk out of the diner.

"Nothing."

"Will, talk to me," Max said. "Did I make a mistake when I asked you to come to Royal?"

"No. It is not affecting my work. In fact, I think I am getting close to finding the hub that Maverick is using to run most of the cyberbullying he's doing. He uses a bunch of different accounts, but they are all fed from the same source…or at least that's what I'm starting to suspect."

Max sat back in the bench and nodded. "Good. But I wasn't referring to your work. You have been sending me reports at all hours of the day with updates."

"Then what are you asking?" Will was trying to focus on the conversation with his boss, but he couldn't keep his mind from wandering to Amberley.

"We're friends, right?" Max asked.

"Yeah. But unless you want to hear about what a sad mess I've become you should lay off this questioning right now," Will warned his friend. Max had known him before he'd married Lucy. He was one of the few people who really knew him well enough to understand what he'd gone through when he'd lost Lucy. How marriage had changed him and how her death had sent him to a darker place.

"What's up?"

"Nothing. Just the mix of pretty girl, messed-up guy and trying to do the right thing," Will said.

He took a sip of his coffee and leaned forward because he didn't need everyone in the diner to hear his business. "For the love of me, Max, every damn time I try to do what I know is right it backfires."

"Then stop trying," Max said.

"If it was that easy," Will said.

"It is. You said that you tried to do the right thing and it backfired. Maybe it was the wrong action," Max said. "All I know is that life isn't like a program. You fix the code and make it work, but there is always something unexpected. You know?"

Will leaned back. Like Lucy dying in the hospital after Faye's birth. "Yeah. I do know. Thanks, Max."

Max nodded. "People are getting more tense as this Maverick remains at large. I know you are doing all you can, but right now, because no one knows who Maverick is, everyone suspects each other. If you can get me something…well, the sooner the better."

"I will. Like I mentioned I think I have a lead on something that should lead to Maverick. I just needed to understand the server set up at the Texas Cattleman's Club."

"I put you on the guest list so you can go check it out."

"Thanks. I want to add the access tracking to the main terminal and the server. I'm pretty sure it's got to be an inside job."

"I think there is a connection there, too," Max said. "So you don't want anyone to know why you are there."

"Yeah."

"A date would be good camouflage."

"Of course it would," Will said.

"Just trying to help a buddy out. You look like you need a nudge toward her."

"Thanks… Not a nudge. I need to get out of my own way. Every time I'm around her I forget things… Lucy. And then when I'm alone I'm not sure that's what I should have done."

"Only you can answer that for yourself, but you can't keep punishing yourself for living," Max said. "I'm going to ask Chelsea to make you a dinner reservation at the club for tonight. Get a date or not—it's up to you."

They discussed how Will would deploy the tracker physically on the server. They didn't want to do it remotely, in case Maverick was able to see the code in the program. Max and he parted company and instead of heading back to the Flying E, Will went to one of the boutiques in town and bought a gauzy dress in a small flower print for Amberley. The dress had a skirt that he suspected would end just above her knee and a scooped neckline. He also purchased a pretty necklace that had a large amber gemstone pendant in the center that would rest nicely above the neckline of the dress.

He had it wrapped and then wrote a note of apology on the card and asked for it to be delivered to her.

He checked his watch and then went to the Fall Festival to meet Erin and Faye. Faye looked cute as could be in her denim overalls and brown undershirt. He held his daughter and knew that he'd be mad as hell if he'd been the one to die and Lucy was hesitating to get on with her life.

But it was harder on the heart than it was on the head. And as much as he knew what he needed to do, it was like Max had said—this wasn't code that he could correct with a few strokes of the keyboard. It was so much easier and conversely more complicated than that. He had no idea what he was really going to do about Amberley, but he'd made a move today. No more backing away.

If Amberley gave him this third chance, he wasn't going to waste it.

When he got back to the ranch, he dropped off Erin and Faye at the guest house since it was Faye's nap time and then he got in the golf cart and drove over to the stables to look for Amberley.

She was running the barrels when he got there and he watched her move with the horse and knew that she was worth the risk he was taking. He had spent a lot of time pretending that he could walk away from her, but the truth was he knew he couldn't.

He wanted her.

Not just physically, though that was a big part of

it. He also wanted that joie de vivre that she seemed to bring to him when he was around her.

He liked the man he could be when he thought of spending time with her.

She noticed him and drew her horse to a stop. She dismounted and walked over to the fence around the barrels, and he went to meet her.

"What's your deal?"

She hadn't meant to sound so confrontational. She'd gone back to the ranch and intended to waste away the rest of the day in front of the television. But instead she'd felt trapped in her house. She'd felt restless and edgy and just as she was about to leave, that package from Will had arrived.

With a handwritten apology note and a gorgeous dress and necklace. Who did something like that?

It was safe to say that no man she'd dated before had made such a gesture. But Will was different. And they had never dated. What had possessed him to do such a thing?

She was tired of playing games. It didn't suit her.

"My deal?"

"Yeah. We shared a great kiss and I started to think I could really like this guy and then you just up and disappear, not even a word about not showing up for our scheduled ride. You must think all country girls are just looking for a big-city man to marry them and take them away from all this, but you're wrong. I like this life. I like it just the way it is, and when I kissed you it was because I thought we had a real connection," she said, opening the gate and stepping out of the ring. "And it's clear to me that we have absolutely no connection at all by the way you keep backing out of stuff, but then you send me that dress and necklace and that apology. It sounds heartfelt, Will. And I'm tired of feeling stupid because I think one thing and your actions say something else. So what's your deal?"

He rocked back on his heels, as if he was trying to absorb the force of her aggression. She knew she was being hostile right now but she was tired of feeling the fool. The way he had treated her, the way she'd interpreted his actions…well, she wasn't having it anymore. She'd been nice and if he went to Clay and complained, she knew Clay well enough that she'd be honest with him and she was pretty sure he'd side with her.

"I am sorry. The note was meant to be heartfelt," he said, holding his hands up to his shoulders. "I like you, Amberley. When we are together I forget about the emptiness that I usually feel when I step away from my computer. But then I hold Faye and it comes back. I'm trying to get out of the swamp that I've been trapped in since Lucy died. And I can't figure it out. I'm not playing a game with you. I promise. I was going to invite you to dinner, but on second thought—"

"Do you really want to have dinner with me?" she asked, cutting him off. His explanation made her sad for him. She could feel his pain when he spoke. She, of all people, understood how hard it was to move on after a tragic loss. She could be his friend. Just his friend. That was something she could handle.

"Yes. I do."

"Okay, then let's have dinner. But as friends. We

can be friends, right?" she asked. "You can tell me about Lucy and maybe we can figure out a way to get you free of your swamp. It doesn't have to be anything more than that."

She could be his friend. Sure, she had wanted more, but the last few days had convinced her that wasn't wise. The anger and the despair from his rejection hadn't been what she'd expected. She had uncovered something buried deep inside her that she didn't like.

She wanted to celebrate being young and alive. Not feel old and bitter. She'd never been bitter about the hand that life had dealt her and she hated that this thing she felt for Will was eliciting that response in her.

"Friends?"

"Yes. Seems like a good place to start."

"Okay. Friends. Then I should tell you that I need a date for cover. I want to install a program on the server at the Texas Cattleman's Club, and in case it's an inside job, I don't really want anyone to know what I'm doing."

"So I'm your cover?"

"That's the plan, but I would also like it to be a date," he said. "I am tired of where I am and would like to get to a better place."

Sure, he would. As friends, she reminded herself. "I can do that. And I can provide some cover for you. What time is dinner?"

"Eight. That gives me time to spend with Faye before she goes to bed," he said.

"That works for me. How is she? I really enjoyed playing with her the other night."

"She's good. A little cranky earlier today, but that's just from teething. She's already got one tooth so this is another new one. She bit me last night when we were playing. She's been drooling a lot, so I was letting her chew on my finger and then *ouch*."

Amberley smiled at him like she would if he was a friend. She could do this. Keep her feelings on neutral terms. If only he wasn't so darn cute when he talked about his daughter.

He walked away and she turned her attention to her horse, brushing Montgomery and talking to the animal. He listened to her the way she suspected she'd listened to Faye. Montgomery lowered his head and butted her in the chest when she was done and she hugged him back, wishing she could understand men half as well as she understood horses.

Will took his time getting dressed for dinner after Erin and he had put Faye to bed. Erin was video chatting with her boyfriend back in Seattle, so he knew that she was set for the evening. He went into his office to check his computers again and took the small USB flash drive that he'd loaded his tracker program onto and put it in his pocket.

He was nervous.

He wasn't sure if that was a good thing or a bad thing. Faye always made him feel pretty okay…well, a little sad and bad that she didn't have her mom, but she had that sweet smile, which kind of helped to center him at times.

This was different. He went to the mirror in the guest bathroom and checked his tie again. He favored skinny ties no matter if they were in fashion or not.

He didn't think of himself as a slave to trends and preferred a look he thought worked for him. He'd spiked up his hair on the top and traded his Converse for some loafers his mom had sent him after her last trip to Italy.

He went in to check on Faye and kissed her on the top of her head before letting Erin know he was leaving for the evening.

He walked out of the house, took a deep breath of the fall evening air and realized how much he liked Texas. To be fair, October was a far cry from July, when he knew the temperature would be unbearable. But right now, this cool, dry night was exactly what he wanted.

He drove over to Amberley's house, having texted her earlier to tell her he'd pick her up. There was a bunch of pumpkins on her front step and a bale of hay with a scarecrow holding a sign that said Happy Fall, Y'all on it. He smiled as he saw it. He leaped up the stairs to her front porch and knocked on the door.

"It's open. Come in."

He did as she asked and stepped into the hallway of her place. The house smelled like apples and cinnamon, which reminded him of his parents' place. There was a thick carpeted runner in the foyer that led to the living room.

"I'll be right there. Sorry, I'm trying to curl my hair but it's being stubborn," she called out from the back of the house. "I am almost done."

"No problem," he said, following the sound of her voice. He found her standing in front of a mirror at the end of the hallway off the living room. He stopped when he saw her as his breath caught in his throat.

She was beautiful.

She'd looked pretty the other week after she'd been out, but this was different. Her hair had been pulled up into a chignon and that tendril she was messing with was curling against her cheek.

"Sorry. But in magazines this always looks so perfect and, of course, the reality is my stubborn hair won't curl the right way."

"I don't think it's a problem," he said.

She turned to face him and he had to swallow. The dress he'd picked out was fitted on the top and then flared out from her waist ending just above her knees. And she'd paired the dress with a pair of strappy sandals. The amber pendant fell on her chest, drawing his eyes to the V-neck of the dress.

"You are gorgeous," he said.

She blushed.

"Don't be embarrassed, it's just the truth," he said.

"Thanks for saying that. I don't get dressed up often, which is why I was trying this new updo. I figured I should at least make the effort. Plus, the folks of Royal aren't used to seeing me in anything but jeans and a straw cowboy hat. Do you think Maverick is working in the club or even a member…? Oh, that would really stink if he was a member, wouldn't it?"

"It would. I'm not a member, as you know, but I am aware of how close-knit the members are," Will said. "Are you ready to go?"

"Yes. Let me grab my purse and shawl. I figured that would be nicer than my jean jacket."

He smiled at the way she said it. She looked sophisticated and polished, almost out of his league, but she was still Amberley.

She disappeared into the doorway next to the hall mirror and reappeared a minute later. "Let's go."

He followed her through her home. It was small and neat, but very much Amberley. Not like the guest house, which was almost too perfectly decorated—this place had a more lived-in quality. It was her home. "How long have you lived here?"

"I got the job when I was nineteen…so that's five years."

"Wow, you were young. Were you worried about moving away from home?" he asked.

"Not really. Dad and Clay have known each other for a while. And it's not like it's that far if I want to go home for a visit," she said. "Plus Clay has an excellent stable and he lets me have time off to rodeo when I want to—it's the best place for me."

She was animated when she spoke of her father and her job and her life, and he realized he wanted to see her like this always.

She'd suggested they be friends and he knew now that was the only route for the two of them. Because he wanted her to stay the way she was just now. With her skin glowing, her eyes animated as she talked about the things in her life she loved. Getting involved with him could only bring her down. And even though he knew he felt like he was missing out on something special, her smile and her happiness was worth it.

# Six

The Texas Cattleman's Club dining room was busy when they arrived. Since Maverick had started his assault on members of the club, and on Royal, some of the friendliness that Amberley had always associated with the town was gone. Everyone was a little bit on edge. She wasn't going to pretend she understood what Will was doing with the computer, but she'd Googled him and read up on him.

They were dining as guests of Chelsea Hunt and she'd met them early at the bar.

If anyone could unearth Maverick it was Will Brady. He was a whiz at tracking down cyber criminals and had made millions selling the code he had designed to the US government. He was gaining a reputation for keeping secrets safe as well, having successfully blocked an all-out assault on one government database by a foreign entity intent on doing harm to the US. Obviously, Will was a well-respected expert in his field.

One of the articles had been accompanied by a picture of him and his late wife dressed up to go to the White House, where Will had been given a commendation.

Seeing that picture of Will's late wife had made the woman very real to Amberley. And she was even more glad she'd decided just to be friends with Will. She liked him. She wasn't going to pretend otherwise. As she went to the bar while he excused himself to go do whatever he had to do in the computer room, she thought more about all Will had lost.

She wanted to be a good friend to Will. He needed a friend.

She remembered how he'd made up a story for her while they'd sat under the stars. No one had done that for her since she was a girl. The men she had dated…they saw the tough cowgirl and they didn't always realize she was vulnerable. But Will treated her differently.

"What'll it be?" the bartender asked her.

"Strawberry margarita, frozen, please," she said.

"Should I open a tab?" the bartender asked.

"No. I'll pay for this. I'm having dinner with someone," she said.

She settled up with the bartender, took her drink to one of the high tables and sat down to wait. She saw a few people she knew from town, but they glanced over her as if they didn't recognize her and she shook her head. She didn't think she looked so different with her hair up.

Finally, one of the parents of her horse-riding students recognized her and came over to chat with her for a few moments. It was nice to have someone to talk to while she was waiting for Will. She felt a little bit out of place here at the club. She didn't come from money. Her father made a good living and the ranch was worth a fair amount, but they weren't wealthy. They were ranchers.

Will walked in a few minutes later and scanned the room before spotting her. He smiled, buttoning his coat as he strode over to her. He looked good in his thin tie and his slim-fitting suit. His hair was slicked back, making him look like he'd just stepped out of one those television shows she loved to binge-watch.

She sighed.

Friends, she reminded herself.

"I didn't order you a drink," she said, wishing now she had.

"That's okay. I'll get one and join you," he said.

He was back in a moment, sitting across from her with a whiskey in one hand. "Sorry to keep you waiting."

"I don't mind. Did you get everything straightened out?"

"I did," he said. "How has it been for you?"

"Funny," she said. "I've seen a few people from town but most didn't recognize me."

"Really?"

"Yup. I'm a woman of mystery," she said. "I like it."

"Me, too. It's nice to be anonymous," he said.

"Are you usually recognized?" she asked. "I read a few articles about you online."

"Did you?" he asked. "That's interesting. But to answer your question, I'm only recognized at home. Mainly it's because I don't live that far from where I grew up. One subdivision over, actually, so I just know everyone when I go to the gym or the grocery store. And most people know about Lucy so it makes things awkward…"

She put her hand over his.

"Do you want to talk about her?" Amberley asked. "When my mom died everyone stopped mentioning her name. It was like she'd never existed and I wanted to talk about her. Finally, one night I lit into my daddy about it. And he said he missed her so much just hearing her name hurt and I told him for me, too, but ignoring her was making her disappear," Amberley said, feeling the sting of tears as she remembered her mom. She'd been gone for years now, but there were times like this when she still missed her and it felt fresh.

"I…I'm a little bit of both. I don't know if I want to talk about her," Will admitted. He took his hand from under hers and swallowed his drink in one long gulp.

"If you want to, I'm here for you," she said.

He nodded. "I'm going to go and check on our table."

She watched him walk away and she wondered if she'd said too much. But she knew that she couldn't have kept silent. He had admitted to her that he was stuck in a swamp and there was no clear path out of it. She suspected it was because he didn't know how to move on and still hold on to the past. And while Amberley knew she was no expert, she'd done her best to keep her mom alive while accepting the woman her dad had started dating when she'd turned eighteen.

So maybe she'd be able to help him.

Dinner started out a little stiff but soon they relaxed into a good conversation, mostly centering on music and books. They differed in that everything he owned was digital—both books and music—while Amberley had inherited her mother's record collection when she'd moved out and had a turntable in her house, where she listened to old country and rock from the '80s.

"What about scratches?"

"Well, that does make for some awkward moments when I'm singing along to a song that I've learned with all the skips in it. Records do that," she said with a wink. "And then I realize there's an entire phrase I've missed."

"You know I could show you how to download all the albums you already own on your phone so you could listen to them when you are riding," he said.

"I know how to do that, Will," she said. "I just prefer to listen to the albums at home. It reminds me of when I was growing up. Like Mom loved Michael Bolton and when I listen to his album I can remember Dad coming and the two of them dancing around. And I have a lot of CDs, too. Between the two of them I think they owned every album they loved on cassette, CD and vinyl. It's crazy," she said. "Dad stopped listening to it all after Mom died, but I wanted my brothers and sisters to have those memories, so Randy and I would put the albums on when Dad was out of the house."

"How many siblings do you have?"

"Four. Two brothers and two sisters. Randy is three years younger than me, then Janie, Michael and Tawny."

"Sounds like a houseful," he said. He'd always sort of wished for a bigger family but he'd been the only child and had gotten used to it.

"What about you?" she asked.

"Only child."

"Spoiled," she said, winking at him.

"Probably," he admitted. "Lucy and I had planned to have at least two kids. She said we should have an even number—she had two sisters and said one of them was always left out."

"It was that way at home a bit when Mom was still alive, but once she died and I became the boss when Dad wasn't home the dynamic changed."

"How old were you?" he asked.

"Thirteen," she said. "You know you could always have more kids if you remarry."

"Uh, I'm barely able to think about going on a date, I'm not sure more kids are in the cards for me," he said. "What about you? Do you hate the idea of being a mom since you kind of had to be one to your siblings?"

She sat back in her chair and tucked that tendril she'd spent so much time trying to curl behind her ear. She shook her head. "No. I sort of always wanted to have a family of my own."

There was something in the way she was talking that made him think she thought she wouldn't have a family of her own. "You're young. You can have a family someday."

She chewed her lower lip for a minute and then shook her head. "I can't. I physically can't have kids."

He was surprised and wanted to ask her more about it, but it seemed obvious to him that she didn't want to discuss it further. She started eating her dinner again and this time didn't look up.

He reached over and put his hand on top of hers, stopping her from taking another bite, and she looked up. There was pain in her eyes and it echoed the loss he felt in his soul when he thought about Lucy being gone.

"I'm sorry."

She nodded. "Thanks. Wow, I bet you're glad this isn't a real date."

"It is a real date," he said. Because he knew now that there was no way he could walk away from her. Yes, he had been hesitating, but when he'd bought the dress for her things had changed and he wasn't going to let it go back to where he'd been when he'd first come to Texas.

"No, we said friends."

"Friends can go on dates. How else do you think friends become lovers?"

She flushed. He loved her creamy complexion and the fact that her face easily broadcast her emotions. He guessed it went hand-in-hand with her bluntness. Amberley didn't hide any part of who she was.

"I can't deal if you are going to blow hot and cold again," she said. "I wasn't kidding around this afternoon. I mean, I understand where you are coming from—"

"Amberley? I told Chris that was you," Macy Richardson said, coming over to her. Macy's family had been members of the Texas Cattleman's Club forever. Chris had grown up here in Royal on the wrong sides of the tracks. But he'd gone away and made his fortune, only to come back to claim Macy and a membership at the club. Their daughter took riding lessons from Amberley.

"It is me," she said. "Probably didn't recognize me without my cowboy hat on. Macy and Chris, this is Will Brady. He's a guest of Chelsea Hunt's."

Will stood up and shook Macy's and Chris's hands. "I hear you're in town to help catch Maverick."

"I am," Will said.

"Good. I'm sure you're going to get the job done. Chelsea has a lot of good things to say about you," Macy said. "We will leave you to your dinner."

A few other members stopped by to chat with them, including Clay and Sophia, who seemed to be enjoying their night out.

When the interruptions were over, Will picked up the thread of their conversation. Amberley's accusations about his behavior were fair, and he owed her a response.

"You're right. I'm not going to do that to you again. I said friends to lovers. We can take this slow," he said.

But a part of him knew that slow was going to be hard with her. It almost felt like if it happened in a rush it would be easier for him to move past the memory of Lucy, but as he watched Amberley he knew that he was always moving forward. He was excited about the prospect of something fresh and new with her. He wasn't about to give up now that he had her. He could do slow, but he wouldn't do never.

"So books… Do you have a bunch of dog-eared paperbacks instead of ebooks?" he asked, changing the subject and trying to pretend like everything was normal.

"Dog-eared? I love my books—I don't treat them poorly. In fact, sometimes I buy the paperback and then read it on my tablet because I want to keep it in good shape," she admitted.

He had to laugh at the way she said it and then he noticed how she smiled when he laughed. Something shifted and settled inside of him and he realized that he wasn't going to let her ride out of his life until he knew her much better.

Will drove her home at the end of the night, playing a new track he'd downloaded of Childish Gambino. It had a funky sound that reminded her of some of the jazzy music her dad liked from the '80s.

"This is really interesting. I love it," she said.

"I thought you might like it," he said.

"Why?"

"Because I do and we seem to have similar taste in music," he said.

"You think so?"

He nodded. "Tonight I have learned we are more alike than either of us would have guessed."

She swallowed hard—he meant the loss. It was funny that grief should unite them, but then her grandmother always said her mom was up there watching out for her, so maybe that was the reason behind this.

"Were you surprised?" she asked.

"Yes, and shame on me for that. Because from

the moment you showed up on my front porch with Cara, I knew you weren't like any other woman I'd met before. A part of me put it down to you being a Texan, but I knew there was something about you that was just different from every other woman," he said.

"Well, not everyone can be born in the great state of Texas," she said with a wink. "You can't really hold that against other women."

He laughed, as she hoped he would. She noticed that he got her sometimes odd sense of humor and it made her feel good. As much as she'd sort of always crushed out city guys that she'd met, he was different. Maybe that was why she kept giving him a second chance.

"I wouldn't," he said solemnly.

"So do you have any country music on your device?"

"Big and Rich," he said.

"They're okay but I think you need to listen to some old-school country. I'll give you some of Dad's old cassettes," she said, again teasing him because she knew he would just download the songs. And he was right that some songs sounded better digitally remastered, but for the sake of not agreeing with him she was going to stick by her guns.

He groaned. "Just give me a list. Actually, give me a name and I'll put it on right now."

"How?"

"Verbal commands," he said.

"Does that work for you?" she asked.

"All the time. Why?"

"Well, Siri hates me. Whatever I say she changes

it to something crazy. I mean, it's not like I'm not speaking English," she said.

"Siri can't hate you, she's a computer program," Will said.

"Well, she does. One time I texted my cousin Eve and told her where to meet me and do you know what that phone sent her?"

"What?" he asked.

"'Meet me where we once flew the summer wind,'" Amberley said.

He burst out laughing. "You do have a bit of an accent."

"No crap," she said. "But that is crazy."

"When we get to your place I'll fix it so your phone can understand you," he said.

"You can do that?"

"Hell, yes," he said. "I might not be any good with people but I'm excellent with tech."

She looked over at him, his features illuminated whenever they passed under a streetlamp as they drove through Royal. "You're good with people."

"Some of them. I tend to lose my patience. But with tech I'm always good."

She hadn't seen that impatient side of him. She wondered if that was because he was only letting her see what he wanted. Maybe the grieving widower was all he wanted her to know about him. But then why would he be talking to her now? She was making herself a little crazy.

They had both been beat up by life and were doing their best to survive. And she didn't doubt that he liked her. She'd seen the way he watched her and she knew when a man wanted her.

The truth was she didn't want to be hurt again and her mind might have been saying that friends was enough for her, but she knew in her heart that she'd already started liking him.

She liked that he cared about Royal even though it wasn't his town. She liked the way he was with his daughter, even though raising her without his mother was obviously hurting him. She just plain liked him and that wasn't how she wanted to be feeling about him.

Friends.

That was easy. She was supposed to be keeping things friendly. Instead she was falling for him.

It would have been easier if she knew that he would stay, but he was a flight risk. She knew he was just tiptoeing through an emotional minefield, trying to figure out how to move on. And of course once Maverick was found there was no reason for Will to stay in Texas. And then she shifted things in her mind. What if he was a mustang stallion that just took a little longer to gentle to the saddle? What if she just approached him with stealth, could she win him that way?

And was she really going to try to win him over?

She twisted her head and looked out at the dark landscape as they left Royal and headed toward the Flying E. She saw the moon up there following her and then she spotted Venus and thought of her own special angel, and not for the first time in her adult life, she wished her mom was here to talk to. She needed some advice on what to do next. She wasn't someone to hedge her bets and she wanted to be all in with Will. But a part of her was afraid that it was just wishful thinking on her part.

He turned onto the Flying E property and slowed the car, as they were on the dirt road and not paved highway. When he stopped in front of her house she turned to face him.

He shut off the car and sat there for a long moment and she felt a tingle go through her entire body that wasn't unlike what she felt when she was sitting on the back of Montgomery waiting for a barrel run to start.

"So, you want to come in?"

# Seven

The dinner hadn't gone as Will had expected and this end to the evening was no different. He'd told himself he wouldn't kiss her good-night. They'd said they'd go slow. Maybe if he repeated it enough times it would stick and he'd get the taste of her off his tongue.

Unfortunately, he was never going to get the vision of her wearing the gauzy, long-sleeved dress he'd bought for her out of his mind. And it didn't help matters that the hem of her dress had ridden up her legs. In the light of the moon and the illumination of the dashboard lights he could see the tops of her thighs.

He clenched his hands around the steering wheel to keep from reaching over and touching her. Lust was strong and sharp and it was burning out all the cells in his brain, making it impossible for him to think. He wanted to be suave and smooth, all the things he liked to think he usually was around a woman, but tonight he wasn't.

He'd told her things he'd never said to anyone else. Like making up stories under the stars and just talking about stuff. Not business or his baby, but stuff that he'd locked away when Lucy died. And all the sophistication he'd thought he'd cultivated over the years was gone. He wanted her and really there wasn't room for anything else. Maybe it was the way she'd watched him as he'd driven back to the ranch.

Hell, he didn't know.

Frankly, he didn't care.

"You really want me to come in?" he asked, his voice sounding rough. He cleared it but he knew short of burying himself hilt-deep between her legs there was nothing he could do about it.

"Do you want to come in?" she asked.

"Hell."

She turned in her seat and the fabric of the dress was pulled taut against the curves of her breasts and he could only stare at her body as she leaned in close. A wave of her perfume surrounded him and now he knew he wasn't leaving.

He reached across the gearbox in the middle of the two bucket seats and wrapped his hand around the back of her head. He slid his fingers along the back of her neck, and his hand brushed against the part where she'd twisted up her hair—he wanted it free and flowing around her shoulders but right now he wanted her mouth more.

He needed to feel her lips under his. To prove to himself that lust had addled his thinking. That there was no way she tasted as good as he remembered. She couldn't.

No woman could taste like sin and heaven at the same time.

He tried to justify this kiss just to prove to himself that it had been the absence of kissing in the past year that had made hers unforgettable.

But as he leaned in closer, watching as her lips parted and her tongue darted out to wet her lips, he knew that was a lie. There was a jolt of pure sexual need that went through him and his erection stirred, pressing tight against his pants. He wanted to shift to relieve some of the pressure but he needed the pain to keep him grounded. To remind himself this wasn't a fantasy but something that was truly happening.

Now.

He brushed his lips over hers and her hand came up to rest against his chest. Her fingers moved under his tie to the buttons of his shirt and slipped through. She brushed the tip of one finger over his skin just as he thrust his tongue deep into her mouth. She moaned, shifting on the seat to scoot closer to him. He felt her arms wrap around his neck and shoulders as she drew herself closer to him. He grabbed her waist, squeezing her as he caressed his way around to her back. She felt like a ball of fire in his arms. Like a mustang that was wild and would take him on the ride of his life if he could hold on long enough.

He had a feeling deep in his soul that he could never tame her.

Amberley was going to be the ride of his life, he knew that. And for a second the grief he'd shoved into a box before he'd gone out with her tonight tried to rear its ugly head, and in response he lifted his head and looked down into her face.

Her hair was starting to come loose from the chignon, thanks to his hands in her hair, and there was a flush on her face, her lips were parted. And her pretty brown eyes were watching him. A little bit with patience and a lot with need.

She needed this as much as he did.

Tonight had shown him that they were both broken in ways that the world would never see. He felt honored that she'd let him see the truth that was the real Amberley.

He put his forehead against hers, their breathing comingled as he wrapped both arms around her and lifted her from the seat. It took a little maneuvering and it wasn't comfortable at all, but he managed to move into the passenger seat and get her settled on his lap.

"That was…I didn't realize you were so strong," she said, softly.

"I'm not."

"You are. I'm not a lightweight," she said.

"Yes, you are. You are perfect," he said.

She put her fingers over his mouth. "Don't. I'm not perfect and you really don't think I am. No lies. This is…what we've both wanted since that moment in the field when you got off your horse. And I don't want to ruin it, but honesty…that has to be where this comes from."

He wanted that, too. Wanted this sweet Southern girl who was blunt and real and made him want things he wasn't sure he was ready for. But walking away wasn't going to happen.

He needed her.

But he didn't want to talk and if he was being honest with himself he didn't want to think at all.

Instead, he reached for the seat release and pushed it all the way back. She shifted around until she straddled him. He reached up and pulled the pins from her hair, then gently brought it forward until it hung in thick waves around her shoulders.

Carefully, slowly, he drew the fabric of the skirt part of her dress up to her waist until he could touch her thighs. They were smooth and soft but there was the underlying muscled hardness of her legs. She shifted against him, her hands framing his jaw as she tilted her head to the left. Her hair brushed against his neck as she lowered her mouth and sucked on his lower lip. She thrust her tongue deep into his mouth as she lowered her body against him.

And his pants were too tight. He reached between their bodies, his knuckles brushing against the crotch of her panties, and he felt the warmth of her there. But he focused on undoing his pants and sighed when he was free of the restriction of cloth.

He took her thigh in one hand and then squeezed, sliding his hand under the fabric of her panties and taking her butt in his hand. He drew her forward until she was rubbing over him.

He groaned and tore his mouth from hers.

He wanted to feel her naked against him.

"Shift up," he said.

"What?"

"I want to take your panties off."

She nodded, bracing herself on the seat behind him. She moved until he was able to draw her underwear down her legs and off. He tossed it on the driver's seat and then turned his attention to her breasts, which were in his face. He buried his head in her cleavage, turning his head to the left and dropping sweet kisses against her exposed flesh. She shivered and shifted her shoulders as she settled back on his lap, moving over him, and suddenly he didn't know how long he could last with her on top of him.

She was hot and wet and wanted him.

He found the zipper at the back of her dress and drew it down, and the bodice gaped enough for him to nudge the fabric aside until her breast was visible. She wore a demi bra that bared part of the full globe of her breast. He reached up and pulled the lacy fabric down until her nipple was visible and then leaned forward to suck it into his mouth. With his other hand, he caressed her back, drew his nail down the line of her spine to the small of her back, then cupped her butt and drew her forward again.

He encouraged her to move against him. She started to rock, rubbing her center over his shaft, and he felt a jolt at the base of his spine as his erection grew again.

He suckled harder on her nipple and she put her hands on his shoulders, rubbing against him with more urgency. He reached between their bodies, parting her until he could rub her clit with his finger. She groaned his name and put her hands in his hair, forcing his head back until her mouth fell on his. She thrust her tongue deep into his mouth, her tongue mimicking the movements of her hips.

He felt like he was about to explode and started dropping little nips all over the curves of both of her breasts and her neck. He tangled one hand in her hair as he traced the opening of her body, then pushed his finger slowly up into her.

She made a wild sound that just drove him higher and he thrust his finger up inside her, feeling her body tighten around it. Then he added a second finger and she shifted, until she had her hands braced on his shoulders. She rode him as fiercely as she'd ridden her horse as she chased the barrels in the ring.

He rubbed her with his thumb while continuing to thrust his fingers inside her and then she threw her head back and called his name in a loud voice as she shuddered in his arms before collapsing against him.

He kept his fingers in her body and wrapped his arm around her back, holding her to him. He was on the edge and wanted to come but a part of him wouldn't allow it. Giving her pleasure was one thing but taking it for himself was something he wasn't ready to do.

She shifted and he moved his fingers from her body. He was tempted to bring them to his mouth and lick them clean. Taste her in that intimate way. But he didn't. He felt her shift her hips and the tip of him was right there, poised at the entrance of her body.

He tightened his buttocks and shifted his hips without thinking, entering her without meaning to.

She felt so damn good. Her body wrapped tightly around his length. It was almost as if she was made for him.

She was tight and it was only as she shifted and he felt himself moving deeper into her that he realized what he was doing. He was in the front seat of his car, hooking up with Amberley.

Amberley.

He'd promised himself that he wasn't going to hurt her and he knew if he let this go any further…

He couldn't do it. He couldn't have sex with her and then lie in bed with her. He couldn't just take her on the front seat of his car. Their first time should be special.

He wanted to be better than he knew he was.

She tightened her inner muscles around him and he knew he was going to lose it right then. So he lifted her up and off him. Turned her on his lap so that she was seated facing to the side. Gingerly he reached for his underwear and tucked himself back into it. He was so on edge it would only take one or two strokes for him to come, but he wasn't going to do that.

Not now.

She deserved better than this. Bold and brash Amberley, who had always given him a kind of honesty that made him want to meet her more than halfway.

Now that his mind was back in the game and he wasn't being ruled by his hormones he realized that a part of him had chosen the front of the car because it wasn't the bedroom.

Like the bedroom was only for…

Lucy.

"Uh, what's going on here?" Amberley asked.

He couldn't talk right now. The only thing he was capable of saying would be a long string of her curse words. And she certainly didn't need to hear that.

"Will? It's okay. Whatever it is you're thinking, it's okay."

"It's not okay," he said.

She put her hands on his face and forced him to

look up at her. She leaned down and kissed him so softly and gently that he knew he didn't deserve to have her in his life.

"Yes, it is. Am I the first…since Lucy?"

He nodded. "It's not that I don't—"

"You don't have to explain," she said. "I am going to go into my house now."

He couldn't stop her even though a part of him wanted to. He wasn't ready to make love to a woman who wasn't his wife. It didn't matter that he knew Lucy was gone and that Amberley was sitting here looking more tempting that a woman had a right to.

He wasn't ready.

Damn.

He had a half-naked woman in his lap and he was about to let her walk away.

"I'm sorry," he said abruptly. There had been a lot of firsts since Lucy had died and he'd never thought about this situation. It had felt natural and right… and then it hadn't.

"Don't be. We're friends."

"Friends don't do what we just did," he said.

"Some of them do," she returned. "'Night, Will."

She opened the door and got out of the car, straightening the top of her dress. He reached out and caught her hand. Brought it to his lips and kissed the back of it. He wished he had words to tell her what this night meant to him. How she was changing him and the way he looked at life and himself, but he could only gaze up at her. She tugged her hand free and touched his lips before turning and walking away.

He watched her leave, knowing he should go after her. But he didn't. He just sat there for a few more minutes until he saw her door close and then he got out and walked around to the driver's side of the car and got in. He was breathing like he'd run a fifty-yard dash, then he put his head on the steering wheel, unable to move.

He was torn. His conscience said to go back home and sleep in his empty bed. Let the frustration he felt make sleep impossible because he deserved to suffer.

He was moving on when Lucy couldn't. But he knew that was survivor's guilt talking. He took a deep breath. But all he could smell was sex and Amberley, and he wanted her again. His mind might be preaching patience but his groin was saying to hell with that and to take what he needed. But he couldn't.

It wouldn't be right for Amberley.

He knew this was a first.

The therapist he'd seen after Lucy's death said each first was going to be like a milestone and everything would continue to get easier. Hell, it couldn't get any harder than this. But damn, when was that going to happen? He felt like Don Quixote tilting at windmills and not getting anywhere. He was chasing something that was always just out of reach. But for tonight— tonight he'd almost touched it.

He'd almost given himself permission to move on. But he wasn't ready. What if he never was? What if by the time he was, Amberley had given up on him? Was she the one?

She'd certainly felt like someone important as he'd held her in his arms. He wanted more from her. Wanted more for himself than he'd taken tonight. He just wasn't sure what kind of sign he was waiting for.

It wasn't like Lucy was going to tell him it was

okay to move on. She couldn't. He knew he was the only one who could decide when it was time.

Was it time?

Maybe it wasn't time that was the important thing, it was the person. And it had felt very right with Amberley.

He finally felt like he'd settled down enough to drive back to the guest house he was staying in. As he got out of the car, he fastened his pants and then looked down and saw her panties on his seat.

He lifted them up, tucked them into his pocket and walked into the house feeling like a man torn in two. A man with both the past and the future pulling at him.

He didn't know what he was going to have with Amberley, but as he walked into the house and locked up behind him, he realized that Erin had left a light on for him and he went down the hall to Faye's bedroom.

He looked down on his sleeping little girl and felt that punch in the heart, as he knew he had to make sure that she didn't lose both her mom and her dad that day that Lucy had died. He knew that she deserved to have a father who was participating in life, not one who was locked away in his office and spending his days and nights in the cyberworld because he was afraid to live in the real one.

He leaned over the side of the crib and kissed her forehead.

And he could only hope that Amberley had meant it when she said she forgave him for tonight because he wasn't done with that cowgirl yet.

# Eight

Amberley didn't sleep well that night. She wasn't a heartless monster—she understood where Will was coming from. And when they were at dinner at the club she'd realized that he was going to take some extra time if they were going to be more than friends. And being friends…well, how could she not be his friend.

She was hurt. She didn't hook up and sleep around, not anymore. She had found a place for herself where she'd started to adjust to her life. She'd begun to feel like she'd found a peace that had always been just out of reach. Then Will Brady showed up, arousing feelings from her past and reawakening the passion she'd thought she'd buried a long time ago.

But as she stared down at her breakfast cereal she knew she had wanted some kind of romantic fantasy.

That was the problem with watching as much television as she did and reading as many books. There were times when she just wanted her life to have a little more romance than it did.

Last night in his car, Will had made her feel things that she hadn't ever felt before. It had been more intense than the other times she'd had sex.

She wasn't really eating her cereal so she carried the bowl to the sink, and even though she knew she should clean it out right now, she just dumped the bowl in the sink, rinsed the cereal down the drain and then left it.

She had told Clay that she'd break in one of the newer horses and she intended to use Sunday morning to do it. She had a lesson this afternoon and then she needed to keep practicing her barrel riding, as she was signed up for a rodeo at the beginning of November.

But this morning all she had to do was get Squire ready for riding and lessons. The hands mostly had their own horses or used some of the saddle horses that Clay kept on the ranch. And Amberley's job was to make sure they were all in good shape and exercised if they weren't being used.

She heard some sounds coming from the stall set away from the other animals at the end of the stables and turned in that direction. She saw Sophie, Clay's pregnant wife, standing outside the stall talking to the bull inside of it.

"Sophie? Everything okay?" Amberley asked as she walked down toward her.

The stall held Iron Heart…the very same bull that had ended Clay's bull-riding career. Clay had saved the animal from being euthanized and brought him to the Flying E ranch.

"Yeah, just talking about stubbornness with some-one who understands it."

Amberley had to laugh. "Clay."

Sophie nodded. "You'd think I was the first woman to ever be pregnant."

Babies again. It seemed that no matter how hard she tried she couldn't get away from pregnancy or babies. "I think it's sweet how protective he is."

"Well, that's probably because you're not the one being smothered," Sophie said with a small smile.

"I was once the one being ignored and told not to have a baby," Amberley said. She hadn't meant to. She was pretty sure that no one here knew about her past except her doctor in town.

"Oh, Amberley, I'm so sorry. Did you—"

"No. I had a miscarriage," Amberley said. "Gosh, I don't know why I'm telling you all this. I guess just to say that having Clay dote on you is a very good thing."

"I agree. Just wish he wasn't so stubborn all the time."

Amberley knew exactly how Sophie felt. "Aren't all men?"

"They are," Sophie said and then waved goodbye as she left the barn.

Amberley went back to Squire's stall, brushed and saddled the horse and then took him out for a ride. But she wasn't alone. Not in her mind. She remem-bered the way that Will had ridden when she'd taken him out here. She remembered how he'd looked when he'd gotten off his horse and looked up at her. Asked her for something she hadn't wanted to give him at the time.

Now she was wondering if that had been a mistake.

She was trying not to feel cheap and used. She'd meant it last night when she'd said she understood him calling things off. She had. She couldn't imagine the emotions he was going through as he tried to process his grief and move on from losing his wife. She only could funnel it through her experiences of losing her mom and of losing...

She shook her head to shove that thought away and focused on the ride. Squire wasn't really in the mood to run and when Amberley tried to force the issue he bucked and she hung on the first time, but when he did it again, she was knocked off and fell to the ground, landing hard on her shoulder.

Angry at herself for being distracted, she got up and took Squire's reins and started walking back to the stables. But the horse nudged her shoulder and she looked into those eyes and decided he was ready for another chance. She got back in the saddle and they took a leisurely gallop across the field, and she suddenly stopped thinking as she leaned low over Squire and whispered to him. Told him how he was born to run and that she was only here to guide him.

She had one of those moments where everything shifted inside her. Maybe it had been being bucked off the back of the horse that had shaken her and made her see things differently.

But she knew she couldn't keep doing everything in the exact same way. Squire liked being talked to. It had been a long time since she'd had a horse that needed to hear her voice. Mostly she communicated with clicks of her tongue and the movement of her thighs.

She realized that Will was like Squire and last night…well, last night he'd bucked her off, but if she was careful she could find a way to get him back into the stable. She shook her head.

Did she want to work that hard for a man whose life was somewhere else?

She drew in a sharp breath and realized that it didn't matter where his life was, he was going to be one big ol' regret if she didn't do everything she could to claim him. That she wasn't going to be able to just walk away. But she'd known that.

That was the reason why she'd said just to be friends even knowing there was no way she'd ever be satisfied with less than everything he had to give.

Last night he'd taken the first step in moving out of the past. She was willing to give him a little breathing room, but she wasn't going to let him retreat again.

She got back to the barn and stabled Squire and then went to her place to shower and change. She found that there was a note taped to her front door. She opened it.

Amberley,
    Thank you for an incredible evening. I'd like to take you out to dinner tonight. Please be ready at seven. Wear something glamorous.
Will

This was the romance she'd been wishing for. And as she opened her front door and went to her bedroom to try to find the right dress, she knew that he wasn't running this time. And her heart did that little fluttery thing when she thought about him.

Will had taken care of everything for his date with Amberley. In the meantime, he was busy at his computer. The program he'd loaded onto the server at the Texas Cattleman's Club was spitting out all kinds of data and Will focused on analyzing it.

Erin had gone to town to run an errand and Faye was sitting on his lap chewing on one of her teething toys and babbling to herself as she liked to do while he worked. He squeezed his little girl closer to him as he continued working. A few articles popped up that he hadn't read before.

One was about a recluse who seemed to have a beef with just about everyone in Royal. Adam Haskell.

The reason his name had come up in the database was that he had written several strongly worded letters to the members of the town commission as well as local business owners. He might not leave his house very often, but he was very active online using Yelp and other local forums to criticize most of Royal. Will used his smartpen to send the articles and the name to Max to get his feedback. Perhaps his friend would have more intel on Haskell.

Faye shifted around on his lap and he turned to set her on the floor. She crawled toward the big plastic keyboard he'd picked up for her in town recently and then shifted to her feet and took two wobbling steps.

She walked.

His baby girl...

She dropped back down and started crawling

again. Will forgot the computers and got down on the floor.

"Faye, come to Daddy," he said.

She looked at him and gave him that drooly grin of hers and then turned and crawled to him.

The doorbell rang and he scooped Faye into his arms and carried her with him as he went to answer it.

Amberley.

"Hi," she said. "I wasn't sure how I was supposed to let you know I was available for our date tonight."

"I thought you'd text."

"Oh, sorry," she said. "I was here so I thought I'd just stop by."

"It's okay. Want to come in?" he asked, stepping back so she could enter. Faye was already smiling and babbling at Amberley.

"If you're not busy," Amberley said.

"I'm not busy. But this one just took two wobbling steps. Want to see if you can help me get her to walk?" he asked.

"Did she?" Amberley asked. "I'd love to help."

He carried Faye into the living room and then he was kind of at a loss. He placed her on the ground and she crawled around and then sat up and looked at him.

"Let me help. You sit over there," Amberley said, scooping Faye up and moving a few feet from him. Then she set Faye down on her feet and held Faye's hands in each of hers.

Faye wobbled a bit and Will realized he wanted to get this on camera.

"Wait. Let me set up my camera. I don't want to miss this," he said.

"Go ahead. We are going to practice, aren't we?"

Amberley asked, squatting down next to Faye and talking to her.

She smiled at Faye and Will watched the two of them together. They were cute, his girls, but he didn't let himself dwell too much on that. Instead he got his camera set up so that he would be able to capture the entire walk from one side of the room to the other. Then he went back to sit down so his baby could walk to him.

"Okay, I'm ready," Will said.

"Are *you* ready?" Amberley asked Faye.

She wobbled and Amberley let Faye hold on to her fingers and she started moving slowly, taking one step and then another. Will hit the remote so that the camera would start recording. Amberley let go of one of Faye's hands, and then the other, and his daughter smiled at him as she started walking toward him.

He clapped his hands and called her and she came right to him. He felt tears stinging his eyes as he lifted her into his arms, hugging her and praising her for doing a good job.

"She's such a rock star," Amberley said.

"Sit down," Will said. "Let's see if she will walk back to you."

Amberley did. "Faye, come to me."

Will set her on her feet and steadied her, then she took off again in that unsteady gait, walking to Amberley, who kept talking to her the entire time.

She scooped Faye up when she got to her and kissed the top of her head and Will realized that he'd found someone special in Amberley. She had a big heart and she deserved a man who would cherish that heart and give her the family she'd always craved. He wanted to believe he could be that man but he still had his doubts.

They spent another half hour letting Faye walk back and forth between them until Erin got back home.

"Look what Faye has mastered," Will said. "Amberley, go over there."

She did and they got Faye set up to walk over to her and Will noticed a look on Erin's face that he'd never seen before. It was almost as if she was disappointed that she hadn't been here for Faye's first steps. And suddenly he realized this was the first milestone in Faye's life that he hadn't shared with Erin.

"Sorry you missed her first steps," Will said. "I recorded it, though. She's so eager to go."

"She is. She's growing up so fast," Erin said.

"Yes, she is," Will agreed.

"Well, I'll leave you two alone," Erin said. "Are you still going out tonight?"

"Yes, I'm going out with Amberley."

"Oh, that's nice," Erin said.

Amberley left a few minutes later because she still had a lot to do, but Will felt deep inside that something had changed between them and he couldn't help getting his hopes up.

Amberley wasn't sure what she'd expected but the limousine Will pulled up in wasn't it. Will wore a dinner jacket and formal shirt and bow tie. He had his hair spiked and there was excitement and anticipation in those forest green eyes of his. She'd twisted her hair up and tonight the style and her hair seemed to be on the same page.

The dress she'd picked was a fitted dress in a deep purple color with sheer sleeves and a tiny gold belt. She'd paired it with some strappy gold heels that matched the belt. She put on the amber pendant he'd given her and some pearl drop earrings that her dad had given her when she'd turned eighteen. She felt further from her cowgirl self than she ever had before, yet perfectly at home in her skin.

"Damn, you look good," he said.

"Ditto," she said with a wink. "Why do we have a limo?"

"In case things get heated in the car again," he said.

"I assumed when you said you were spending the night that you meant at my place," she said.

"I did," he said. "I just really wanted to shower you with luxury and a limo seemed the right choice. Are you ready to go?"

She nodded. She didn't bother locking her door since the only way on or off the ranch was through the main drive. Will put his hand on the small of her back as they walked to the car. The driver was waiting by the door and he held it open for her. She wasn't sure how to get into the car and still look ladylike.

"Well, you can dress the girl up but that's about it," she said. "How the heck am I supposed to get into the car?"

"You sit down, ma'am, then swing your legs inside," the driver said.

"Thanks," she said. She wasn't embarrassed at having to ask. The truth was if she didn't know how to do something, unless she asked about it, she was never going to learn. She sat down and looked up at

Will as she swung her legs into the car and then she scooted over on the seat and he just smiled at her and then climbed in the way she would have.

"Next time we rent one of these I'm going to insist you wear a kilt so you have to do the same crazy maneuver I had to do," she said.

"Deal," he said.

The driver closed the door and she realized the back of the limo was very intimate. The lighting was low and Will put his arm along the back of the seat and drew her into the curve of his body.

"Thank you for coming out with me tonight," he said.

"Thanks for asking me out. You are spoiling me."

"Figured I had to make up for it since you already know I'm spoiled," he said with a grin that was both cocky and sweet.

"I was just being a bit jealous because I'm one of five and we always had to share everything. You haven't ever really acted spoiled around me," she said.

"Thanks," he said sardonically. The car started moving.

"Where are we going?"

"It's a surprise," he said, taking a silk blindfold from his pocket. "In fact, I'm going to have to insist you put this on."

"Uh, I'm not into any of that kinky *Fifty Shades* stuff," she said. She'd read the books, and while it had been exciting on the page, it wasn't really her thing.

"Understood. This is just to preserve the surprise I have in store for you."

"Okay," she said, turning to allow him to put the blindfold on her.

As soon as he did it, she felt more vulnerable than she would have expected. She reached out to touch him, her hand falling to his thigh. She felt the brush of his breath against her neck and then the warmth of his lips against her skin. She turned her head and felt the line of his jaw against her lips and followed it until their lips met.

Will let her set the pace, which she liked. But then he sucked her lip into his mouth as he rubbed his thumb over the pulse beating at the spot where her neck met her collarbone. She closed her eyes.

The scent of his aftershave and the heat of his body surrounded her.

The limo stopped and Will stopped kissing her.

Damn. He had distracted her. She hadn't been paying attention to anything. Not even how long they'd been in the car.

She reached up to take off the blindfold. "Leave it," he said.

"Will."

"It's part of the surprise," he said. "Trust me?"

Trust him.

She wasn't sure...which was a complete lie. She did trust him or she wouldn't be here. Or maybe it didn't matter if she trusted him or not. She wanted to be here and she was going to do whatever he asked.

Except for the kinky stuff...maybe.

She nodded.

"Good. Now scoot this way," he said, drawing her across the seat. She felt a blast of cold air as the door of the limo was opened and then Will kept his hand on hers, drawing her forward until she was on the edge of the seat.

"Swing your legs around," he said.

She did.

The ground beneath her sandals felt like dirt, not pavement.

"Where are we?"

He didn't answer her question. Instead he lifted her into his arms. "Please come back for us in two hours."

"Yes, sir," the driver said, and Amberley wrapped her arms around Will's shoulders, listening to the sound of the limo driving away.

Then Will started walking and the breeze blew around them a bit chilly until she felt a blast of heat, but they hadn't gone inside. He set her on her feet and took off the blindfold and she saw that they were on a wooden platform with those large infrared heating things positioned around a table. There were twinkle lights strung over the top of the table set for two and covered chafing dishes on a buffet next to it.

The ranch land spread out as far as the eye could see. The sky had started to darken and as she glanced up she saw her angel star.

"Surprised?"

More than he would ever know. It was as if he'd glimpsed into her soul and saw every romantic notion she'd ever had and then amped it up to provide this evening for her. Which meant her heart was in for a whole heap of trouble.

# Nine

After almost losing her life at eighteen, Amber had promised herself she was going to live in the moment. And it was something that she'd always strived to do. On the back of a horse it was easy—there was no time to worry about if she was behaving the right way or if someone could see her imperfections. She just hadn't always felt comfortable in her own skin. But tonight she did. In town running errands it was a struggle, which was why she usually had to brace herself before she left her truck and walked among everyone else.

It was easier in Royal because no one knew her history the way folks back in Tyler did. But tonight was one of the few times where she felt totally present and like nothing else mattered.

She faltered a little when she saw the dishes he'd

had made for them. Some of them looked so fancy she was tempted just to stare at them instead of eat them. But Will put her at ease. He was snapping photos and then telling her that he was posting the photos of them online. She figured it was something like the photo story app that Cara had shown her but she wasn't interested.

She didn't want to connect with a world that was bigger than the ranch or Royal and maybe a few folks back in Tyler. That was good enough for her.

Will looked like she imagined a prince would look. He was polished and he talked easily and kept the conversation moving along from topic to topic. He knew horses and led her onto the topic of polo ponies and where she saw the breeding changes leading that field. And it didn't matter that she was dressed like a woman and not a cowgirl—she felt at ease talking about the animals.

"I did read an article last month that talked about a breeding program that a Saudi prince was spearheading. I think it's interesting in that he is working on increasing agility while maintaining stamina."

"That makes sense. I knew a guy in college who had gone to Europe to learn a centuries-old custom of Spanish horse dancing. It is basically training the horse to do very practiced moves, not unlike the Olympic horse events but even more controlled. He used some of those practices when we were playing polo and they worked," Will said.

"There really is room for crossover in all types of training. I was recently trying a technique with Montgomery that I saw used in the Olympics. Barrel racing is speed and mastery not only over the horse, but also over yourself."

"How often do you practice?" he asked.

"I try to get a couple of hours in every day. I am only really participating now when I can get away from the ranch," she said.

"And I couldn't tell the pattern you were using, but is there one? Or do you just have to circle all of the barrels in the least amount of time."

She took a bite of her dinner. "You have to go in a cloverleaf pattern and the one who does it the quickest is named the winner. They use an electric eye to do the timing. The key is to get as close to the barrels as you can so that you are taking the shortest route around them all."

"I'd love to watch you compete sometime," he said.

"Sure. I'll let you know the next time I'm going to a rodeo. I try to stay local here in Texas."

"Cool," he said and she wondered what that meant. Was he going to be in Texas for a while?

It wasn't really a response but she was living in the now. So that meant not pointing out that he could be back in Seattle before her next rodeo. Or would he?

She didn't ask the question because, to be honest, that would make things more complicated. Give her another thing to worry about it and that wasn't what she wanted right now.

"I've never had a guy buy me clothes before. Not even my dad. He used to have my grandma buy us stuff or take us shopping," Amberley said.

"Was it odd? It just reminded me of you," he said.

"Well, you were right. I would never have picked it out. I was surprised when I put it on," she said.

"I'm not surprised, I could picture you in it as soon as I saw it."

"Well, aren't you clever?" she said, winking at him. He was too charming for his own good. She suspected he knew it, as well, because he kept moving through life like nothing could touch him.

She wondered if that was how he had dealt with losing his wife all along or if it was just with her that he ran. Because some of the time he'd seemed to be okay. But then she remembered the other night, when he'd stopped himself from making love to her.

And she wondered if he was pretending like she was. She had gotten pretty damn good at believing the lie she told herself that she was okay. She wanted it to stop being a lie. And she knew she wanted to help Will get to a place where he was okay, too.

She suspected that it would happen in its own time and she knew she had to be patient, but a big part of her was afraid that time was going to take him back to Seattle before she could witness him getting there.

"So there I was standing in the middle of the river in Montana with a client that Dad wanted to impress, and he's asking me where I learned my fly-fishing technique, and all I could think of was if I say the Wii, Dad's never going to forgive me," Will said to Amberley as they finished up their meal. They had been having the most carefree conversation, and Amberley loved how he was telling all these personal stories from his childhood.

"What'd you do? I would have straight up said a video game," she said.

"I said natural instinct," Will said as he took a

sip of his wine. "Then my dad came over and said, 'Yup, that boy has a natural instinct for bull.' The client started laughing and I did, too, and honestly it was one of the first times my dad and I connected."

"That's funny. So did the client do what your dad wanted?" Amberley asked.

"Yes. Dad offered me a job after that, but as much fun as the trip to Montana was I knew that I didn't want to have to work that hard to charm people. Computers are easier," he said. "So I turned down the job and that pissed the old man off but I already had the job offer from Max so he got it."

"What does Max do?" Amberley asked.

"He's an ex-hacker-turned-billionaire tech genius. He owns St. Cloud Security Solutions. I'm the CTO for the company...the Chief Technology Officer."

"Dad would have been happy for me to stay on our ranch," Amberley said. "But I knew if I did then I'd spend the rest of my life there. It would have been easy to hide out there and just keep doing what I'd been doing."

"You wanted more," he said.

"I did. I still do. I like working for Clay and Sophie now that they are a couple, but I really would like to have my own stables someday," she said. If she had one dream it was that. She'd let horses take over the parts that she'd thought she'd fill with kids and a husband.

"Why would you have been hiding out if you had stayed at home?" he asked. "You seem like you grab life by the—I mean, you're pretty gutsy."

She smiled at the way he said that. She had tried grabbing life by the balls, but it had grabbed back, and her father said that actions had consequences, which she'd never gotten until that summer.

She took a deep breath. She'd thought telling Will about the hysterectomy would be the hard part, but this was a big part of who she was and why she was here in Royal.

"Um, well, I… This is sort of a downer, maybe we should save it for another night," she said.

Will nodded. "If that's what you want. But I want to know more about you, Amberley. Not the stuff that everyone can find out. The real you. And I think whatever made you want to hide is probably important."

She pushed her plate forward and folded her arms over each other on the table as she leaned forward. It was cozy and intimate at the table. Will had created an oasis for them in the middle of the Texas night.

"I took a job working at a dude ranch the summer I graduated from high school. I was thinking about what I'd do next and I knew I wasn't going to college. It just wasn't for me."

"Makes sense. You have a lot of natural ability with horses and I read about your rodeo wins online."

"You did?" she asked. "I didn't realize you'd looked me up."

"Yeah. I wanted to know more about you even as I was running from you and pretending that you didn't fascinate me."

"That's corny and sweet," she said.

"Thanks, I think."

Will made her feel like she mattered. It was kind, and it wasn't that others hadn't done that but he made her feel like she mattered to him. That it was personal and intimate and she hadn't had that before.

"So, you're on a dude ranch…"

She sat back in the chair and the words were there in her mind and she practiced them before saying them. It was easy in her head to remember what had happened. The cheap wine they'd bought at the convenience store. The way he'd never driven a pickup truck, so he had convinced her to let him drive. And then when he'd parked it and moved over to make out with her in the front seat until it had gone much farther.

Then of course she'd gotten pregnant and had expected Sam to be, well, a better man than he was. Of course, he'd said he was back to his real life and he'd help her financially but wanted nothing to do with her or the baby. It had hurt and there were times when his rejection haunted her. It made it easier for her to isolate herself on the ranch. But she wasn't going to say any of that to Will.

"There had been a group of guys from back east staying as guests at the ranch. They'd decked themselves out in Western clothes and they were flirty and fun and I ended up hooking with one of them. It was my first time and not his, and I'm afraid that freaked him a little bit and then…" She paused. She wasn't sure she could say the next part.

She looked at Will. He'd stopped eating and was watching her carefully.

She took a deep breath and the words spilled out quickly. Like tearing off a bandage, she did it as fast as she could. "I got pregnant. But there were complications, I started hemorrhaging and I almost died. I did lose the baby, and the only way to save me was for me to have a hysterectomy."

She stopped talking and it felt too quiet. Like even the animals and insects that had been in the background before were surprised by her words. She blinked and realized how much she hated telling this story. She never wanted to do it again.

Will didn't say anything and she started to regret telling him, and then he got up and walked around the table. He pulled her to her feet and into his arms and hugged her close. He didn't say anything to her, just wrapped her in his body, and the panic and the pain that had always been buried with that story started to fade a little bit as he held her and made her feel like she was okay.

That she wasn't damaged and broken.

Will didn't know the words to make everything all right and he could tell by the rusty way the story had come out that she was still a little broken from everything that had happened. He knew because no matter how many firsts he had after Lucy's death there were still things that bothered him. And there was no way that he was ever going to be completely washed clean of the past.

And now he knew that Amberley wasn't going to be, either. She was deeply scarred, as he was.

Hell, he wanted to do something to fix this thing that he couldn't fix.

He thought about how caring about someone could suck sometimes. He'd loved Lucy but had been unable to save her and he was starting to care more deeply for Amberley than he wanted to admit and there was no way in hell he could ever fix what had happened to her. No matter how much he wanted to.

"Siri, play Amberley playlist."

The playlist started and it was Jack Johnson's "Better Together." It was the perfect song for how he felt at this moment. He pulled her into the curve of his body and took one hand in his and kept his other wrapped around her waist as he danced her around the table, singing underneath his breath in that off-key way of his.

"You have a playlist for me?" she asked, tipping her head to the side and resting her cheek against his shoulder.

"I do. It's a bunch of songs that you might not have on vinyl," he said, hoping for a smile. He'd made the playlist this afternoon after she'd left his house. He'd wanted to give her something.

She rewarded him with a little half smile. And then he kept dancing and singing to her. He knew there were some pains that words couldn't heal and that time could only scab over. He had been debating his own pain for a year, trying to figure out if he was going to scar or just have a scab that he kept scratching and refreshing the hurt.

"I like this one," she said.

"I do, too," he said.

He wanted them to be better together. They could bring out the best in each other. Tonight he felt they'd jumped over that first hurdle. But he knew each of them was going to have more obstacles that they would bring to the relationship.

"I think we are going to be more than friends," he said.

"Me, too. I want more than that from you," she said. "But I don't want to make another mistake. I picked a guy who had nothing in common with me before. A man who didn't look at the world the same way I do."

"I care about you, cowgirl," he admitted.

"Me, too, city boy," she said with a grin.

The song changed to "SexyBack" and she just arched one eyebrow at him.

"Oops. Not sure how this got on there," he said.

"Maybe you were thinking about the way our last date ended," she said with a sassy grin.

Music had done what he couldn't as there were sweet and fun songs in the playlist, and after about five songs he noticed she wasn't tense and the tightness around her mouth had faded. She was laughing and smiling and while he still ached for her and the pain she'd gone through, he felt better for having cheered her up.

"So what do you think? Is there a place for the twenty-first-century technology in your music life?" he asked.

"You're a complete goofball, Will. I told you I use the music app on my phone," she said.

"You did but you said it was just for stuff you already loved."

"Not all the songs you selected are newer," she pointed out. "I think you like my kind of music."

"I do like it. And I was trying to ease you into it. Keep the shock value low," he said, aware that they were both talking about something inconsequential to keep from talking about the real emotions that were lying there between them. The truth that was there in the silence under the music that just kept playing on.

"Thank you."

"You're welcome," he said. "How does dessert sound?"

"Sweet?"

Some of her spunk was coming back and that was exactly what he'd been hoping for. "Good, because I asked for pineapple upside-down cheesecake with a salted caramel sauce."

"That sounds interesting," she said.

"Exactly what I was aiming for." He held her chair out for her and she sat back down.

He cleared away the dinner dishes and then brought back dessert. Everything had been set up by a private chef he'd hired in Royal. The dishes had been labeled and set up so that he could easily find them.

"Coffee or an after-dinner drink?" he asked.

"Coffee would be nice," she said.

"Decaf?" he asked.

"God, no," she said.

Another thing they had in common. He poured them each a cup of coffee from the carafe that had been prepared and then took his seat across from her again. He ignored the questions that still rattled around in his head. Instead he looked around at the night sky.

"My app still isn't doing what I want it to, so I'm not sure we are going to see anything fabulous in the sky tonight," Will said. He was unsure how to get the conversation back on track now.

"That's okay. I'm pretty happy sitting here staring at you," she said.

"Yeah?"

"Yup," she said. "Did that thing you did at the club last night work?" she asked.

"I think it might have. Do you know Adam Haskell?"

"Know him personally? No," she said. "But I do know his reputation. He seems to have a gripe about everyone and everything in town. Do you know he gave my riding lessons a low score on Yelp even though he's never taken a class from me?"

"I'm not surprised. He showed up in a relay link that I was chasing and then when I searched on his name it seemed to make sense that he might be the one releasing everyone's secrets. Do you know if he has any computer knowledge?" Will asked. Being able to post a bad review on Yelp and trolling people on social networks didn't take any real knowledge of computers or hacking. And a part of him had thought that Maverick was more skilled than Haskell seemed to be.

# Ten

Will was just about to ask Amberley more questions about Haskell when his phone pinged. He ignored it, after making sure it wasn't Erin. Then it pinged again and started ringing.

"Sorry about this but I think I need to take this," Will said.

"Go ahead," Amberley said.

"Brady," he said, answering his phone.

"St. Cloud," Max said. "Where the hell are you? It looks like Haskell might be our man. I need you to come to Royal now. He's leading the cops on a high-speed car chase and I'm with a judge, the sheriff and a lawyer right now getting a warrant to search his property. I need you to analyze what we find and tell me if he's our man."

Will wasn't ready to end his evening with Amberley but business had to come first. This business, anyway. Once Maverick was caught he would be free to focus on Amberley and see where this was leading.

"I'll be there as quickly as I can," he said.

"Good. I'm texting you Haskell's address. Meet me there."

He ended the call and then looked over at Amberley, who was watching him carefully. "Haskell is on the run and Max is getting permission for me to go through his computer. I'm sorry to cut our date short—"

"No, don't be. I want that bastard Maverick caught as much as everyone else in Royal does. What can I do?"

"I could probably use your help going through things at Haskell's if you want to come with me."

"Will the cops let me help?"

"I don't know," he said. "But I didn't want our night to end."

"Me, either. I think I would. I don't really want to go home yet."

"Okay. Let me get the limo and we will head out."

The limo driver was quick to retrieve them and Will had him take them to his car, tipped the driver to move a box from the trunk over to his car while he and Amberley went inside and then sent the driver home. He checked in on Faye and updated Erin on what was happening before he and Amberley drove into town.

"I never imagined your life would be like this. I figured you just did things on your computer and that was it."

Will laughed. "Usually it's not this exciting. In

a big city Haskell could have slipped away anonymously. And if he was smarter he'd be driving sensibly instead of leading the cops on a high-speed chase."

"I know. He's not the brightest bulb according to the gossip I've heard at the diner."

"Really?"

"Yes, why?" she asked.

"It's nothing," he said. But in his mind there was a new wrinkle to Haskell being Maverick. It would take someone really smart to set up the kind of cover that Will had encountered while trolling the web for Maverick's true identity. It seemed a bit far-fetched that someone people considered not so bright would be able to do something like this on his own.

Was he working with someone?

Will was confident he'd be able to find the answers on Haskell's computer.

"Catching cyber criminals isn't usually like this. Though one time I did have to chase a guy down an alleyway. He'd had a program running on the police scanner to alert him if cops were dispatched to his property. It was a clever bit of code," Will said. He'd tried to convince the hacker to give up breaking into secure systems and bring him over to work for him but the guy wasn't interested.

"That must have been… Was it scary? I mean, are hackers and cyber criminals usually armed?"

"Some of them are. But usually I find the evidence and I don't go with the cops to arrest a criminal unless they are on some sort of mobile relay, where I have to track them while the cops move in. One time I had to wear a bulletproof vest and was stationed in a SWAT truck. There were all these guys with guns and riot gear on and there I was with my laptop...I felt like the biggest nerd."

"You could never be a nerd," she said.

"Thanks. But I can be. I'm sorry our date has taken a crazy turn."

"I'm not. Honestly this is the most exciting thing I've ever done," Amberley said.

He shook his head. There was pure joy in her voice and he realized again how young she was. True, there were only four years between them and she'd had a very harrowing experience when she was eighteen, but the way she was almost clapping her hands together at the thought of being part of the investigation enchanted him. And turned him on.

"Why are you looking at me like that?" she asked.

"Like what?" he countered, trying to sound innocent, not like he'd been imagining her wrapped around him while he kissed her senseless.

"You know," she said.

"Uh, this is the place," Will said as he turned into the driveway of a run-down ranch-style house. The yard was overgrown and there was a big sign that said Keep Off the Grass and No Solicitors.

As they got out of the car, Will noticed there was also a sign in the front window that read Protected by Smith & Wesson.

"Not the friendliest of men," Amberley said. "So what do we do now?"

Max was waiting outside for them and a patrol car was parked at the curb with the lights flashing. Some of the neighbors poked their heads out of the front door but most weren't interested.

"Thanks for coming. The sheriff wants us to help go over the house with his team just to be an extra set of computer expert eyes. He thinks we might see something relevant that his officers would overlook since it's not the kind of crime they are used to dealing with," Max said. "Did I interrupt a date?"

"Yes."

"I'm sorry," Max said. "Dang, I wish this had happened another night."

"Me, too. But it didn't. So let's get this taken care of," Will said.

Max knew that this was the first real date that Will had been on since Lucy's death.

"Do you want to take his computer back to your place?" Max asked.

"Let me see the setup first," Will said. "Do you know Amberley Holbrook? She's the horse master at Clay's ranch."

"Nice to meet you Amberley," Max said.

"Same."

They went into Haskell's house and the cops were gathering other evidence while Max, Will and Amberley found his computer. "This doesn't look very sophisticated."

"No," Will agreed. "It looks like it's about ten years old."

Not that you needed a new or sophisticated machine to hack. Most of the time if he ran from a DOS prompt he could get into over-the-counter software and some social media sites.

Will hit the mouse to see if there had been a program running or if there was a security login.

And then he sat down in the dirty chair to get

to work. He lost himself in the computer programming...or tried to. But the smell of Amberley's perfume lingered in the room and he couldn't help but think this was one time when he didn't want work distracting him from his real life.

Tonight he'd come closer than ever to finding something with Amberley that he hadn't wanted to admit had been missing in his life.

Max and Will talked quietly while the computer ran some program. Everyone had something to do and she was just standing in the corner trying not to get in anyone's way.

She hadn't seen Will work before. She stood there watching him when she thought no one was looking. He was intense as his fingers moved over the keyboard. He took a small dongle from his key ring and plugged it into the USB drive and first lines of text started scrolling on the screen, which meant nothing to her, but Will nodded and then started typing on the keyboard.

"He's one of the best in the world."

She glanced over her shoulder at Max St. Cloud, who stood next to her. She didn't know much about the man except he was Will's partner at St. Cloud Security Systems. She also knew he was engaged to Natalie Valentine, a local wedding dress designer.

"He's awesome," she said, then realized how lame that sounded. "Sorry, I'm really better with horses than people."

Max laughed in a kind way. "It's okay. I should probably leave you alone but I was curious about you."

That didn't sound very reassuring.

"Why?"

"Will hasn't done anything but work since... Faye's birth. I think you're the first woman he's been out with," Max said.

"I know," she said. She was the first. That's why she should be cautious about falling for Will. He was a city guy who'd lost his spouse, so in her mind there were danger signs all around him. But he was also the guy who'd made her a special playlist and could ride like he'd been born in the saddle.

"Good," Max said. "Want to help me look for USB drives, other storage devices, a tablet, maybe an external hard drive?"

"Sure," Amberley said. "I know what some of those things are but what's an external hard drive?"

Max smiled. "Should be a rectangle shape and thin. Follow me, the lead detective needs to give us some gloves and tell us how to search."

Amberley followed him into the other room and after a brief explanation of what they were to do and orders to track down an officer and let him know if they found anything, they were both sent to look.

"If you take the living room and I take the bedroom we might be able to finish this search quickly and get you back on your date," Max said.

"Sounds good," she said.

She followed Max out of the room where Will was working and went into the living room. It was dusty and cluttered, but as Amberley walked around the room she noticed a system. There was a pile of *Royal Gazettes* next to his recliner. The weekly newspaper was stacked up almost to the arm of the chair. She glanced down at the paper on top. It was the one from two weeks ago that had run the story of Will coming to town to help find and stop Maverick.

He'd underlined the word *Maverick*. That was interesting. It could be a clue or maybe Haskell was just ticked off that someone else was ruining the lives of Royal's citizens and taking over his role.

Amberley sorted through the top papers and noticed that he'd used his black pen to mark every story relating to the cyber menace. Was it a kind of trophy for him? Seeing the stories about himself in the paper? She set them in a neat stack on the seat of the chair to show to the officers who were in the house and then started looking through the mess on the side table. There were prescription pill bottles and a community college book on computer software that looked to be about three years old. She stuck that on her pile of stuff and kept moving.

She found some other things that were personal and she realized how odd it was to be going through someone else's house. Haskell always seemed like an old curmudgeon to her when she'd seen him in town but she found a picture of him on one of the bookshelves with a girl from when he'd been in his twenties. He'd been smiling at the camera and he had his arms wrapped around the woman. Amberley didn't recognize her but she wondered what had happened to her.

Was she the reason why Haskell hated the residents of Royal so much now?

"Find anything?" Max asked as he entered the room.

"Not the hard drive, but I did find these papers,

where he has underlined every mention of Maverick. Not really hard evidence but I saw on a crime show that serial criminals like to keep references to their crime as a sort of trophy. So this might mean something. And I found this old computer book on his table. Maybe he was brushing up his skills?" Amberley said. "There's a lot of junk and dust in this room."

"In this house," Max said. "I think the papers might be a lead. And the computer book, let me see that, please."

She handed it to Max. He opened the book and read some of Haskell's handwritten notes. "Let me see if Will can make anything of this."

She followed Max back into the area where Will was. Will turned when they entered.

"He was definitely using an external source," Will told them. "I think if we find that we might find the evidence we need. Did you two find anything?"

"We found this," Max said, handing it over to Will. "It was an MS training class. So not anything in here that would help him mask his online presence. So we're done here?"

"I think so," Will said.

"I'll let everyone know," Max said, leaving the room.

Will went back to the small home office and Amberley followed him, watching from the doorway as he pounded his fists on the desk.

Going in to check on Will hadn't seemed like a bad idea until she put her hands on his shoulders and he pulled her closer to him. He was frustrated—she could see that. He stood up and she looked into his eyes and she wanted to say something or do something to help him not feel so hampered by this investigation.

"Let's finish this up so we can get back to our date," Will said. "I'm not close to being finished with you."

She hoped she looked calmer than she felt because every part of her was on fire and she knew that she'd changed. That sharing the past with Will had freed her in a way she hadn't expected it to.

The secret that she'd always hid from the men she'd hooked up with had been a weight she hadn't even been aware of until now. Until she was free of it. She heard the cops talking and Max went in to talk to Will and she just stood there in the cluttered, dusty living room, knowing that her entire world had changed.

A new hope sprang to life inside her and she wondered if she'd found a man she could trust.

# Eleven

"I should get you back home," Will told her as they walked out of Haskell's house.

"Okay," Amberley said, glancing at her watch. "I have to be up early for the horses."

"Wait a second," he said, turning and leaving her by his car to go over to where Max stood.

She watched as he spoke to Max, his business partner and friend, and remembered how Max had talked to her. She wasn't sure if he'd been warning her to be careful with his friend, or just warning her that Will might not be ready for whatever was happening between them.

She rubbed her hand along the back of her neck and shivered a bit. The night was chilly and she was outside without a coat on. But it wasn't too cold. She just suddenly felt very unsure.

And she didn't like it. It wasn't as if Max had said anything that she hadn't been aware of, she knew that Will hadn't dated since Lucy's death. She knew that she might be someone he cared for but she might also be the woman he was using to help him get over losing his wife. But hearing it from someone else's mouth was making her think that maybe she wasn't being smart.

Her heart didn't care and neither did her body. In fact, maybe her being his temporary woman was exactly the right thing for her. He was her first in many ways, too. The first guy she'd told about losing the baby. The first guy she'd really cared about since she was eighteen.

She'd thought she loved Sam. Well…at least cared about him. But this thing she felt for Will was so much stronger. She didn't know if it was real, either. And it was harder than she had anticipated to keep her cool. Not to let her emotions overwhelm her. But when Will came back over, shrugged out of his jacket and draped it over her shoulders, she felt like she was fighting a losing battle inside of herself.

"Max is going to text me if he hears anything," Will said. "Let's go home."

Home.

An image of her, Will and Faye popped into her mind and she didn't want to shove it out. She wanted it to be true. Watching Faye take her first steps today and feeling that punch of joy in her stomach had made her realize that she could have a family. She didn't have to give birth to love a child. And while a part of her realized that it was dangerous to think that way about Will and Faye, another part of her was already putting herself in the picture.

"Okay."

He held open the door for her and she slid into the passenger seat. She slipped her arms into the sleeves of Will's jacket. It smelled like his aftershave and after she fastened her seat belt she put her hands in the pockets and felt something…

She pulled it out. It was a photo. She glanced down at it and saw Lucy. He was carrying around a picture of his wife. The door opened and she shoved the photo back in her pocket, but it caught on the fabric and he noticed her hand as he slid behind the wheel.

"What's that?" he asked.

She felt like there was a weight in the pit of her stomach… "This."

She handed it to him.

He took it and as he did she noticed there was typed information on the back of the photo. And she realized what it was. She had a card like that with her mom's picture on it that she'd gotten at her funeral. It was Lucy's funeral card.

"I—I haven't worn that jacket since the day we buried her," Will said. "I didn't even realize it was in there."

He looked down at the picture and ran his thumb over her features and Amberley felt like she'd interrupted a very private moment. She shouldn't be in the car with him. Or wearing his jacket or even falling for him. She didn't know where Will was in his head but he wasn't with her. Would he ever fully be able to be with her?

That thought hurt more than she'd expected it to.

"She would have liked you," Will said.

"Would she?" Amberley asked.

Watching Will gently caress his late wife's picture gave Amberley an odd feeling. Like when she had cut herself with a knife cooking dinner and she knew she'd cut herself, but it didn't start bleeding right away or hurt for a few seconds. The wound was there. She was just in denial about how deep it went.

"Yes. It's not…I'm not holding on to the past," Will said. "This isn't like the other night."

"Please, you don't have to explain."

"But I want to. Lucy is gone and she's a part of my past," Will said. "She'll always be a part of my life because of Faye."

"I know that. Really I do. I'm not upset," she said. She was trying to make the words true by saying them with conviction but in her heart, she was sad. And she felt just a little bit sorry for herself.

"Amberley."

She looked over at him and she'd never seen him so intense before.

"I want you to know that I'm not dating you just to try to move on from Lucy's death. And I know that we haven't had much time together but I'm not fooling around with you and using you."

She wanted to believe him. He had said the words that she could have asked him to say but she wasn't too sure they were the truth.

Will dropped off Amberley at her place, where she shrugged out of his jacket and gave it back to him. "Thanks for a very interesting date."

"You're welcome," he said. He wanted to come in.

His gut said that he shouldn't just let her walk away, but he didn't know if pushing her now was the right thing to do. So he waited until she was safely inside her house and then drove back to his place.

But when he got there he just sat in the car holding Lucy's picture. Life with Lucy had been uncomplicated. They'd met in college and both of them had come from similar backgrounds. Everyone had said they were a match made in heaven. And while he loved her and cared for her, he knew they'd been growing apart in the months before Faye's birth.

Sometimes he suspected his guilt stemmed from that. That he'd been drifting out of their marriage when she'd died. He went home and the house was quiet with everyone sleeping. He checked in on Faye.

He had the funeral card that Amberley had found earlier and brought it into Faye's room with him. When he looked down at his sleeping daughter's face he could see the resemblance to Lucy. It was growing stronger every day and it made him miss his wife.

He felt a pang in his heart when he thought about raising their daughter alone. And there was a part of him that wondered if he'd ever really be able to bring another woman into their lives. He liked Amberley. He wanted her fiercely but he didn't know if he was right for her.

If she was just a good-time girl, then he wouldn't hesitate to get involved, but everything had changed tonight when she'd told him about the child she'd lost. There was a hidden vulnerability to her that he couldn't ignore now that he'd glimpsed it. And no matter how hot they might burn together he sensed that she was going to want more from him. And he knew she deserved more from him. He couldn't do it.

After a restless night he woke up early and went into the kitchen, where Erin was feeding Faye breakfast. He poured himself a cup of coffee and then sat down.

"How was your date?" Erin asked.

"It was okay. We did get a break in the Maverick case last night."

"That's good," Erin said. "So does that mean we won't be here much longer?"

"I'm not sure yet," Will said. "Why?"

"Just wondering if I should start packing up our stuff. I've got to run a few errands in town this morning," Erin said.

"We'll probably be here at least until the end of the month," he said.

"Okay," she said.

"I'll watch Faye while you go to town," Will said.

"Are you sure?" she asked.

"Yes. I missed spending time with her last night and you had to work overtime."

"You know I don't mind."

Will nodded at her. "I do know that. But I also know errands go quicker without Faye."

"True. Thanks, Will."

"No problem," he said. He moved around to take the spoon from Faye. "Go on. I've got breakfast."

Erin quickly left the room. He touched his daughter's face and she cooed and blinked up at him.

"Hello, angel," he said. "You're hungry this morning."

She kicked her legs and arms and smiled at him. "Dadada."

"That's right. Daddy's here," he said as he scooped her up into his arms.

He held her close and buried his face in the soft curls at the top of her head. He changed her diaper and then carried her into his office. "Ready to help Daddy work?"

"Dadadada," Faye said.

"I'll take that as a yes," he said, then grabbed his laptop and Faye's little toy computer and sat down in the big double chair in the corner. He put his laptop on his lap after he'd set down Faye and she reached for her toy and mimicked his motions.

Then she looked over at him and smiled.

He smiled back at her as she started pounding on the keys with her fingers. His little computer whiz.

He knew he should be looking up some of the information he had found on Haskell's computer, but Amberley was on his mind and he typed her name into the search bar instead. He saw the pictures of her in the rodeo and then did a deeper search and found an old newspaper article from when she was a junior in high school. It was a profile of her as the junior barrel-racing champ with her horse. She looked so young and innocent.

Only seeing that photo of her and comparing it with the woman he knew now showed how much life had changed her. He leaned back and Faye crawled over to him and climbed on his lap the way she did. He lifted her with one hand and shifted his computer out of her way with the other.

She looked at the picture on the screen.

He looked down at her.

"Dadada," she said. Then babbled a string of words that made no sense to him.

Had she recognized Amberley? They'd played together for an entire afternoon but would that be enough for her to recognize her?

And was he doing Faye a disservice by allowing her to get attached to Amberley when Will wasn't sure what was going to happen between them. Sure he'd told her he saw a future with her, but now he was having second thoughts. How could he promise her something like a future when he wasn't even sure where he was going to be in a month's time. He was pretty sure he wasn't going to stay in Royal. His entire family was in Bellevue. His parents and Faye's maternal grandparents. But Lucy's sisters didn't live in Bellevue; one of them was in Oregon and the other in San Francisco.

And after she'd seen that picture of Lucy in his pocket was she going to want to be with him? Did she think he was still hung up on his wife?

Hell.

There were no answers, only more confusion and a little bit of sadness because if there was ever a woman he wanted in his life it was Amberley. She suited him. She wasn't his twin, which was probably why he enjoyed her so much. She was blunt and funny and unafraid to admit when something confused her. She was sassy and spunky and he wanted her to have all the happiness that he saw on her face in that picture when she'd been sixteen.

He didn't want to be the man who'd completed

what the jerk from the dude ranch had started. The man who showed her that she couldn't trust.

But how could he do that for Amberley and not risk hurting himself. He'd promised himself that he would never fall in love again when he'd held Lucy's hand as she lay dying. He'd never felt that abandoned and alone before and he'd promised himself that he'd never feel that way again.

Amberley went about her business all morning, ignoring Will and anyone who wasn't four-legged. Cara arrived on Monday afternoon with the latest news about Adam Haskell. After he'd crashed his car and been captured, an ambulance had transported him to the hospital. Apparently his condition was still critical.

"Sheriff Battle impounded the car. I heard they had to medevac Mr. Haskell to the hospital after he crashed on the highway," Cara said.

"Sounds like it was nuts," Amberley said.

That meant that Will was probably going to be done here in Royal. Everyone seemed to agree that Haskell was Maverick and she was afraid that Will was going to leave now. It hardly mattered that she was still upset with him for the way their date had ended and angry at herself for letting pride make her send him away. But she was tired of trying to compete against a ghost for him.

But she couldn't change the past. She knew that better than anyone.

"Why do you think they were after Haskell? Maybe they finally got tired of his crappy online reviews."

Amberley glanced over at Cara, who was smiling and texting while she was talking to her. "What do you know about Haskell?" Amberley asked. Cara's family had lived in Royal for generations.

Cara looked up from her phone at Amberley. "Not much. He really didn't like high school kids. One time I tried to sell him a magazine subscription and he was a jerk."

"Why did you even bother?"

"Someone dared me," Cara said.

They worked in silence for twenty minutes until they were done with the horses, and Amberley wanted to pretend she'd found some inner peace about Will, but she hadn't.

"Amberley?"

"Yes."

"Will you watch me run the barrels? I need to gain a second or two and I can't figure out where," Cara said.

"Sure. The barrels are set up. I'll go and walk the path while you saddle up." Amberley walked out of the barn and over to the ring to double-check that everything was where it should be.

She noticed that Erin was walking toward the stables with Faye in her arms. The little girl was wearing a pair of denim overalls and a rust-colored long-sleeved shirt underneath it.

"Hi, Erin," Amberley said as the other woman came over to her. Faye held her hands out toward Amberley and she reached over to let her grab on to her finger as the baby babbled at her.

"Hiya," Erin said. "We were out for our afternoon

walk and I thought she might like to see some of the horses."

"Perfect. Cara is going to be out in a minute with her horse to practice. That will be fun to watch."

Amberley couldn't help thinking that Erin was here for something other than to watch the horses. And when Cara came out and noticed they had company, she gave Amberley a look.

"Warm up, Cara. Then let me know when you're ready to take your run," she said. She had a stopwatch on her phone that she'd use to time Cara after she warmed up.

"I didn't realize you were working," Erin said.

"It's okay. You haven't been over to the stables to ride. Do you like horses?" Amberley asked.

"I don't know. I mean, I read books with horses in them growing up but I've never been on one," Erin said.

"We can fix that. Do you want to go for a ride?" she asked.

"Yeah. Sort of. I'm not sure when, though," Erin said.

"Well, the best way to get to know horses is grooming them. And I think even little Miss Faye would like to be in the stables. When Cara is done with her run we could go and meet the horses," Amberley said.

"I'd like that," Erin said.

Faye squirmed around and reached for Amberley. Erin arched an eyebrow at her and held Faye out toward her. Amberley took the little girl in her arms and hugged her. She was going to miss Faye when she and Will left. And though she hadn't spent that much time with the baby she knew she'd become attached to her.

Not her smartest move.

But then everything about Will Brady rattled her.

Cara rode over to the fence and smiled down at Faye.

"Who is this little cutie?"

"Faye Brady. Will's daughter," Amberley said.

"She's adorable," Cara said.

Amberley agreed and she realized that she wanted this little girl to be hers. She wanted that image of the family that had popped into her head last night to be real and she knew it couldn't be. Finding Haskell meant Will would be leaving. Maverick was done terrorizing Royal and Will Brady was going to be leaving Texas and taking a piece of her heart with him.

She handed Faye back to Erin as Cara started doing her run. And Amberley tried to settle up with the fact that this was her life.

# Twelve

Sheriff Battle, Will was told, had found a hard drive and some other incriminating evidence in Haskell's car. The police had brought it over to him this afternoon and Will was trying to break the security code to access the info within. The coding was different from anything he'd found on Haskell's home computer. It was more complex and nuanced than what he'd seen before.

Will was on the fence as to whether the same programmer could be responsible for both codes. Haskell had used a complex passcode on his computer, but the security on the hard drive was different. Will used all the skills he'd developed as a hacker back in his teenage days, before he'd settled down to working on the right side of the law.

He kept Max and the sheriff up-to-date on his

progress and after spending six hours working at a cramped desk, he got into the hard drive and found all of the files that Maverick had used to blackmail and scandalize Royal.

"This is it," Will said, calling over the sheriff. "All the files and the paths he used to upload the information are on here. This is pretty much your smoking gun."

"Just what I wanted to hear," Sheriff Battle said. He pulled his cell phone from his pocket. "I'm going to call the hospital and see if he's awake for questioning. Wonder if he has asked for a lawyer yet? Thanks for your help, Will."

"No problem, Sheriff," Will said.

The sheriff turned away and Will heard him ask for Dr. Lucas Wakefield. Will's own phone pinged and he saw that he had a text from Max, who was coming into the building. He went to meet him in the hallway.

"The hard drive had all the evidence the sheriff needs to charge Haskell. He's on the phone to the hospital right now to see if Haskell can be questioned. I'm a little concerned that the coding and some of the scripts on the hard drive were way too sophisticated compared to the home computer, but maybe he was just trying to cover his trail," Will said. "I'll put together some questions about that for the sheriff to ask when they interrogate Haskell."

"There won't be an interrogation," Sheriff Battle said as he came into the hallway. Will and Max turned to face him. "Haskell is dead."

The crash had involved Haskell's car flipping over when he hit a guard rail on the highway. They'd had to use the jaws of life to get him out of the car and then he'd been medevaced to the hospital.

"Well, hell," Will said. He didn't like the lack of closure on this case. He was used to catching hackers and seeing them brought to justice. The entire thing with Haskell was making the back of his neck itch. Something wasn't right. It had been too easy to find the hard drive in his vehicle. Though to be fair, Haskell probably hadn't expected to crash his car and die.

Max had some stronger expletives and the sheriff looked none too happy, either. Will didn't know about the other two but he was beyond ticked off. Hacking was one thing and unmasking cyberbullies was something that he was known for. It frustrated him that he was having such a difficult time unmasking Maverick. And it ticked him off even more to think that the man who'd had the messy house and seemed to have only taken a computer class at the community college had outsmarted everyone in Royal for months before he was fatally injured in a car crash.

Things weren't adding up as far as Will was concerned.

"What were you saying about maybe there being more than one person involved?" Sheriff Battle asked Will.

"It was just a theory. I can't confirm it without information from Haskell. He might have been smarter than everyone thought and used the town's perception of him as cover," Will said.

"Do you feel confident that I can tell the townspeople that Haskell was Maverick?" the sheriff asked him.

No. He didn't. And that wasn't like him. Had he let Amberley distract him from his job? Had he missed something obvious that he shouldn't have? He couldn't say and both men were looking at him for an answer. "The hard drive belonged to Maverick," Will said. "That is definite. But there is no real proof that it was Haskell's or that he programmed it."

"That's not good enough," the sheriff said.

"You could announce that Maverick's been caught and see what happens," Max suggested.

"I'm still running that program from the club's server and I can use the code on the hard drive to start a trace back…to see if I can tie the code to any known hackers on the dark web," Will said.

"Okay. Let's do it. I'm going to hold a press conference and say that we believe Haskell was Maverick. If there are no more attacks then… Hell, this isn't the way I like to do a job. It's half guesswork," Sheriff Battle said.

"I wish we had more to go on but without talking to Haskell there's just not enough on the drive or his personal computer to tie the two together," Will said.

He didn't like it. It felt to him like there was something more going on here.

"Well, I guess we're going to have to play the cards we've been dealt," the sheriff said.

"It could be a group effort," Will said. "In which case exposing Haskell might convince the other members or his partner to go underground."

The sheriff went out to make his announcement and Max took one look at Will and said, "Let's go get a drink."

The two of them went over to the Texas Cattleman's Club, and about thirty-five minutes later the television over the bar was carrying the press conference announcing that Maverick had been identified. A lot of people in the club were surprised but not overly so.

"He always had a beef with the townsfolk of Royal," someone remarked.

"Guess it was his way of getting back at all those supposed slights."

Max took a swallow of his scotch and Will did the same. He couldn't shake the feeling that something wasn't right. Chelsea Hunt joined them a few minutes later.

Will only had to glance at her to know she didn't believe that the trouble with Maverick was over, either. "Scotch?"

"Yes," Chelsea said as she sat down next to Max. "The sheriff brought me up to speed before he started his press conference."

"This isn't the way I expected this to end," Max said.

"Something tells me this isn't over," Will said. "It just doesn't feel like it."

And he was right.

He got a text three hours later when he was halfway back to the ranch that nude pictures of Chelsea Hunt had shown up on the website Skinterest.

The release of the photos seemed to be timed to embarrass the sheriff's department. Will pulled the car over to call Max; he didn't know Chelsea well enough to call her.

"St. Cloud," Max said.

"It's Will. I'm not back at my computer yet but I wanted to let you know that I can run a trace to see if the posting of the nude photos was time delayed or if they were put up after the sheriff's news conference."

"Good. This has gotten out of hand," Max said. "Chels is beyond ticked off. We need to know if it was Haskell."

"I'll do what I can. I'll be in touch soon," he said, hanging up.

The culprit had identified himself as Maverick and there was no doubt in anyone's mind that he was to blame since the way the photos were released was similar to the other scandals Maverick had caused. And after all, Chelsea was the one who'd been spear-heading the effort to stop Maverick and she and Max were old buddies, which was how Will and Max had ended up in Royal.

Will remotely started the trace from the Skinter-est site and then texted Max back that he should have something in a few hours. He was pissed. It felt like Maverick was thumbing his nose at them. He'd waited until after Sheriff Battle's press conference and, of course, the news that Adam Haskell had died in the hospital. It wasn't that the track was cold; they still had a few leads, but it was damn sure not as hot as it once had been.

Max told him to take the afternoon and evening off and they'd regroup tomorrow to figure out what to do next.

Next?

Will didn't bother to text Max back after that, he just got back on the road. He knew where he needed to be now and it wasn't the guest house he'd called home these last few weeks.

It didn't even matter to him that the way he'd left things with Amberley was less than ideal. He needed her. Needed to see her.

She was another loose end here in Royal and he was tired of running. Tired of feeling like he was losing. He needed to talk to her and…well, more. But he didn't dwell on these things as he pulled up in front of her house.

He sat in the car for a good ten minutes, debating between going up to her door and going somewhere else.

Maybe he would be better suited going to town and finding a rowdy bar and drinking and maybe getting into a fight to work out his frustration. But then her front door opened and she leaned there against the doorjamb wearing a pair of faded jeans and a top that hugged her curves. Her hair was pulled back in its customary braid.

She chewed her lower lip as their eyes met.

He turned off his car, shutting off the sound of screaming death metal that he'd put on because it suited his mood, and got out.

"We lost Maverick. It wasn't Haskell."

"I heard the news," she said. "Cara was texting with one of her friends in town when the Skinterest link popped up."

"I'm so…I don't know why I came here. I'm frustrated and edgy and I just couldn't go home and the only place I want to be is with you."

She nodded. "Then come on in."

He crossed her yard in angry steps and climbed

up the stairs. She stepped back to give him room to walk past her. But as soon as he stepped inside and smelled the fragrance of apples and cinnamon, his temper started to calm.

"I've got whiskey or beer, if you want to drink. I've got a deck of cards if you want to play poker. I would say we could go for a ride but I'm not a big fan of riding when you're upset. I think it puts the horse in danger," she said.

"I don't want to ride horses," he said.

"Good. So what's it going to be? Did I list anything that sounds good to you?" she asked.

"No," he said. "I want you. I can't think of anything except your mouth under mine and my body inside yours."

She flushed but didn't move from where she stood with her back against the cream-colored wall. Then, with a nudge of her toe, she pushed the front door. It closed with a thud and she stepped away from the wall.

"Where do you want me?" she asked.

"Are you sure?" he asked. Because even as he was walking toward her, his blood running heavy in his veins, he wanted to give her a chance to say no.

"Yes. Make that a 'hell, yes.' I have been aching for you, Will. Every night when I go to bed I'm flooded with fantasies of you and me together. That orgasm you gave me was nice but it only whetted my appetite and left me hungry for more."

"I'm hungry, too," he said.

Will walked forward until not even an inch of space separated them. He pulled her into his arms, kissing her slowly, thoroughly and very deeply. He caught her earlobe between his teeth and breathed into her ear, then said, "I'm not sure how long I can last."

She shivered delicately, her hands clutching his shoulders, before she stepped back half an inch.

"That's okay," she said, and it was. She had been dreaming of this moment—when he would forget about everything except her, when he needed her more than anything else. She wasn't about to let him slip away again without knowing what it was like to make love to him.

She tugged the hem of her thermal shirt higher, drawing it up her body, and he touched her stomach. His hands were big and warm, rubbing over her as she pulled the shirt up and over her head. She tossed it on the floor and he put his hands on her waist, turning her to face the mirror in the hallway.

He undid the button of her jeans and then slowly lowered the zipper. She stared at them in the hall mirror, concentrating on his hands moving over her body. Then, she glanced up to see he was watching her in the mirror, as well.

Their eyes met and he brought his mouth to her ear, and whispered directly into it, "I love the way you look in my arms."

He stepped back, tugged at her jeans and then slid them down her legs. She shimmied out of them, leaving her clad in only a pair of whisper-thin white cotton panties. Delicately she stepped out of the jeans pooled at her ankles, balancing herself by putting one hand on the table in front of her.

The movement thrust her breasts forward. He unclasped her bra, her breasts falling free into his waiting hands. She looked in the mirror as a pulse of pure desire went through her. He stood behind her, his erection nestled into the small of her back. His hands cupped her breasts, and his eyes never left her body as his fingers swirled around her nipples.

She turned in his arms, reaching up to pull his head down to hers. Her mouth opened under his and she wanted to take it slow but she couldn't. She was on fire for him. He was everything she ever wanted in a man and he was here in her arms.

He slid his hands down her back and grasped her buttocks, pulling her forward until he could rub the crown of his erection against her center. She felt the thick ridge of his shaft against her through the fabric of his pants. He reached between them to caress her between her legs.

He lowered his head, using his teeth to delicately hold her nipple while he flicked it with his tongue, and she moaned his name. She brought her hands up to his hair and held his head to her. He lifted his head and blew against her skin. Her nipples stood out. He ran the tip of one finger around her aroused flesh. She trembled in his arms.

Lowering his head, he took the other nipple in his mouth and suckled her. She held him to her with a strength that surprised her. She never wanted to let him go.

Her fingers drifted down his back and then slid around front to work on the buttons of his shirt. She pushed his shirt open. He growled deep in his throat when she leaned forward to brush kisses against his chest.

He pulled her to him and lifted her slightly so that her nipples brushed his chest. Holding her carefully, he rotated his shoulders and rubbed against her. Blood roared in her ears. She reached for his erection as he shoved her panties down her legs. He was so hard as she stroked him. She needed him inside her body.

He caressed her thighs. She moaned as he neared her center and then sighed when he brushed his fingertips across the entrance to her body.

He slipped one finger into her and hesitated for a second, looking down into her eyes. She didn't want his fingers in her, she wanted him. She bit down on her lower lip and with minute movements of her hips tried to move his touch where she needed it. But then she realized what she was doing and reached between them, tugging on his wrist.

"What?"

"I want you inside me," she said. Her words were raw and blunt and she felt the shudder that went through him.

He plunged two fingers into her humid body. She squirmed against him. "I will be."

"I need you now."

He set her on her feet and turned her to face the mirror.

"What are you doing?" she asked, looking over her shoulder at him.

"I want you to watch us as I make love to you. Bend forward slightly."

She did as he asked. Her eyes watched his in the mirror. "Take your shirt off, please. I want to see your chest."

He smiled at her as he finished taking off the shirt

she'd unbuttoned. His tie was tangled in the collar but he managed to get them both off. He leaned over her, covering her body with his larger one.

He bent his legs and rubbed himself at the entrance of her body. She pushed back against him but he didn't enter her. He was teasing her and she was about to burn up in his arms.

"Will."

"Just a second," he said. "Keep your eyes on mine in the mirror."

"Yes," she said, meeting his forest green gaze with her own.

He bit down on her shoulder and then he cupped both of her breasts in his hands, plucking at her aroused nipples. He slipped one hand down her body, parting her intimate flesh before he adjusted his stance. Bending his knees and positioning himself, he entered her with one long, hard stroke.

She moaned his name and her head fell forward, leaving the curve of her neck open and vulnerable to him. He bit softly at her neck and she felt the reaction all the way to her toes when she squirmed in his arms and thrust her hips back toward him, wanting to take him deeper.

He caressed her stomach and her breasts. Whispered erotic words of praise in her ears.

She moved more frantically in his arms, her climax so close and getting closer each time he drove deep. His breath brushed over her neck and shoulder as he started to move faster, more frantically, pounding deep into her.

He slid one hand down her abdomen, through the slick folds of her sex. Finding her center. He stroked the aroused flesh with an up-and-down movement that felt exquisite and drove her closer and closer to her climax.

He circled that aroused bit of flesh between her legs with his forefinger then scraped it very carefully with his nail. She screamed his name and tightened around his shaft. Will pulled one hand from her body and locked his fingers on hers on the hall table. Then penetrated her as deeply as he could. Biting down on the back of her neck, he came long and hard.

Their eyes met in the mirror and she knew that she wasn't falling for him. She'd fallen. She wanted this man with more than her body. She wanted him with her heart and with her soul.

# Thirteen

Will lifted Amberley into his arms and carried her into the living room. She had deserved romance and a night to remember and he'd given her sex. He wanted it to be more. Because she was more than a hookup to him.

"Are you feeling relaxed now?" she asked with a grin.

"I'm definitely calmer than I was when I arrived," he said, pulling her onto his lap and holding her closer. "I'm sorry if I was too—"

"You were fine. We both needed that. For the first time I feel like you let your guard down around me," she said.

He had.

He shouldn't have because that meant he was letting her in and he wasn't sure there was room in the gray and gloomy parts of his soul. He had been too good at keeping everyone at arm's length. And now he was unsure what would come next.

"Want to talk about it?" she asked.

"No."

"Sorry. I thought maybe if you talked about what Maverick was doing I could help. Offer some insights."

Of course.

Maverick.

She hadn't read his mind and seen the tortured way he was trying to figure out how to hold on to her and not let go of Lucy. He had to get past that. This was the first time he'd made love to a woman since his wife's death. Maybe the second time like their second date would help him move forward.

"I hadn't thought of it that way," he said.

"I'm not sure why I offered to talk except that I'm nervous. I don't know what to do now."

"What do you usually do?" he asked.

She flushed. "I don't have a habit. I'm still new to this."

"Oh…" That was telling. She'd never trusted a man enough to have him in her house.

And here he was.

"Okay, well, do you want me to leave?" he asked.

"No. Will, you are the one guy that I really want to stay. I need you here."

She needed him.

Those words warmed his heart and made him feel invincible. Like he would do anything for her.

He knew that feeling.

He was falling in love with her.

His heart, which he'd thought was down for the count, was beating again and beating for this woman.

"How about if you go get a shower while I set up a little surprise for you in the bedroom."

"What kind of surprise? I thought you came here without thinking about it?"

"Enough with the questions, cowgirl, it's a yes or no, that's it."

"Yes."

"Stay in the bathroom until I come and get you," he said.

"I will."

She walked away and he watched her leave. He wanted to make sure he committed as much of Amberley to memory as he could. He stayed there on the couch for another minute then stood, fastened his jeans and put on his shirt.

He saw her jeans, shirt and underwear strewn in the hallway and remembered the animalistic passion that had taken over him.

Maybe that was what it had taken to break through the icy wall he'd put around his heart. But there was no going back now.

He folded her clothes and set them on the table by the door and then went out to his car and opened the trunk, where he had placed the box from their romantic dinner. The box he was supposed to have put to good use then. Well, now was definitely the right time.

He opened the box and took out the CD he'd made for her. She liked old-school stuff and he thought the music mix he'd burned onto it would be a nice surprise for her the next time she got in her truck.

He opened the door to the cab, which she never kept locked, pulled down the visor and grabbed the keys. He turned the key to the accessory position and ejected the CD she had in there. Garth Brooks.

He wasn't surprised. He pushed in the CD he'd made for her and then shut off the truck and got out after putting the keys back up in the visor.

He reentered the house and heard her singing in the shower and smiled to himself.

He wanted this night to be perfect. He wanted to give her a gift that was equal to what she'd given him when she'd welcomed him into her life and her body.

Luckily the flowers he'd had in the box were still somewhat preserved and he took his time placing rose petals in a path from the bathroom door leading to the bed. Then he strewed them on the bed. Next he took the candles out of the box and put them on different surfaces. They were fragrant lavender and he lit them before stepping back to admire his handiwork.

He heard the shower shut off. But he wasn't ready yet. He took one of the low wattage Wi-Fi stereo bulbs that he'd placed in the box and installed it in the lamp next to her bed.

Then he cued up his "Amberley" playlist and connected his iPhone wirelessly to the lightbulb. He hit Play and went to the bathroom door, realizing he was overdressed for this. He took off his clothes, neatly folding them on the comfy chair in the corner of the room.

"Will? Are you out there?"

"I am. Stay there," he ordered.

He walked over to the bathroom and opened the

door, quickly stepping inside so he wouldn't ruin the surprise that waited for her.

He washed up quickly at the sink while she combed her hair. "I need you to close your eyes."

"I'm still not—"

"Into the kinky stuff. I know," he said with a laugh.

She made him happy. And he hadn't realized what a gift joy was until he'd spent so long without it in his life.

"Can I open my eyes now?" she asked.

"Yes."

She wasn't sure what she'd been expecting but this was the perfect romantic fantasy. There were rose petals under her feet, candles burning around the room and soft, sensual music playing.

Will put his hands on her shoulders and guided her to the bed.

"Surprised?"

"Yes!"

She turned in his arms and he took her mouth in his, letting his hands wander over her body, still amazed that she was here in his arms.

She buried her red face against his chest. "I wasn't sure if I would see you again or if you were going to leave and go back to Bellevue without saying goodbye."

Her words hurt him but he couldn't argue with them. He hated that he'd done this to her. That his own grief and doubts had been transferred to her.

"I promise I would never leave without saying goodbye," he said. Then to distract her, he picked up a handful of the rose petals that littered the bed and, turning her onto her back, he dropped them over her breasts.

She shivered and her nipples tightened. He arranged the petals on each of her breasts so that her nipples were surrounded by the soft rose petals. "I'm not surprised. You're a noticing kind of guy."

He leaned down to lick each nipple until it tightened. Then he blew gently on the tips. She raked her nails down his back.

"Are you listening to me?" she demanded.

He made a murmuring sound, unable to tear his gaze from her body. He'd never get enough of looking at her or touching her—he was starting to fall for her and that felt like a betrayal. Something he wouldn't let himself think about tonight.

"I'm listening to your body," he said, gathering more rose petals. He shifted farther down her body and dropped some on her stomach.

Her hand covered his. She leaned up, displacing the petals on her breasts. She took the petals on her stomach and moved them around until they formed a circle around her belly button.

He did just that, taking his time to fix the petals and draw her nipples out by suckling them. He moved the petals on her stomach, nibbling at each inch of skin underneath before replacing the rose petals. Then he kneeled between her thighs and looked down at her.

He picked up another handful of petals and dropped them over the red hair between her legs. She swallowed, her hands shifting on the bed next to her hips.

"Open yourself for me," he said.

Her legs moved but he took her hands in his, bringing them to her mound. She hesitated but then she pulled those lower lips apart. The pink of her flesh looked so delicate and soft with the red rose petals around it.

"Hold still," he said.

He arranged the petals so that her delicate feminine flesh was the center. He leaned down, blowing lightly on her before tonguing that soft flesh. She lifted her hips toward his mouth.

He drew her flesh into his mouth, sucking carefully on her. He crushed more petals in both of his fists and drew them up her thighs, rubbing the petals into her skin, pushing her legs farther apart until he could reach her dewy core. He pushed his finger into her body and drew out some of her moisture, then lifted his head and looked up her body.

Her eyes were closed, her head tipped back, her shoulders arched, throwing her breasts forward with their berry hard tips, begging for more attention. Her entire body was a creamy delight accented by the bloodred petals.

He lowered his head again, hungry for more of her. He feasted on her body the way a starving man would. He brought her to the brink of climax but held her there, wanting to draw out the moment of completion until she was begging him for it.

Her hands left her body, grasped his head as she thrust her hips up toward his face. But he pulled back so that she didn't get the contact she craved.

"Will, please."

He scraped his teeth over her clitoris and she screamed as her orgasm rocked through her body.

He kept his mouth on her until her body stopped shuddering and then slid up her.

"Your turn," she said, pushing him over onto his back.

She took his erection in her hand and he felt a drop of pre-cum at the head. She leaned down to lick it off him. Then took a handful of the rose petals and rubbed them up and down his penis.

She followed her hand with her tongue, teasing him with quick licks and light touches. She massaged the petals against his sac and then pressed a few more even lower. Her mouth encircled the tip of him and she began to suck.

He arched on the bed, thrusting up into her before he realized what he was doing. He pulled her from his body, wanting to be inside her when he came. Not in her mouth.

He pulled her up his body until she straddled his hips. Then using his grip on her hips, he pulled her down while he pushed his erection into her body.

He thrust harder and harder, trying to get deeper. He pulled her legs forward, forcing them farther apart until she settled even closer to him.

He slid deeper into her. She arched her back, reaching up to entwine her arms around his shoulders. He thrust harder and felt every nerve in his body tensing. Reaching between their bodies, he touched her between her legs until he felt her body start to tighten around him.

He came in a rush, continuing to thrust into her until his body was drained. He then collapsed on the bed, laying his head between her breasts. He didn't want to let her go. But he wasn't sure he deserved to keep her.

* * *

*I would never leave without saying goodbye.*

The words suddenly popped into her head as Will got up to grab them both some water from the kitchen.

He'd said he wouldn't leave without saying goodbye.

But that meant he was still planning to leave.

She sat up, pulling the blanket with her to cover her nakedness.

He came back in with two bottles of water and a tray of cheese and crackers. "Thought you might want a snack."

"Thanks," she said.

He sat on the edge of the bed and she crossed her legs underneath her. Why had he done all of this? Created the kind of romantic fantasy that made her think…well, that he could love her. And he was only going to leave?

He handed her a bottle of water and she took it, putting it on the nightstand beside her bed.

"Will, can I ask you something?"

"Sure," he said.

"Did you say you won't leave without saying goodbye?"

"Yes. I wouldn't want you to wonder if I'd gone," he said.

"So you are still planning to leave?" she asked.

He twisted to face her.

"Yes. You know my life is back in Bellevue," he said. "I'm just here to do a job."

He was here to do a job.

She'd known that. From the beginning there had

been no-trespassing signs all over him and she'd tried to convince herself that she knew better.

But now she knew she hadn't.

"Then what the hell is all of this?"

He stood up and paced away from the bed over to the chair where his clothes were and pulled on his pants.

"It was romance. The proper ending to our date last night. I wanted to show you how much you mean to me."

She wasn't following the logic of that. "If I mean something to you then why are you planning to leave? Or did you think we'd try long-distance dating?"

"No, I didn't think that. Your life is here, Amberley, I know that. My world… Faye's world is in Bellevue."

"Don't you mean Lucy's world?" she asked. "Faye seems to like Royal pretty well and as she's not even a year old I think that she'd adjust. You said yourself Lucy's parents travel and your folks seem to have the funds to visit you wherever you are."

"It's my world, too," he said. "I care about you, Amberley, more than I expected to care about another woman again, but this…isn't what I expected. I made a promise to myself that I'd never let another woman into my life the way I did with Lucy. Losing her broke me. It was only Faye and friends like Max that kept me from disappearing. And I can't do that again."

She wasn't sure why not. "I'm willing to risk everything for you."

She watched his face. It was a kaleidoscope of emotions and, for a brief moment, as his mouth softened into that gentle smile of his, she thought she'd gotten through to him.

"I'm not. It's not just myself I have to think of. It's Faye, as well," he said. "And it's not fair to you to put you through that. You've lost enough."

"Lost enough? Will, I think…I think I love you. I don't want to lose you," she said. "If you asked me to go with you to Bellevue, I would." She knew she was leaving herself completely open but she had lost a lot in her young life. First her mom, then her innocence and then her baby. And she'd thought she'd stay locked away for the rest of her life but Will had brought her back to the land of the living.

If she didn't ride all out trying to win him over, then she would be living with regret for the rest of her life.

"You would?" he asked.

"Yes. That's what you do when you love someone."

Saying she loved him was getting easier. She got up from the bed and walked over to him. She put her hand on his chest and looked up into his eyes.

"I know your heart was broken and battered when Lucy died. I know that you are afraid to risk it again. But I think we can have a wonderful life together. I just need to know that you're the kind of man who will stand by my side and not turn tail and run."

He put his hand over hers and didn't say a word. He lowered his head and kissed her, slowly, deeply, and she felt like she'd gotten through to him. Like she'd finally broken the wall around his heart.

He lifted her in his arms and carried her back to the bed. "Will?"

Instead of answering he kissed her. The kiss was

long and deep and she felt like it was never going to
end. And it didn't end until he'd made love to her
again.

She wanted to talk. It felt like they needed to but
he pulled her closer to him and she started to drift
off to sleep in his arms. His hand was so soothing,
rubbing up and down her back, and she wondered if
words were really needed. She'd finally found the life
she'd always wanted in the arms of the man she loved.

When she woke in the morning she sat up and realized she was alone in bed.

"Will?"

She got up and walked through the house but it
was almost silent. She had always liked this time
of the morning. She wondered if Will would like to
take a morning ride. She wanted to show him the
south pasture.

The clock echoed through the house and she realized it was very quiet.

Too quiet.

It was empty except for her.

He hadn't made love to her last night. It hadn't
been the joining of two hearts that she'd thought it
was. That had been his way of saying goodbye.

Tears burned her eyes and she sank down on the
floor, pulling her knees to her chest and pressing
her head against them. Why was she so unlovable?
What was it about her that made men leave? And why
couldn't she find a man who was as honorable as she
believed him to be?

# Fourteen

Amberley had thought she was ready for whatever happened with Will, but waking up alone… She should have expected it, but she hadn't and she was tired. She called Clay's house and asked for some time off. He wasn't too pleased to be down a person right around the big Halloween festival they were hosting this coming weekend and she promised she was just taking a quick trip home and she'd be back for that.

But there were times when a girl needed to be home. She wanted to see her brothers and sisters and just be Amberley, not the complicated mess she'd become since that city slicker had come into her life with his spiked hair and tight jeans. He'd looked at her with those hungry eyes and then left her wanting more.

Enough.

She wasn't going to find answers in her own head. She needed space and she needed to stop focusing on Will Brady. He had left. He'd said goodbye in a way she'd never really expected him to.

She got Montgomery into his horse trailer and then hit the road. She wasn't going to even glance at the guest house where Will and Faye were staying, but she couldn't help her eyes drifting that way as she pulled by his place. His car was in the drive, like that mattered. He wasn't in the right frame of mind to be her man. In a way she guessed he was still Lucy's.

She tried to tell herself she hadn't been a fool again but the truth was she felt like an idiot. What a way to be starting a long drive. She hit a button on the radio and the CD she had cued up wasn't one she'd put in there. She ejected it and read the Sharpie-written label.

Old-School Mix Tape For My Cowgirl.

She felt tears sting the backs of her eyes.

God, why did he do this? Something so sweet and simple that could make her believe that there was more between the two of them than she knew there was. She'd given him three chances and each time he'd wormed his way even deeper into her heart. And yet she was still sitting here by herself.

She couldn't resist it and finally put the CD back into the player and the first song that came on was "SexyBack."

She started to laugh and then it turned to tears.

He'd set the bar pretty high and it left both of them

room to fall. He'd made her expect things from him that she'd never thought she'd find with anyone else.

She hit the forward button and it jumped to the next track. That Jack Johnson song that he'd danced with her to. The one that had cured her broken heart and her battered inner woman who'd felt broken because she couldn't have her own child. He'd danced with her and made that all okay.

And maybe…

Maybe what?

"Hell, you're an idiot, Amberley. You used to be smart but now you are one big fat dummy. He's messed up."

But she knew that wasn't true or fair. He was broken, too. And she'd thought they were falling in love, that they would be able to cure each other, but instead…they were both even more battered than before. She should have known better.

Her and city guys didn't mix. Did she need some big-ass neon sign to spell it out?

She had no idea as the miles passed but the flat Texas landscape dotted with old oil derricks changed to the greener pastures of the hill country and she just kept driving. She'd expected the pain of leaving to lessen the farther she got from the Flying E ranch but it didn't. So when she stopped to let Montgomery out of the trailer and give him some water, she couldn't help herself. She wrapped her arms around her horse's neck and allowed herself to cry. Montgomery just neighed and rubbed his head against hers.

She put him back in the trailer, wiped her eyes and got back on the road again, pulling onto the dirt road that led to her family ranch just after sunset. She pulled over before she got to the house, putting her head on the steering wheel.

"God, please let me fall out of love with him," she said.

She put the truck back in gear and drove up to the old ranch house where she'd grown up, and the comfort she'd wanted to find there was waiting.

Her siblings all ran out to meet her. Her brothers took Montgomery to the stables while her sisters dragged her into the kitchen to help them finish baking cookies. They chatted around her and the ache in her heart grew. She knew she'd wanted this kind of family for herself and while it was true Will wasn't the last man on the planet, he'd touched her deep in her soul.

She'd started dreaming again about her future, had allowed herself to hope that she could have a family like this of her own, and now it was gone.

It was going to take a lot for her to trust a man enough to want to dream about sharing her life with him. And she was pretty damn sure she wasn't going to be able to love again.

He dad came in and didn't seem surprised to see her.

"Clay called and said you were heading this way. Everything okay?" he asked.

"Yes. Just missed seeing you all and we always carve pumpkins together," Amberley said.

"Yay. Dad said you might not make it home this year," her sister said. "But we knew you wouldn't disappoint us."

"That's right. Dad just knows how busy life is on

the ranch. I was lucky to get a few days off before the Halloween rodeo we're having on the Flying E."

Her dad nodded but she could tell that he knew she was here for more than a seasonal activity. Her siblings brought out the pumpkins and they all gathered around the table and worked on their masterpieces. She sang along to her dad's old "Monster Mash" album from K-Tel that he'd had as a boy growing up.

Tawny slipped her arms around Amberley as they were each picking a pumpkin to carve. "I'm glad you're home. I missed you."

"I missed you, too," Amberley said. "Daddy sent me a video of your barrel run last weekend. Looking good, little missy."

"Thank you. Randy said one day I might be as fast as you," Tawny said.

Amberley ruffled her fifteen-year-old sister's hair. "I'm guessing you're going to be faster than me one day soon."

"She might," Daddy said. "Randy's got himself a girl."

"Dad."

"Do you?" Amberley asked. "How come that's never come up when you call me?"

"A man's allowed to have some secrets."

"Unless Daddy knows them," Michael said.

"How did Daddy find out?" Randy asked.

"I might have told him that you were sweet on someone in town," Michael said.

Randy lunged toward Michael and the two of them started to scuffle the way they did and Amberley laughed as she went over and pulled Randy off his younger brother. "Want to talk about her?"

"No. Let's carve pumpkins," Randy said.

And they did. Each of them worked on their own gourd, talking and teasing each other. Amberley just absorbed it all. As much as she loved the quiet of her cottage she had missed the noise of family. She felt her heart break just a little bit more. When she was in Will's arms it was easy to tell herself that she could have had this with him. Could have had the family of her own that she'd always craved.

After everyone was done carving they took their jack-o'-lanterns to the front porch and put candles inside them. They then stood back to admire their handiwork. Her dad came over and draped his arm around Amberley's shoulder.

"You okay, girl?" he asked.

"I will be," she said.

"You need to talk?"

"Not yet, Daddy. I just needed some hugs and to remember what family felt like," she said.

Her father didn't say anything else, just drew her close for a big bear hug that made her acknowledge that she was going to be okay. She was a Holbrook and they didn't break...well, not for good.

Her heart was still bruised but being back with her family made her realize that the problem wasn't with her. It was with Will. He'd told her that he was in a world of firsts and she should have given him space, or at the very least tried to protect her heart a little more because he wasn't ready for love. And a part of her realized he might never be.

* * *

Will locked himself away in his office, telling Erin that he couldn't be disturbed. There were no leads on Maverick and that was fine with him. He wasn't in any state of mind to track down a kid who'd hacked his parents' Facebook accounts, much less a cyberbully who was too clever for his own good.

His door opened just as he was reaching for the bottle of scotch he kept in his desk. He was going to get drunk and then in a few days he was going to pack up and go back to Bellevue. But he didn't want to leave Amberley. He wished there was a way to talk to Lucy. To tell her he was sorry for their fighting and that he had never thought he'd find someone to love again. But that he had.

He loved Amberley. He knew that deep in his soul. But he had been too afraid to stay. He realized that losing her the way he'd lost Lucy would break him completely. That he'd never survive that. So instead of staying, he left.

"I said I'm busy."

Will saw his partner standing in the doorway with Chelsea. She looked tougher than the last time he'd seen her and he couldn't say he blamed her. "Come in. Sorry for being so rude a moment ago."

"That's fine," Chelsea said. "I've been biting everyone's heads off, as well. Did you find anything on the remote trace you did?"

Max followed her into his office and they both sat down on the couch against the wall. Will turned back to his computer.

"Yes. The coding was the same as what we recovered on the hard drive and I can tell you that it wasn't a time-delayed post. The person who put the photos up definitely has a Skinterest profile so I have been working on getting into that," Will said. "I should have an answer for you in a few days."

"Thank you," Chelsea said. "I am not above hacking the site if I have to. I'm done playing games with Maverick."

"I think we all are," Will said.

Chelsea's phone went off and she shook her head. "I have to get back to town. Thanks for your help on this project, Will."

"I wish I could have gotten to Haskell before he ran," Will said.

"Me, too," Max said. "Go on without me, Chels. I need to talk to my partner."

She nodded and then left. Max reached over, pushing the door shut.

"Give me everything you have so far," Max said.

"Why?"

"Because I think you have been working this too hard. You need a break."

"Uh, we're partners. I don't work for you," Will said.

"We are also friends. And you need a break," Max said. "I think you've been too busy. I think you should take a break."

Will turned in his chair to look at Max. He didn't want to do this. He needed time before he was going to be anything other than a douche to anyone who spoke to him.

"I can't."

"You can," Max said. "This isn't about Maverick."

"How do you know?"

"Because I saw the way the two of you were the other night," Max said.

"I don't know what you saw," Will said.

"Lying to me is one thing, I just hope you aren't lying to yourself," Max said.

His friend had always had a pretty good bullshit detector. "Hell."

Max laughed and then walked over to Will's desk, looked in the bottom drawer and took out the scotch. "Got any glasses?"

Will opened another drawer and took out two glasses. Max poured them both a generous amount and then went to sit on the chair in the corner where Will and Faye usually sat.

He took a swallow and Will did as well, realizing that Max was waiting for him to talk.

"I—I think I'm in love with her. And I don't know if I should be. What if I let her down? What if I can't be the man she needs me to be."

"Good. It's about time. Lucy wouldn't have wanted you to die when she did."

"But I did, Max. I lost some part of myself when she died that day. It was so unexpected."

"I know. I remember. But time has passed and she'd forgive you for moving on."

"I don't want to forget her," he said after a few minutes had passed. That was his fear along with the one that something would happen to Amberley now that he had let her into his heart, as well.

"You won't. Faye looks like Lucy and as she grows up, she'll remind you of her, I'm sure of that," Max said. "But if you are still punishing yourself you won't see it. All you will ever see is your grief."

Will knew Max was right. "I think I feel guilty that I have this new love in my life. You know Lucy and I were having some problems before...well, before everything. Just fighting about how to raise Faye and if Lucy should quit her job."

"You aren't responsible for her death," Max said. "You were fighting—all couples do that. It had nothing to do with what happened to Lucy."

"Logically I know that. But..." Will looked down in his drink. "It's hard to forgive myself."

"You're the only one who can do that," Max said, finishing his drink. "But I do know that you have to move forward. So that's why I'm going to do you a favor."

"You are?"

"Yup. You are on official leave from St. Cloud."

He leaned forward in his chair. "Are you serious?"

"Sort of. I'm not firing you but I think you need to take some time off. Don't worry about the investigation, we got this without you. You've been working nonstop and grieving and I think it's time you started living again."

"What if she won't take me back?" Will asked his friend.

"If she loves you, she will," Max said.

Max got up to leave a few minutes later and Will said goodbye to his friend, then walked him out. He realized that he'd been stuck in the past because of guilt, but also because of fear. And he wasn't afraid anymore. Amberley had said she loved him, and he'd made love to her and walked away rather than let her see how vulnerable that made him.

And he did love her.

He wanted to make his life with her. He scooped Faye up off the floor where she was playing and swung her around in his arms. His baby girl laughed and Will kissed her on the top of her head.

"Are you okay?" Erin asked.

"I'm better than okay," he said.

In fact he needed to get making plans. He needed to show a certain cowgirl that he wanted to be in her life and that he could fit into it.

He asked Erin to keep an eye on Faye while he went to find Clay Everett. He was going to need some serious lessons in being a Texas man if he was going to win over Amberley. He knew he'd hurt her and he hoped she could forgive him. Because he was determined to spend the rest of his life showing her how wrong he'd been and how much he loved her.

Amberley felt refreshed from her time with her family but she was glad to be back on the Flying E. The time away had given her some perspective. Will was in a tough spot and maybe he'd get past it and come back to her. But if he didn't…well, she knew that she wasn't the kind of woman to give her heart lightly. And she also wasn't the kind of woman to wallow in self-pity. She loved him and though living without him wasn't what she wanted, she'd give him time to realize what he was missing out on.

"Hi, Amberley," Clay called as she walked over to the area where the rodeo was set up on the Flying E. She saw Emily and Tom Knox, who had recently announced they were expecting a baby boy. Brandee Lawless was there taking a break from all the wedding planning she'd been doing and Natalie and Max were hanging together near the bleachers.

They had two rings set up and some bleachers for townsfolk. All of the kids from town were dressed up in their Halloween costumes.

"Hey, Clay. I just finished my shift at the dummy steer booth. The kids love roping those horns mounted in the hay bales. Where do you need me now?" she asked. She might have decided that she could give Will time, but she had discovered that it was easier to do that if she stayed busy.

"I'm glad to hear it," Clay said. "Why don't you take a break?"

She sighed. "I'd rather keep busy."

"I think you might want to check out the next contestant in the steer-roping competition," Clay said. "A certain city slicker is determined to prove he's got what it takes to be a cowboy."

"Will?"

Clay just shrugged.

"Are you crazy? He can ride. But roping a steer? That's dangerous," Amberley said.

"The man has something to prove," Clay said.

"Yeah, that he's lost his mind," Amberley said, taking off at a run toward the steer-roping ring. She pushed her way to the front of the crowd and saw Erin and Faye standing there. Erin just shook her head when Amberley walked up to her.

"Can you believe this? I always thought he was a smart guy," Erin said. "I'm afraid to watch this."

"Me, too. What is he thinking?"

"That he must prove something," Erin said. "Or

maybe he isn't. You know how guys and testosterone are."

She did. But Will had always seemed different. She leaned on the railing and looked across the way at the bay where the steer was waiting to be released and then saw Will waiting, as well.

"Will Brady!" she yelled.

He looked over to her.

"You're going to get yourself killed."

"Well, I love you, cowgirl and I need to prove that I'm worthy to be your man. So if I die at least I'll die happy."

What?

He loved her.

She didn't have a chance to respond as the steer was released and Will went into action. He roped the steer on his second try and in a few seconds he had it subdued. He'd had a good teacher and she suspected it had been Clay Everett. She ran around the ring to where Will was as he entered and threw herself into his arms.

He caught her.

"Did you mean it?" she asked.

"Yes. I love you."

"I love you, too."

He kissed her long and hard, and cheers and applause broke out. When he set her on her feet Erin brought Faye over to them. Will wrapped the two of them in his arms.

"Now my world is right. I have both of my girls back here in my arms."

He led them away from the crowd.

"I'm sorry I left the way I did. I was afraid of

letting you down and of not being the man you needed."

"It's okay. I kept forgetting that you were going through firsts and that I promised you time."

"I've had all the time I need."

"I'm glad."

Later that evening, after Faye had been bathed and put to bed, Will carried Amberley down the hall to the bedroom.

He put her on her feet next to the bed. "I can't believe you're really here, cowgirl."

"I can't believe you participated in a steer-roping competition for me," she said. He was everything she had always wanted in a man and never thought she'd find.

He was perfect for her.

He leaned down and kissed her so tenderly.

"Believe it, Amberley. There is nothing I won't do for you."

He undressed her slowly, caressing her skin and then following the path of his hands with his mouth. She couldn't think as he stood back up and lifted her onto the bed. He bent down to capture the tip of her breast in his mouth. He sucked her deep in his mouth, his teeth lightly scraping against her sensitive flesh. His other hand played at her other breast, arousing her, making her arch against him in need.

She reached between them and took his erection in her hand, bringing him closer to her. She spread her legs wider so that she was totally open to him. "I need you now."

He lifted his head; the tips of her breasts were

damp from his mouth and very tight. He rubbed his chest over them before sliding deep into her body.

She slid her hands down his back, cupping his butt as he thrust deeper into her. Their eyes met—staring deep into his eyes made her feel like their souls were meeting. She'd never believed in finding Mr. Right. Everything that had happened to her at eighteen had made it seem as if that wasn't in the cards for her. Everything that was until she met Will.

She felt her body start to tighten around him, catching her by surprise. She climaxed before him. He gripped her hips, holding her down and thrusting into her two more times before he came with a loud grunt of her name.

She slid her hands up his back and kissed him deeply. "You are so much wilder than that steer I tried to tame earlier."

His deep laughter washed over her and she felt like she'd found her place here in his arms. The family she'd always craved and never thought she'd have.

He held her afterward, pulling her into his arms and tucking her up against his side. She wrapped her arm around him and listened to the solid beating of his heart. She understood that Will was going to need her by his side, not because he didn't respect her need to be independent, but because of the way Lucy had been taken from him.

She understood him so much better now than she ever could have before. And because she had her own weaknesses, she didn't want him to feel that way with her. Will had given her back something she wasn't sure she could have found on her own.

"Are you sleeping?" he asked.

She felt the vibration of his words through his chest under her ear. She shifted in his embrace, tipping her head so she could see the underside of his jaw.

"No. Too much to think about." This had been at once the most terrifying and exciting day of her life. She felt like if she went to sleep she might wake up and find none of it had happened. "I'm not sure I can live in Bellevue. I mean, my life—"

"We're not going to live in Bellevue. I'm going to buy a ranch right here in Royal. Someplace where you can have as many horses as you want and we can raise Faye and maybe adopt some brothers and sisters for her."

"You'd do that?"

"Yes. Frankly, the thought of you being pregnant would have scared the crap out of me. I wouldn't have wanted to risk losing you and there are plenty of kids in the world who need parents," he said, rubbing his hand down her back. "Does a big family sound good to you?"

"It does," she said.

He rubbed his hand up and down her arm. "Perfect. So I guess you're going to have to marry me."

She propped herself up on his chest, looking down at him in the shadowy night. "Are you asking me?"

He laughed at that. "No. I'm telling you. You want to, but you might come up with a reason why we should wait and I'm not going to."

"Are you sure?"

He rolled over so that she was under him. Her legs parted and he settled against her. His arms braced on either side of her body, he caught her head in his hands and brought his mouth down hard on hers. When he came up for air, long minutes later, he said, "I promise I most definitely am."

She believed him. Will wasn't the kind of man to make promises lightly. When he gave his word, he kept it.

"Will?"

"Right here," he said, sinking back down next to her on the bed.

"I love you, city slicker."

"And I love you, cowgirl."

\* \* \* \* \*

# LET'S TALK

For exclusive extracts, competitions
and special offers, find us online:

 facebook.com/millsandboon

🐦 @MillsandBoon

📷 @MillsandBoonUK

**Get in touch on 01413 063232**

For all the latest titles coming soon, visit
**millsandboon.co.uk/nextmonth**